Guile and Spin

a cricket novel

STUART LARNER

This first paperback edition published in 2013 by FeedARead.com Publishing – Arts Council funded

First published as ebook Kindle Direct Publishing 2012

A CIP catalogue record for this title is available from the British
Library.

DEDICATION

To all my family, friends, and fellow players, for their guile and
spin.
And especially to my wife Rosie.

.

CHAPTER ONE

They said the recession would be tough, but I didn't know it would be like this. I was in a dead-end job managing a small town sports centre that was overdue for demolition. I wanted to go to London, study sports psychology and coach high level tennis pros. There was no way that could happen. I was lucky even to have this job. The whole building stank and the walls streamed with condensation. The toilets blocked frequently, and I had to clear these myself since the caretaker was so part-time he was hardly ever there.

Then my boss said he could help me. I just had to do this one thing first. I had to save the town's Sports and Leisure Service.

It was an impossible idea. How was I supposed to do that?

Merely by resurrecting the town cricket club to get grant money. That's how.

But, get involved in cricket to save my own job? Cricket. Such a boring and hopeless game. At school I had never liked the hard ball.

I couldn't do it.

Then I met Fardeep and Claire.

And that's when things got really bad, even though I didn't know it at the time. I thought they were improving.

"Look, I've invited some people here to help you," said my boss, Sir Richard Gregory, ushering me into the restaurant ahead of him. Though yet early evening, the curry smell in the narrow restaurant was strong enough to have been brewing all afternoon. Red lamps on red-flocked walls bowed over the dozen or so tables down the room. A waiter took our coats with a quiet "please yes".

Three people finishing their starters of kebab and poppadoms looked up as we crossed the room to their table.

"This is Claire. She is a new teacher at St Margaret's Junior School." He introduced a blonde in her early twenties. Her hair was twisted into a pile on top of her head. She wore a sharply cut navy blue business suit and skirt. Her tailored jacket fitted precisely around her toned athletic figure.

"Hi, pleased to meet you," she said. "I've heard a lot about you." She smiled and held eye contact for a little while longer than I expected. It was both unnerving and enticing.

Sir Richard nodded at the second person at the table. "You know Rod, of course."

Rod Sterling the captain of Scoving Cricket Club, and local builder. In common with many other people, I had never liked Rod Sterling. He was so competitive that he would even turn discussion of the weather into a battle. When it rained, he would make me feel that it was my fault. When the sun shone, I would feel almost indebted to him that he had been able to arrange that loan of brightness for me. His blue eyes always seemed to pierce and probe me like ice-cold lasers for every advantage he could get. His fine light ginger hair was short and beautified into little waves. He was slightly suntanned, and still keen to prove that at fifty-two he was really only twenty-two and could play cricket and lead a cricket team better than anyone else. He just grunted rather than saying hello properly.

"And this is Fardeep Singh, the great Indian cricketer," Sir Richard said, introducing the third person - a stocky Indian, complete with navy blue turban, beard, and a guru's piercing jet-black eyes. He stood up and bowed.

"Good evening, Jeremy," his breath was heavy with garlic.

"I'm sorry," I said. "I have to say that I don't know anything about cricket, I really don't. You'll have to count me out. But I'm sure it must be a very good game."

"Oh, do not worry," said Fardeep, wobbling his head. "There is no problem here. Many people, they think cricket is boring because nothing ever seems to happen. But it does. Cricket is like a still pool – with the life bubbling under the surface."

He narrowed his eyes and waggled his fingers horizontally in front of him like something swimming.

"You are a manager so you probably like chess, yes? But does anything happen in chess? No. It seems very still like cricket. The pieces stand on the board and do not move. But the mind moves. The mind is very active. It must think so many different things on so many different levels. Then when something does happen, it happens in a terrifyingly short flash of time."

His eyes glinted as he flung his arms wide in delight, holding the pose to us all.

"But I can't do it. I don't know anything about cricket," I reiterated.

"Never mind, I can teach you what to do," said Fardeep. "There is no problem here. Too many people think that it is the sport of a few. It is not. It is for all. When they realise that it is part of their culture, their history, then they will embrace it with open arms. Watch now. I will show you something special now. I will show you the three deliveries of the great Jadugar Singh from many years ago."

He reached out for some leftover kebab and bhaji, and squeezed it together in his hand.

"What do you mean Jadugar Singh? That doesn't seem a proper Sikh name," said Claire, raising an eyebrow.

"Oh, do not worry. This was long before then, long before the Sikhs properly got started, and long before the English think they brought cricket to India. He was bowling long before your Battle of Hastings," dismissed Fardeep as he squeezed the food hard into a ball, soaking the oil off onto a napkin.

Closing his eyes, he touched the ball to his brow below the bottom of his turban, as if he was making a magical spell, loudly sucking on some of the beard around his bottom lip. I wondered whether it was a joke, or a new way of saying grace, as he started to roll the ball in between his hands to firm it up.

"Jadugar Singh was a great cricketer and one of the first spin bowlers in early Indian cricket. He could bowl a ball whose spin would hypnotise a tiger in mid-pounce."

I looked at the others at our table in turn. They were all studying Fardeep intently. None dared to speak, all of us as malleable in his presence as though we were that ball of kebab and fried onion that he was firming between his fingers.

Fardeep flicked the hardened ball of food against his palm so that it gripped and spun vertically up his hand to the end of his fingers where he caught it.

Claire squealed with delight.

He looked to each of us in turn for our reactions before he leaned forward to make himself heard above a loud peak of conversation from the table behind. "These three deliveries, he taught them to his son before he died, and so they were passed on down the generations. Then my father taught them to me. They are the most revered of all the secret deliveries of the spinners of the Parthan Rajas. Few people have heard of these, and even fewer can bowl them."

"Sounds like they were the original Kings of Spin," Claire said.

There was suddenly a striking silence from the table behind indicating they were listening in.

"First there is the scorpion. It will appear to drop just before it pitches and then shoot forward to sting you with its tail," he said, holding a knife in his down-turned left hand like a small bat.

"Oh, scorpions! I don't like scorpions. They're not very nice. Not very nice at all. They're poisonous too." She grimaced.

A cascade of metal sitar notes fell opportunely from the loudspeakers as if to announce his presentation. Fortuitous, or perhaps he recognised the track and knew the music well.

With a complex twist of his right wrist, he tossed the ball onto his plate and it accelerated after the bounce so quickly and sharply towards him that he hardly had time to parry it with his knife.

"See. You must be on your guard. See. It will shoot like a spear along the ground. So you must play forward and use your bat like a shield. Like this, see." He motioned with his knife again as I imagined all great cricketers do when they are talking about dangerous kebabs at the dinner table.

I heard someone behind me say, "Did yuh cop that?"

Fardeep looked over to see the interest from the other table, and sensed a growing audience. Holding the ball up for all to see under the wall-lamp, he rolled it in his fingers with large gestures as the tabla rhythm picked up louder and faster.

"I need to get this ball really smooth so you will see there are no tricks," he announced. "It is all spin."

Feeling that I might be blocking Fardeep's view of the table behind, I made myself smaller in my chair.

Claire leant forward to whisper urgently to me. "Hey, don't do that! You'll only encourage them, and they don't need it."

"Second, there is the crab. It will roll sideways and change direction. So you must watch it with your bat and you must handle it carefully when it is near."

"Crabs? I don't like crabs. I got nipped on the toe once by a crab in a rockpool in Scarborough when I was young." She grimaced.

"Yes, and if you do not watch it carefully it will nip you again," Fardeep laughed. "Your bat must be like a net when you guide the crab away. You see it will be trying to get under my bat now. Watch."

He gripped the kebab in a slightly different manner and tossed it onto the plate, and the kebab spun on its own axis. As he prodded it with his knife it ran away from him, circling all the way round the edge of the plate to return to his knife.

There was a murmur of "Oi mate, cool!" from behind as Fardeep's kebab bounced around in response to his prodding.

Next, he waved the ball in the air at both tables.

"Third, and most dangerous of all, there is the cobra. It will bounce and then spit at you. You must be like a mongoose if you want to play the cobra. You must be ready and when it strikes then you must have your bat up high to strike back."

"Oh, I certainly don't like snakes," Claire said. "They're horrible. Especially poisonous ones, the ones they charm. But I like mongooses. Or do you call them mongeese? I think they're cute, like meerkats."

Raising his knife high he flicked the kebab hard onto the plate. As it bounced up into the air he struck it with perfect timing across the room.

It hit the wall with a splat.

"Good shot!" came from the table behind. I turned and caught the eye of one of the lads. He had a fat face and bulky shoulders and was raising a glass of lager in his fist. His eyes lit up as he chirped "Heehaw! Cop that! Go for it, mate!" He had a long scar on his right cheek that changed into a curl as he laughed.

The waiter hurried across to clear our table. He immediately took the kebab dish saying, "You like food, sir?"

Sir Richard and I muttered in agreement and gave our order.

Then Sir Richard said, "Well, now to business. Rather than calling a special meeting to discuss this, I am taking the opportunity of talking about it at this Christmas night-out since we are all here anyway and a full exploration of the issues can be systematised. Now, you all got my e-mail?"

We nodded.

"And you have read the two attachments? The first one from the County Council, and the second from the government?" asked Sir Richard.

I just smiled back, hoping that I wasn't going to be asked any details about them.

"Actually," Rod said. "I've been busy with my business and trying to get sponsors for Scoving."

Sir Richard scowled. His bushy eyebrows gave his stare the intensity of an owl. An ex-rugby player, now in his sixties, he sat squarely, elbows out, his broad frame not letting any point pass him.

He uttered a kind of disgusted harrumph and said, "It would have been good, Rod, if you had read them. But actually, since then, an opportunity has arisen and we have some new objectives. That is why I have asked Fardeep here to meet us before he flies back tomorrow."

Fardeep was smiling proudly as if it were an honour to be mentioned.

"Well, I've read them," said Claire. "The first attachment is the cuts, the second is the new source of funding. The baddie and then the goodie. That's right, isn't it?"

She nodded to the table generally, giving support to Sir Richard especially. It struck me how she and I might have a common interest in supporting people: I was a tennis coach and she was a teacher.

"Yes, you could say that," said Sir Richard. "As you know England has just won the World Twenty-Twenty Grand Decennial Supercup of Supercups. This all amounts to about one hundred and fifty million pounds from prizes, bets, and sponsorship deals for the National Board. Fantastic things are planned and new stadia promised."

We had all seen it on television. It had produced more riotous behaviour than the open top bus and the winning of the Ashes in 2005. This time around the team had all been knighted, not just given an MBE. All the cricket grounds had been thrown open in a day of national celebration as big outdoor screens carried repeated highlights of the match to drunken crowds that played impromptu cricket in dozens of little groups on the outfield.

One hundred and fifty million pounds. A wonderful injection for the sport, yet a drop in the ocean compared to what international bookmakers took.

Rod interrupted, "Excuse me, but can you make it short? Only I've got to pick up my son. He'll be depending on me. It's just that I've got the only car now as his Mazda's at the garage."

Sir Richard gritted his teeth, ignoring the remark, and said, "Trouble is, it's going to be taxed heavily."

"Typical!" Claire exclaimed.

The waiter arrived with our food and lagers, and water for Sir Richard.

After a sip I asked casually, "So, is it really that bad, surely not?"

As soon as I had said it, Sir Richard snorted and a look of horror passed fleetingly over Claire's face.

"Yes it is," he said. "Your job is already threatened, Jeremy, and your private work. Your sports centre has no repair budget left and is crumbling away. The government will give some money back to the councils to run their other sports. But only if the councils develop the cricket that would have happened if the government hadn't halved their budgets as it has done. And to help us bid for the money, Fardeep here is a visiting professional coach funded between the National Board and our best local club, Appleton Water. But it's very precarious money and very short-lived. It's called redistributed reclaiming."

"Yes," said Fardeep. "It is like a game of twenty-twenty itself. You have to play and go for it. If you don't then you'll lose anyway. But you can win. I will put my name to your bid."

Rod spoke with his mouth half-full, "Hah! It doesn't affect me. I'm a builder, not a local council employee like you."

Sir Richard swallowed, and then said, "Maybe not. But it does affect the funding for your general cricket and football infrastructure. We're going to lose a lot of the annual budget for certain unless we can succeed with the grant application. Anyway, that's it."

As I took my first mouthful of kebab and mango chutney there was a hiss from the loudspeakers high in the corners indicating the restaurant CD was about to start again. The tinny flow of the notes of an Evening Raga began to cascade. The high-pitched twang from the sitar seemed to curve around the peppery mix of meat, ginger, and mango in my mouth. Overhead a large copper-coloured ceiling fan slowly rotated against the background of a slow tabla beat.

I adjusted my tie. We were all wearing suits and I was beginning to boil in mine under the influence of the food and the hot radiators.

My thirst grew as the hot spices smarted my mouth, and my glass was soon empty. The foamy remains of my last lager clung mournfully up the sides.

Over Fardeep's shoulder I could see our waiter filling some fluted glasses with lager from the stainless steel tap. It streamed into the crystal like the Raga dancing and celebrating being golden and alive.

One of the young men on the table behind us gave a scornful laugh about a football player, and then they fell quietly back to eating and mumbling agreement. There was the sound of a poppadom being crunched.

The waiter pivoted from the bar with a tray of four brilliant glasses of lager, ice-cold with condensation streaming down the outside, misting the light golden liquor. He started towards us with a full tray just as another spoonful of curry stung my mouth, and I put down my fork and moved my glass to the middle of the table to clear some room to my right for the lager. Yet he carried on past to the people behind.

"Cheers mate," I heard one say, as the glasses were plonked on their table. I could almost feel the cool sensation of a cold glass brought to my lips as I heard one of them take a long swallow and breathe out with a satisfied gasp. I finally managed to re-order a glass as the waiter passed us on his way back.

Rod shuffled in his seat. "So what cricket project had you in mind?"

"Repropagation of cricket communities," said Sir Richard. "I think we should develop a team."

"Where, Appleton Water? That posh modern private place on the hill? They've got enough money already. It's coming out of their ears! Best give it to my club, Scoving."

"No," Claire interrupted. "We want the money for schools and the local community. It should go to a junior school team."

Sir Richard shook his head at them both. "No. Apparently this has to be for new initiatives, not for clubs and organisations that have got money already. I think we should resurrect an old club." Then he said in a quiet voice, "Moxham."

"What? No way! We don't want that again! They were the biggest bunch of swindlers in history!" Rod dropped his fork onto his plate.

Claire asked, "Why? What happened?"

Rod stared straight at her and lowered his voice. "It's best that you don't know. Cheating, thieving scoundrels!"

"Well, I'll admit there was some controversy," said Sir Richard. "But it's all gone now."

"You'll bet your life it's all gone – and that's the way it should stay!" Rod shouted.

Sir Richard shrugged. "Well that's the kind of bid they would support – especially managed by a council sports centre manager so nothing can go wrong. They won't support any other. And unless we do it – and a Moxham Cricket Heritage Project was what they wanted when I spoke to the Council – unless we do it, then we'll all be deconstituted in less than two years."

"Nah! I'm not going to," said Rod. "I can't go through all that again between my club and Moxham. I'm sorry. I've got my building business to worry about. I'll take my leave now."

Fardeep tilted his head from side to side and moved his right hand as though he was still spinning a ball. "Now calm down everyone. There is no problem here."

"No, that's right," said Rod. "There's no problem. There's not going to be one as far as I'm concerned."

Rod rose from the table. "Thanks for the meal RG. I've nothing else to help you with if that's what you're discussing. Giving it to Scoving or a junior side somewhere - I'm in favour of this all right. But not falling back into all that again. And you

Jeremy, not liking cricket. You've got sense. You'd be wise to keep out of it and stick to your tennis. You don't need to get involved in cricket if you're inside the sports centre. I know what's best for the game in this area."

As he passed the bowing waiters near the door, he tossed his head back scornfully at our table.

The sitar and tabla suddenly got louder and then fell into a glissando like a sad anticlimax.

"That wasn't very helpful," said Claire, folding her arms.

Sir Richard turned to me. "Well, it's bad. Considering his is one of the most successful clubs around here, I thought that he would have helped."

Fardeep nodded. "Things must go very deep with him. What was it?"

"Well, it's hard to say," frowned Sir Richard. "Apparently, Moxham and Scoving had a bit of a mutual dialectical discourse about ten years ago after some controversial claims about cheating and silverware going missing. Moxham had won the League Cup and sent it away to have their names engraved on it, but then claimed that it was stolen. So it was never seen again."

Sir Richard took a sip of water.

Fardeep mouthed, "What, never?"

"No. Rod didn't believe them because his team Scoving lost controversially to them in another competition. He and Turner the main man from Moxham never spoke to each other again. They both took it bad. Moxham lost their main players, and then they folded the next season. Scoving just about managed to stay together, but it was a big row."

Fardeep shook his head. "That's very bad."

We were all silent for a moment.

Then Sir Richard brushed his jacket and said, "Anyway, redistributed programisation. It's down to us now. Particularly you Jeremy, if you want your job and your tennis coaching to survive. I think you'd better do this. Resurrect Moxham Cricket Club."

Looking straight at me, Fardeep said, "Remember Jeremy, cricket is a great game. I will teach you when I come back in February."

"And I can help," beamed Claire. "We have to succeed." She moved her hands nearer to me across the table.

Now that, I thought, was very enticing. It would be wonderful to be the recipient of some help from Claire. I could imagine some late indoor evenings here, lying down on the sofa with bottles of wine, even snuggling up with a candlelit copy of the Laws of Cricket. Who knows where it might all lead?

Then my heart leapt as she said, "But we must succeed, Jeremy. We must succeed for the future of the whole district. Please say you'll do this for me."

CHAPTER TWO

I was still unhappy about the whole thing as I climbed into Sir Richard's Range Rover for my lift back home. Claire had already set off in her car and Fardeep had gone back to his hotel ready for his early morning train to Heathrow.

"We need it to succeed," Sir Richard said, turning the ignition. "You can't leave it all in the hands of an amateur like Rod with his own interests."

He peered into the darkness of the main street ahead and turned on the fan full to blow the mist from the windscreen for a minute before we could set off. "Rod will knock anything down. You just can't trust him."

"I'm sorry but I just can't do it," I said. "I don't know enough about cricket. I'm just a manager of a sports centre where some kids come for an hour's table tennis or badminton or the odd game of indoor football. I just book out the gear and do a bit of tennis coaching up the road. I haven't got the depth of expertise for this – and that's what you want. Someone with a great understanding of cricket."

"Well, you'll lose your job if you don't." He turned towards me. "And endanger everybody else's. Maybe the health of the borough as well. It'll all go. Moxham Sports Centre, council-aided sports grounds, the council fitness education initiative. Already the swimming pool is colder and not as clean as it used to be. Leaking roofs on every building. All that funding – we desperately need to get it back. We need to recover our designated service levels. It's all dependent on this cricket project succeeding."

I knew I would have to disappoint him. I had a terrible feeling again like earlier in the restaurant when I couldn't move.

Whether he sensed my inner state or whether he thought I was being pig-headed and resistant I don't know. His voice was faint over the windscreen's loud fan. "You told me when we last met that you wanted to build up the coaching more and especially the mental side of it. Sports psychology will be all the rage soon, not just in tennis and golf. It'll be good for you to get applying it to a team game like cricket. There's market opportunities and dissemination challenge there."

I saw the opportunity he described, but something told me it didn't seem right for me. Something involving a hard red ball.

"You could be promoted to a project officer for the time you were doing it. Just give it a go for us, please." He squeezed his face up. "Fardeep will help you in February when he's back from his business in India. Even if it failed I would give you good references. You could then go and get a good job down London where there's more opportunities – if that's what you want to do."

"But I don't want to go to London. I'm happy here."

As soon as I said it I realised I was on shaky ground. There were very few opportunities here for sports psychology and in the oncoming climate there might now be even less. London would be the next place to develop but it would mean giving up my cosy life of office work and private tennis coaching.

"I have contacts down there, Jeremy. I run a national consultancy firm that specialises in these projects. Fardeep is a coaching consultant and Claire is our junior's and women's consultant. If you did well in this Moxham Project, you could come on board with us as a national advisor. It would get you opportunities in the private fitness industry. They're looking for people all the time. I can help you if you can just help us with this for a few months. Look, just think about it and I'll speak to you again in a few days."

We drove out of the town and the speed-limit-ends sign shone white in the full headlights as Sir Richard put his foot down.

His last comment flared something in me. I did not want to be left to think about it as though I was being left there like meat on a hook to be inspected later to see if the toughness had bled out in the meantime.

"So why Moxham?" I asked, thinking he might be less resistant and more persuadable whilst he was driving.

"There is no groundswell for any other club. And it fits in with the general county-wide Heritage Regeneration Project. With Moxham there is this strong history, even stronger than Scoving.

Then there was this little glitch. I think that's what turned people off. But it is now a simple case of reputation rebranding."

"Sounds like a big glitch to me!"

"No. Basically there is vast goodwill and talent about still in the Moxham area. Admittedly some has gone to the other neighbouring clubs of Darbury and Lampton Ambo, but it will come back. Moxham could be turned on again and shine more brilliantly than before."

Undeterred by having to concentrate on driving, he slowly went through the argument about tax and national funding again.

A damp misty darkness haunted the far extent of the headlights where the frosted hedgerow, grass verge, and bare black trees met the road. The branches grew white as they neared us and turned into skeletal ghosts as they streamed past.

I tried to think of another way of saying "Why me?" as I looked at the three-quarter moon through the side window. There was a halo around it.

We had become silent as he concentrated on picking the line into a right-hand bend.

"I don't know if they grit these roads," he said in a suddenly worried voice, the car lurching as he braked. The back of the car wiggled into the bend.

"Whoa! Did you feel that?" he exclaimed.

As we slowly pulled out of the corner he drew in breath and muttered, "It's not a good night for driving a car."

Unnerved by the car's odd movement, my attention fell to any slight inconsistencies in the road.

Ahead was a right-hand bend lit by another car's headlights. But the headlights didn't move and remained at a glaring angle.

Sir Richard slowed the car down to a crawl and then stopped about twenty yards before the lights. It was a Fiesta. Its rear end was in the ditch on our side of the road.

I got out. Immediately my feet slipped on the icy road. I sidled carefully onto the verge, where I found walking on the grass easier, though uneven and wet. The cold air tore at my face.

As I slithered along to the Fiesta I realised its engine was not running.

I saw a head slumped forward onto the wheel. It was a young woman. At that moment she looked up.

It was Claire.

CHAPTER THREE

I put my hands on the front of the car for support.

I shouted back to Sir Richard "It's Claire. Stay in the car. It's much too dangerous, and don't try to bring the car down this side, you'll lose it."

"Is she all right?" he shouted.

I opened the car door.

"Claire? Claire?" I asked.

She muttered something.

"Are you all right?"

"I'm OK." Clearer this time.

"Can you move?"

She grunted, and groggily stretched a leg out of the car.

I put an arm round her, pulling her towards me. There was a whiff of lavender scent as I pulled her arm over my shoulder and lifted. All along the grass verge to the Range Rover she stumbled on the uneven ground and leant on me with all her weight.

I had a strange thought that I wasn't just holding her body at all. It was as though she wanted me to do this, she wanted to lean on me. And I wanted her dependency, to lean against me. It was exciting. As we reached the Range Rover she became lighter, as she became more awake. Now we had achieved close contact she loosened her hold on me. Yet she did not let me go completely. She still held an arm around my neck as I sat her on the front passenger seat of the Range Rover.

"Are you OK? What happened?" asked Sir Richard.

"I don't know." She brought her other hand to her forehead. "It just spun round on the bend. My neck." She rubbed it.

"We'll take you to the hospital," said Sir Richard.

"No. I'll be OK. The hospital's miles away. Just a lift home. My flatmate Amy will still be up."

"It's best to go to hospital," insisted Sir Richard.

"No, not the hospital," she whined. "Just give me a lift back. I'm OK. I've not broken anything. I'm OK!"

The last 'OK' was spoken so forcefully that I could see that we had to give in to her. I wanted to do more for her. She was drawing me in but also setting a limit. Maybe she had not broken anything. Her car was not smashed up. It looked as though it had just spun on the ice, putting the back end in the ditch. All the wheels were off the highway, so there was no obstruction.

"All right then, if not the hospital then back home to your flatmate to look after you," decided Sir Richard. "Anyway, no sense in phoning a garage tonight either. Too icy. Sort it out tomorrow."

He turned to me and gestured. "Just turn it all off and lock it. Bring her bag, and we'll take her home to recuperate."

So I got her stuff out of her car and locked it. Then we drove carefully to the front of the old staff annexe of St Margaret's School, and watched her as she was met in the open doorway by another young woman dressed in a thin pink dressing gown over jeans.

As we drove off, I mused how light her body had grown considering how groggy she initially appeared. I had never encountered that before. Groggy people usually stayed as dead weights all along. Though I had heard of people who suddenly developed superhuman power to pick up weighty objects in the stress of the moment, it was not that I had been transformed into a superman. It just seemed that there was a natural affinity here between rescuer and victim.

CHAPTER FOUR

"Want a cake?" I asked, close up to her ear, in my best jokily seductive deep voice.

Claire spun round. "Oh, that's good timing!" She brightened.

Spying her across the room, I hurried to be right behind her in the queue at the coffee bar counter. Though there was no one else heading for the queue, my eagerness still made me take fast strong steps.

I could smell her lavender scent as she turned to speak to me and then to look down at the cakes under the large glass counter with the curved top. Her hair was let down today, not piled up formally like at the evening meal. She was dressed in tight blue jeans and pullover with a scarf and jacket on top of that.

I had rung on Saturday the day after the night in the restaurant. I had got through only to her flatmate who said that she was still asleep, but she would tell her that I had rung when she awoke.

I wanted to get more involved with her, but my ambivalence over the cricket was a hurdle.

Perhaps there was a way to get involved without having to take on the cricket role? Maybe I should follow up the crash scenario. After all, I was her rescuer. With luck, Sir Richard would find someone else to do that cricket stuff. I'll just talk about her and me.

So I had phoned again on Monday and found out she would be going into town and would be in Marmaduke's at the end of the afternoon. Good. Monday was my day off.

Marmaduke's was an exclusive coffee bar attached to the Imperial Hotel, where Fardeep had stayed, and was adjacent to Moxham Railway Station. Marmaduke's discerning customers received coffee in large beakers and sat in woven cane chairs at tables with free newspapers. Its stone floor was laid out in black and white Flemish squares. It had white walls and a low ceiling supported by plain white Roman columns. Background music and large indoor plants under intense spotlights gave the appearance of bright sunshine, suggesting an atmosphere of being somewhere Mediterranean.

And the cake display was renowned. These cakes were mini-monuments to comfort eating. Each was an artistic statement, a coded sculpture of a balance between flavours, laid on a plate in its own little world where the language was happiness, and the currency was fat and sugar.

She surveyed the glass cabinet. There was a simple sponge, a blackcurrant cheesecake, individual blueberry muffins, cinnamon biscuits, gingerbread men, but also the big cream cakes; the overpowering black forest gateau, creamed walnut cake, apple pie and cream in a little silver jug to pour on thickly, carrot cake, raspberry Pavlova, puffed meringue macaroons, apple doughnut with cream and Danish pastry.

"Which cake do you want then, an apple doughnut or a Danish pastry?" I said, taking my chance to try to influence the course of her mind.

I watched her lips quiver over the prospect of the delights. There was something about her that made me put aside my Sports and Leisure worries. That hectic long weekend duty with lots of complaints about unclean changing rooms and the rundown state of the rackets and other equipment we hired out. Something about her lavender perfume just bore it all away. That same something made me delight in the time she was taking to decide on the cake.

She frowned slightly while she made up her mind and then she said, "Yes, I'll have the apple doughnut!"

I asked for the same.

The girl behind the counter was of striking appearance: a dumpy brunette with hair combed over one side exposing an ear with a piercing. She wore heavy mascara. The tip of her tongue came to her lips as she precariously raised a second apple doughnut with a rather under-sized pair of cake tongs onto a plate.

I paid for the tea and cakes and read her nameplate "Charlotte" on the left breast pocket of her tunic as I waited for the change.

We sat down with the cakes and coffee at a vacant table by a large palm. However, though we sat in the Mediterranean atmosphere, the Pennine stone was never far away. Through the front window we could see part of Moxham's main street, and through the back window the distant hills leading up to the Old Man Tor. Just through the French windows behind us was a little Pennine stone courtyard. Years ago there were pens and stabling for animals destined for the market train. Lines of old mortar left between the stones of the courtyard walls showed where the partitions between the pens had originally been. I felt that I had also been waiting and now my next phase had come.

I watched her eat the doughnut. A smidgeon of cream and apple syrup stuck to her fingers after the first bite. She put it down on the plate and licked her fingers one by one lovingly as though she was kissing little children.

"How are you?" I asked.

"Not too bad, still a bit shaky."

"You didn't need to go to the hospital then?"

She shook her head and trembled. "No thanks. I can't stand those places."

"What about the car?"

"Oh, a garage has picked it up. It wasn't too bad in the end. Just ended up stuck backwards in that ditch. It should be back today. Thanks for your help."

"That's OK. The least we could do. But are you sure you're OK? Your flatmate said you haven't been out for two days."

"Yes. I had some palpitations."

"Oh?"

"Yes, well, it reminded me of something that happened a couple of years ago."

She looked down at the cake.

"I thought I'd got over it, but obviously I haven't." She shrugged her shoulders. "Sometimes it comes back."

"Want to tell me about it?"

"Not much to say really. Just got a bit shook up. It was a few years ago now. I got in this guy's car and he drove like a maniac."

She blanched. "We ended up off the road. I thought I would die, and I thought the others in the car were dead."

She tightened her grip on the coffee cup but did not lift it. "I hadn't thought about it for a few months. Then my skid pan antics the other night…"

She forced a laugh. The head was still down but I could see she was grimacing.

She reached in her bag for a tissue and blew her nose. "Anyway, your words were helpful at the time."

I smiled and said I could not remember what I had said.

She touched a corner of the tissue to her eye and said, "That's because you're a natural. It's the coaching coming out."

"Must have been the pulling-people-round routine. The one I use between the sets on the tennis court when they're love-five down." I didn't mean love, or did I?

I took a sip of my coffee, and asked her what her interests were.

"Yoga, dancing and cricket," she said. "My turn. Are you a vegetarian?"

"No, but I'd rather give up meat than vegetables. What cars do you like?"

"Sports cars. But I can only afford a little Fiesta. And you?"

"Oh, I have a SUV," I said, but not giving away it was a very small SUV – a Suzuki Jimny.

"Really? Do you go off-roading in it?"

"No."

"I would like to go, but sports cars are my favourite. I know someone who has a Mazda MX-5 convertible and I've been out in it a couple of times with him."

This didn't sound so good that she might have a boyfriend. But I persisted with the interests in an effort to draw her away from discussing other people.

I said, "Do you like sweets or savouries?"

"Savouries."

"Ah, but you have eaten an apple doughnut. That's sweet," I teased her.

"That's true. But the apple is very tangy and it offsets the sweet, and besides I don't like savoury in the afternoon."

Clever answer.

"OK, my turn back," she said. "Who would you like to play you in a film of your life?"

I thought about that one, then I said, "I don't know his name but it's the one who plays Jason Bourne in the Bourne series."

"Oh, so you consider yourself a jumper, eh?" she asked.

"Yes, I do a lot of falling for people,"

She raised an eyebrow, sipped her coffee, then put the cup down, looked up and asked suddenly, "Have you thought anymore about the cricket project?"

"Well, honestly, as I've said, I'm not the one to be doing this."

"You are. You're the only one who can do it. And furthermore, Rod is so self-interested he's hopeless."

She gave me that wide-eyed heart-quivering stare she had given me in the restaurant.

"He would be better than me," I said.

"No he wouldn't. He can't be relied on. You saw him in action that night. And he has got no support, whereas Moxham would be good. And there's nothing better for the council than an employee like yourself who could devote their time to it."

"But that would provoke friction amongst the clubs."

"Yet it's the council's choice. And I think it's a good idea. Fits in with all their strategies."

I shook my head. "Well, I wish someone else would do it. I don't know anything about cricket."

She put her hands towards me on the table.

"No, but are you against it in principle? I mean, can you see the value of it?"

"Oh yes, I can see the value of it. It's just that I don't know anything about cricket and I can't stand the game."

"Yes, but we'll all lose our jobs unless somebody does something. And you've got the time and the connections in your job at the sports centre to be able to carry it through."

"Well, I'd make a mess of it," I put my hands flatly on the table.

She moved my empty apple doughnut plate to one side, reached further into my space, her hands just hovering above mine, and pleaded straight into my face, "Look, you must do it - because only you can do it. Without it, the whole of the sports service in this area will go down - including school sports."

I went silent. Her eyes were not moving from my face.

"I will help you," she pleaded. "I really will, I've played cricket before. I know a bit about it. I was in a women's team at teacher training college, and I teach it to the children in the summer."

The more I said I did not know anything about cricket, the more she might feel compelled to help me. I liked this idea.

"Also Fardeep will be back soon in mid-February and he will help us," she continued. "You heard Sir Richard. There is some consultancy money, so he will get some expenses for coaching. And he is a great coach. We will do this. I know we can."

Just then, Eine Kleine Nachtmusik started in my breast pocket. I reached for my mobile.

It was Sir Richard. It must be something important, phoning me on my day off.

"Well, have you thought about it?" he asked.

Surprised by the suddenness of the phone call and the aptness of the question, I replied I was still working on it.

"Very good," he said in a firm, presumptive manner as though I had moved along his decision continuum.

Then he changed the subject and asked about Claire and I told him she was here and he asked to be put on to her.

She put the phone to her ear, glanced at me, then looked over the courtyard window and smiled, "Fine now thanks."

A pause. "Yes, we were just discussing it. I'm working on him," she joked. "Yes. Bye."

She passed the phone back to me.

"Well, look," Sir Richard said. "I don't want you to feel as though we're putting pressure on you. Have a think about it. Perhaps we'll speak after Christmas. You give me a ring in the New Year. Just let it percolate at your own pace."

He hung up.

This was better. I was to give him a ring. I felt more in control, at my own pace.

I looked across the table at Claire. Yes, I could do whatever I liked. I was now in a position of power rather than being in a position of being coerced.

Before either of us could speak a little hip-hop tune came from her bag. She took out her mobile. A text.

"Sorry, but I have to go to meet Amy, my flatmate." She mimed a big beseeching apology, turning her mouth down at the corner. "She's waiting. Just finished at the hairdresser's, and she's giving me a lift back."

She got up and, giving a little wave, said cheekily, "See you soon, Captain. Ciao!"

I watched her go out of the door.

Attractive women don't usually eat the cream cakes I recommend. Even more, I liked the idea she could turn out to be helping me.

Helping me with the project, yes, but also helping me to sort out my life. My instinct over the last few years had been to keep my head down and to try to carry on as a duty manager at the sports centre, still doing the odd couple of hours a week of private tennis coaching indoors or at Appleton Water's courts in the summer. But the complaints of the weekend had shown me how decrepit and rundown the place was becoming. The odd flood in a changing room one day, the fused lights in the main hall the next. Even the new lighting circuits blew up. I hadn't seen it coming but I could see now that the whole structure was falling apart and from what they had all said last Friday night the Sports and Leisure Section may be going totally bankrupt. Although I hadn't really wanted to get involved with any of this at the outset, I knew now that somebody would eventually have to.

But if I didn't watch it, I might be sucked in too far here. I would have to tread a fine line: in close enough to reap the rewards, but not so close as to be responsible. Then I would be a free agent.

I thought about her interests. They were not all that different from mine. She did like cream cakes, and I could persuade her. She could persuade me to do things likewise. She did not say much about the friend with the sports car. She did not actually say that she did have a boyfriend. So maybe she didn't. Perhaps the coast was clear in that respect. However, people who charmed others, as she most certainly could, kept their own cards close to their chest.

I had often wondered if my life were to change, how would it happen. Would it be like an earthquake, or would it be a slow imperceptible change?

I could not make out whether my life had been turned upside down or whether it was upside down before and had now been turned right way up, or indeed how many turns it had been given.

It often happens that the person chosen for something important is the one who knows nothing.

CHAPTER FIVE

It was on one of those drizzly dreary January mornings that I regard as a Catch-22 challenge to go to work. Bad if you go and still bad if you don't. The damp chilly air pierced my top jacket and searched for signs of motivational weakness as I pulled the door to the flat shut and climbed into the Jimny.

I turned down onto the main road that leads eventually to Moxham. Through the sparse hedgerow on my right I could see the newly and extensively built Appleton Water Sports Resource Centre on the top of the hill. It dominated the countryside, always in my sight while I drove.

It was a complex building, high-walled redbrick with black-tiled, multi-hipped, stacked roofs housing small halls, state-of-the-science gyms, and changing rooms. Behind it the enormous sweeping green arch roof of the multi-sports Great Hall, huge as an aircraft hangar.

Through all the glass of the main building the light beamed out this morning like a newly-landed spaceship calling the people to come and boost their bodies and optimism. A factory putting out its steamy smoke through the boiler chimney as though it was the by-product exhaust from the exercising process. Appleton Water body pumpers were very early risers, much earlier than Moxhamites.

The traffic slowed past the front driveway gates. I could see right up the drive. A flagged walkway zigzagged artistically across a gravel car park with half a dozen sports cars and large 4x4s, and then curved round up to the front entrance. Bordering the edge of the path against the gravel was an array of bicycle stands, like animals sticking out their legs and heads down to feed at a shore.

The car was beginning to heat up now and I wound the window down a little to let in some fresh morning air.

I changed gear as the road curved to the right and caught a glimpse of the seating surrounding the cricket pitch at the back, just visible round the corner of the Hall. On a little sunken plateau in front of the complex were six tennis courts: three grass, three hard-court. It was here that I came by appointment to do a few hours freelance coaching each week during the summer for anyone able to pay the fees that this private health company charged.

During the winter I would sometimes coach one or two keen beginner tennis players indoors at Moxham if they could not pay the extra money to go to the better indoor facilities at Appleton Water.

I thought of how magnificent this site was, and of how really I would like to be in charge of an independent private sports centre like this rather than the council one at Moxham.

Moxham was in ruins and needed tremendous money just to keep it going. No wonder people were going out of town to the modern fully-equipped one at Appleton Water. If only we could succeed in this bid and claim back the money that was overdue to the area to modernise the Moxham centre. Yet the lead person would have to be a cricketer and, though I was a sports centre manager, my knowledge of cricket was rudimentary. I had barely played it at school, whereas I had been interested in tennis right from the start and had become quite reasonable at it, and now held a Club Coach Award.

So someone else was needed to be the prime mover. Then I could help them, and the beautiful Claire could also help me to help them. However, what if they got someone and she worked closely with them, better than with me? Would I not then be cut out of the loop?

The dilemma closed in on me as the grey drabness of Moxham town did. Its buildings began to infiltrate the fields and I wound the window up defensively.

I pulled round the back of the converted old church hall that was the Moxham Sports Centre. Dirty, decaying, single-glazed, draughty casement windows. I parked in my usual spot close alongside the wall on the passenger side to allow cars to pass up the back alley. As I reversed my rear bumper touched the smelly dustbins overflowing with black bags. A kind of morning greeting between inanimate objects that somehow knew their position.

As usual I was first into the centre and I jiggled open the door with my old heavy key. It was a bad fit; it had been for years.

Every time it had to be manipulated afresh. Each time I was relieved anew as it opened and made a note to myself to chase up a new key, but each time the note was forced from my mind by the urgency of the burglar alarm beeping its thirty second countdown as I hurried to the control panel in the light of the open doorway. I entered the code, unchanged from the factory setting for years because we could never work out how to reset it.

The air inside was musty, damp and cold, with an added tang of rotting wood, excess polish and stale changing rooms. The central heating boiler had been at a bare minimum during the night to stop the building freezing and was sleepily humming awake in the background.

I switched on the lights. Welcome to the bunker. A fluorescent tube down the side passageway to the changing rooms didn't stop flickering. The bucket that I had set near it to catch a drip last night was now overflowing onto the floor. It wouldn't be much longer before the whole place fused.

Fortunately nothing yet had dropped onto the computer on the reception desk or into my little converted storeroom that serves as a back office, though I supposed it was only a matter of time.

Past the reception desk was a wider darker corridor that went down to the little gym room and the Hall behind. Our hall was not Great like Appleton Water. It was barely enough for a children's indoor football game, and had an old cricket net kept folded up against the back wall.

I turned the computer on in the office and dodged past the ceiling drip to get a mug of coffee from the little kitchen.

When I got back, I re-read the e-mail from Sir Richard about meeting up today lunchtime that I had replied to the other day. 13.30 in his office in Moxham Town Hall.

I started checking the staff weekly time sheets, and waited for Ann my deputy and the first customers to come in.

About a quarter of an hour later the front door opened and there was a breezy shout of "Hi!".

It was Ann, her large shoulder bag bustling and rubbing against the door as she came bashing in. She was the same age as me and still single. A slightly dumpy brunette, she had a gentle honest face and a way of welcoming everyone and saying "Hi!" to them before they were within normal social range. That was why she was a receptionist. Her reception preceded her.

"I'll put the kettle on. Do you want a biscuit with it?" she shouted.

She made her interactions with people more flowery than a simple series of grunts that Charles our No3 might do. Indeed, she seemed to go over and above the normal bounds of human social interaction, especially when it came to me. It was a form of over-mothering and here was a case in point. Yet, it was a case where she had come unstuck today.

"There aren't any biscuits," I shouted back. "I've already looked. Charles finished them off over the weekend."

She came to my doorway.

"Ah, but I've bought some." She waved a packet of half-covered digestives.

I made a move towards the packet but she withdrew, leaving only her head round the door and a teasing "Ah hah hah! Not yet. Not until coffee time."

"But it's coffee time now," I said.

"I'll open them in a minute. Just let me get my coat off first."

I heard the clang of her locker behind the reception desk and then her feet down the corridor into the kitchen.

She came back a few minutes later with three biscuits on a plate with a fresh mug of coffee.

"What's your schedule for today?" she asked.

"I've got a meeting with Sir Richard at 1.30 in the Town Hall."

"I'll make you a sandwich to eat before you go. We've got cooked meat in the kitchen we need to use up."

"Fine."

"Then when you get back I'll go out into town and bring back a cake for afternoon tea. You'll need to recover from a meeting with him I suspect."

A cake. We had some old cakes here, but I knew what kind she was thinking of. She was thinking of going into Marmaduke's and getting one of those cream ones. Not wishing to be outdone by my recounting to her a few weeks ago of how I had assisted in the recuperation of an accident victim by feeding her with cream cakes in Marmaduke's, she had been awaiting her turn to play the doctor. Now my recovery from the grilling session with Sir Richard Gregory would give her a chance.

"Look," I said. "I'm just going to tell him once again what I've told him before – that I can't do it, it's not for me – and just to see if he's got anyone else yet."

"Watch your step with him, Jeremy. I don't trust him and the other two. They've all come from nowhere. All together overnight. Sir Richard from down south. I've never heard of him before now. And what was he doing paying for all those big restaurant meals for people? Splashing out like that. Where did he get the money for it?"

"It's all legitimate from expenses," I defended.

"Expenses? Ah yes! The previous bosses never did that. Not as long as I've been here. You never knew the others. They wouldn't bother. They had no expenses. Then there's that Fardeep character. I've never heard of him either. In fact, I've tried to Google him and his name doesn't come up. If he's that famous a cricketer you'd have thought that it would have done."

"Ann, I don't know. He seemed pretty genuine to me. Maybe you have to look him up in a specialist almanac or something."

"Well, if he was only in something obscure then he wouldn't be as famous as people make him out to be, would he? Anyway, what about that Claire? What's such a young woman doing getting mixed up in cricket? If she's any good she wouldn't be here in Moxham. And do you think it was a genuine accident you recovered her from that night? I don't think so."

"Well, she seems a nice genuine person to me."

I looked down at my PC screen and fiddled with the mouse. She moved in closer.

"She's got some other motive I reckon. She'll probably be off in a year. In fact, I've heard that she was in a shortlist of six for St Margaret's and she got the job even though she's hardly out of teacher training college and there were more qualified candidates there who were just passed over. The head's secretary told me. And guess who was on the interviewing panel?"

I shrugged.

"Sir Richard Gregory, no less," she said. "Now how did he get onto an internal interviewing panel for a junior school, when he's a council employee and project consultant?"

"Perhaps he was an external assessor."

"External assessor? He's an assessor all right!" she snorted. "Anyway, my advice is that it'll all come to no good. This place isn't that bad. I know we're having a bit of a struggle during the recession, but you just need to stay here and stick it out with me. Yes, the place needs a coat of paint, and some new lighting in the hall – they're going to do that you say – and you'll feel better after that's done. And the roof patched up. But if we put up with a little bit of inconvenience now this council will see us all right in the long term. They're a good lot. This business about us losing all these jobs and the whole place collapsing is all scaremongering put about by Sir Richard Gregory. You don't hear the top bosses talking about it like that. They're more positive."

"They wouldn't say things because they've got a service to protect. They couldn't say anything in case it damaged morale."

"Hold on now, you're beginning to talk like them. They've got you brainwashed. You be careful. You'll end up all stressed and that'll be good for no one. Cricket's not your game. You make sure you get someone else to do it. Perhaps Rod. He might be a bit proud, but he's good. Stick to your few hours of tennis coaching."

Just then, the front door opened and Ann returned to the desk.

"Hi," I heard her say. "Can I help? Is it two for the badminton as usual?"

There was a grunt. "Yes, and can we have better rackets this time. They weren't so good the ones that bloke gave us last time. The strings were soft."

I recognised the voice from last week. Two older men in tracksuits and trainers carrying sports bags.

"Yes of course. I'll get out a selection for you to choose from."

I heard several rackets clatter onto the counter.

"Um well, thank you. These are better. We'll take these two." His voice was now more relaxed.

That's why she was a natural receptionist. I don't think I could have been as understanding and accommodating as Ann was.

She seemed to take it on as a vocation, to find a way to make everyone happy. Even though it meant that she had to give up something and be humble at the outset, she knew that eventually it would make everyone a winner.

I realised how much the centre depended on her and how everyone was happier when she was on duty. And, although I didn't realise it at the time, especially me.

CHAPTER SIX

"Happy New Year Jeremy. Thanks for coming. I'll be with you in a second." From behind his desk, with eyes fixed on his PC screen, Sir Richard waved vaguely as I entered his office.

"Oh, Happy New year to you as well," I said, trying to be bright and not falling into an automatic belated acknowledgement of the New Year as I had been doing to the flab-fighters that morning. I was also trying to keep detached for the negotiations that I knew would be coming.

"The keys are on the table over there," he said.

This thing about the keys froze me. They were not on my agenda. I had not actually come here to see the keys of the defunct Moxham Cricket Club. I had only agreed to come for a few minutes after lunch to see if he had found somebody to take on the project yet. Possibly, I might then agree to having my arm twisted to help in some fairly minimal way the dynamic and wretched soul. That way I could have all the charisma of the action without needing to take any responsibility. And I could also have a certain person "help" me in turn, though I had not seen her since Marmaduke's. She had gone down South to her parents for Christmas.

"But you know, I've only come to discuss things further without commitment," I said.

"Of course" he assured me, his eyes screwing up as he clicked the mouse. "Although I thought I'd better get the keys anyway so we can see where we're up to. Just to look at them."

I shrugged.

"Where? I can't see them." I looked around.

The smell of beeswax polish stank out the room. It would have been elegant if it had not been applied to such a ridiculously pungent extent. I wondered what or whom they were trying to protect the wood from. His office was a strange mixture of poverty and power. The room was too small and the desk too big. It was dark mahogany and spread across from one corner into the middle.

Sir Richard was so far back into the corner behind it that he looked more like a prisoner than an executive leader. His glasses were down over his nose, his jacket off to reveal his grey cardigan.

On the wall to his left was a casement window with an old style big-vaned radiator set up in front of it like the rib cage of a white dinosaur. His overcoat, still damp and smelling musty from the morning sleet, was hung over one end like a hood over the dinosaur's head.

The whole room had oak-panelled wainscoting to half-way up the wall. To his right was screwed a whiteboard which extended down to overlap the top of the wainscoting. It looked like it was just stuck on, as though the room's occupant had arrived without preparation.

On the whiteboard were notices on different coloured paper and a wall planner. Different pieces of A4 were stapled in sheaves of twos or threes, and attached to the whiteboard's edges with blue tack.

A couple of thick, worn, case note folders and a few pages of fresh balance sheets were scattered across the desk. The wire from his PC trailed to the mains socket in the wall above the wainscoting.

It was the office of a man who was not going to stay here long, as though the ancient radiator and panelling were just tolerating him for the moment and had not made up their minds about him. It was the office of someone who wielded power but knew that he was a transient figure.

This air of impermanence about his presence made me wonder if my turn was next. If this was how he was accommodated then no one was safe. He had been a captain of industry and had been co-opted by the council. This culture had made him and could break him.

There were two bucket-shaped armchairs with high backs and arms. I recognised the type, where you felt you had to tuck all of yourself in as if you were going on a dangerous rollercoaster. As soon as you sat down you felt imprisoned. But that was in contrast to Sir Richard's cheery style of interaction. On the surface you felt cheered to meet him, but there was something spooky about the way that his furniture kept you in your place.

"In the tin," he said, giving his mouse a final click and leaning back in his chair. He turned to me and pointed behind me to a heavy dark oak table with a dirty green leather top.

I picked up an old biscuit tin, but didn't open it. "I'm only here to discuss it further, to see if you've found somebody else to do it instead of me."

He didn't nod or show acknowledgement, but said, "I've had a word with the chief accountant. He says that if you like you can be given an honorarium as a project development officer and we can increase some of the hours of the part-timers to cover you whilst you're not on duty there for one day a week."

The thought of going back into the sports centre for just one day less each week was attractive. Seven hours less each week having to hire out duff equipment, getting the disgruntlement of customers, especially when none of it was my fault. If the project succeeded there would be new money coming. Everything would be upgraded with new equipment, the roof repaired, and I could probably get some more tennis hours.

"Sure there's nobody else?"

"No. we've been through all that. Nobody is in the right position in the organisation. You'll get lots of help: Claire, Fardeep. Probably not Rod, no. But see if you can make contact with Turner the old Moxham man. I've his address and telephone number. Fraternise and proliferate."

He stood up.

"Let's go and have a look at the ground. It'll only take a few minutes' drive across town to look at the building. Just an option reconnoitre. That's all. You'll then be in a proper position to decide. You've got an extra few minutes, I'm sure."

I opened my mouth to speak, but suddenly realised then that I was holding the biscuit tin with the keys in. To try to squirm out of things I would have to give him the keys back, and that would make a bad impression. I suppose it was all right for me to just hold the tin like this for the moment. I wasn't agreeing to anything.

"My secretary got the keys from the key store in the council cellar. The keys were returned to the council for safe-keeping because the land is all owned by the council originally. There's a housing association and the garden centre nearby and both tried to buy the land in the meantime, but the council wasn't selling it. Their option appraisals suggested asset retention. Have a look."

I wrenched it open.

Inside was an old scrunched up brown envelope. I brought the envelope close to my face to peer inside. A smell of grass from a bright English summer morning. A tennis coaching day for me, a cricket day for others.

I emptied the contents of the envelope onto the table. There was an assortment of keys tied up with string. A few pieces of dirt and old grass cuttings came out with them and sprinkled themselves across the keys like magic dust.

Keys had always fascinated me. The more ornate the key, the more wonderful might be that other world beyond.

I picked up the keys and thought of what hands had used them. How they had opened the locks in anticipation early on a brilliant summer morning, the sun high and burning onto the field. A glorious June morning without a cloud in the sky and the keys opening up a hot day of cricket.

Those same hands might have locked away victory or defeat at the end of the day.

Suddenly there was tapping at the window. It was another sleet shower starting. A Mercedes car with full headlamps on and windscreen wipers was trying to manoeuvre round the yard below. The summer that had come, bright and beautiful with the grass cuttings, had in the next instant returned to winter.

An old label card of the sort used on suitcases before the modern plastic snap wrapper was tied to the keys. The old card part of the label had gone but there was still the little brown cardboard ring of the eyelet. I thought of the cardboard labels of old coach and train journeys. It was as if these keys had been on a journey themselves and were now coming back through time. Though their labels were lost, they remained together as a team. Their brass warmed up so quickly in my hands.

Holding the bunch in my left hand, I fingered the largest key with my right. It had an elaborate filigree handle shaped like an ace of clubs, and its shaft ended with sturdy teeth on the bitting.

"That must be the front door to the pavilion. They knew how to make keys in those days," he said. "Not like the modern pavilion at Appleton Water. That's all electronic and computerised there."

The locks must have been made by a master locksmith decades ago. No wonder the council were keen on reviving Moxham rather than any other team. No other club grounds would ever come close to rival the majesty of the splendour of the pavilion judging from that one key alone.

It put into perspective the old rundown Moxham sports centre in which I worked. It was strange that no great noise should have been made about promoting the heritage of Moxham before. How many more of these gems was the council quietly sitting on and just letting decay? Surely somebody round and about must know of the ground and its history? Surely not all just dirty records kept in the town hall cellar?

The key slipped comfortably in my hand as I brought the next key round on the ring. This was much heavier and not so filigreed in the handle but had a stouter bow at the handle end and the shaft was stubbed. The blade ended in a single beefy square of brass with a large notch in the middle of each side edge drawn in like a waist so that the blade looked like two triangles joined at their vertices. Here was nothing so intricate, but a strong lock none the less.

"That must be for the back door," I said to Sir Richard. "The strongest and oldest key there."

Next on the string were two long and thin keys, and a third was slightly shorter. It would fit a tumbler lock in the bottom of a padlock.

"They're probably for outbuildings," he said. "Maybe the shed for the mower and the padlock on the gate. Any way we'll see. Investigate and revisualise. In fact, this is how it used to look," he said, picking up a painting from the floor behind his desk and turning it round to show me.

A painting of a cricket ground on a bright summer's day. A classical view, with the green playing field at the bottom of the picture, a match in progress, and the pavilion and buildings at the top of the picture. It was crudely painted with distorted perspective by a thick and heavy hand. It had been forced from a wide angle to get the whole ground in with its buildings.

The pavilion was at the top and the scorebox to the left and the garage to the right. It was exactly as I had imagined it from my reverie with the keys.

The pavilion was a magnificent structure. There was a generous veranda on which players relaxed in easy chairs. It was clear that there were many rooms inside, perhaps a large central room, and there were figures in white looking out from the windows either side of a grand central double doorway. I felt that I could almost see inside that central area. It might have had a notice board at the back for team news, a kitchen servery, a ladies toilet, changing rooms, toilets and showers.

The roof was pitched and red-tiled. I could just make out that the steps in the middle leading up to the veranda had ornately carved banister rails.

To the left of the pavilion was a small shed behind a wooden flat-roofed scorebox on which was displayed the score at 111 for 3, and two figures inside, one waving an arm to the umpire on the field who was signalling with arms high. The players were painted in awkward postures, and one of the batsmen was following through a flamboyant stroke.

To the far right outside the green playing area was the grey car park with a prefabricated concrete-walled garage with a flat sloping roof, the door slightly ajar to show part of a mowing machine of sorts.

The cars in the car park seemed to be from the fifties or sixties because I recognised the models of the cars.

In the bottom right was an artist's signature "Turner".

"Surely not <u>the</u> Turner?" I asked.

"No. Of course not. But the father of one of the Moxham cricketers."

I thought that if it was in any way the remotest bit now like the splendour of that bygone age, then surely it must be worth saving.

He looked at it proudly, and then said. "Well that's how it was about forty or fifty years ago. I'm afraid I've been told that there's been some neglect and vandalism since there was last a team there. The horticultural department say it will certainly be overgrown because no one from the council has been there for eight years. Anyway, let's investigate."

I suggested we take my little Suzuki 4x4 Jimny because afterwards I could just drop Sir Richard off outside the Town Hall and carry on back to the sports centre without delay. I didn't have a lot of time since I would have to relieve Ann who needed her afternoon break from the reception desk. The sleet had stopped a few minutes ago but the skies were still heavy and would bring some more. Sir Richard sat in the front seat with the biscuit tin on his lap.

We took the short route, driving out onto the main street and out of town to the East, turning right opposite Blade Farm and went up Nova Lane. Nova Lane was a narrow street at the side of the housing estate that marked its lower boundary with the back gardens on the right and the fields on the left surrounding Moxham. We were going clockwise round the outskirts of the town.

The sleet started again heavily. "It's along here somewhere. You would have thought there would have been a sign telling people where it was," he muttered, peering through the hard-working windscreen wipers.

"Ah. There. Romiley Lane. Up there." He pointed to a narrow unmade track, hidden between large bushes and just passable in a small car.

The overhanging hawthorn and elder screeched against the car as we drove up the track and I couldn't tell if it was welcoming or resisting us. I wondered if we would eventually get by or whether we should have to reverse back.

We craned our necks eager to see the gateway. Sir Richard had now opened the box, had the key to the gate's padlock, and was ready to jump out.

"Right here, can you get in here? It's a concealed entrance I think, you have to turn a right hairpin to get in," he said.

A sign appeared amongst the bushes. Its faded black lettering on rotting wood was vandalised "Moxy Prick Club".

We turned a very sharp hairpin right and there was the gateway. The five bar gate was wide open, rotten and hanging by only its bottom hinge.

I drove through a little way then paused. I scanned the field for the pavilion, garage, scorebox, and toilet block but could not see them. Instead, up at the top of the field was the remains of a building, blackened and charred. It was totally decrepit. Only three sides and no roof. Some wooden steps led up to the front where there seemed to have been a door at one time. Nearby two other separate piles of bricks and burnt wood.

"Are you sure we have the right field?" I asked.

"Yes," he said. "I'm afraid so."

CHAPTER SEVEN

The Jimny laboured on the long wet grass. We drove slowly north up the right side of the field towards the three ruins. I hoped that this debris was some fantastic trick or even misperception on my part and that the old pavilion would suddenly appear from behind there as if by magic. Yet as we neared the ruins their reality grew stronger the more I tried to disbelieve it. Over the eastern hedge to our right we could see only the backs of houses on the estate, and ahead over the hedge on the northern side just the massive greenhouse of the garden centre.

"Why didn't the residents phone the police?" I asked Sir Richard as we got out. "They would have seen or heard something for sure."

"Perhaps they didn't phone the police because they didn't know anything was happening. This didn't happen overnight, Jeremy. It happened bit by bit, drip by drip."

He kicked some rotten wooden planks in frustration that were lying loose as we walked across the final few yards. "Years ago there would have been a puncture in the roof – a little drip when it rained- nothing for anyone to get worried about. It would have been patched up quickly. Then the patch would have leaked, gradually bit by bit. Drip by drip. I suppose eventually it would become tolerated as a joke. Then when the Old Moxham team wound up there was no one to maintain it."

He shrugged and looked towards the hedgerows.

"So of course the kids would play here, and when a little bit of wood got rotten they would prise and poke at it because they had nothing else to do. If it was rotten then it was nobody's." He kicked another plank. It flipped over to reveal yellowed grass, worms and mud underneath.

We walked past the remains of the garage. The stone walls were weathered with green moss. Tufts of grass were growing in the top of the flat roof which had collapsed forward over the red doorway.

I peered in. A sturdy shelf with rusted tins and an old bird's-nest had collapsed on the back wall.

The sleet stung my face as I looked round for shelter. Instinctively I made for the pavilion.

But it was a paltry and pathetic shelter. The front façade of the building was still there but it had virtually no roof now, just a hipped framework of bare rafters with a few roof tiles still covering a back corner.

"It's a bit different from the painting," Sir Richard complained.

I half-closed my eyes and saw it in front of me. There were the steps up to the front, the veranda and windows and then the pitch of the roof. But I could not hold the image of its former glory strongly enough in my mind to offset my outrage. In fact, it seemed that the more I tried to picture it as it was in the painting, the more painful it was when I eventually lost concentration and returned to reality and the present ruins.

I mounted the three wide brick steps to the front doorway. Inside was a central lounge area, and two corridors leading off it: one either side of a kitchen servery at the back.

Everywhere was wet and half of the floorboards had been ripped up so I had to step from one to another, slowly testing each new board with part of my weight first, watching out for nails. Small shards of green glass crunched underfoot.

"Don't go in any further - it might still collapse!" cried Sir Richard from the entrance. "It needs a risk assessment first."

Like visiting a ghoulish scene, I had to keep on looking.

The outlines of bricks showed where walls had lost their plaster. To the right, behind me near the bottom in a corner, unashamedly declared, black against the dirt white walls, the words "Charlotte 4 Alan".

"I think someone's been in and the roof has collapsed as much as it's going to for now," I said.

Behind the servery the plumbing had been pulled away at odd angles. Pipes and wires lay half-wrenched from the wall like exposed nerves.

Pinned to the back wall of the kitchen was a notice whose ink had run and was inside a plastic wallet curling at the edges: "Please switch kettle off after use."

Sir Richard called from the doorway "This is a bit like the entrance to your Moxham sports centre, isn't it? This servery here is where your reception desk is? With the toilets to the left?"

I gave a shudder. Yes, the toilets would be up that left passageway. In that moment my memory of Moxham sports centre coalesced with my eerie experience now. A brief flash, then it passed again. Yet there was no door like that here, just a doorway. The door frame had been ripped from the jamb to expose the bricks.

"Yes," I said, snapping myself out of it. "But it's not the sports centre."

"Yes, but it could be. It could be if you don't do something about it."

I dismissed it as a tired reverie, sighed, and kicked at some plaster on the floor to steady myself.

Across the top of the notice board to the left of the servery were still the words "Moxham Cricket", but the rest had rotted away. The remains of one notice was still attached to the board by drawing pins in three of its corners. It was just possible to make out "Subscriptions 1999 now due" and some names which were smudged, but in the bottom corner more clearly "W K TURNER, Honorary Treasurer."

Sir Richard said: "That looks like your notice board."

And once again I could only gasp at what seemed a visual transformation in front of my eyes. My board in the sports centre was crowded with notices of different colours and, though this board here was rotten and broken, I could see how my familiar notices would look here in their shades of blue, fluorescent yellow and emergency red.

Up the right passageway there was only darkness as parts of the roof still remained on the back. Yet it was too risky to go in further. Anything could collapse on top of me.

As I looked down into that dark space I began to imagine myself back at the sports centre again, and could hear the cries of children playing football in the hall, and the thud of the ball against the inside of the door. It stayed for a couple of seconds or so, and then I retraced my steps and walked solemnly around the outside of the building in the sleet.

Beyond the pavilion the outside toilet block with scorer's hut was as bad as the garage. Though the roof was slightly better, most of the front of the hut was missing. On the floor a broken metal-framed canvas chair and an empty water bottle, and three lager cans – the rubbish of many seasons ago.

Sir Richard was following me round, the keys still in his hands, but there was no sign anywhere of doors, let alone locks, to try them in.

I thought, right that's it. Forget it. Nothing here. I can't take forward something that isn't here.

No one could blame me if I just walked away like everyone else. I need not care if I really didn't want to.

But if I did not care, no one else would. So where would it stop?

Then a strange calmness came over me as I realised that this had nothing to do with cricket. I need not fear that. My anger turned to pity, pity for how run-down this place had become, and strangely I found myself smiling inanely with a feeling of gratitude. Gratitude in part to Sir Richard for showing me this, but mainly to these ruins on this sleeting midwinter day for having shown me a path. Gratitude indeed for seeing where my life might lead and what my calling was.

"OK" I said. "Let's go. I can't stand this any more. You're right. I'm going to have to do something. It's got to be me. Just don't let me have to do it all alone."

Sir Richard smiled. "Good. That's the right decision. You'll get Fardeep and Claire and a whole team to help you. And I'll keep in touch. Just sort out a night in a few weeks when we can start using the hall for nets practice. I'll have some notices printed that you can put up throughout Moxham. That's all you have to do. Just diarise and delegate."

He nodded towards the ruins, screwing his face against the sleet. "I'll tell them to bulldoze this and we'll get a new pavilion set up."

"Great, you mean we'll rebuild it?"

"No. That would be more of a problem. It requires an architect's revisualisation and would cost too much money. We haven't got it. But we could in the future one day if we succeed with the bid. "

Then after looking round the field he pointed to the car park. "Only it'll have to be a temporary structure over there till the bid succeeds. Just a cabin from stock to show the project inspection panel we are serious."

I nodded and we walked back to the car.

It took several attempts to turn round out of the tight hairpin entrance the way we had come.

Sir Richard balanced the biscuit tin of keys on his lap like he had done during the journey here. Only this time it was different. Whereas before they had rattled and chattered excitedly loose in the box as if they were bursting to get out, now they made no noise sealed back again into their crumpled paper.

I felt that my imagination had been mugged by those keys. For a few minutes I had imagined their glory, only to be dashed by the revelation of their orphanage. The keys were the only substantial things that remained about Moxham Cricket Club. The rest was fantasy and memory.

It occurred to me in my fragile mood that it all might have been one of Sir Richard's management ploys to give me the illusion of being free to decide, but subtly persuading me by shock tactics.

I asked him if he knew that the ground would be bad before we went there.

"A bit," he said, looking out of the side window and avoiding my gaze. "Although I didn't expect it to be that bad. I am as shocked as you."

At that time I believed him.

CHAPTER EIGHT

It was early Wednesday morning a few weeks later in Moxham Sports Centre and I was at the PC in my office.

I heard the main door open and Ann shout "Hi!" as she entered. She always knew if I was there because she could see my light, though we could not see each other. There was a pause, and then she appeared at my doorway still with her coat on and carrying a riding hat. She put it on and posed, hat cocked, hand on tilted hip.

"How do I look?"

"Horsey?" I asked.

"Don't forget it's my day off this afternoon."

Then I remembered. She was having a visit from an old friend and she had specially planned this afternoon off in advance.

"I've been able to book the same horses that Cindy and I had last summer. I booked them weeks ago when I knew she was coming. Mine's called Chestnut. It was glorious then and we went for miles. And today is such a lovely day, a rare early spring day." She closed her eyes and breathed in deeply.

"Wow, you must really be looking forward to it."

"Yes. Isn't it great?"

The main door opened again. It was the postman with the internal post from the Town Hall. Ann went to the reception desk and came back with a large brown envelope.

"I think these are the notices at last," I said, taking the envelope.

Intrigued, she watched me open it. Inside was a sheaf of bright red A4 posters advertising the Nets Practice next Wednesday.

It had taken Sir Richard weeks to get these printed. I think because he wanted to use a picture of a famous cricketer and he had to wait for copyright permission which probably never arrived. So, at the finish, the council promotions department decided to take an old photograph and blur it so that it was unrecognisable.

However, it still looked pretty impressive: a side view of a batsman taking a large aggressive stride with the bat raised ready to drive.

"Oh no!" I said. "Sir Richard says here in his note that we need to put them up all round town so that people who come into town midweek will have enough notice for next Wednesday. Today really is the last day to put them up. Damn! Because of my work schedule today I've only got my lunch hour so I'll have to do it then, otherwise it will be too late."

"I don't think that's good planning," she said. "Why can't they find someone else to put them up? You're getting involved too much as I've said."

"Well, it's all got so delayed. It'll fail unless I do it now. It's been left too long."

"Jeremy, it's not fair of them landing all this on you."

"I know, but there's no one else."

"You'll make yourself ill rushing about like this in your lunch hour. I'm worried about you."

I studied Sir Richard's note again and looked at the batsman frozen at the moment of attack.

"I think I'd better help you," she suddenly said, her wide eyes showing concern. "I'll get Cindy to help me. We'll go riding later on. Chestnut is very popular, but hers will probably still be available later in the afternoon."

"But it's nice weather today and you've planned it for ages. It's really rare at this time of year to get such a couple of hours of sunshine. And you haven't seen Cindy for months. I can see this is really important to you. I can't let you do that."

"Oh, I can still meet her and we can go round town instead, round the shops. I know she'd like to go riding but the riding school can give us a session with that particular horse on another day. We'll just take the horses that are available later on in the afternoon for a quick trip. They will understand. I know the riding school people."

"Yes, but it'll be dark by then and you won't get a proper ride."

"She might be able to stop off again on the way back down from her business trip in a few days."

I hadn't thought she'd be so kind and self-sacrificing. A weight lifted off my mind.

"But I won't go putting them up where others can easily do it themselves," she said sternly, taking a thick sheaf of the posters from me.

"Oh no. Fine. Sir Richard is doing the council offices and Claire is doing the school and the youth club. You just go round a few shops with Cindy. I'll do the swimming pool and the post office."

"What about Marmaduke's? Claire goes in there a lot. Will she put one up in there?"

"I'm not sure if Claire will be in there today. She may be in at lunchtime. I suppose I could go into Marmaduke's." I flustered, cuddling one of the posters carefully to me.

I did want to see Claire again, but I wasn't certain she would be in town today. She sometimes got a few hours break because she was part-time, but it was unpredictable and she was usually asked to stay on at St Margaret's and work through. If I did go in and wait for the off-chance of seeing her then I would not have time to do the swimming pool and post office because they are in a completely different direction. If I did not put up those notices, then she and Sir Richard would be mad with me for failing in the project. Regretfully, in order to keep her sweet I would have to give up the opportunity of seeing her today.

"I will be there because it's next to the railway station where I'm meeting Cindy." Ann said. "Give me a notice for there. Claire might turn up, she might not. That's typical of her type. I'll put it up if you can't rely on whether she'll make it to town or not in her off-time. Especially when you are giving up your own time, that's a bit rich."

I reluctantly and carefully handed over the poster I was cradling, as though it was the most precious one from the whole envelope, and she snatched it roughly.

"That's it. Now I'll make some coffee," she said with a triumphant smile as though she had won some kind of minor victory, and placed the posters possessively on her reception desk.

In my lunch hour I dashed through town to the swimming pool and the post office, giving myself indigestion with a tough cheese and beef sandwich as I walked.

Later that evening as I drove home along Moxham High Street I caught flashes of Ann's posters in the shop windows. Most shop windows showed them. To have convinced so many shopkeepers, even ones that normally do not display notices, showed how diligent Ann and her friend had been. The red posters burned like beacons announcing the resurgence of Moxham, alerting all in the town. Each one was a bright spark of hope for our project.

With each one I saw, they crowded more so in my mind with another kind of presence. A presence beyond words, a significance I couldn't understand, or perhaps I wasn't ready to understand then.

CHAPTER NINE

I looked at my watch again. 7.40 pm. Ten minutes after start time, first nets night in the Moxham Sports Centre hall and still no one else there except me.

I drew out the cricket netting from the far wall. Its curtain rollers clattered along the ceiling tracks, echoing across the empty hall. Though I was pulling out a piece of sports equipment for action it seemed to me more like drawing a curtain across a project.

Nets would be held on Wednesday evenings until the start of the season. At this first meeting in mid-February I would know if a real cricket champion would come forward to restart the club.

I glanced at the door again. I desperately wanted it to open and a lot of people to come through there. Real cricketers, who could play properly, not just people like me. Real cricketers who had a passion for the game, who stayed up all night to watch live broadcasts from Australia. People who booked their holidays as part of tours to the subcontinent to see the great players in action. But were there any in Moxham, and would they come tonight? Even if only one such person would come down that corridor by chance; even if they put their head round the door looking desperately for the toilet (with a family waiting outside on double yellows in the rain); even if only one such person would discover us and would volunteer to take the idea forward - then my livelihood and the sports and leisure provision in the county could be saved.

I walked over and opened the door just to check if anyone was there, rehearsing a fantasy of being trampled by a stampede of people who had been waiting ready to rush in at the appointed time as they do at the start of the New Year Sales.

Few people ever came in the evenings after eight. Only perhaps a hard core of three or four regulars who would just flash their membership cards and needed nothing from reception on their way to the little gym. This was their quiet time. They knew the setup better than anyone and were accepting by now of the seedy smell of this tired building at the end of a day. The indoor footballers had gone, and I had wedged the male changing room door open to allow the warm pungency of shower air and pheromone deodorants to diffuse out of the changing room window. Yet it had also succeeded in drifting into the empty dirty white corridor with its glaring fluorescent tube lighting which ran down to the reception desk at the far end. There Claire sat with a notice on the desk saying "Cricket Nets" and an arrow pointing back up this way.

She heard me open the hall door and dragged her attention away from the evening paper to give me a commiserative smile.

She wasn't an employee of the sports and leisure section but since I was the only one in the building tonight I would therefore have to split my time between the reception desk and the cricket in the hall. She had volunteered to staff the reception area and had been given a lift here by a school colleague. I wondered whether this was because she was getting keen on me. Certainly, she wouldn't have offered to sit in at the reception desk if she didn't like me.

"Let Ann have the evening off," she had said. "You and I can handle it all by ourselves."

Ann was still uncertain about the whole project. She would help me if I was desperate and there were no others who could help, but she didn't like helping them if she didn't have to. Going out in the fresh air, shopping and distributing notices, was one thing, but sitting at the reception desk for yet another boring evening in the sports centre when she had been there all week was another.

"Mind she doesn't mess with the way I've set up the computer," Ann had said as she left at five o'clock.

"Don't worry. She won't be trying anything like that," I had reassured her.

"Ah, yes, but you never know. I know her sort. I wouldn't be surprised if she's a hacker. And mind she doesn't go through my desk and mess up my filing system. Also I don't like the idea of somebody adjusting my chair. I've worked out that setting for my own legs and back exactly."

"She won't. She'll just sit on the chair and watch the door," I said as Ann left.

Now, installed on that chair, Claire looked very appropriate in a tracksuit, a change from her formal clothes. It fitted in with the council's efforts to echo a sporty lifestyle for the visitors. There was a nice neat athleticism about her body. I imagined it warm inside her tracksuit, soft and cuddly wool. With her long hair tied in a pony-tail she looked as though she was going to play cricket herself.

I felt a little sad that I would be separated from her. I mean, here was a golden opportunity for me to get her on her own. I should be up at the front desk with her chatting. But she had not arrived till almost just before the appointed start time. Meanwhile I had to immediately prepare the hall because the indoor footballers had not left until a few minutes before our start. I was occupied just when I should be chatting up Claire.

Suddenly she turned her attention back to the entrance door to look outside. My heart leapt as I thought she was watching someone I could not see coming into the building. Then just as quickly as this moment had come, she slumped her head wearily back down onto her shoulders, turned to me and shook her head to acknowledge the false alarm.

I went back into the Hall, quietly turning the handle in studied precision, as though not wishing to disturb my luck for tonight. I watched myself close the handle and couldn't believe how timorous I had become in the deserted silence of my own sports centre.

I placed the set of sprung self-righting cricket stumps down the far end inside the netting where a batsman would be. A feeling of indignation welled up inside me that no one else was here. Then it occurred to me that I should have closed that door with a slam to make the point to whatever gods in charge of the fate of this building might be watching. I should have let them know with a defiant door bang that I was here and ready for action and would now fight against any further deterioration in service.

I plonked a cone down on the open end to serve as the bowler's stumps and breathed out forcefully.

Yes, I thought, I will open this door again and bang it in frustration to signify to anyone who needed to know that this was not a quiet part of the universe that would go down without resistance till closing time. I will disturb the gods.

Gritting my teeth in anger I marched over and grasped the handle and wrenched it open. The full power of my tug caught me off balance as it was simultaneously propelled with force towards me from the other side. Right in front of me was a sturdy figure in white trainers, dark tracksuit bottoms and white pullover, all topped with the unmistakeable navy blue turban and beard.

"Hah! Jeremy!" Fardeep's loud voice filled the hall as he strode in. "What? No one here yet?"

"Give them a little time," I said, trying to instill hope against the inevitable conclusion that anyone would reach from surveying an empty hall ten minutes after an appointed starting time.

"What about Claire, is she not coming in to join us? We need a few more people. Can we use her?" He scratched his beard and looked at me as if I was guilty of not using everybody that I could.

"It's OK," I said. "She's volunteering to stay there and show people the way. She might join us later when everyone has come. I don't think that she plays much cricket. She might be a good fielder on account of teaching rounders and such."

He shrugged.

"Yes, maybe. Maybe she will surprise us all," and he walked thoughtfully over to the netting.

He swirled his arms around a couple of times and bent his body at the hips from one side to the other.

"Let's have a little go while we're waiting," he said, lifting his knees and stepping a sprightly little dance to warm up his body.

"Perhaps we ought to wait till someone else comes first," I mused, afraid that I might come to be regarded as the champion of the cause if others came and found me taking an early lead.

"Nonsense!" he smiled, "Have you got a bat and ball?"

"Well, yes, an old bat and tennis and cricket balls from the storeroom but I don't know if we have time before the main group of people arrive."

"Nonsense! There is always time, Jeremy. Let me give you some batting coaching. That is what you need, isn't it?"

I needed coaching with everything since I had absolutely no idea. I had been looking at the cricket websites that he had recommended in his e-mail a few weeks ago, and I had tried following some of the exercises there with little enthusiasm. It seemed to me that hitting a tennis ball off an upturned paper cup using a cricket bat was a little bit too much like golf to be useful for cricket, even though it was recommended to take a stride and put your body into it.

I had played cricket when very young but I was never any good at the game. I was always out cheaply and was hit by the ball a few times, and preferred a sport with a softer ball like tennis.

"I will throw you a few balls and you can see how you get on." He picked up a tennis ball and spun it in his hand. "When people come they will see us working here and then they can watch us as part of a teaching workshop and join in."

I liked the idea of other people joining in and taking over but didn't like the idea of them watching me beforehand to see how hopeless I was.

"All right," I said. "But not fast. I can't do that".

"No"

"And not with a hard ball."

"No. With a tennis ball. Go in the net and I will drop some balls for you to hit just like in the videos but we will not use an upturned cup as a tee. I will drop the ball for you to hit on the bounce. I will just drop them gently, OK? There is no problem here."

He let a ball fall gently from waist height, and caught it after the bounce to demonstrate his point.

"But first I will show you how to grip the bat properly. Put it on the ground and pick it up like you would an axe because the bat and the axe are one. The bat will cut through the opposition's bowling like felling a tree. "

I did as he said.

"See, you are holding the bat handle like an eagle's talons grips its prey. You are squeezing the life from your strokes. Yes, you must hold it firmly by the top hand, but the bottom hand must be gentle and guiding."

He pointed to my thumb and forefinger.

"Now see that your hands are aligned. The V formed by the webbing cleft between the first finger and thumb of one hand is directly in line along the handle with the V of your other hand."

I had thought about all that before in tennis. In tennis we would occasionally use a double-handed grip and I had explored the dynamics of how the two hands should grip the handle in relation to one another. We'd worked it all out from the standard single-handed grips. But I didn't know it also applied so precisely to cricket. I thought you just tried to hit it.

"Look. Let us go down to near the stumps. I will drop the ball here just at the extent of your stride and I want you to let it bounce and then take a stride and hit it just as it comes up."

He motioned with his left hand, the back of it directly away from him forward as though he was playing a shot.

At first I had thought that this was going to be relatively easy. All I had to do was to repeat near enough what had been in the videos. I also had tennis skills so it was easy to use these. I knew all about how tennis balls bounced.

My first shot was a lazy attempt. It was more of a dab which sent the ball in the air. It was obviously a kind of hybrid aerial tennis-cum-cricket shot.

"No, no, no!" Fardeep cried. "You are like a charging rhino. Like a rhino you charge but cannot see – all he has is a horn. He charges mad without control! His prey is tossed in the air by his horn. You are like a rhino- but you must reach like an elephant and kill like a tiger.

"You see the elephant he has a trunk and he reaches forward like you but then curls the trunk back towards him. An elephant's trunk curls in. So you must let the ball come into you. Reach out with your eyes, not your bat and let the ball come into you. Look over the ball as you hit it. Over your front foot. Down. And I want to see the top of your head as you look down."

I bent my head down and let him move my arms and bat into position under my eyes.

"Bend your knees like a tiger pouncing, you see. Your weight must go into the ball. Your weight must be whipped into it. The tiger's prey is underneath him when he kills."

He snarled "tiger" as he dropped the next ball.

I thought, yes, I'll whip into it. I'll kill it with a swipe from my tiger's claw when the ball is underneath my eyes like he says.

But it ended up no more than an airy flick.

"No! Do not force the body to go where you think it needs to go. The body learns its space from the head. If the eyes stay on the ball the head will bring the body to the right place. Look at the ball as it hits the bat. Can you see it do so?"

I wondered how you can see the moment when the ball hits the bat. The mind and eye is not fast enough for that, surely. Even in tennis we cannot see the ball on the racket. We only think we can.

He bounced another ball. I patted this one again but I couldn't see the moment the ball hit the bat. I saw the ball only a short while before contact and a short while afterwards.

"You must believe that you can see it. To achieve that there is a way. You must behave as though you have seen it. Do ghosts exist?"

"I don't know. I've never seen one," I said as I struck another ball.

"No. That is because your mind does not want to see them. But if you believed in them you'd see them. People haven't seen them, except very few. Clearly those people who want to believe in them will see them. Similarly flying saucers. People want to believe in life from other planets and those who are ready to believe will see them."

He dropped another ball and I struck it and felt the soft splat of a tennis ball and a bat, and saw the ball speeding away. I had a surge of accomplishment.

"See! Yes! You have done it. That is subliminal perception. So it is with you. Your eyes can see the ball, but your mind will not let them. You must always look for it even though you don't think you can see it. Stare deeply down into the ball. Even though you don't know it … part of your mind will see it."

Excited, I struck another ball, but not as cleanly as the last one.

"You must be perfectly calm to be able to look into the eye of the shot and see the ball in there. It is a secret which you must learn. It is all slow motion. Your bat will come down very slowly even though you are there hitting it. In reality it is moving at very fast speed, but to you - you will see it slow. It is like time stopped."

"Yes, but I don't think I'll have the time to see any faster balls," I said.

"Yes you will. There is always time," he said. "I will prove you have twice as much time as you think. And you will have it because you will make more space in your mind."

He nodded as I looked up to query what he meant.

"I will show you. Sit down over there on that bench against the wall. I will show you what I mean."

Rather puzzled I sat on the bench at the open end of the netting near the door.

"Now," he said, sitting on the bench beside me. I could smell a strong scent of garlic coming from him. His voice dropped and slowed.

"Now relax. Look at your watch, at the seconds display. See how fast it is moving? Yes. Now remember that speed. Now close your eyes and relax. Clear your mind and just concentrate on your breathing. Gently in and out. Think of nothing but the breath coming in and out. Relax."

He continued with this soft hypnotic tone for what could have been almost a minute. I often used relaxation techniques so this was natural for me.

"Now you are centred. Keep your eyes closed, but raise your watch hand in front of your face. Now, when I say 'Go' I want you to open your eyes and the first thing I want you to see is the seconds display of your watch. You will see how the first second you see passes very slowly."

Bemused, I raised my hand as he said. I hadn't tried this part of relaxation before and wondered what he was getting at.

"Now, are you ready? Then open your eyes and look."

I opened my eyes and I saw the seconds display by chance was on 51, and it seemed to stop there, taking such a long time to change to 52. After that the seconds went at their normal speed to 53 and then 54.

A flush of excitement came over me. I turned to face him and he laughed. The overpowering smell of garlic and the dark eyes flared in his triumph.

"See. That is what is happening. That is how it should be. You have emptied your mind so you can see all of the moment. The moment is as long as your mind can make it. Then when the display changes to show the next second your mind is distracted. The world has taken over again and your mind is full of the change and back to normal speed."

He raised both of his hands together as if he was holding the next point out in front of him like a bowl.

"The secret of getting into the zone in batting is to train yourself to empty your mind so you can stay in that first second. Just for the time of a second is all you need. Make time pass like that very slowly, by emptying your mind. That is what happens when you are in the zone. Think of nothing but the ball. Your mind is so empty that you can see everything. Time is slow and you have so much time for your reactions."

I giggled in wonder at the simple elegance of the idea.

"So," he continued. "With the fastest balls: do not be afraid of them because the more you look at them the more you will see. As you watch it more so it will appear to slow down. You will have more time. You have more time than you think. It is only your own fear and your refusal to look that shortens your time. If you do not look all the time you do not have the time to see. Empty your mind and think only of the ball. It will appear to slow down.

"Come back now down to the net. Take your stance as before. Only this time, really clear your mind. In your practice you must spend time to relax and meditate. You will see more if you allow yourself to see. If you can stay calm you will see the way. No matter how good and clear your eyes, it is only when we clear our mind that we can truly see."

He dropped another ball, and as I was still focused on the watch experiment I was able to see it in detail. I saw how it bounced and rotated. In its short travel I saw it was a dirty yellowish green tennis ball. I saw how it slowed as it reached the top of its bounce. I saw my bat come slowly down and then the ball rocketed away along the ground.

I was not attempting to force it or control it. I was not being the batsman or the bat. I was the whole piece of cricket. Before this moment if someone had said, do you believe in ghosts and flying saucers? I would have said no because I hadn't seen them or experienced them. I do believe now.

As the ball sped away across the hall floor it hit the entrance door. I marvelled at my timing but the sound broke my concentration and in that moment my mind began to dwell on the fact that no one had turned up yet. 'Yet'- I said to myself I was going to use that word. 'No one had turned up "yet"'. Implying that someone still might and I wondered whether it would be better to check it periodically to see if there was anyone there. But perhaps one look too many might mean that I was disturbing my luck by tempting fate. Or there again, perhaps I should look because that's how I managed to get Fardeep to appear.

With part of my attention now on that door I missed the next ball.

"No," said Fardeep. "It must be like a meditation. Prepare your mind open. Do not think. Just watch what happens to the ball. Watch yourself hit it. Your strokes will be without thought, at the reflex level. The best batsmen are those whose minds have been trained. If you get excited or dismayed then you must let go and bring your attention back to the ball, and only to the ball. Forget the last one. If you want something, just still your mind. Let your mind be the space between thoughts."

I did. I took a deep breath, centring myself. I brought my mind back to that space between the thoughts, ready for the next ball.

And then the door opened.

CHAPTER TEN

The door opened and two young men in their early twenties came in.

"Is this the cricket? A woman said it was down here," said the first one, striding into the hall carrying a kit bag over his shoulder. He had fair hair which was slightly curled on top. Of medium height, he had an upturned nose so that to some people he might look cute, but to others it might appear as though his face was pressed forward against a window in an effort to pry into your business.

He came straight up to us, with a slight smile on his face which softened the force of his approach.

"Yes!" both Fardeep and I exclaimed at the same time.

"Is this all there are then?" he asked, looking round the hall, as though there might be others lurking about that he had not seen.

"You're the first," I said extending a hand. "My name's Jeremy and this is Fardeep."

"Luke," he said, shaking hands with us both, "and this is Simon."

Simon, of similar build, had short dark hair, and a larger kitbag which he dumped on the ground in front of him with a clunk. "Any more coming?" he asked.

"I'm hoping so," I said, but then wished afterwards that I should have said something more encouraging, for he turned his mouth down glumly at one side. Still, I could have pretended that there were hordes of people coming but then I would have been found out. At least this way I was being honest even though it hurt me and embarrassed me to admit that this was all there was so far – just us.

"What do you do, bat or bowl?" asked Fardeep.

"A bit of both," Luke replied.

"And you?" Fardeep asked Simon.

"More batting than bowling," Simon said, walking towards the lane of netting and peering down.

"Do you have any matting for this?" he asked. "After all, on a hard floor like this the balls are going to ping about."

I didn't like the idea of a hard ball pinging about, especially if I was one who might be pinged by it. So I desperately searched my brain and remembered the matting in the storeroom.

"I think there's something in the equipment store – some matting we could use," I said, trying to give an air of the sports centre being well-equipped with lots of modern pieces of kit.

We went to the storeroom across from the hall and Fardeep seized upon the only roll of matting in there. It was dirty and old. He grunted in an attempt to move it, saying, "Here, help me with this judo matting."

It wasn't really thick enough for the purpose of protecting people in a fall at judo, being not much thicker than carpet underlay and probably was the original cricket matting for the hall years ago. However, I liked it being called "judo matting", even though we did not have judo classes at the sports centre. It gave the impression that we had a more extensive collection of equipment than we actually had. So I didn't correct him.

We manhandled the matting and laid it down the lane in front of the set of stumps at the far end.

"Get some pads on then. Have you brought any?" asked Fardeep of Luke and Simon.

"Of course I have," instantly replied Simon, seeming a little affronted as if his competence as a batsman had been challenged.

Simon opened up his kit bag and within a few minutes had donned his pads and gloves, and was walking down inside the lane to bat.

He took a classical stance with his bat tucked behind his right toe in front of the stumps and played the balls from Fardeep and Luke fluently. I suspected that Fardeep bowled very easy balls on purpose, for although they were bowled with a beautiful flowing action, they did not have any of the vicious spin that he had used on the kebab and bhaji mixture at our dinner before Christmas.

Luke bowled with a leap like he was serving in tennis.

Fardeep congratulated each of us every time we did the slightest thing. Of Simon's batting strokes he said that each was wonderful and superb. Of Luke's bowling he said that he liked each ball and that it was masterful.

At Fardeep's invitation I stood and bowled a few balls down slowly. I had half-remembered how to do it from my schooldays, but I had no accuracy compared to Fardeep and Luke. Mine were landing wide either side of the batsman, mainly down the leg side.

Fardeep remarked on how the ball moved and dipped even though it was quite off target.

"Perhaps you can bring your arm a little higher and not let it fall over to your right. Reach tall like a leaping gazelle. Then your balls will be straighter."

Occasionally Fardeep would bowl a spinning ball, but he made it so wide that it was fairly harmless and its theatrical spin could be seen easily. The ones that he bowled on the line of the stumps were quite accurate and might have got Simon out if they had been bowled faster or they had been dipping as well as spinning.

After about twenty minutes Fardeep called on Simon to come out of the net and for Luke to put his pads on and bat. Whilst Simon was taking his pads off Fardeep took the opportunity to talk to him in depth.

"If you can double the speed of the bat through the ball, then you can double the power, but that does not mean that you should be hitting it hard and fast. No. Because that would mean that you were jerking your body."

He mimicked a driving shot with his arms.

"Aim to speed it up during the follow-through. Remember the follow-through is not just for afterwards, but it is actually part of the shot. When a leopard leaps he does not just stop when he has the prey. He carries through with his jump. The follow-through might happen after the ball has gone, but its shape and attitude is set up by the shot. If the follow-through is right then the shot must have been executed correctly. It's all part of the one sequence. If you plan for the future the present will happen just right."

Luke had put on his pads and was just about to go down inside to the batting end of the net when the door opened again and Sir Richard and Claire walked in. He was wearing his overcoat with the collar up and unbuttoned in front to reveal his dark suit underneath. His footsteps from his formal shoes rang loudly in the hall in contrast to the soft steps of Claire in her trainers.

"Is this all there is?" Sir Richard asked, looking round the room and frowning in surprise.

"So far," I answered and felt criticism as though it was my fault that so few had come.

I was pleased to see Claire but I was just a little worried about the desk and who was manning it. I wondered if there should be somebody else on reception in case a lot more people came and needed directing down here. I was torn between missing an opportunity for something to happen and missing some time with Claire.

So I decided to ask, "Shouldn't Claire be back on the reception desk?"

Claire just looked gently at Sir Richard for guidance who said critically, "Well, if this is all who've come and there is only twenty minutes left then there's hardly any point in her going back down there. I bet no one else is coming now. So why not? Do we have a credibility issue or a viability threshold or what?"

"Something like that," I explained. "When I put up a notice here there were a few comments about people not wanting to change club. Some didn't like the idea of the old team being resurrected and their money (as they saw it) going to Moxham. A couple saw it as an opportunity and they're here tonight but the others weren't too keen."

Luke added, "No one else is here because kids don't play in the sports centre much. They tend to play football in the street or the park, or they're part of other teams. There are no established pure junior sides in the area, other than at Appleton Water."

Simon nodded. "Yeh, this sports hall has been used by two other teams from the outskirts of Moxham in the past: Lampton Ambo and Darbury. They already have their current players." He spoke as if he was giving a lecture.

Sir Richard raised his eyebrows in frustration.

"Well, I suppose this is it, then," he sighed. "We'll have to try to get some more from somewhere. Try that person Turner connected with the old Moxham Club. He might know people. Otherwise I'm not sure who."

We knew that Fardeep would have to go back to India in our mid-summer, so he would not form a stable part of our side. We would only have him for occasional coaching, not for playing. He was contracted to Appleton Water for that. I doubt whether we could afford to pay his match fees. They would be too much for a normal club, especially a nascent one like ours.

Sir Richard and Claire watched as we started to bowl to Luke. Simon bowled with a slinging action from his shoulder, like hurling a javelin in a low trajectory: making it straight and low. It was quite accurate.

Fardeep bowled a flighty one, and then I bowled one which was totally inaccurate and went wildly off course.

Luke began hitting them fluently and was moving smoothly to the ball without error in a balanced series of strokes.

Fardeep, as he had done before when Simon had been batting, congratulated Luke with an ever-rising series of superlatives, whose exclamations served to inflate the batsman's ego. Successive balls were dispatched in extravagant and balanced action with the bat raised in a flourishing follow-through.

Each bowler would wince in horror as his best delivery was clouted and the people waiting to bowl behind him could only close their eyes and grimace about their upcoming turn.

Finally after a few more of these exhibition shots Claire took my ball from me and said "Seems like you could do with more help in the bowling department tonight."

Simon, the next bowler in turn, smiled in surprise as Claire unexpectedly jumped the queue. "OK. Give it a try," he shrugged.

I didn't believe that Claire could bowl. Surely only a throw or an underarm chuck like she might be doing with her pupils. Yet, if she was keener than me and knew more about cricket than me, then surely she couldn't be worse. It seemed that our shortage of players was proving to need desperate measures and I wanted to give her encouragement to see what she could do in what was predominantly a man's sport.

"Just need to smooth up one side," she said, leaning down forward to polish the ball vigorously on the outside of her thigh.

Simon raised an eyebrow, and looked at me as I was intrigued to see her mock the habits of fast bowlers.

I thought that this was excellent spoof-acting, totally task-focused, mimicking exactly the self-absorbed concentration of a ferocious fast bowler.

"OK, run-up from here," said Simon, pointing to a mark on the floor a few yards before the stumps at the bowling end. "You can try under-arm if you've never bowled properly over-arm before."

But she took no notice of him. Impervious to those around her, she measured with firm footing four steps from the cone that served as the near stumps and then leapt a final half-step to a mark on the gym floor used for basketball.

Still looking down on the floor she turned on her mark to face Luke the batsman and set her feet exactly together on the spot. Holding the ball up in front of her chest she set the seam position between her fingers like I'd seen them do on the television. She stared at the ball and raised herself up on her toes and leant forward, her eyes now focused ahead at a spot near the batsman.

Simon was still giving out the body language that he wanted her to start her run-up to bowl from his spot.

"Get nearer, it's easier," he urged.

But she paid no attention to him. Sir Richard watched expectantly. She was putting on an insightful show of what it was like to be a completely internally focused bowler. I wondered where she had learnt this. Probably from the television. She was obviously good at mimicry and might have been an impressionist on the stage when she was a little girl. I wondered how far the joke could go and at what stage she would pull out of her act, go "Da dah!" and bow for a round of applause.

But she still remained focused, and as her body weight took her head forward she took a stride, and then another. And another. And more fluid and longer.

She turned side-on, jumped, left hand reaching high.

Her action froze and hung balanced for a split second.

She landed on her left front foot and her right arm came whipping through.

As the ball left her hand there was something which her wrist did, but I am not sure what it was because it was too fast to see.

She let out a short cry from the effort.

I watched Luke as his head fixed on the ball flying towards him and he raised his bat. He took an instinctive half-step forward.

As the ball neared him, even though it still had some way to travel, I knew that he had not taken a large enough stride forward and the spinning ball was quickly dipping before him.

Looking back now I think I knew at that point what was to happen next, but it happened so fast that I could hardly register what I was seeing. I had to re-run the action in my mind's eye like a video just to convince myself it was true.

CHAPTER ELEVEN

Luke moved fluently into position as the ball bounced before him. However, his bat had come through too early to meet the ball, which shot straight through the gap left by his bat. It clattered into the metal stumps.

Claire threw her arms up wildly at full stretch and shouted out "Yes!"

"Wow!" I exclaimed. "Where did you learn to do that?"

"I just know," she shrugged her shoulders smugly.

Simon was speechless, but Fardeep and Sir Richard nodded knowingly.

"No, come on now," I said. "You must have learnt from somewhere."

"I got some experience at school. And down south where I lived before here, there is more women's cricket. However, there isn't a women's team here, yet," she emphasised the word 'yet'. "So I thought it would be best to get the county funding and the new Moxham team sorted out before I started rocking the boat and stirring things up too much."

"You've certainly stirred things up here," I said. "You'll have to play in this new Moxham team. In fact you can take over the lead."

"No," interrupted Sir Richard quickly. "It can't be. The council would not want her as the main name. She is not an employee of Sports and Leisure. She's in the Education sector. However, there's no reason why she couldn't assist you so long as you remain the vanguard as you are now."

The vanguard? I wondered how I had suddenly become the 'vanguard' from a mere putter-up of notices.

"Hey, don't forget me!" came a voice from the batting end of the net. "Are we still playing? You won't get me again like that!" Luke rolled Claire's ball back along the floor to us.

Simon started off the bowling again, but Luke was more defensive this time and after several more balls from each of us it was clear he was not going to take any chances. Now he had become dour and drab in his shots, just patting the ball back to us. In fact, just about one of the most boring things that I hated about cricket was this stonewalling approach that Luke had now adopted out of ultra-caution.

We carried on for another ten minutes or so. During this quiet phase Fardeep whispered to me as I stood by him in turn to bowl "Next week, come early and I will show you a special trick." He touched the side of his nose with his finger, and then turned away from me without further explanation and ran up to bowl.

I waited for him to turn round and come back and mouthed "What?", but he merely touched his nose again to indicate that we should say no more in front of the others.

I bowled my ball and then the door opened again.

Two men came in. It was Rod Stirling and his son Mark. We stopped as Rod slowly came over to us with a conceited swagger. His tanned complexion was radiant as usual, giving his skin a plastic appearance almost as if he was wearing make-up. He was wearing a leather jacket with zip front, expensive jeans, and posh brown cowboy-style boots.

"Hah! Is this all that's here, then?" he laughed.

But before any of us could answer him, Mark following behind him had said "What? You've got a lot here!" He looked round the hall in an exaggerated way, craning his head to look behind us and raising his eyebrows in mock surprise as he pretended to count a dozen others with his head. He was tall and thin with pale taut skin, resembling something like a set of traffic lights with green eyes, fine red hair, and a port wine stain on his neck. He copied almost everything his father did. They were like a double act of threatening baddies in a gangster movie.

"You'll never get it off the ground." Rod went on. "People have got their own clubs. They're settled in their ways. They'll never move."

"Nope, never move," reiterated Mark coming alongside him.

Surprised by the sudden intrusion I desperately searched my brain for a quick put-down reply, but I could find none. Seeing no response from us had the effect of letting them carry on in the same vein.

"Not so good, then, the maintenance here," said Rod, nonchalantly casting his experienced builder's eye on a radiator cover and reaching inside it to wiggle a loose valve knob.

He drew his finger along the top of the radiator cover and pulled a face as he looked at the dirt he had collected.

"Not so good the cleaning here, eh Mark?" he asked of his son.

"No, Dad, not so good the cleaning here. Nor the infrastructure."

Then playfully coming over to Claire and putting his arm around her waist, Mark added "But you've got a good infrastructure," and pulled her towards him.

Out of the corner of my eye I saw Sir Richard tense up as Mark hauled her over, and soften as she uncoiled herself neatly from him by pirouetting swiftly with a crooked smile that revealed toleration rather than acceptance. She made sure that she held the final flourish of her escape with a long stare and smile in my direction. I think she wanted to see my reaction as she narrowed her eyes and pursed her lips fleetingly, and then turned back to a scowl as she looked at Mark. Then, like a cat tired of us both, she walked over to her bowling mark and ran up to bowl another accurate ball, which Luke played defensively back.

Sir Richard found his voice at last. "They might not come from other clubs but we'll bring a lot of people back to cricket who haven't played for ages. There's a lot of history in Moxham. We'll get more players. This is just early days."

Rod pulled a face. "No, they won't come to Moxham when they've got others nearby. You need to give the money to established clubs like Appleton Water or Scoving."

"Look, we've been through all this before. Appleton Water has got private money coming out of its ears, and Scoving? You've got an organised set-up there but it's out on a limb. There's no heritage like there is at Moxham."

"Heritage?" ridiculed Rod in distaste. "They stole that and they dumped it. You know that!"

Rod waited for a reaction then, as Sir Richard did not give one, he addressed us all as he turned to go. "You all know, as regards Scoving being an outlier, it might be in the west but it's got lots of land for development, and history in the nearby villages."

"But not cricket history." I let him have this parting shot.

"Hah! We'll see who gets the money. We're also putting in a bid to the county sports council. Moxham won't have it all their own way," he said, pointing his finger at Sir Richard. "No doubt you'll bring Turner back again. But his tripe about heritage and history is all lies. Council bids take time and you haven't got it. I know about the new deadline."

I startled at the mention of a new deadline and turned to Sir Richard who was biting his lip, half-turning to us to say something, but cautiously watching them go.

"Come on. I'll give you a lift back," said Mark, leading Claire by the arm towards the door.

She didn't resist this time, but kept an eye on me to make sure I was watching her. As she passed through the doorway she shouted back over her shoulder "Let me know when you are going to see Turner, Jeremy, I want to be there as well to get some background for my class project."

"I'll ring you," I shouted to her but Mark tugged her towards him through the doorway. He turned and gave a proud aggressive stare in my direction as he left.

The door closed and Sir Richard turned back to us. "I just heard tonight and came to tell you after nets. The County has brought forward the deadline for the bids. We've got just till a week on Friday to get it to the main county council offices. Jeremy, you'd better get hold of W K Turner quick. I'll give you his full details."

He drew out a silver pen and a small notebook, leafed through it, copied it onto another page, and tore it off.

In a deadly serious voice, the most serious I have ever heard him, he handed me the note saying, "There's no time to lose. Action is of the essence."

Fardeep with a worried expression pointed to me. "Yes, Jeremy, you make sure you see him. You must act fast now. It's very important."

They were right. There was no further time to lose as far as the project went, but also as far as Claire and I were concerned. It annoyed me the way that son of a snake had been coiling around her. Unless I acted fast she would be taken. She was still interested in me, I was sure, but I would have to make a move when we met up to go to Turner's house.

CHAPTER TWELVE

It was the next Saturday morning in February, a few days after the first nets night. One of those bright early false spring mornings which would only last a couple of hours before sinking back into dreary winter again. Now it was the time for something special to be done, or an answer to be found, like an early squirrel unearthing a stored acorn: the morning that I would take Claire to meet W K Turner.

As I drove away from the sports centre and up to St Margaret's School I felt guilty for the situation I had left at work. It takes two to staff the reception and cook the chips for the children's Saturday morning session in the hall. Yet Ann would have to do it all by herself because Charles had phoned in sick even though he had previously agreed to come in to cover at short notice whilst I went to see Turner.

"You go. I'll be all right," Ann had said regardless. "You go and see Turner. It's important."

Perhaps Ann could cope. She would shortcut some health and safety regulations by getting one of the older children to help her to plate the chips and pizza for the younger children, or to keep a watch on reception as she ran backwards and forwards between the desk and the deep fat fryer.

"No, don't worry about me, I'll cope. You go and see Turner like you've planned. Go and see him. You've less than a week to get the bid in. He'll be a good man if you can get him on your side, convince him. But I'm not sure you will – he's still got a lot of feelings about the incident between Moxham and Scoving from the past. But if you can get him - he'll be a lot more use to you than the others." She sniffed. I knew whom she meant, but I didn't rise to it. I hadn't told her that I would be taking Claire.

I felt guilty that I was spending all this time away. But there again I wasn't really. I might have to follow up some leads this afternoon or do extra work on what Turner would tell me and then I might have to send it on to Sir Richard. I would do this in my own spare time. Ann would have the whole of Sunday off.

Besides, my body was still stiff from the nets earlier in the week and I might not have been able to do a lot of frantic work with the children. So all that was how I justified to myself my cruelty - putting my compassion aside and being a cold-blooded manager. Certain things had to be done and somebody had to do them.

As I carried along that road out of town up to St Margaret's School I knew here was an opportunity, albeit with cruel repercussions on others, but it was an opportunity nonetheless, to get closer to Claire. And I wanted that. The occasion had empowered something extra in my mind, a little degree of excitement which grew. An excitement that I would now be alone with Claire for this visit, driving her there and back. It reminded me of the time in Marmaduke's when I felt I could control what cream cake she had. I didn't know I would feel like that again.

I eased my stiff back out of my car and with a raised heartbeat I pressed the doorbell to Claire's flat. Hers was the upstairs one with its own outside entrance door in the little block just inside the grounds. The caretaker and his wife lived in the one underneath.

I thought about what I would be doing today with her. I should find out about the state of her relationship with Mark and then see if I could take her to lunch at Marmaduke's.

There was a clomping noise of someone coming downstairs in boots and the door opened. Claire was in a long grey cashmere blend coat. Today she was an official, like a teacher or reporter, not in the tracksuit of a sports and leisure person. It was partly undone at the lower buttons and it flashed her knees below her skirt as she walked.

"Hi! Let's go!" and she had skipped past me to the Jimny and waited for me to open the door for her, which I did with mannered ceremony. We laughed at this, at how formal we had made it, for it confirmed that she wanted me not to be formal but to be close. There was that lavender scent again.

I eased myself into the driver's seat and drove us down Nova Lane. Yet we didn't go as far as Romiley Lane and the overgrown track to the cricket ground. When I mentioned it she said that Sir Richard had shown her those weeks ago. Today we were looking for 20 Greenhazel Avenue, the house of W K Turner.

I felt like asking her about Mark, trying to gauge her relationship with him, wondered if I had a chance or not. Had it all been some device to get me to take on this role, or did she genuinely like me? I was afraid she might not give me the reply I wanted.

If I asked how she knew Mark, she might say, "Oh, he's my boyfriend".

Alternatively, she just might say, "Oh, he's just a friend".

Or even, "He's an idiot, why didn't you give me a lift back last Wednesday? I hate him and his Dad!"

However, just then, when I had plucked up courage to tackle the subject and was about to open my mouth, she shouted: "There! Greenhazel Avenue!"

An old white sign on posts partially overgrown by someone's hedge marked the entrance to a short run of small semi-detached houses. Claire calculated the house was the one at the very bottom of the avenue. I drove down onto a patch of muddy ground that served as a parking space and turnaround, squeezing alongside two large rusting white vans.

A thick privet hedge formed a tall shield around the small front garden of number twenty.

The front gate was barely three feet high and consisted of about half a dozen inch-thick cylindrical pickets formed into a gate by two crosspieces and a diagonal. The pickets had points on their top, and the bottom ends were rounded and notched. They were old upside down cricket stumps.

I unlatched it easily and Claire stepped gracefully through.

There was a concrete step about four feet deep in front of the door. It had a thick white line painted along its front edge which I assumed was a safety line.

"Ha," she said, "this must be the crease."

There was no bell push but a brass stirrup-shaped knocker, whose horizontal handle had bands of different thicknesses along its length.

"If I'm not mistaken, that's in the design of a bail," Claire mused.

I rapped loudly on the front door and we waited.

Over the telephone earlier in the week I had introduced myself and asked if we could come and talk to him at the weekend.

I told him we were writing a history of Moxham and its cricket for a government grant to upgrade the area, and that Claire, a local schoolteacher, had set her class to do a project on it.

There was a rustling sound from behind the door and it opened onto a tall, thin grey-haired man in his late fifties or early sixties with a white goatee beard and blue eyes. He had lanky arms and a thick white cricket pullover with some tea stains down the front.

"Mr Turner? I'm Jeremy Freeman and this is Claire Spedman. You know, we spoke on the phone?"

"Better come in then," he opened the door wider to reveal a narrow hallway and stairs. There was the smell of recently-fried bacon.

In the hall was a painting of the Moxham ground by a local artist. It was similar to the one that Sir Richard had shown me a couple of months earlier, but from a slightly different angle. There were once again many perspective errors, but it was compelling none the less.

As we paused by the painting an old woman's frail voice called from the kitchen.

"Who is it, Will?"

"It's them from the council and school, Mum." He shouted back down the hall.

"Who?"

"It's all right, Mum, it's about the cricket," he shouted, as he showed us into the front room.

"Oh," was the reply.

It was a room from the nineteen fifties, with a fabric-covered three-piece suite with antimacassars, heavy central rugs on a linoleum-covered floor, glass china display cabinet, a two-barred electric fire in the cream tiled hearth, but no television or radio.

As the first armchair already had a folded newspaper on it, I eased my stiff back into the other chair across the room alongside the cabinet. Claire sat on the sofa in front of the fire.

"What is it you want to know?" he said, sitting down and moving the newspaper onto his lap.

"Well, we'd like some information about the history of cricket in the area. Sir Richard Gregory at the council said that he thought you'd be the person to ask."

"Who?" he asked.

"Sir Richard Gregory, the Culture and Leisure Director of Moxham council," I said, leaning forward and bringing my elbows to the arms of the chair.

"Never heard of him," came the gruff reply.

"Yet he seemed to have heard of you."

"In a good way, of course," added Claire. Her eyes twinkled brightly with reassuring honesty. "He says you would know a lot about the history and could help us with the project." She nodded to encourage him.

"Huh, well I don't know about that," he said, folding the newspaper tighter. "Moxham cricket is dead and gone now. There's not many who'll want to hear about it."

"Oh yes there are. The whole of my class at school, for instance, and people in general will want to know about the history of the area. The children are very keen."

The faint trace of a smile came to Turner's face, but it passed quickly as if he thought it might be flattery and said with a questioning look sideways "Oh aye?"

"Yes," I said, and decided to go for the whole tale now since he was showing signs of softening with Claire. "It's like this. As I said over the phone, the government has taxed English Cricket's profit of hundreds of millions of pounds from the international twenty-twenty programme."

He whistled. "Well, we've all heard a lot about that. Finally our boys came good."

"Yes. And we'll get a lot of it back to sports and leisure via grants if councils can show that they have appropriate schemes for promoting general sports services themselves. Legally it has to be given to councils that have new cricket because it's cricket money. Without this money a council will now find it difficult to keep its sports centres open for everything else because of all the cuts."

Turner frowned. "So when cricket finally wins something it's taken away to bolster up some failing part of something else."

"Yes. The council wants the local cricket to show it is thriving – not just a few teams and a sleepy league but a regenerating league. The best way to do that is to show that we have new cricket coming back and to tie it in with things like healthy lifestyle, heritage, and tourism."

Claire added, "So then we can show that cricket is regenerating the community as well as improving sports. Money is piled in by the government because it can tick all of its lifestyle and health boxes".

"In this area we can make a good bid because we can tie it in with culture and history," I said. "That makes it stronger, like the cricket adds to the heritage, and heritage is what government is mad on at the moment."

"I see," he looked down at his folded paper. "History and heritage and things like that are all right. I can tell you a lot about that."

I was pleased that he was coming onto our side.

"In fact," he pointed to the glass case, "in that glass cabinet there's some interesting stuff."

I looked into the cabinet by the side of my chair. There were three silver badges on dark blue velvet backboards, each in individual boxes.

"Those are performance medallions from when Moxham won the league three years running 1991-3. Including the league centenary year 1992. They knew how to commemorate you in those days."

Though they were unadorned discs with basic inscriptions, it was still remarkable that each player had been given one in a local amateur league. They took commemoration seriously. On the glass shelf below were team photos, mainly posed full face in the classical way in cricket whites, front row sitting, back row standing, and an official in a suit on either side.

To the right of this was a photograph of him being presented with a large cup. It seemed unposed, as though it had caught Turner in a private moment with eyes down and head bowed before he might have said "Thank you" and held it up to the camera.

"That's the centenary year cup," he said. He fell silent, as though he was secretly mourning something for a second and then before I could make any comment he quickly got up and said, "Come with me and I'll show you some more stuff upstairs."

He plonked the newspaper back down on his chair with a flourish.

I hauled myself stiffly out of the chair and followed him. Claire watched me with interest as I struggled up.

As we went up the stairs there was something strange and chunky about the balustrade. Then I realised what it was: each baluster was an old cricket bat screwed through the top of the handle to the banister. Some of the twenty or so bats were light-coloured and relatively new and had red marks from the ball's impact. Others were stripped of their rubber handle grip, old and brown and cracked with history.

He opened the door at the top of the landing to a small room.

The doorknob was an old cricket ball. He pointed to it when he saw Claire smiling at it: "That's the ball I got five wickets with in the final match in 1993. I took off my wicket-keeping pads and had a bowl. You turn it like a leg-break going into the room and an off-break coming out."

We followed him inside. A smell of old cardboard and linseed oil greeted us. Against the walls were a bookcase, a small desk and chair, and a small glass-fronted cabinet, similar to the one downstairs.

He opened the cabinet and selected an old worn green book from a row.

"These are the original Moxham scorebooks. The complete set from 1911 when the club was founded."

He smoothed its weathered cover. "These were great games. See, 1984. Morton. A great player. Hit two sixes and sixteen fours in his 127.

"Then this next one. Rain shortened this match. We only needed 21 off the last six overs when the heavens opened and they wouldn't come back out to finish off."

He breathed out in disgruntlement but replaced the book carefully in sequence.

Next to the scorebooks was a collection of half a dozen yellow paper-covered Wisden cricket almanacs, mainly from the 1980's and 1990's. On the shelf underneath, a collection of other cricket books lay haphazardly on their side. I recognised an old MCC cricket coaching book, and Mike Brearley's 'Art of Captaincy'.

Round the walls were framed newspaper photos of people batting on village greens, and a picture of two batsmen walking out to bat, one obviously Turner when he was younger.

"Here, this might be of interest," he said, getting a large scrapbook out of the cabinet and opening it on the desk.

He pointed to a newspaper cutting of a full cricket team and to himself in the front row.

"That's our winning team from the league centenary year," he said.

Next were several pages of pictures of women and girls, either in pairs or as single portraits, stretching back several decades. They were dressed in cricket whites, the earlier ones in skirts, the modern ones in trousers. Occasionally there was a photo of a full team of women. Later on, some in casual clothes and aprons were jokingly holding up kettles.

"The tea ladies had their own cricket teams," he said. "Fifty years worth. Some very good fielders. Terrific."

"Can we contact any of these for interview?" asked Claire.

"Well, some of them are still in the area, but I haven't got their addresses. Just the last one, Margaret."

He pointed warmly to a large woman with a cheery face and smiled. He paused, then his tone darkened as he remembered "She's at Scoving now," and he abruptly turned the page.

"Also the kids may be interested in some of these pictures here," he said. "We had to cut the outfield for a cup match and the mower's engine failed. We used a horse to drag it."

There was a picture of a farmer leading a horse with what looked like half a mower behind it and two cricketers following with broom and shovel.

"Yes. Dobbins was made honorary horse member for a day. His dues were collected from behind him."

He closed the book and put it back in the cabinet.

Next, he took out a cricket ball whose leather casing came unpeeled to reveal the hard inner corkwood core.

"This ball got into a terrible condition towards the end of a match and we didn't know what to do. We had no other. They had all been lost so we had to carry on with this - the worst ball you could imagine.

"Anyway their big hitter was still in and they needed ten off the last six balls to win. They hit a single and then another single, then a two and the ball was now in a right state. So they had three deliveries left. He missed it and then he had to hit six off the last two. Anyway, we tossed it up and he hit it. Only he literally hit the cover off it. Our fielder dived for the leather which had lobbed up and was near the wicket, but the inside part of the ball had gone for six. The batting side tried to claim victory and we tried to claim the catch, but of course the ball was dead as soon as it split into two. The end result was that we had to abandon the match because we didn't have another ball, and there was still one more delivery left.

"Anyway, that is the bit of leather casing, and there is the inner cork sphere."

"That's remarkable," I said.

"Yes, according to Rice's "Curiosities of Cricket" it's only happened on two other occasions: in Australia, and in Hong Kong many years ago. But they had other balls they could finish the matches with. We didn't. Our match is still waiting to be concluded if we could ever get all those people together again on the field for the final ball. But I know we can't because Sid died a couple of years ago and he was the fielder who caught part of the leather cover."

"That would be good to show the children," Claire said. "I'm sure they'd love to hear more about that, Mr Turner."

"Oh, don't call me Mr Turner. Most people call me Wicket."

"OK, Wicket," she nodded.

As he put the ball carefully back in the cabinet, he said "Yep. I'd better put Sid's ball back together again. Show him some respect. He was cremated and the ashes were scattered up there on the field by his family."

My eye drifted from the cabinet to the pattern of the yellow wallpaper. As I looked at it in more detail, I could see that it consisted of small squares with a series of red dots and numbers and the occasional letter W on a yellow background.

"That pattern's an extract from the Australian bowling scorebook of the 1999 World Cup at Lord's," he said. "You can get other matches printed on ties and scarves."

84

Then in a frame by itself on the opposite wall was a poem, decorated in the margin by drawings of bats, balls, and stumps.

The Batsman's Prayer
As I walk out up to the crease
I feel this day is gold,
For I will play with inner peace
And let my strokes be bold.

I will thank the ardent groundsman
Who made this pitch today,
And bowlers scheming with their plan
Good balls for me to play.

I face in awe the umpire
Who gave me guard to stand
And needs nought else to end my power
But the finger of one hand.

I strive with my batting fellow
To call a comfy run,
Whether from wide or willow -
The scorer writes what's done.

No matter how short my innings
Or yet how long I stayed,
Best of my losses and winnings
Is a game that's fairly played.

"Ah, by Renral," Claire said approvingly, reading the signature.

"Yes, I met him years ago. He was signing in a bookshop." He paused to gather his thoughts and read through part of the poem again to himself. Then he asked, "So what's this new cricket you are going to start up then?"

I looked back at him blankly. He looked back at me. He hadn't got it.

I couldn't believe that we had spent all this time discussing and reminiscing and me speaking over the phone to him and he still did not realise that we wanted to restart Moxham, not reinvent any other club.

"It's Moxham," Claire said quietly, unsure of what his reaction might be.

"Oh aye?" he raised an eyebrow.

"We would like you to get involved," I said quietly and waited for his reaction.

"What? No way! There's no way that can happen! I don't want to go back down there, and I can't play like I used to. That was over eight years ago, and what's between me and Rod is in the past and gone."

But it wasn't all gone. I could see it in his eyes. They suddenly no longer had the inspiring openness that comes with telling cricket stories. There was the cold hardness of anger that had been kept frozen for years like a steel sword kept in a deep cave of ice.

"I know that Rod accused you of stealing when in fact you'd been burgled," I said in an understanding tone.

"Yes, but we could never prove we were innocent. Rod had the ear of the league then."

"Yes, but even worse now." I said. "He's still on the league board. In fact, he's almost the secretary as well the way he interferes and he's going to try to get the money for himself. All the rest of the clubs can go to hell as far as he's concerned. His and Appleton Water will be the best two clubs, guaranteed, and will get more power and money. He knows Appleton Water won't get funding because they've got good facilities already. Therefore, he reckons that he will get it all. He has contacts above Moxham Council directly into County Hall itself through his building business. So that's what Rod is up to and the league will become unbalanced: just the two top dogs and no one else will get any resources."

"You can't trust that Rod." He shook his head. "We were innocent, definitely. 'Case unproven' they said. But if you ask me, I reckon it was Rod who had a hand in it. Rod didn't like us winning that cup. He thought it was his, right up till the last ball. I think we were burgled – burgled by him. I wouldn't be surprised if you searched his place you'd find that silverware. But the police never searched. And they should have done!"

"So you'll help us with the bid?" urged Claire. "Can you come and talk to my class at school next Tuesday? If we include work by children in the bid it will show that we're keen on developing the whole infrastructure – which is what the money is about. The bid has to be in by next Friday."

Wicket looked from Claire to me and then out of the window in thought.

"Well to stop Stirling you're gonna have to have a good team again. One with a good batsman, preferably one with a grudge, and a big hitter at that. And I can't think of a better one than Peter Kammer."

He turned round with a relish. "Kammer the Hammer we call him. He's good and will clobber whatever's served up to him. Guaranteed. He held the record for the number of sixes for the under-sixteens one year. Peter was playing for Darbury against Scoving at the time. Yes, he had just left Scoving to go to Darbury and they didn't like it and tried to get back at him. His mother came and gave a bollocking to the league about it. You'll find him at Mechkwik in town. He's one of the mechanics there."

"Kammer?" I queried. "In Moxham?"

I remembered seeing the surname on the staff wages sheet I sign each week to send to Salaries and Wages. Mary Kammer is an attendant at Moxham Pool who also does a couple of hours of children's swimming lessons a week. This must be her husband.

"Go and have a word with him. You'll recognise him because he's got a scar down the side of his cheek." He pointed to his right cheek. "Sterling's son gave it him when he was fifteen. He wasn't wearing a helmet. Anyway, Kammer will definitely be interested in playing against that bastard again."

I thought jolly good, that's an excellent recommendation, but Claire thought differently. Her cheeks unexpectedly flushed as she stared at him, her body stiff.

"Don't you dare call him names! What do you mean by that?"

"Sterling and the whole of his family are crap," said Wicket.

"That's not true. Take that back!" She pointed at him. "They are friends of mine and human beings and they deserve better. I won't have anything said against Mark."

"No. Wait a minute." I held up a hand. "Just hold on here. Let's not dwell on the past. These sporting events do happen, but don't drag it up again. Forget it."

"Well, it's very hard for me to forgive Rod for what he's done," said Wicket.

"Yes, I can see that about the father," said Claire. "But don't say that the son is also tarred with the same brush. He was young and it was an accident."

"Yes, maybe, but if you ask Peter Kammer he'll have a different view," he said.

"Well, yes, he can have a different view. They'll both have different views," I said.

"Huh!" she said, smiling as though in her own mind she'd somehow won an argument.

I was struck by how quickly she could change from being irate back to normal again. Her affection for Mark might also be just a passing whim. If such emotional variability was anything to go by it showed that I also, once in her affections, could be quite as easily dropped. That is, unless I could find a surer footing in her life.

As we were leaving Wicket handed us a yellowing typewritten manuscript.

"Have a read of this. It was my dad's. You might find it useful."

It was on foolscap paper, bound together by a string through a hole in one corner and entitled 'The History of Moxham Cricket by G K Turner'. It had evidently been typed on an old typewriter with dirty typeface as the e's and o's were filled in. There were occasional alterations and insertions by hand in navy blue fountain pen ink.

"You can let me have it back next week. I'll bring the scrapbook and some other stuff to the school on Tuesday. So yeh, I'll help you. I don't want Scoving getting any of the money. They'll waste it. If anywhere, it has to go to Moxham. Also I'll try to get some players. Stodgy and Neil, two old pals of mine, they've a score to settle with Rod, I'm sure. I've been thinking about this for years, how to get even. And now's the time."

Now was the time indeed. Our team was building. We had Luke and Simon from the nets. Though Fardeep couldn't play for us a lot because of his coaching commitment to the league, we had Claire, myself and now Wicket. Wicket might get two others. That made seven, but we still needed more.

I would call in at Mechkwik at the end of the afternoon to try to speak to Peter Kammer, but first I wanted to see how close I could get to Claire.

CHAPTER THIRTEEN

I eased myself stiffly into the driving seat after we had left Turner's and felt a twinge of pain across the small of my back. Claire saw me wince.

"Ow," she said. "That looks bad."

"Yes, still a bit stiff after the nets."

"Do you have a medical condition there?" she pointed to my back.

"No. Just soreness."

"Well, have you thought of massage for it? I'm a qualified sports therapist."

My heart leapt, but I tried not to appear too eager. "Oh, I don't think I've ever had that. Is it easy to arrange?"

"No problem. I could do it. That is, if you are prepared to come to me rather than a clinic."

"I don't want to put you to too much trouble. Where were you thinking of?"

"There's my flat. I have some massage oil there and the space to work."

"Ah hah. But when?"

"When could you make it?"

"Any time to fit in with you."

"Well, since you look as if you're in pain, then the sooner the better. Today?"

"Good. After lunch at Marmaduke's?"

"Yes. Let's eat first. You'll be more relaxed then, and it will have a better effect."

I started the car and drove off back to town. We had only gone half a mile or so along Nova Lane with the estate on our left when there was a little hip hop tune from Claire's mobile.

"Hello…. Yes….No, listen, no. I can't speak to you now…. Yes, I know…..Mmm….Mmm."

She uttered the last "Mmm" in a delectably deep voice. Then realising that I must be listening, she hurriedly signed off with "No, I can't speak to you now. Save it for later. Ciao!"

She shuffled in her seat and looked out of the side window. Seeing I was glancing at her, she said. "Hah. Just Mark. He's a fool sometimes."

"It didn't sound foolish at your end. "

"No. he's nothing. He's an idiot. He's after something. I don't know what."

"Oh?"

"Yeh. He's nothing to me. He's a pain really."

We turned up onto the main road by Blade Farm and there was that little hip hop tune again.

"Hello? Yes. Yes, Sir Richard. We've just been there now....Yes....We've got something for you. The History of Moxham by Turner's Dad....Yeh....What?....OK. I'll tell Jeremy to read it....You'll call in to pick it up at the sports centre tomorrow?....Fine....Yes....Well, that's what I thought....I agree...."

Then she turned away towards the side window and spoke in a quieter voice, with her other hand cupped over the phone. "Yes, that's what I'm going to do…Yes....I'll make sure....Don't worry....I've got a way....Yes....Ciao!"

She turned to me quickly. "That was Sir Richard," she said as though I hadn't gathered who it was.

"Yes? What did he say?"

"Not much. He just said that he'd pick up that old booklet thing from you tomorrow after you've read it. That's all."

"Is that all?"

"Yeh. Nothing else."

That couldn't be all. I wondered why Sir Richard would be phoning her to pass a message onto me when I was supposed to be the project officer, not her. Perhaps he realised that I would be driving and didn't want to disturb me so he phoned her first. Surely he would call and be prepared to leave a message, knowing that I would get right back to him? It didn't make sense.

I found it difficult to ask her directly about all this. Somehow or other I didn't think I could get a straight answer and I didn't want to disturb our atmosphere or endanger my chances of getting the Claire Special Massage.

Within a few minutes we had pulled up in the railway station car park. I eased myself out gingerly just to signal to her that I was still in need of her treatment. She winced, showing the sympathy I wanted.

In Marmaduke's we had the Lunchtime Lasagne and took the only free table - near the counter. I felt self-conscious as Claire stood watching to offer help as I carefully lowered my tray and eased into my seat.

I thought that several people were watching us. I wondered if Ann would be here. Why that thought entered my head I don't know. She would be working like a slave back at the sports centre and would certainly not be here to see me with Claire. To see me with Claire? It was none of her business.

Yet I did see the counter assistant watching me. The dumpy one with dark hair all combed over to one side to uncover a large earring. As before, she wore her name badge 'Charlotte' high on her chest.

Claire repeated again that Fardeep would help with the project, as would Wicket, and that I should go to Mechkwik at the end of the afternoon to try to catch Peter Kammer.

She said she'd get Wicket to tell the horse story on Tuesday and get the class to write cricket stories. Perhaps even about playing cricket in outer space, or retrieving balls from magic gardens.

I was looking through the history document.

"This is mainly about the early teams and the results of some matches. It's not all that interesting and seems hard going," I said.

"Well I'm sure Sir Richard will be able to use a few quotes from it. For instance, that bit about the original owners of the field and then how the council took it over in the last ten years to maintain it."

"Ah, but they didn't maintain it," I said. "That's the problem. That's the nightmare situation."

"Well. Huh. Talk about nightmare. I've still got mine from that accident years ago."

"I'm sorry to hear it, but I've been having some funny dreams of late myself."

"Oh yes, "she asked, "What?"

"Well I was in a room trying to get out and there was a door and this door led out to a beautiful sunlit garden," I said.

"Only I couldn't go through it – it was like glass or something there - as though the door was a French window which wouldn't open. The more I wanted to get out and go there the more I panicked. And then I heard this voice, this soothing voice saying "Do not go out, do not go out". Then this beautiful music and then the glass door opened and as soon as I tried to go out this roaring monster appeared and I ran back in."

"Hah! You'd better find a way to defeat the monster next time you have that dream. You don't want to be stuck indoors all the time!" She laughed.

"Let's go if you're ready. I'll drop you back home before I go to Mechkwik." I stood up and winced with pain.

"Let me give you that massage first. You seem pretty cranked," she said.

So we drove to her flat at St Margaret's. I held the handrail as I painfully hauled myself up the stairs inside the building.

"What about your flatmate?" I asked.

"Oh, Amy is not in. Go in the lounge." She gestured to the door on the left. "Get your jacket off and lift your shirt and pullover and get ready. I'll get the massage cream."

"What only shirt and pullover lift up? Don't you need to work on more of me?" I joked.

"Oh no. Not today. Anyway that's all that's wrong with you, isn't it – just your back?" She moved to the bathroom down the hall.

I opened the door. There was no massage table or bed, just a white leather three- piece-suite, TV, coffee table, and bookcase.

I sat down on the sofa very carefully.

"Don't we need a bigger area?" I asked as she came back in with a towel and some massage cream.

"No, I can handle it here."

"But it's a bit cramped, isn't it? Don't you need more room to do stuff?"

"What kind of stuff?"

"Well, you know, massage stuff. Perhaps we should be using another room. I mean, wouldn't it be better rather than on the sofa, doing it on a bed – you'd have more room?"

"No. It's all right. I've got enough room here. More of a congenial environment. We've got music."

She spread a towel on the sofa. "Lie down here on this."

She put some music on from underneath the TV stand. Sitar music. Smooth transcending raindrops of notes twanging into a pool of echoes. I wondered what a strange coincidence that she should have the same kind of record as that restaurant before Christmas.

I closed my eyes and lay face down, and soon the music changed to the sound of the seashore. I heard her squelch the cream out of the tube. At first her fingers were cold, but gradually they warmed up.

Occasionally a tickle made me jump as she moved round to the side of my back, but when I tensed and laughed she glided back to my spine with wonderful languid movements.

She spoke in a voice softly and slowly as if we were both in a dream.

"Just imagine now that you are getting into a boat, a boat with white sails to sail away across the ocean. You want to come in that boat, don't you? Just keep lying there and imagine you're in that boat with me on that calm sea and you're just sailing slowly on the ocean on a nice day with blue sky and you're just drifting along. You've got no worries. Just float away in that boat on the ocean. The calm, calm ocean. Just rest a while like that."

I floated along on that calm sea as the tide and the gentle breeze bore me effortlessly in a realm of peace. Occasionally her hands would flow around a sore spot in my back, as the incoming tide flows around a sharp half-submerged shell, ebbing and then flowing back to test and tease it by degrees. At other times, her fingers would dance along my skin like fronds of seaweed lifted by the sea.

"Now I'm going to count to three and when I reach three you can wake up. One: waking up. Two: being more awake. Three: you're wide awake now."

I opened my eyes. I must have been asleep for a quarter of an hour or so. I lifted my head and saw a mug of herbal tea on the coffee table. I drank the tea with Claire there watching me from an armchair, smiling.

"You'll join our group, won't you?" she asked. "I know Sir Richard has mentioned consultancy work to you in the beginning before Christmas. It's not just the Moxham project, but it's an opportunity to be part of a wider national project. If you do well with Moxham, then leave someone in charge there and come and join us. You'll earn stacks. Think about it."

Still relaxed from her massage, I felt as though I might agree to anything she suggested.

We finished our mugs together and she motioned towards the door.

"Time for you to go to Mechkwik."

And so it was in the dreamlike aftermath of that session that I arose smoothly and without any pain, and set off towards town and the Mechkwik Auto Centre.

CHAPTER FOURTEEN

"Yes sir, how can I help?" the man sang his trained greeting without looking up, banging with one dirty finger at the keyboard on the long counter in Mechkwik. Along the wall on the left was an observation window into the workshop. The sound of hammering and blaring music came through a doorway up by the counter. It seemed to me that everything in here would always be banged or forcefully applied to something else. The keyboard no doubt at one time had required only a feather touch. Now extreme pounding seemed to be the only way.

Even the low coffee table, coffee machine and the half a dozen plastic chairs around the walls looked hammered. A customer in a suit huddled in a corner over an old well-thumbed car magazine.

"I'm looking to speak to Peter Kammer for a minute if he's here," I said.

"Pete!" the man turned and yelled through the open doorway into the workshop. "Somebody for you!"

A mechanic in dirty red overalls was underneath a dark Ford saloon on the hydraulic lift, tensing a spanner against a nut.

"Who?" he shouted back, his voice as rough as an unbaffled exhaust.

The man at the counter continued to bang away, his eyes intent on his work, and the mechanic under the car froze and waited for more information from my direction. He might have decided that I was a new customer and, considering the lateness of the hour he would not want to get involved in another job, so he stayed hiding on the other side of the exhaust.

He was a large muscular man in his mid-twenties, just under six feet. Lit by an inspection lamp, his face was bright yet grubby; a scar was visible on his right cheek.

I decided to end the stalemate and took a stride to put my head round into the workshop, breathing in the smell of warm engine oil and hot new rubber.

"I can't let you go in there I'm afraid – health and safety," the man at the counter suddenly took an interest in my movements.

I deferred to him by freezing in the doorway.

"Is it possible to speak? It'll only take a minute." I shouted into the workshop above the pop music.

The walls, once painted white and red, were grey and maroon with dirt. An oily rag hung like a curtain underneath the front of the workshop bench on which stood a plastic bottle of coca-cola half-drunk. Above the bench were wooden boards with clips on which hung spanners and screwdrivers in order of increasing size like organ pipes in sequence. The calendar for February showed a topless girl leaning over a pile of tyres.

"What's it 'bout?" shouted Peter Kammer, wrenching his last word as if it were a stiff nut.

"About the sports and leisure service. About cricket," I shouted back.

He paused with both hands on the wrench, grimaced as he applied pressure, then he squeezed out the words "I'll come out in a minute. Hang on."

He tugged hard at a spanner with both hands, and it finally gave.

Picking up a piece of wood, he laid it at the front of the exhaust box and hit it forcefully with a hammer to separate the back end from the front.

The banging was brief, rapid, and deadly. It was absolutely accurate. There were no little preliminary taps to size up the area, just the brutal precision from a forearm without compromise. Five short sharp strong strikes.

The loud blows stirred the only customer to life. He stood up halfway, still holding the car magazine, and peered through the observation window into the workshop with a worried expression. He turned round to look at the man at the counter who gave him a reassuring nod.

The exhaust separated and Kammer tossed the back end nonchalantly into a corner of the workshop with an ear-splitting clang. It bounced up off the red floor and was cushioned by a pile of old tyres like a crash on a race circuit.

Yet, although it was an awkward object that weighed several kilos, it left his hands with such a smooth effortless balletic motion. It appeared almost as if it was in slow motion, like a wrestler being thrown out of the ring.

He held the pose with a sense of achievement, as if he were in some fantasy that the world's press was gathering to record such a brilliant toss of an old exhaust pipe into a corner. He was only being paid to repair them, but he had made that final fling his own.

On the floor beside him was a shining new exhaust bending up like the sculpture of a kind of giant metal worm from outer space.

He installed the new pipe, checked the assembly, drove it back out onto the forecourt.

He came into reception wiping his hands on a rag. "Finished" he said to the man at the counter.

Then he turned to me.

"Yes sir, how can I help?" The scar twitched on his cheek.

I explained I was trying to restart Moxham and did he want to play since I understood that according to Wicket, he had played in the past, and that we had the occasional services of a visiting international coach, Fardeep Singh.

"Oh, Fardeep yeh- that's that Indian geezer –I've heard of him – in fact I've seen him. He was in the restaurant one night when we went in for a curry. He was on the table in front of us. He was a case, spinning food about! He kept Sterling pretty quiet!" he laughed.

"You know Rod Sterling?" I asked.

"I played for Scoving once. When I was young, under fifteen. I had to play out for a draw to save points in the league table, which is what Sterling got us to do. But we could have won. Sterling didn't want to take the risk."

He looked down regretfully. It was a tale he had told before, but I could tell it still irked him and he hadn't got it out of his system.

"That's one of the reasons why I left Scoving. Things like that," he emphasised. "Anyway, I've got too much to do on Saturdays now. Working all the hours God sends since getting married. We've got a little kid on the way. So, no mate. I wouldn't be able to play for you. I get about one weekend off in three."

"But Turner gave me your name! He said you'd be OK about it," I protested.

"What? Wicket? Oh yes, I know him. He was good, he was. He coached me when I was at Moxham for a while. Then there was the trouble and I ended up at Darbury. I shouldn't have done that. It ended in disaster. Then I quit."

"But we are only going to play a few matches this year - just the Enterprise Cup. It's open to unaffiliated friendly clubs," I said. "We only play on Sundays. Next year we will get a place in the league. We need to put in a bid to save the sports centre and sport and leisure in general."

"A bid to save the sports centre? Well, it needs it. Things are getting bad at the swimming baths. Mary says there's not much cleaning being done anymore. Doors are half-hanging off their hinges, lockers not shutting properly. They had a gang in there from Nottingham who found a way to jam the lockers so they looked shut, but they weren't. Then they came back a few minutes later when nobody was about, opened them easily and nicked people's stuff out. Hundreds of pounds of wallets and phones and stuff gone in an instant."

I winced. Though rather exaggerated, it summed up what had happened at the baths about six months ago.

"Your wife? Mary Kammer? She works at the pool? Ah, I thought so. I sign her pay claims regularly."

There was a silence from him as though a penny was slowly dropping through a machine and he said slowly "Oh, that's different. Yeh, cool mate. We will need Mary's job to continue because she'll go back to work afterward."

A faraway look came into his eyes. "Yes, it'll be good to play with Wicket again."

"Well, we are short of players. Do you know any others and how we can find them?

"Yeh sure mate. There are loads you can get. All you have to do is put up a notice."

I explained we'd done that without success and waited as he thought further.

"I've seen some play in the streets last summer. They're pretty fast and whippy. We just have to go out and ask them. The old Darbury Ground. Hang on and I'll show you where they hang out. I pass them on the way home. They're round the outskirts of

Moxham, east side as well. I'll show you if you've got half an hour."

"Yes. You mean now?"

"Yes. Let me just phone the missus. I'll tell her I'll be late and I'll pick up the Chinese on my way back. Then we can go. Cool, mate."

Night was falling. I had a slight trepidation about going out at night to meet gangs of youths. But how dangerous can they be when we just want to talk to them, offering them something to their advantage? Besides, I should feel protected by Peter. He knows the scene. An impulsive daredevil.

Peter led me to his car on the side of the forecourt. It was an old Ford with a newly replaced front assembly scooped up like an enormous shovel close to the ground. This part was still in its matt grey undercoating whereas the rest of the car was a dark red. It had mildly tinted windows. A spoiler had been added on the boot.

Indicators flickered as Peter held out a key fob.

I climbed down into the passenger seat that hugged me with a smell of fresh leather. Yet it was not a luxurious hug; it was a safety hug given by a car capable of fast acceleration.

Peter's steering wheel was small like a racing driver's, bare steel with holes cut in the blades to lighten it and a leather cover on the ring. Compared to his bulky frame it looked absurdly small.

The engine started with a deep roar from in front and beneath us like a lion that had been awoken, dangerously alert, angry. Then it purred in deceptive obedience to the commands of its tamer.

We set off slowly and the car pulsed with music, every panel vibrated with a penetrating beat. An alien voice from the sat-nav kept on cutting into the music as it announced which street we were going along or passing right or left. Hardly necessary going around your home town.

Though not an automatic car, Peter's gear changes were effortless and smooth. A bar of violet light on the dash grew and then receded to mark engine speed.

It felt like we were going on safari after big game, travelling in a disco inside a military tank.

"Yee haw!" He shouted. "Let's find some players! Yee haw!"

He accelerated wildly going up to the traffic lights on the main street and pulled up sharply when they turned to red. The seatbelt cut across my chest. The violet light display inside the cab flared and then grew dim, like a firework celebrating a moment of human achievement.

The streets were busy, it being just after half past five. Cars formed slow queues along the town's main street going from the towns behind us in the East to the villages in the West.

We slowed where the road narrowed and the shops closed in on either side, concentrating the sound of our thumping voodoo. We passed a succession of scowls: those opening the Methodist church hall for an evening meeting and the early regulars smoking outside the Rose and Crown.

Soon we came to the end of the shops. A group of lads were playing football in a small parking yard against the wall of the last shop.

Peter parked the car across the road from them to be out of the line of fire from stray balls.

"Let's try these, I think I recognise a couple of them," said Peter, and we got out of the car.

There were five players in all. Two forwards, two defenders and a goalkeeper.

One of the forwards was dressed in jeans and a red Manchester United shirt, the other in a black Manchester United shirt, thin material in this February air. The first forward turned and pirouetted with the ball, squeezing it with one foot pressed against the other, so that it flipped up to his knee. He stepped over it as it bounced and he kicked it past a challenging defender to the other forward who received it effortlessly on his left foot, and transferred it to his right. He did a 360 spin away from the defender marking him, dribbled the ball round the back of the first defender, and kicked it forcefully past the goalkeeper onto the wall.

There were two girls watching at the side, one of them was texting on her mobile, the other chewing gum.

At this point Peter joined the group, and after a cheery "Hi Mate!" came directly to the point about cricket and asked if they fancied joining Moxham.

"Who?" The red-shirted forward asked.

I was just about to explain further when the goalkeeper shrugged and said "No. We play for Darbury. So, what's this Moxham thing? We don't fancy splitting and leaving for another club."

"Yeh," continued the red-shirted forward. "We're settled here. We get a game every Saturday and the cup on Sundays. Anyway, what's this Moxham team? Never heard of it."

"How much will you pay us?" the other black-shirted forward joked.

I explained where it was, and that it was being revived after lying dormant for eight years. Their eyes were glazing over in non-recognition. They must have been only eight or nine years old when Moxham finished.

"Oh, yeh. That. That's waste land. You mean they used to play cricket there?" asked the goalkeeper, his eyes wide.

I nodded.

"Well, no we don't want to go there." The red-shirted one pulled a face. "No that's wasteland, man."

I half-turned away and said, "Give me a ring at the sports centre if you change your mind. I'm at the desk most days."

"Thanks, but we're sorted already," the red-shirted forward said as we walked away.

Peter turned to me as we got back in the car. "What do they mean it's a wasteland?"

"Well," I hummed without wanting to reveal that really it was being bulldozed soon. "It's not in its best condition at the moment."

"What do you mean?"

"We're going to have to get the grass cut a bit, and also tidied up," I intimated.

"Fair enough, I suppose if it hasn't been used for a few years it can get overgrown. I remember they've got a really good pavilion there. Mind you, it was decaying a bit then, some of the floorboards had the odd splinter and you couldn't be in your socks in the changing room."

"Oh no, it's a bit like that today still," I admitted.

"Yeh. I remember it needed some paint here and there. Especially on some of the colonial columns on the veranda."

"Yes of course, things like that do need attention from time to time," I agreed.

"Also that fancy green beading around the doorways will probably need a touch up. People used to catch it with their bags going in and out. I don't suppose that's improved over time."

"No. It hasn't. It might even have got a bit worse," I conceded.

"Hmm. So you'll need a painting party soon? I'll see what I can do this coming week on my days off."

"Oh," I flustered. "Perhaps not this coming week. The council will be coming to check it over, and then it'll be ready for us to look at. Give it a week or so, and then we can have a good look at the ground. Anyway," I nodded to the football game, "that group don't know what they're missing. They're too scared to jump to another club and be involved in something at its start. Too scared to help build something back into the community. For them everything revolves around that western end of town."

"Yes" he said, "That's the trouble with that group. They are too small, too isolated in Darbury. Let's try the East."

CHAPTER FIFTEEN

The engine roared again and the stereo thumped the start of another cacophonic ride. He drove a few yards at high acceleration, slammed on the brakes and the car swung like a Wurlitzer. We were now facing the other way and he raced to take a right fork in the middle of the shopping centre.

"Let's just check here first," said Peter, wiggling the small steering wheel as we came to the crossroads and the floodlit church near the southern centre of town.

Beyond the low churchyard wall could be seen a little graveyard, its semi-lit headstones tilting at odd angles, a classic scene from a gothic horror movie. Some stones were in small groups: they might have been from the same family or made by the same stonemason. Others, older, stood resolutely alone. Black and reliable, a patient congregation.

In front of this wall on its own little grass verge was the town war memorial: a squarely-hewn cross of York stone set on top of several tiers arranged like a wedding cake.

On either side of the monument was a badly-coppiced sycamore, their crowns now tufted heads of chaotic bristles.

This long low wall would have been excellent for kids to gather by and climb, yet it was strange that there were none here tonight.

Peter stopped the car and thought about what to do.

Thinking back to the hive of activity at the last place, I couldn't believe there was no one here. It seemed a perfect meeting place. Surely someone would be jumping on the monument, or skateboarding on its lower tiers. But there was only the silence of the tilted gravestones.

He sighed and drove on, left through town, down the main street and into the east. After almost a mile, and lit by the very last streetlamp going out of town, was a gravel ash car park in front of a large warehouse. At one end of the car park stood three trailers without their lorries. Two of the trailers had a container on them;

the third was a flatbed which had fabric sides with one side open, revealing it was empty.

At the other end of the park six or so young lads in mid-teens were playing football.

I noticed how the defending players kept missing the ball. One in particular, dressed in black jeans and a black T-shirt with gothic lettering, stumbled when the attacking forward came near, several times went down the wrong path, and was consistently wrong-footed. In desperation he once stuck out his foot so far sideways that he almost did the splits, yet was still unable to stop the ball. Even the goalkeeper moved the wrong way as the forward kicked the ball past him.

The goal was marked by a couple of coats on the ground and the ball had travelled about thirty or forty yards past them to roll underneath the trailers. Dejectedly the goalkeeper commenced what I guessed was yet another weary journey to retrieve the ball. He came trudging back, bouncing the ball, thoughtfully trying to plan another counter-move.

Setting the ball down, he kicked it with an enormous and mannered swing of his right leg. However, he succeeded in catching only part of the ball, so that it only rolled along the ground. Thereupon, the opposing scorer nonchalantly despatched it back past him, consigning the goalkeeper to another journey back to the trailers.

The ineptitude of the defenders and the goalkeeper was more remarkable than the skill of the attacking forwards who were merely tapping the ball. Some of the defenders' escapades were laughable, but I knew that I shouldn't mock. After all, I had come to try to entice them into playing cricket, and if they were unskilled they might be a more tractable entity than the collection of highly skilled precious individuals we had seen in the west.

We got out of the car and approached the group, asking if they ever played cricket. They said they played at Lampton Ambo. Like the previous Darbury group, they were unwilling to change or to come along to the nets to see, even though Peter assured them that it was a good club and that they could be in at the start of great things.

"My dad wouldn't like it," said one. "I help him in the club and sometimes play on Saturdays."

I informed him it would be Sundays at first this year and only a few matches in all for a try at the Enterprise Cup.

"No mate. Not another club. My dad still wouldn't like it."

"It's too far," moaned a second, pulling a face in disgust. "We've got no transport there."

We walked slowly back to the car. They started playing again and one of them shouted. I turned round. Peter was already looking back to see if they were attempting to speak to us with some last minute change of mind. But the shout was by one of the defenders, berating the goalkeeper for letting another goal through.

We got back in the car slowly, and Peter sat down heavily.

"Right," he said, "It's getting late, but it's not all over yet." He looked at his watch, gritted his teeth, and smartly turned the engine on.

It roared into life and there was a screech of ash from the car park as we spun round again. We headed back to town, thudding the ground on a marathon hunt for vanishing prey.

"I know where there may be some," Peter said thoughtfully. "There is one more place to look."

We went into town again and turned north up the Foss Walk Road, a side street leading out of town.

The street soon widened uphill and in the fork at the top of the hill was an old recreation ground which had lost most of its fencing.

Larking about a remaining piece of the fence was a group of four lads of mixed race in their mid-teens. Two appeared to be Asian in origin, one Afro-Caribbean, one white. They were not doing anything organised. Not playing football, just hanging about. One of the Asians and the Afro-Caribbean were leaning on the fence; the white boy was sitting on a mountain bike. The other Asian would occasionally take a couple of steps away from the group in a dance and then rejoin them.

Peter stopped the car. It seemed that this would be our last group. We had searched the entire town: west, south-central, east, and now north.

The other groups were linked to clubs in the next villages past where they lived. Here up this side of town there was no club, for the old Moxham ground was well to the south.

They did not look to me like players who could be organised enough into a team game. The other groups had been actively athletic and keen on sports. These did not appear to do much other than hang around, merely doing a kind of jig or jumping on or off a fence.

"Let's have a look," said Peter, easing the car slowly up the hill towards the group.

As we approached the Asian who had been dancing had stopped, yet still occasionally swung his legs while he talked to the white cyclist. The other Asian and the Afro-Caribbean who had been on the fence were now bowling a tennis ball to each other with high actions. This, I thought, was at least some kind of cricket.

We watched several passes between them. The Asian, stocky and muscular in a zipped-up grey top with baseball cap and well-fitting jeans, was hurling the ball right-handed. His Afro-Caribbean partner was tall and thin with a light blue top, and also wore a baseball cap. He was bowling it back, also with force, but left-handed.

They seemed to delight in seeing how much spin they could impart to the ball with their high twirling actions and laughed when the ball spun sharply away. Yet each always rescued the situation at the last second with a sudden smart diving interception.

Then one pass was so off-target that the tall left-handed darker-skinned one had to reach too far to retrieve it. He missed, and the third boy, the slightly shorter Asian who had been dancing and talking to the white boy on the bike, suddenly seized his chance, snatched the ball, and ran with it downhill on the opposite side of the road from us.

The left-handed Afro-Caribbean, infuriated by being beaten, picked up a clod of earth and threw it at the Asian running downhill. It struck him in the back between the shoulder blades. The impact made him release the ball which bounced in front of our slowly moving car. The running boy recovered in a couple of steps and dived towards the ball, vaulting over the bonnet of our still moving car, and rolled with the ball into the bushes on our left.

Peter slammed on the brake and my head almost hit the windscreen but was saved by the tight bucket seat and safety belt.

It all happened so fast I was unsure what did happen, but felt that the vaulting Asian must be seriously injured.

"What the…?" shouted Peter.

"Sorry about that mister," shouted the stocky right-handed Asian with the zipped-up grey top who had come running down the hill.

Then, recognising Peter, he cried "Hey, Pete! How goes it? You still want me on Saturday mate?"

Peter was still in a state of shock and could only splutter "What? Anas? Anas? What?"

"You want me on Saturday?" he asked again.

"What? Anas? What are you doing here?" then he looked around, and said "Oh my God! Where's your mate, is he all right?"

To our left the bonnet-hurdling acrobat was now extricating himself from the bushes, and came up grinning. "What is it? I'm all right. We're just playing."

Peter shouted at him from inside the car "You idiot! You could have got killed! That was a dangerous thing to do. Do you always play like that?"

"It's OK. I knew what I was doing. We were just playing," the acrobat rebuffed him, grinning widely.

"Well, can't you play in some other way?"

"There's nowhere else to go without spending money and this is the only place near here," Anas said in the acrobat's defence.

Peter shook his head. Collecting himself, he said "Yes Anas. Usual general cleaning in the garage. That was pretty stupid then, those acrobatics." Then he added, "And pretty nifty."

"Yeh," Anas laughed. "Jafar's good."

"That was amazing!" I said, having recovered from the shock. "And your friend up there who threw the dirt bomb. What a throw! Yeh, now look, call them all here. We've got a proposition for you all."

"What is it? We ain't doing nothing, honest!" Anas protested.

Peter looked askance at me, waving his hand downwards to indicate that he felt that he should be doing the negotiating.

"We need to ask them something, Anas," Peter said.

Anas turned and waved the other two down the hill towards us. They came down together reluctantly, the cycle brakes squealing as the white cyclist wiggled to keep balance with the slowly walking guilty-looking left-handed Afro-Caribbean thrower.

"So you've nothing to do in the evening?" Peter asked when they were all together.

"No," the white cyclist said. "Like I've got my bike, but there's no buses so you wouldn't be able to get anywhere."

"Yeh, it's bad here," the left-handed thrower said. "In this park the swings are bad. People cut the tyre seats so the wires come out. Then they're sometimes folded up high so that little kids can't use them."

"So why don't you go to town?" I asked.

"There's gangs there. They hang around the back of the Rose and Crown drinking. You get into trouble sometimes; people come and take your footballs off you, and I've had three footballs nicked off me," said Anas.

"What about other sport?" I asked.

"There's nothing to do. The pulley in the playground is not safe. That rope is the only one left and it's worn." Anas pointed up the hill.

"Yeh. We need the sand renewed each month. It's disgusting! You find lumps of glass, dog poo and cans in it!" the cyclist said.

"There should be more slides and swings here. There used to be more in the past," the thrower said.

"I'd like bike tracks, BMX tracks," said the cyclist, lifting his back wheels and making the bike stand on the front.

"Sometimes other groups come up here from town and wreck the grass with fires," Jafar the acrobat said. "It should be floodlit like the church."

"Well, listen, would you like to play cricket?" I asked with an upbeat air.

"No. We've tried that before and it was no good. So we don't do nothing now. We just hang about," said Jafar.

"Yeh, it's like we don't do nothing here. There ain't nothing to do. Others play cricket all right but we've never been able to play it. We can't get a look in," said Anas.

"Like at Lampton Ambo, like me and my mate went to Lampton Ambo," said the cyclist. "Like we put our name down for teams once. And they said yeh yeh man, you're picked, you can play. You come on Saturday. And so I was looking forward to it all week, especially when the schoolwork stress was on. Then when I got there on the day they said you're not playing and they put this other geezer in instead who was an old geezer and he could do nothing.".

The thrower added, "He was so old he could hardly run and he didn't hit the ball properly. He just touched it once and missed it all the other times."

The cyclist took back the story again. "They had no runs at all. Then when they came to bowl this tall old bloke he just stands there and loops it up in the air real slow, and the other bloke who is as old as him can hardly see the ball at all and kept on missing it."

"Yeh," the thrower interrupted again. "And I tell you it's hopeless. They didn't have any umpires and they got two of their own batsmen to stand in rather than asking me. But I suppose I couldn't have done it because I didn't know the rules anyway that well. But they could have just asked me to judge whether they had made their ground or not when they were trying to run them out. I could have done that at least."

"Nah. That's right," the others echoed.

"Oh well, look," I said. "Come down to the sports centre in town next Wednesday and we'll see if we can teach you to play and get you a game. We're having regular nets there."

They stared blankly back at me. I might have gone too fast for them. They probably like to complain about facilities, but not commit themselves to using them.

"Our sessions go on through till our first match. For the next couple of months, then outside. You know Peter, he will be there, and Fardeep Singh is our coach. Have you ever heard of him?"

They shook their heads.

"He's a very good coach from India. He's coached a lot of good players. And, well, I'm Jeremy, the sports centre manager – who are you?"

I went round the group: Alan the white cyclist; Dwayne, his friend, the Afro-Caribbean left-handed thrower; Anas who was Peter's Saturday helper; and Jafar the acrobat over the bonnet.

After some small talk Peter said he had to go home and so we left them. I wasn't sure if they would turn up on Wednesday, but at least I had given them an extra sports option in their lives.

As Peter drove us back to my car parked by Mechkwik he turned off the radio and asked "So, what did you think of them?"

"Well that was a good throw from that Dwayne," I said.

"Superb wasn't it? He would be a handy lad to have in your team. Very accurate, fast and whippy. And left-handed."

"Yes, and then there's Jafar the acrobat – he must be a tremendous fielder."

"It certainly looks like it. What a hurdler!" laughed Peter.

"Then there was Alan on the bike – we didn't see much of what he could do," I said thoughtfully.

"No – but at that age he would be quite athletic, much like the others," assured Peter. "And then there's my mate Anas – he should be reasonable as well. Always reliable when he comes to work on Saturdays. He and Jafar are both Muslim."

"Let's hope they all turn up at the nets on Wednesday," I ventured.

We were silent in thought for a while, and then just as I was getting out of the car Peter said, "Tell me about Scoving. Has Rod still got that son of his?"

"Yes. I think so. I think he still plays for them."

He shook his head. "In the juniors he was a tearaway then. Even in practice he was a dangerous bowler. I wouldn't like to face him again on the field in a match. It could get nasty. Do you think we'll have to?"

As I was out of the car I could only lean back in and say "No, probably not. Scoving's well to the west of the area and they'll play teams over there in the Enterprise Cup. They'll probably get knocked out there. We'll play local Moxham clubs before we finally have to play one of the big teams like Appleton Water."

"Well if you think that this year you're just entering the Enterprise Cup, I can tell you that Scoving played in it in the past, so did Moxham." He bit his lip. "And that's when all the trouble was. I don't think anybody in their right mind would want another fixture arranged like that. It would kill this project off right from the beginning, create a terrible scene."

"No. I don't think we'll meet them. I don't think we'll have much to do with Scoving. I think we'll be put in different draws from them. See you."

I closed the door with a firm reassuring action.

CHAPTER SIXTEEN

This was an awkward place and time to meet, but it was the only time we could all get together. School finishing time, Tuesday. Sir Richard had called us all together to put final touches to our bid at Claire's school where Wicket had just finished telling some cricket stories to the children.

As I drove up in the Jimny from the Sports Centre, Ann's last words echoed in my ears asking me why I should want to be involved with a crew that I could not trust. Yet those words just vanished on driving through the school gateway.

I was once again going to be close to Claire, and this time I would have the added pleasure of seeing another facet to her: to see what she was like at school, and what her classroom was like.

I eased my way through a riot of children leaving school and drove towards an empty bay in the car park between Sir Richard's Range Rover and a silver sports car.

Just as I was manoeuvring a young girl came screaming past chased by two others. I braked hard, my head jolting forward even though I had the seat belt on. It brought back all the horrors of that split second in Peter's car a few nights ago.

Fortunately, I managed the final inches without incident and squeezed out of my car, taking care not to open my door against the silver sports car. It was a Mazda MX-5 convertible. I did not expect teachers in a junior school to drive around in these. On the other side of it was Claire's, a more familiar Fiesta.

As I passed the first classroom I saw inside a male teacher tidying up the children's artwork on a table near the door. He turned round. It was Mark. He scowled as I passed.

Further along the corridor an open glass door had 'Miss Spedman, Year 3' in a riot of colours and fonts.

Inside I was hit by the stuffy smell of sweat. Although the children's bodies had gone, their warm exuberance hung in the air.

There were children's paintings and drawings of cricket scenes on the walls. A number of pieces of cardboard art imitating wickets and bats were on tables at the sides of the room, with short compositions on the walls written in children's hands.

Sir Richard, Claire, and Wicket were already gathered round a folder on the front desk, illuminated by the early March sunset from the large window.

"Right then," Sir Richard began reading aloud from the folder. "First the Summary, then '…a new building of quality and distinction, reclaiming the heritage of the Club…'. By the way, I've put some of the heritage information from that paper by Wicket's father in there. OK so far? '…A shared commitment to regenerating our communities…. Friends of Moxham Cricket Club Sport Facilities and Physical Activity Strategy will contribute to Objective Two of the County Strategy 2008-2013 …'. You've all seen the interim drafts and had time to think. I reckon we're certain to get the six million funding, eh?"

We all nodded.

"And great editing and presentation work by the people in our national consultancy office, GSS, in London," he said. "If you want to join us, Jeremy, you can. As I've said before, there's a wide world out there. Lots of opportunities."

"Maybe I'll think about it," I said, glancing at Claire.

Claire nodded at me. Then, turning to Sir Richard, she said, "Go back to the section on local support."

Sir Richard flipped back the pages and Claire asked, "There … 'Friends of Moxham Cricket Club'… what's that?"

"Community involvement," said Sir Richard. "It's only just been formed and seems to be just a couple of people so far."

"And about time too," I added. "We desperately need things to look as though they are happening. Peter Kammer was asking me some awkward questions about the ground the other night. I managed to skirt round them to avoid having to show him the ground and risk putting him off."

Then I realised that sounded negative and added, "Of course, I'd like him to go and visit it and show commitment and curiosity."

"Yes," said Sir Richard. "But not for a few weeks yet."

"Why? What's happening then?" asked Wicket.

"The new pavilion will be coming," said Sir Richard.

"What do you mean, 'Coming'?" asked Wicket cautiously. "I thought they build those kinds of things on site and took months over it. How can it just come?"

"Coming on the back of a lorry," said Sir Richard. "Modern building techniques."

"Ah yes, but it won't be a patch on the old Moxham pavilion," said Wicket. "Those were the days. We had running water and electricity – lights and power. We had a full kitchen and changing rooms with a shower."

"Let's not dwell on that," said Sir Richard. "This is going to be a cabin for us to get changed in and to go to the toilet in. It's come from a football club who don't need it anymore because they've built their own. It's a reclaimed resource. Near-zero asset depletion. To show the inspectors who control the money for the grant that we are willing to get something off the ground ourselves. It'll be an indicator of our motivation. We'll hear the outcome of the bid by the end of the summer."

"About the same time as the Cup finishing?" asked Wicket.

"Yes, but we don't need to win the Cup to be awarded the project money. That's decided on potential, progress, motivation, and management indicators like that. We just have to put up a good show in the Cup – which I think we will.

"Now there are two other bids besides ours. One is Appleton Water. For an upgrade. An Upgrade! To use the club as a social recreational centre for two and three day conferences. They've got almost a million pound facility at the moment and now they're asking for seventy thousand extra! They've got a nerve! They won't get that. However, here's the other one … Rod's."

He brought a stapled document out of a folder. "Scoving Sports. … Heritage of Scoving. History of cricket in Scoving, Current situation, Future proposals, Advantages for the area…Extra car parking and bar and promotion £300,000. The Club intends to be proactive with its marketing. Outside consultants have identified a need…'"

"A what, who?" asked Wicket.

"He's just got his brother to write him a letter from London," said Sir Richard. " '…to promote and advertise the new facilities by a brochure with detailed information for the banqueting side of the business...' "

"What banqueting? It's just a bloody wooden hut!" said Wicket.

Sir Richard smiled, and continued, " '... cultural strategies option appraisal, by promoting increased use of the clubhouse, this will produce increased interest in the Scoving area, thus allowing visitors to stay in much sought-after reclusive hotels...' "

"Huh! Hotels which his brother has a share in, no doubt," muttered Wicket.

"Hah!" said Sir Richard. "If his bid goes through then the whole infra-structure of the county sports programme will be jeopardised because it makes no provision in it for regeneration."

I said, "They'll obviously see it's a load of bunkum and accept ours!"

"Unless they give all the money to Appleton Water," said Wicket. "They might want to play safe with a safe bet."

"Yes, but," Sir Richard paused, and his voice darkened. "There is a worse scenario that the County might decide the whole area was full of uncoordinated bids not worth spending the money on. If so, no one would get anything."

"Yes, but ours has got the entire general county infrastructure in," I protested. "That's what they're after ... isn't it? That's why we're doing this. To save our jobs, the sports programme, the county, the country, the world, the planet. So you see they've got to give it to us."

"Not necessarily," interrupted a voice from the doorway. It was Mark who had come unnoticed into the room.

He swaggered over. "Oh yes. I see what you're looking at. That's fast work, getting a copy of our bid."

Claire softened and leaned back into him as he came from behind and put an arm round her. I didn't like the way he did that. I was about to tell him to leave her alone when she spoke.

"We just wanted to see what you've got," she murmured cooingly into his ear, with an intimacy that was possibly too controlling to be genuine.

Mark frowned at the Moxham bid on the table and looked straight at me.

"Anyway, what's all that stuff in the appendix of your bid – children's drawings in support?" He mocked. "It's amateur – they'll see it's all poor quality stuff straight away. Six million? They'll reject it out of hand. You've got no chance. Particularly when we've got evidence about what went on with Moxham."

Claire pulled away, saying "Come on now Mark, don't knock all our hard work here. The bid will come in useful for the district as a whole. Who knows – you might want to join the national consultancy as well at the end of it all!"

I blanched. I could not stand the idea of him joining Sir Richard's consultancy as well. He would get in the way of me and Claire.

Wicket stared at him, steeling himself for what Mark might say next.

"Dad says that he has very firm evidence that you know where all the cups from the old Moxham club in 2000 have gone." Mark said assertively as Wicket shook his head. "And he says that he's going to go to the inspectors at County level with the evidence if anything goes wrong with the bids."

Mark started to leave the room, winking and smiling at Wicket. "And he will, he will."

Stunned, we watched him through the internal window as he crossed the hall still with a commanding swagger like his father.

"Well this is a show-down now!" said Sir Richard turning to us in anger.

CHAPTER SEVENTEEN

I was standing at the reception area in the Moxham Sports Centre on nets night, awaiting the early appearance of Fardeep for a personal session he had promised.

"You've got the nets again now tonight with perhaps more people," said Ann at her desk. "So I can stay for an extra hour on reception if you like. I can get some of the invoices done and then go straight to mother's."

"You don't have to," I said. "There's lots of time for you to do them when you're next on duty."

"But they're at a critical stage in sorting now and I don't want them messed up by anyone. It'll be interesting for me to see who turns up."

Ann was keen to support me in a little local cricket revival, but I don't think she wanted me to get very involved with the future consultancy aspect of the project team as Sir Richard had invited me to do.

I checked my watch: 7:10.

"Fardeep's late. I'm supposed to be having a personal session with him before the start."

"Huh!" Ann said. "I suppose you have to make allowances for these geniuses. But it's a bit rich for him to cut into your time like this, as though you had nothing better to do. Oh, and by the way, I've looked up their consultancy GSS on the internet. There is a GSS, but it's to do with computers and obviously nothing to do with sports projects. There are others even more unlikely - to do with airline cargo, boats, churches and bottled gas. But with a firm supposed to be handling six million pounds, you'd have thought there would be a website. After all, Sir Richard Gregory has his own."

"Well, have you used the right search terms?"

"I have. And different engines. Dozens of them. I tell you, something stinks."

"I can't discuss it now. Fardeep's just got out of his car."

"Perhaps he might know? Ask him."

Yet Fardeep was inside and upon me before I could think. He had his arm around me and was whisking me down the corridor towards the hall before I could utter a word.

"Ah Jeremy! Let us go in! Let us have that personal session I mentioned to you. Quick, before the others come! The receptionist will wait here for the rest of the team."

Ann looked on, waiting for me to ask him there and then. She winced one of her extremely rare disapprovals at the way he had breezed in late and had taken her role for granted without a word to her.

As he closed the door to the hall after us he said. "Sit down here on this bench and I will explain this session to you. All the great players have their own special way of clearing the mind. For it is how you concentrate that points to your greatness. Great players are single-minded and focus strongly. If they lose focus then they can regain it quickly. Now look at this charm."

He opened his hand. "It is a jewel from the Amritsar Temple. Feel it. It is yours. I am giving it to you as a gift."

It was a soft plastic amber domed button, yet it glittered with complex facets.

"There are many Indian symbols I could give you. But this is special. It is like an eye. If you look into the centre it will give you great sight. If you do that and meditate with it every day then you will be able to control your powers of attention. When you go out before a game, hold it, close your eyes, and say these words to yourself: EK- DO- TIN- CAR- PAC- CHE. Then open your eyes to look into the jewel again. Then close them again and say the words again. Remember, cricket is counted in sixes. So you will open and close your eyes six times in this exercise. Then when you go out to bat, you will be fantastically improved and you will focus much better. Try it out!"

I closed my eyes and held the charm. I said the words with his help, and then opened them again. As I repeated this process I really did feel that I was settling down ready for the practice session to come. All other past thoughts had been forgotten, including my promise to Ann to ask him about GSS.

"So, whenever you get into a panic while you are playing, then just close your eyes, and think of the jewel. Think of being inside the jewel and looking. Inside the jewel you are protected and

119

can see clearly. It is calmness of mind that brings clarity of vision. Think of the jewel, then open your eyes again and you will be able to focus instantly. Try it tonight when you are waiting to bat in the nets. Just touch the jewel in your pocket. Imagine you are deep inside the jewel, protected from all harm and with clear vision looking out."

I must admit that this seemed a good idea. When I had been bowling or batting my mind often wandered. This was a way in which I would bring it back, and protect me from the guilt of my mistakes.

"But do not overexpose yourself to it. After the game, put it straight back into your bag again. The charm must stay in the bag until just before you bat. Otherwise, it will go stale on you. Here, put it in the side pocket with all your things in there."

Our session was interrupted by the arrival of Luke, Simon, and Claire. Luke set about putting his pads on as the others limbered up to bowl. I watched Claire swing her arms gracefully and then measure her run up as she had done last time. She bowled flowingly to a cautious Luke.

Wicket was next arriving. I introduced him to Fardeep, who put his hands together in prayer and bowed his head as though he was giving due deference to a village elder and said "Thank you for giving the information for the project. I have seen the next draft. Sir Richard is still working on it. It is good."

"Glad to be of use. Anything to stop that devil Rod and his son Mark trying to put something up to scupper us."

"Will you keep wicket for us today?" asked Fardeep and gestured to the nets.

Wicket screwed up his eyes in thought.

"No. I don't think there's enough room for me behind there today."

"I'll move the stumps," I said and took a step towards the nets.

"No. Don't do that," said Wicket. "If we move them up, we'll have to move this end and then there won't be enough room for the bowler's run up. So, no, best leave them where they are."

"Oh," I said. "I'm sorry we haven't got a bigger hall."

"Never mind, I don't need to practice that today," said Wicket. "Leave it for a few weeks until we practice outside. It's difficult to dive and catch indoors. The floor is so hard. "

"Oh yes, very true," said Fardeep. "We don't want anyone to get hurt before the season starts. There is plenty of time for practice. Plenty of time."

Wicket nodded and picked up a ball.

"Would you like me to give you some coaching advice as we go along?" asked Fardeep. "I will be giving it to the others."

"No thanks," said Wicket gruffly as he was bowling a practice ball. Distracted by the question, it went wide and he grimaced as it thudded into the bottom corner of the netting.

As we queued up to bowl I manoeuvred myself next to Claire and asked about what Mark had said at the end of yesterday's meeting at the school.

"Oh him! It's nothing," she said. "He's a total liar. It's Rod's inflated views putting it into his mind. Your turn to bowl."

She gestured to the stumps as the previous bowler was collecting his ball and leaving the net. She returned quickly to studying the ball in her hand. It seemed that the bowling queue was not the place to have an in-depth discussion with her about potential boyfriends or what they meant about the history of Moxham.

After a quarter of an hour we had settled down into a rhythm, and Simon had started his turn as the next batsman.

Suddenly, Peter sprang into the hall.

"Pip! Pip! Whoa! How are you, Jeremy mate? Who's batting next?" He flung his heavy kit bag into a corner with a bang.

Fardeep nodded at me.

"Well, er, I suppose I was going to, er, unless you want to?" I stammered.

"Fine, yes, of course, don't mind if I do," said Peter, putting on his pads.

Soon after Fardeep shouted "Last few!" to Simon and we finished our turn. Peter strolled down, pulling his cap over the right side of his head and trailing his bat on the ground behind him. Unlike Luke and Simon, he did not cradle his bat like a precision instrument or a samurai sword, but dragged it along like a huge hammer that was going to be worked in a forge. I wondered how heavy it was since even he was having trouble carrying it in one hand.

I was first to bowl to him, and I feared my ball would be immediately blasted for six. However, I need not have worried for he carefully watched the ball down towards him and merely touched it defensively.

I thought how genteel and how kind such a potentially aggressive batsman was to the bowling. How different he was to the brute force of the mechanic in the garage. Where had this hammer aspect gone?

We bowled six balls, and he played them carefully with respect, as though they were eggs that had been entrusted to him for safekeeping and he was merely helping them to nest down for the night by guiding them to one side or the other. They curled away slowly like crown green bowls at the end of their run.

I cast off my fear of what he could do and relaxed into a slower kind of cricket. It was remarkable that what he had hauled like a sledgehammer could be used so daintily.

However, as soon as he had guided six of our balls, his posture changed as if a switch had been flicked. I was unlucky enough to bowl the seventh. A darker and murderous air took him over. He gritted his teeth and lifted his bat much higher than before, and took a stride towards me. I was still in my false sense of drifting off to sleep and did not appreciate there was going to be any particular new event. The bat came down at lightning speed and the ball thundered back inches over my head. It continued straight onto the wall behind blasting like a cannon ball against a castle. Bits of paint flew off where it smashed. The sound of the explosion echoed round the hall.

The next ball from Luke was also given the same treatment, if not more forcefully, for not only did it take some of the paintwork off but it rebounded a considerable way towards us. Wicket was in danger of being hit in the back had he not turned round and caught the ball as it came off the wall, shouting "How's that?" for the catch. We heard the smack as it hit his hands and, though he did manage to keep hold of the ball, he shook them in pain afterwards.

Peter was undeterred. He launched an even greater blow at a ball from Fardeep. This was a tremendous swipe so full and wild that I feared the entire building would be in danger of demolition. However, he missed and Fardeep's ball flew into the gap that had been created behind his early speeding bat.

"How's that!" shouted Fardeep, jumping in the air with glee.

Fardeep turned to me and said, "Better put your pads on, ready for your turn, Jeremy. And mind you change in a safe area."

As I waited with my pads on ready, I touched my left trouser pocket. I could feel the charm through there as I closed my eyes and did the exercise Fardeep had taught me.

"Last few!" Fardeep shouted to Peter.

Then it was my turn. With the charm in my pocket I had calmed down compared to last week. I was no longer so worked up when I missed the ball. Fortunately, I only missed the ones that missed the stumps. The ones in line I was able to play carefully and defend. Mistakes did not hurt me. I no longer felt as though I had caused the end of the world. I could compose myself, take a deep breath, and start again knowing that my mistake was in the past and I would not be tainted by that event. I felt that I had a clear psychological space between me and the outside world, as though there was at least a foot of solid unbreakable glass. This zone I began to call "my reaction space" and I could watch it and see that I did not have to feel anything personal about what happened in it.

When Fardeep shouted "Last few, Jeremy!" I felt neither disappointment nor relief. I just took it in my stride as a natural progression.

After me, Claire batted next. She had not batted in the nets last week but I remember how she had bowled in a wonderful fluid movement. Indeed, with the first ball Luke bowled to her today she showed all the promise and skills of a semi-professional with an exquisite full follow-through of her arms.

I was excited to bowl to her, and looped my first ball up to make it easy for her. It was one of my terribly inept deliveries, dropping short, but she was unprepared for how facile and slow it was. She was unintentionally through her stroke too early and the ball was lobbing back to me. I dived forward onto my knees and accepted the ball as though in prayer.

I did not scream, "How's that!" but merely asked with a little playful smile "How is that, please?" – whispering it, to try to lessen its impact.

She nodded and retook her stance at the crease, retreating into a shut-in concentration for the rest of her session. I wondered whether it was my skill, her error, or whether she had taken pity on me and had purposely given me the catch as an encouragement.

From then on, each stroke of hers, whether it was a defensive or an attacking one, had that same sense of marvellous mastery of action, of subtle smooth grace. Sometimes she played it down to her right through the slips area with a little petulant spank. At other times, it was a larger stroke, hitting the ball high in the air.

The way that she had so intensely focused on her skill showed me just how coldly she could shut out all distractions and not show her real emotion. So it was in her personal dealings with others, especially me. I was treated kindly at arm's length. Yet surely, she must appreciate what my feelings towards her were? Perhaps she thought she had to remain above all personal contact for the good of the project. However, I wanted to show her that for the good of the project we must acknowledge our mutual attraction. Surely she must see this. Then why does she rebuff me, yet still want me to join the project and the team?

Perhaps she was still attached to Mark. Was it an affair she was struggling to get out of? She allowed Mark to touch her - to a point. She did not want to become too involved with me yet, but still wanted to keep me as an option. That is why she so loudly dismissed him whenever I asked.

Fardeep announced the last round to signify the end of our session and I was immediately saddened that the spectacle had to end.

Claire came out of the nets, took her helmet off, and shook her hair. A few strands hung over her face.

Fardeep said, "Same time next week, everybody."

As the group broke up, I limped over to Claire, holding my back and said it was starting to ache and needed massaging.

"Sure," she said. "Can we quickly use somewhere here? Only we can't go back to my flat because I've got preparation work to do for school tomorrow."

"Well, there are some benches in the gym."

"Fine. Let's go there."

Just then, the door opened and Ann came into the hall followed by the four lads from Saturday night: Anas, Jafar, Dwayne, and Alan.

"They're sorry they're late," Ann announced.

They came slowly in single file sheepishly with their eyes down, not undisciplined or running wild like Saturday.

Fardeep looked at them and said, "Now, Jeremy, can I have a few minutes with them? I will see what they can do."

I nodded, but Ann interrupted, "I'm afraid I have to go to check on my mother. I can't be held responsible for people staying late."

"OK," I said to Ann, sensing her hostility to Fardeep. "You go. I'll lock up. I'll just let Fardeep see what the lads can do."

"Mind my stuff on the desk," Ann said. "There's invoices for the new equipment and sodium lighting. As I've said, I've sorted those into a proper sequence now and I don't want people looking through and messing them up."

"Don't worry. I won't be going through stuff. I won't. Your stuff will be safe. I'll just sit there and watch the door."

Ann took a look at me standing there still holding my back next to Claire. She sniffed, turned, and left with the established players.

Fardeep turned to the boys. "Now then, how much cricket have you played before?"

I closed the hall door and headed to the little gym with Claire.

I opened the door and flicked on the fluorescent light. It was like a cell. There was an old blue carpet and light blue walls, with a high frosted glass window in one, a small TV on a shelf on the other. There were only a few machines and they easily crowded the small room.

"Here we are – there are plenty of soft benches in here for us to lie on." I said.

"Yes. You mean for you to lie on," she said.

"I can give you a massage in return?"

"Oh no. I only want it done a certain way and I know how to do it. If you don't know how, you might do it too hard or the wrong way. Maybe at a later occasion when you've learnt a bit more. You just lift your shirt up and lie down there for now. It'll stop your back hurting so much tomorrow."

Her hands were cold at first but then they warmed up and soon there were those smooth flowing strokes like soft warm waves rippling over a shore, easing round the stiffness in my spine until it had all gone.

After a short while, there were voices in the hall and she said, "Fardeep has finished. It is late. I must go."

"You don't need me to see you back?"

"No thanks I have my car. Ciao!" She was already half-way out of the door, but blew me a kiss.

Over the next weeks through March and then into April I touched Fardeep's charm before I went into bat. I had two more sessions with him – the next week and then a few weeks later. After that, Fardeep would periodically draw me aside to remind me, "Jeremy, that is good. You are using the charm so well".

But another charm held equal power. At night I remembered the way Claire batted and bowled. The way I had seen her pull her eyelashes and blink when she had something in her eye. The way she puckered her lip and blew her cheeks out when someone, usually Peter, had hit her bowling hard. However, when her bowling was going well she would spring up wonderfully high and shout "Yes!"

In contrast, there were those more thoughtful moments when she would stop, stare, and narrow her eyes at me when I was batting as though she was staring at something beyond me, or something she saw in the future. In those moments I wondered what she saw.

CHAPTER EIGHTEEN

It was Monday morning in late April and I was in the Hall in Moxham Sports Centre with the electrician. He was standing by the control box on the wall and looking at the sodium lamp circuit that had been installed to save money and provide better lighting. But the new sodium lamps had begun to malfunction already.

"Well I don't know," he said, one hand on hip, the other bringing a mug of coffee to his mouth. "I've never seen a circuit like this before. The way I've re-fitted them they should come on now. For those two that don't we'll have to order two more bulbs. They're probably reconditioned stock from another council."

"Can we have the fluorescents back on?" I asked.

"Well, I don't know if I can do that. The council wants us to have all energy-saving bulbs and wants us to use the new ones."

"But we can't see. It's only useful for the children's games or football. For cricket we need them all working, or the brighter fluorescent."

"Well, I don't know. Try to go part-time with them. Use it like that. Just fluorescent for cricket till the new sodium lamps come."

Just then the door opened and Ann the receptionist shouted "Excuse me, Jeremy, but there's a call for you. It's Sir Richard."

I picked it up in my office.

"Hello, Jeremy," he said. "We have a problem with the Moxham field. The cabin is coming on Wednesday. We've got a Bobcat mini-bulldozer into the field to bring down the ruins but we can't get the larger skip lorries through because halfway along the western lane is a sycamore which we need to prune more. We need the wider lorries to take the debris away. But we have been told by a supervisor in the gardening section that they won't prune the sycamore anymore and we'll have to use mini-skips. In which case it'll take ages to shift the debris. Can you ring up Nathaniel Broome, the Head of Gardens which is what this lane comes under, and see if he'll authorise pruning the sycamore more? Otherwise it'll take ages to clear the site. My secretary is off today and I have to go to a meeting in London about the bidding process for a couple of days. So can you phone head of gardens and get them to prune it? Also, can you be there on Wednesday to supervise the arrival of the new pavilion? I won't be back till late Wednesday."

I explained the situation to Ann who helped me search our internal directory for estates and gardening.

"Huh! That's another example," she said. "See what I mean about them leaving you to do it all? What's Sir Richard got to go to London for now?"

After several false leads I eventually got through on a mobile number.

"Hello, Mr Broome? It's Jeremy Freeman here from Sports and Leisure. It's about the Moxham field. I wonder if you can help us? We've got a problem with a sycamore in the western lane. Can you cut a bit more off it so we can get our lorries through?"

"Oh we've cut that off already. We've pruned it as much as we can." His voice sounded faint as though it was in a forest at first, and then came through stronger and more focused.

"Yes, but we can't get the maxi-skips through."

"Well you don't need maxi-skips. You can do it all in mini-skips – it won't take much longer and probably save you diesel on smaller lorries."

"No. It <u>will</u> take us longer and be more expensive because we are on a tight schedule and have to have it all cleared today. The pavilion is coming on Wednesday."

"Well if it's coming on Wednesday and it is only Monday then you have today and tomorrow so you can use the mini-skips."

"But we've got a pavilion being delivered on Wednesday and that will be on the back of a lorry, and the cargo will be the size of a maxi-skip and it won't be able to get past the sycamore in the western lane because of the size of its load."

"Well. You can come along the eastern lane with that. That's relatively clear."

"I don't think he'll have enough room."

"Look, we're not cutting down or deforming any more trees. We've cut down what we can because we're good neighbours with your department but we can't go about destroying the tree stock of Moxham."

"But if this doesn't succeed because we can't get the cabin through, then the whole service will be in trouble."

"Oh, I know what kind of cabin it is that's coming. And the lorry that's bringing it. We use them a lot in forestry. They are basically cubes and they'll get through from the east easily. Those lorries are very manoeuvrable, with a crane on as well for tight spots. It'll do that hairpin OK. Anyway we're not going to cut any more in that western lane. That sycamore has been disfigured and half-destroyed and damaged just for the sake of a five-minute lorry. It can come in from the east – it will make the turn OK. They have good wheel lock on those new lorries. I've got to go now. Sorry."

He hung up.

I clutched the phone tightly to my chest and breathed out forcibly.

Just then, the electrician put his head round the door.

"I can't get all the sodiums fully on. I've put the fluorescent circuit back up as an option for the cricket. Rest of the time the council will want you to use the sodium to save running costs. But you can't have both on together otherwise they'll fuse the entire building and set off the alarms."

With my mind still caught up in the ramifications of Mr Broome I could only nod at him. By the time I had registered what he'd said and collected my thoughts the electrician had gone.

CHAPTER NINETEEN

Cricket had not been played here for years. This was a field of bricks and rotten timbers that smelt fusty when I kicked at them under the long spring wet grass. Sir Richard had had the old ruins bulldozed a few days ago and most of it had been cleared away. There was no evidence of there ever having been a pavilion here now. The council had promised a new pavilion, but not a new pavilion of nostalgic English splendour. That era was over: its ruins were buried around me. The council meant just something for the inspectors to see so that we could get a grant towards restoring cricket.

I had volunteered to wait at the northern top of the field and direct its positioning onto those bricks in the car park. As I waited I looked southwards down the field. On my left and all along the bottom was the hedge which had overgrown the lane behind it. We always came to the ground from this eastern end. Although it was overgrown, it was not as difficult as fighting the denser sycamore from the western end. The lorry driver had directions to approach from the east and to make a hairpin turn up into the ground. He was already over two hours late.

Suddenly there was a screeching of branches and I saw the cream-grey roof of a large cabin with flashing amber lights forcing slowly along behind the tops of the thickening spring greenery from the east.

I hurried through the gateway. The lorry was facing me up the lane with an old cabin and small Hiab loader crane on its back. These Swedish cranes were often on delivery lorries. Its arm could be folded away tight behind the cab and when extended they would manage quite large and heavy loads. The cabin was a scruffy pre-owned prefab. The lorry had to back up angrily every few feet and try different angles to force past obstructing bushes.

In the lane the space between the trees would just allow a farmer's tractor to pass. A tractor was of the earth and the hedges had grown to its shape like a memory. But this, this monstrous flatbed lorry with its Hiab loader crane and large wide load was of a shape not of this earth. The hedges seemed to know it. They resisted its passage, pushing themselves up against it, screaming in a scrunching savage battle. The top edges of the cabin roof wrenched the tree branches, bending and snapping them off as it came.

The driver's face strained and the gears crunched as he inched the cabin forwards then backwards, then forwards again.

After a quarter of an hour the driver threw his hands up in exasperation. He put his head out of the window through the foliage and shouted above the laboured engine noise. "I'm getting bloody well stuck here, mate! How much further?"

I pointed behind me to the gateway.

"What?" he spat into the bushes. "No way! It's hard enough getting along this lane. I won't be able to turn sharp into there. No mate! This can only go straight. And right now it can only go one way – straight back to the depot. This bloody engine's overheating! I'm not messing around here anymore."

Deep down I felt glad that this dirty old cabin could not be delivered, for I dreamt that the council would now after all have to rebuild the old pavilion in its Edwardian splendour with its regal veranda where those waiting to bat could lounge and sip lemonade in the afternoon sun.

But then, I thought, that's ridiculous. It's been neglected for years and they won't provide money to rebuild it. No, the project will fail without a pavilion. I resigned myself to accepting this eyesore, and it had to be sited today. The driver would not come back again.

Since he was level with the field's car park, I suggested he use his crane to drop the cabin over the hedge. He tossed his head at the imbecility of my suggestion. He pointed out that the hedge was too high and he would need to come back tomorrow with a mobile extending crane. He doubted if I had the thousands needed for such costly rental.

"I'm sorry, mate," he said. "But I can't get this across there. I can't deliver it. It's not normally we have this kind of problem. In fact, I'm quite good at getting it in spaces where other drivers might not. But this can't be done. Anyway, it's getting dark. Cheerio."

Before I could say anything, he started to move the lorry forward slowly and I had to retreat in front of it and take refuge in the gateway as it struggled past.

I felt helpless. Cricket would never be played here again. I could do nothing but step back and let him scrape slowly past and away onwards into the western part of the lane. The entrance to the haven of golden summers was now, because of its layout, preventing its revival.

Then I saw it. Glimmering in the last rays of the afternoon spring sunlight: the solution that had eluded us all the time. I had been blinded by my anger at the quality of this replacement pavilion; he had been blinded by his frustration and agitation at the difficulty of the lane. As he had now passed the gateway, there was no need to turn. He could go backwards.

The entry into the ground was one prong of a fork and he had come down the other prong into the handle. Now having come down this far he could easily reverse back up the other prong into the car park and unload.

Years ago this must have been the way the players came before it became overgrown. Ever since the start of this restoration project I had been coming down this lane from the east, just because it was more convenient from town. In my Jimny I always just managed the hairpin turn. I had never really liked the narrowness around that sycamore in the western lane, preferring to push past the softer bushes and approach from the east. But I could see now that the way from the west was the natural turn into the field.

I shouted and waved to him to stop but he didn't seem to hear me above the engine noise. The lorry revved, inching laboriously forward, picking up speed as its way became clearer.

It roared in freedom, taking the cabin away from me.

Then it suddenly stopped.

It had reached the sycamore in the western lane.

The lorry alone might just pass through, but there was no way it would squeeze past with the cabin on it. I saw him switch his engine off and drop his head onto the steering wheel in frustration.

"Just back it!" I shouted to him, now banging on his window. "You can do it now! See?" I pointed to the gateway behind him.

The engine roared again and the gearbox scrunched into reverse. There was just enough room for him to swing through and up into the car park in the field. There he stopped and used the Hiab loader crane to slide the cabin onto our prepared base.

He nodded thanks as he drove off. Being free of his wide load he drove smoothly along the lane and purred past that sycamore.

I listened to his engine die away and turned to the cabin. It was splattered with mud and gouged and scored from the branches in the lane, but it would be our pavilion.

And in the lock of the door was a set of keys still tied to the handle. A new season ready to be opened.

CHAPTER TWENTY

"You'd better take a look at Fardeep and those four lads. It's not going well again," Ann said to me at the reception desk in Moxham Sports Centre on the last indoor nets night. The four boys Anas, Jafar, Alan, and Dwayne always came late and stayed on after the rest had gone for Fardeep to coach them.

It was the usual pattern tonight. Everyone had come, had their practice and then gone, including Claire. I would stay on for Fardeep to do his coaching with the late boys. Apart from them, it was just me and Ann in the building.

"OK. I'll check. Are they still on the old bright fluorescent lights? Did you switch over to the new sodium lamps circuit?"

"No I didn't. I wasn't sure how to."

"No problem. That can be my excuse to see how they're getting on."

Through the small window in the hall door I could see Fardeep was standing at the stumps nearest the door where a coach or umpire would stand. The left-handed Dwayne was bowling and Anas was batting down inside the bottom of the netting. Behind Fardeep's back Alan was laughing at Jafar who was doing some dance moves along a wooden gymnastics balance bench. Neither of them appeared to be paying proper attention to the cricket practice.

Anas took a swipe at the ball. He missed it and it clattered into the stumps behind him.

"No, no. That is not the way!" Fardeep shouted.

Not wanting to make an intrusive entrance, I opened the door slowly. On hearing the door, Fardeep turned to me and motioned me inside. The others glanced in my direction and Jafar stopped jumping on the furniture.

"As you were," I said. "You've got a while yet. I've just come in to change the lighting over."

"Oh, plenty of time, there is always plenty of time," said Fardeep.

"Can you give me a hand with it?" I asked Fardeep. "You stand by the normal room switch and when I say "Go!", turn it off, and I'll instantly turn the sodium on. Only we can't have them both on together. They'll blow the fuse the way they've been repaired. The council want me to try to run the sodium as much as possible. I know it's not as good a light as the fluorescent but we have to show willing, so we'll just have it on for a short while."

"Good. There is no problem here. We are only bowling slowly."

I went over to a side wall and opened the sodium lamps control box.

Fardeep went over to the main room switch on the back wall near the door.

However, the large team kit bag was in the way of his getting to the light switch so he bent down and dragged the bag a foot away from the wall into the room.

"Wow! This is heavy Jeremy," he gasped. "Lots of kit in this. Left-handed gloves and pads, and wicket-keeper's pads. You're well off for kit."

Then he put his hand on the switch.

"I am ready. You tell me when."

"Right. One, two, three," I said. "Turn yours off."

As soon as Fardeep turned his switch off I threw mine on. There was barely a blink of darkness before there began a quiet hum and the hall slowly grew brighter as the sodium dawned its dirty yellow light from the lamps overhead.

I closed the box and said, "Main thing to remember is not to flick that fluorescent light switch back on now because the circuit won't support both lighting systems on together. The fuse would blow and we would all be in darkness. It would trip the security alarm with its back-up battery directly to the police station. That's cheap low budget electrics for you. It all blows up together."

I pointed to a little hand-written notice by the switch, 'Do not switch on if sodium is on'.

"Hey," said Jafar looking upwards. "There's one that's not coming on. And there's another going off again."

"Huh. That's progress here," I said. "That shows you there's new faults on the circuit that's supposed to have been repaired. I don't know what they've done."

I said thank you to Fardeep and he thanked me for thanking him and in nodding back acknowledgement to me almost fell over the kitbag to rejoin the lads.

I suppose a lot of keen cricketers would have picked up a ball and joined in bowling next but I didn't. I had done my hour's practice earlier tonight and that was enough. So I just stood in a corner away from the door, vaguely watching.

Fardeep motioned to Alan to bowl.

Alan was a cyclist and approached everything in life by way of circles. He seemed to pedal up to the stumps lifting his knees very high with long easy strides and then he bowled a full cycle of his arms as though he was a monocycle balanced on a spot.

Anas saw the ball early and waited in position to hit it with good timing.

The sharp smack echoed in the hall. I shuddered as the ball sailed high up onto the back wall, narrowly missing Jafar who had started dancing again on the wooden bench.

They took it in turns to bowl to Anas who intermittently played a correct forward defensive shot, or lofted a drive onto the back wall. His batting was regularly punctuated by Fardeep shouting "Well done!". Sometimes, however, Fardeep would shout "No, not like that. What have I told you?" whenever his stumps were hit by balls bowled by Dwayne.

The lofted ones were struck with such force at Jafar that it seemed to be an attempt to knock him off his bench. However, he caught many of those that came within reach, often spectacularly one-handed whilst leaping. It reminded me of his agility when hurdling across Peter's car that night.

When it was his turn in the sequence to bowl Jafar jumped down from the bench always exactly on cue and afterwards returned to the bench to catch the next ball again spectacularly. He was never struck by the balls but once one of them thudded into the notice near the switch.

All three lads turned to look at how close it had come and then looked round at each other. Anas held his bat up in salute, and between them an unspoken idea had taken place.

As the practice progressed Jafar continued catching. However, his skill seemed strangely to leave him when the ball was hit anywhere near the light switch, and indeed several times the ball struck the notice.

Fardeep saw me take a few concerned steps towards the switch and said, "Oh, don't worry Jeremy. They're not that accurate. They can't hit such a small light switch from down there. That is thirty yards away. It is quite safe. There is no problem here. We must try to encourage their batting skills. In a match a good hit like that would be runs if not caught."

He wiggled his head to reassure me in a quiet aside, "But if balls do go near the switch I will surely catch them in time."

Then, turning back to the lads, he shouted, "Well done, Anas. Excellent stroke. Now try that again."

The left-handed Dwayne ran up and slung the ball low and fast into Anas's legs who attempted a cross-bat swipe, not a free-flowing forward bat movement like before. He missed, and the ball clattered into the aluminium cricket stumps.

Alan screamed "Howzat!" at the top of his voice, in vengeful jubilation that Anas, who had hit so many of his balls against the back wall, had at last been bowled.

"No, no, no!" shouted Fardeep to Anas. "That is not the way. What have I told you? You do not listen."

Fardeep shook his head at me. "No. that is not the way these boys should be doing this."

He walked down the lane inside the netting towards the batsman. "Listen here. Give me your bat. I will show you."

Fardeep took stance where Anas had been. "Just try it like this as I said." He swung the bat vertically forward. "Not like this," he swished with the bat across him in a scything horizontal action. "Do not swing the bat like that. You will not hit anything. You are like a farmer cutting the wheat. He thinks he is doing well but he does not notice the rats eating his crops down below. You want to hit the rat that lives amongst the wheat. But you are using it like a sword. How can you kill the rat cutting it across the top? There are no rats there. The rats live on the ground. They are eating his crops there and he will have none left for himself if he lets the rats through.

"You must bring your bat along the ground to meet them. Do not bring it across at waist level like that. You will not kill any rats that way. I have been telling you that for many weeks now. The bat must be played straight so all is in line. Here, now you try."

He handed the bat over and walked back up to the bowling end.

"Now pay attention and watch. You must all be on the lookout and watch what the batsman is doing. Watch what he does like a hawk. He is your prey. You can see what he is doing. You must be ready to counter every move. If he comes out to you then you need to drop one shorter. It will give him that same difficult length. If he goes back then you need to bowl further up to him. It will keep the same length there. Or if he is playing a crossbat shot, then you need to try to bowl it so that you can get underneath his action.

"Now listen please and pay attention. I will bowl like a wolf coming up to the wicket. See my slow long strides. Remember wolves hunt in packs. Remember you are hunting together, taking turns to attack. The batsman is your prey – not your master."

Fardeep gently loped up to bowl. Behind him Jafar silently mimicked by taking a few long strides from the back wall, bending his head down and leaning forward like a wolf, yet holding his arms by his side like a monkey.

Alan and Dwayne both circled their thumbs and forefingers round their eyes to imitate the eyes of a hawk as Jafar came aping up to them.

Fardeep bowled a high looping trajectory. Anas took a step down the wicket and did a wonderful flowing stroke bringing his arms fully through which lofted the ball towards the back of the hall.

Fardeep was finishing his follow-through so that he was directly in the line of the stroke and the light switch was behind him. The ball came straight off the bat at head-height rapidly towards him.

It would surely have done some damage to the wall or the light switch fifteen yards behind, but Fardeep's catch was a brilliant snap reaction, clean and decisive. There was a smack as the ball went into his hands.

"Hah, not this time! You are getting over-confident. You are falling into my trap. I know where you will try to hit it!" shouted Fardeep, tossing the ball up. "Ah hah. Do not worry, Jeremy."

He motioned Jafar to bowl.

Jafar bowled a gentle full toss and Anas saw it coming and decided to give it a good wham again.

Jafar shouted a warning for everyone to move quickly out of the way of the missile.

Once again Fardeep had positioned himself exactly in the ball's path, but this time he was further back, only a yard or so in front of the wall, and was half-turned so that he was presenting his left side to the batsman.

Sensing an opportunity for another brilliant catch he reached his right hand up just as the ball was travelling past him. He managed to get his fingers round it but the ball was travelling at such velocity that it took him off balance to his right and to the rear. His body went with it. He tried to move his right foot out for balance but it was stopped by the kitbag. He fell enthusiastically into a slow dive knowing that the bag would cushion his fall and it would make his catch appear even more spectacular.

Holding the ball in triumph, he instinctively put his hands out to break his fall. The back of his right hand still clutching the ball hit the wall; the full force of his left hand went straight onto the light switch.

As he finished his cry "Howzat!" there was a gigantic bang. The hall was thrown into darkness and a painfully loud alarm bell sounded.

CHAPTER TWENTY-ONE

"It's OK. I've turned this switch back off now. Why doesn't it come on?" Fardeep shouted out of the darkness above the noise of the deafening alarm bell.

"Because I need to reset it again." I shouted. "Hold on. Everybody stay where you are."

I felt along the wall to the circuit box, opened it, and turned off the sodium switch.

Then I felt along towards the door to try to reach the main fuse box in the corridor, but tripped over Fardeep on the floor in the darkness, and fell onto the kitbag.

Besides the noise of the alarm and Fardeep shouting about the switch, I heard the cackle of laughter from the lads.

I managed to stagger up and reach the door.

In the corridor there was a dim light as I felt along for the main sports centre fuse box.

I heard Ann shout, "What's happened, Jeremy? Jeremy?"

"Nothing. It's OK. Stay where you are."

Inside the fuse box was the little torch that I kept there just for power failures like this. Its light was very dim because I hadn't replaced the battery for ages. I tapped it with little improvement. I could just about see to reset the tripped fuse and the lights came back on in the corridor. I shouted back to Fardeep to switch on the hall fluorescent light and went up to reception to phone the police station to stop them coming out.

As I put down the phone, the boys and Fardeep were leaving, having decided that this was the time for them to stop for the day.

Fardeep said to them as they went past, "Next week it is outside nets. You do better next time. You concentrate, lads."

He watched them go, then turned to give a deep sigh to Ann and me.

"How can we take them to the outdoor nets at the ground next week? They are not ready. They will just wreak havoc. Like this tonight. It is now almost May and they have learnt nothing. So many weeks they have been coming. I teach them batting, but the ball is hit in the air to be caught. I teach them bowling, but the ball is always easy to hit because they give it so much air. Fielding, they hurl themselves at the netting. They roll around in it. They try to destroy it. It is impossible to believe these boys will ever learn anything."

"They are just young boys," said Ann. "Give them a chance. They are just teenagers. They get easily distracted. When they are outside next week they will be more focused because there is less about to distract them."

"No," said Fardeep. "They will be even worse because they have the great outdoors and there is nothing there to control them."

"Well I've seen them that night that they jumped in front of Peter's car. They must be pretty good," I said.

"You are joking with me, surely," said Fardeep. "They will not make the grade – they cannot pay attention. In all my years of coaching I have never seen anything like this. They do not want to make the grade."

"They can't be that bad, Fardeep. It's too easy to get disheartened. You've taught beginners before?" asked Ann.

"Not so much. I usually coach elite players. I have tried to teach these the straight drive. I have broken it down into little bits. Leading with your head. Moving your foot. Getting the head over the ball. Leading with the left arm. Following through. I have praised them when they got it right."

"And did they get it right?" Ann asked.

"Occasionally they did, very right. Then they were up to their tricks again. I have given them easy things to do. I have given them hard things to challenge them. I have got them to bat in pairs to see if that is any different. Still they mess about behind my back. They hit the ball too early. They are talented, yes, but they cannot control it. They run around and play with everything."

He wiped the sweat from his brow. He looked down at the floor.

"But you must admit, Fardeep - once in a while they get it right so you must have done them some good," I said.

Fardeep shook his head. "But will they continue to come? They have been coming later and later. If we ask them to come to a derelict ground further away to the south, I don't know if they will."

"We need them. It's too late to get more players. We've got games coming up," I said.

"Ah yes, where are we up to with all that? Have we arranged some more games?" asked Fardeep.

"Well, we have the Enterprise Cup which we are in. That is all. Sir Richard told me that. We were formed too late to apply to join the league this year and to be given fixtures. So we have a friendly practice match against a local celebrity side and then we have the first of the Enterprise Cup games."

"I see, and this Cup, that's a knockout, is it?"

"Yes," I said.

"And if we get knocked out, then what happens?"

"Then we have no more games in that competition, I'm afraid."

"I see, and what other games do you have?" he asked.

"We'll have to see what Sir Richard might be able to fix up."

"You mean that we won't have any more games if we lose our first game of the Cup?"

"Well, that's how it stands at the moment."

"Such hard work should come to nothing," he tutted. "You know I soon won't be able to help you so much. I have a playing arrangement with Appleton Water. I am their professional. I will only be able to coach Moxham a few more weeks. Then the season starts. I won't be able to do so much later on."

"Well, look at it this way: we should be able to win the first match, the friendly. You'll be playing in that. It's at Moxham to mark the inauguration of the club, with players from other teams, and various dignitaries and councillors playing. The opposition's supposed to be chosen to be a weak side," I laughed.

"Yes, but only if we've got a full team. It looks like we might not have one. Tell me, who is this friendly match against?"

"Some team called the County All Stars. It's all fixed up by Sir Richard to be a foregone conclusion. It'll be a carnival atmosphere."

"The County All Stars?" exclaimed Fardeep. "I've heard of them. Rod and Mark play for them sometimes. They are a strong side and have a guest player who is Australian."

"Oh no! What? That's not friendly! They're absolutely hostile, and they will be coming to criticise the club and the ground and to scupper the whole project."

CHAPTER TWENTY-TWO

"Keep holding that pole there. Not much longer now," Claire said to me, her face close up to mine, the closest we had ever been. We were separated by the practice netting that we were erecting around one end of the Moxham pitch.

"Here, hook that ring on the top, and hold that first pole upright," she said, throwing me a ring on the end of a guy rope over the top of the netting.

I hooked it on the top of the first pole, careful to keep holding it upright, and tossed her the knotted end back. As she started to disentangle the line, there was a soft twitch around her mouth. Her tongue came to her lips, and then flicked in and out again with each loop she unravelled from the knot.

I watched her through the taut mesh of nothingness that separated us. I felt somehow that it was my knot as well.

She knew I was watching her as she worked. She said nothing, but eventually stretched it out in triumph to complete the disentanglement and that was when she met my gaze again.

She asked "What?"

"You look beautiful when you unravel," I said quietly.

She smiled, and leaned forward with a mischievous flash of her eyes, she said quietly "I know how to fix guys."

"I can see you do," I laughed.

"It's all to do with getting the right tension," she said, running her fingers down the unravelled guy rope seductively and stretching it taut.

Luke at the next pole suddenly interrupted us with "Hurry up. My arm's getting tired."

She finished on my ropes, and went to Luke's whilst I went to hold up the third pole ready for her.

I noticed that she stood a lot further away from him to disentangle the knotting of his guy ropes.

With two poles up, Luke went to join Simon who had finished hammering in the pegs and had started to put on his batting gear. They did some warm-up exercises and Claire and I were left to work on the other two poles.

"Hello again," I said as she came close to reach in front of my face for the last guy rope end on the last pole.

"Just pass me the guy rope, will you?" she smiled, trying to control her laughter.

"Why do you stand nearer to me than to Luke?" I peered into her face through the netting.

"Because your knots are more difficult than his."

"Is that because I've got you on a shorter rein?" I smirked.

"Maybe." She was bending down to hook a guy rope onto a peg.

"You mean you feel drawn in?"

"Perhaps," she said, finishing the tensioning. "It helps to keep things on a leash so you can see them clearer."

She seemed pleased that she had the final remark to put me at distance again as she stepped back to admire the work. We had made a three-walled enclosure into which we could bowl with space inside behind the stumps for a wicket-keeper to stand.

As usual, Simon was the first to bat and we three bowled to him. He hit crisp shots, moving easily to the pitch of the ball and then after a quarter of an hour, Luke took over and after another quarter of an hour Claire had a bat with her wonderful action.

I decided to bat last because I was waiting for Fardeep to arrive to give me some coaching tips.

Presently a dark green Volkswagen Golf screeched and revved into the gateway. It was Fardeep's car that he had as part of his deal with one of the committee at Appleton Water who ran a local garage. He had been in such a hurry to get here that he had got stuck in the hairpin, having chosen the wrong angle to begin with and was now having to work the car forwards and backwards.

"I am sorry I am late," he said, his face tense and sweaty. He zipped off his tracksuit jacket to reveal a white cricket pullover. "I have just come from teaching the juniors at Appleton Water. They have a big class on these nights. It takes a long time. Especially all the fielding drills. You know the classes are getting bigger all the time. With each week there is more and more children coming. Now where are our four boys? Are they not here yet?" Fardeep looked round.

"Give them time," I said. "I'm sure they'll be along."

"Yes, yes. There is always time. Always time with those four. Always they never come early." Fardeep shook his head and then said "Hah, right now Jeremy. Put your pads on and be ready."

I put on my pads and waited for my turn, touching Fardeep's charm in my pocket, and preparing my mind for the session.

"Now watch Jeremy, watch my arm action." Fardeep said when I got to the crease. "I will just bowl it straight at first."

I watched him tiptoe up to the stumps and bring his arm over, his face fixed in his usual mask of concentration.

The ball came down onto an easy length like in Moxham Sports Hall and it flowed smoothly off the bat.

"That's right Jeremy," said Fardeep. "Just pat them about at first. Don't try hitting them yet."

As Claire bowled to me Fardeep said to her, "Keep your arm up higher; don't let it fall down to the leg side. The arm must go over your head in the direction you are bowling down the pitch. You must not let it come at an angle over your shoulder. I know it's difficult."

Fardeep told Simon "Start with the right arm with the ball more tucked into the chest. Hold this arm close to you as you cock your body like a spring - like a snake that coils up ready to strike. Balance on the back foot. Arms up ready. Your left arm should point up to the sky, then come down, and cut the batsman in half. Then all that energy comes through like a whip. And Luke, you have a tremendous leap like you are serving in tennis. Try to take it easier."

Fardeep could be overpowering with his coaching. Simon and Luke did not discourage him, but occasionally grunted and tried a few things out to show willing.

After a few rounds of bowling I was starting to strike the ball with crisper timing. My vision was as clear as the crystal in my pocket, and my unbreakable zone calmed me and protected me from self-reproach at any mistakes I made.

Fardeep sensed this and said "Yes, well done Jeremy. Now I will bowl you an off-break. See how I will hold my hand, so."

I recognised his grip from previous sessions and rehearsed the angle of my bat-swing. As expected, the ball turned in and my bat was already there to defend it.

"Well done, Jeremy. That is just what the doctor ordered!" Fardeep cried. "Right Jeremy, now I will bowl you a leg-break."

Once again, he held up the ball for me to see with a cocked wrist and spun it with a big flip of his hand.

The ball seemed a normal delivery at first and I instantly started thinking about hitting it in a similar way to the off –breaks, but I soon became aware of something different about its path.

The ball was not so much as slowing down, but dropping vertically in front of me much faster than I had expected. I tried to adjust to the new pitch and my bat continued on its way to try to meet it there, but because of its backspin the ball bounced a full yard in front of where I expected.

Since it was now rising after the bounce, I ended up playing the bat underneath the ball with some force and slicing it up into the air. It would be an easy catch for a fielder.

"Now then Jeremy, watch the ball. This was a leg-break remember. It dips then breaks from the leg-side to the off."

Another flip of his wrist and I managed to prod the ball downward not so long after it had bounced this time.

"Well done, Jeremy. Now we will try a few more of these."

I watched his hands and could see the difference between leg-breaks from a tightly cocked wrist and off-breaks from twirling fingers.

Just then there was booming disco music from the lane behind the trees and a powerful saloon came into the ground with tinted windows and front spoiler, taking it slowly so as not to catch the bodywork on the uneven ground. The music flooded out even louder as Peter got out.

"Pip! Pip! Whoa! Cheers mates! How goes it?" Peter shouted across.

"Very well. Put your pads on Peter. Jeremy will be finished soon," shouted Fardeep.

His next delivery action was the same as an off-break, but its trajectory was slightly different. As well, there was something odd in his face. A twitch of his cheek, it wasn't the usual expressionless mask.

I was right. It spun away from me like a leg-break.

Then the next one I noticed there was that twitch again in his face. A slight twitch by his eye, and the ball spun again in the unexpected direction. So, this was his doosra. The leg-break in disguise, bowled with an off-break kind of action.

Fardeep held up his hand feigning an apology, "I am sorry. My hand just slipped. It is getting tired."

I remembered where I had seen that twitch before. It was one night several weeks ago when we were sitting down after one of the net sessions in the Moxham Sports Centre. We had been waiting for Sir Richard to arrive with some more documents to do with the bid. We had half an hour so we showed Fardeep how to play poker. He had only played it once or twice before, and it had took him some time to get the hang of bluffing. It had been evident in his face.

"What did you say the order was again?" he had asked, holding his cards at such an awkward angle in front of him that others could see them if they looked over.

"Four aces, then four kings, then four queens," I said.

He took another card from the pack and his eyes lit up.

"Is it my turn to bet now?" he fidgeted forward, with that twitch in his eye, the cards now tightly held in front of his nose and mouth trying to conceal a smile. "Can I raise you fifty pence?"

We had to tell him that the maximum raise was five pence. His face fell at this. He had two aces and a run of King-Queen-Jack.

That same twitch was there now, as he said, "Sorry, Jeremy, my hand slipped again. There must be a small lump on the wicket which is producing this peculiar result. It is nothing to do with me."

Well, I thought, two can play at that. I decided not to tell him I had worked it out and I played it as though I couldn't tell what it was. Each time he sent it down I played wrongly on purpose spooning up a catch to a ball dropping short and turning away. He put a lot of spin on his doosra so that it always turned strongly away. Had I not stretched out and lunged wildly they would have been called wide balls each time.

He hadn't realised that I knew, for he said afterwards "Well done Jeremy. You batted well, but I am sorry my arm kept on slipping. It must be the tiredness of the evening."

I had seen through one of the great man's tricks. That powerful thought gave me the magical feeling that one day the whole success of our project might depend on that knowledge, and I must tell no one, otherwise all would be lost.

I've read somewhere about an old Chinese saying that when the student thinks he has learnt more than the teacher, then that is when his real learning will begin.

At this point there was the rumble of an old car engine and an old Ford Escort came into the ground with Wicket at the wheel.

"Ah, Jeremy. Well done. I'm glad you've left me enough room to stand behind the stumps and keep wicket," he shouted across, manhandling his kitbag out of the boot.

"Yes," said Fardeep, "an excellent idea. Good. We couldn't do it at the indoor nets because they weren't long enough. Now we've got this extra room behind. Good. Go on then, get your pads on."

"All right. All right. I'm coming. Give me a chance. I haven't locked the car yet!"

Wicket put his wicket-keeping pads and gloves on and squatted down on his haunches behind the stumps, muttering "Huh! Room enough, but a bit more would have been better."

Claire bowled the first ball, which was slightly wide of the stumps. Peter was not tempted to try to hit it. He watched it go past. Wicket stepped sideways to take it and there was a smack as the ball went cleanly into his gloves.

"Well done. That's good," shouted Fardeep.

"I _have_ done this before you know," Wicket shouted back.

Simon bowled the next ball and Peter played defensively to it. Wicket had moved sideways again to collect the ball if Peter should miss it.

"Yes, good," shouted Fardeep. "Get that left knee slightly back so that you can swing through with the body more. If you take the ball from the off you can bring it to the stumps for a possible stumping."

"Yes, I know," shouted back Wicket. "I was taught the bacon-slicer, you know."

"The bacon-slicer?" asked Fardeep.

"Yes, the bacon-slicer!" shouted Wicket. "That is the movement," he held his arms close to his body in front of him, elbows bent, and swung his hips, turning from his right to his left, and bringing his hands up to the stumps.

"The bacon-slicer," Wicket repeated.

"Ah yes, I see. Well we did not call it that. But I see that you are doing right by swinging your hands into the stumps. Good. But don't be too eager to rise up before the ball comes. You must squat down and wait to see what happens."

"Yes. I know what I'm doing, thank you. I've been playing the game for 50 years now."

"Yes. Good. But I am a coach. Carry on. Just trying to give you advice. There is no problem here."

"No. There is no problem. Thanks."

Then Claire bowled a fairly swift one which Peter nicked and it flew as a catch to Wicket who dropped it and snorted angrily.

"Of course in a match I'd have been standing further back. We haven't got the room here to do that." Wicket shouted.

The next ball shot along the ground and Wicket had got up swiftly to a standing position and just put his legs together to stop it. It rebounded back narrowly missing the stumps. Peter was out of his crease.

Wicket just stifled a cry of 'Howzat!', and Fardeep said, "There, you see you got up too soon again. You should stay down and use your hands. Then you can bring the ball to the stumps exactly and he would have been stumped."

"Huh! Well it's all right for you to say that. I don't see you keeping wicket. Anyway. These things, they all happen too fast. I'm used to doing it this way. It's an old wicket-keeping technique which you modern people might not know too much about."

"Yes, but what I am staying is that you could have stumped him properly if you had used your hands."

"Hang on a minute, you two. I'm trying to concentrate here," shouted Peter to Fardeep and Wicket.

Wicket said nothing but got down into his wicket-keeping stance again behind the stumps. Fardeep went quiet, annoyed that

Peter would not take the trouble to acknowledge his coaching and the insights he was giving people.

Peter played Fardeep's next ball slowly back to him, but with everybody else's balls, and particularly mine, he jumped straight down the pitch and hit them with wonderful flowing strokes back over our heads. Many went into the hedgerow behind us and I spent a lot of time running over to retrieve them.

I spent so long in looking for one in particular that I was joined by Luke after another monstrous swipe had deposited his ball in roughly the same area as mine. Then there were shouts to retrieve yet another before we had found those two.

I looked at my watch. It was getting late and the four boys had still not arrived. We had all batted except Fardeep and Wicket who didn't want to. Fardeep's tiredness from his previous coaching was showing now, and he was taking his time between deliveries.

When I came back to bowl after retrieving yet another ball I said to Fardeep, "The boys are late."

Fardeep shook his head. "I am sorry I lost my temper with the boys last week. Perhaps I have scared them off. I couldn't stand being mocked. In my country they honour teachers. So what are we going to do? Surely we cannot give up on them? That would be giving up on youth."

"I can probably find some other players, but they will be older players," Wicket said as he slung his bag into his car, having decided the session had finished.

Peter, also sensing the end to the evening, said, "Sorry. Got to go and pick up the Chinese. The wife will be hungry and I promised I wouldn't be late."

I watched his car boom out of the gate. It was always a spectacular sight: the roar as it came to life, the thumping of the stereo and the loud revving of the engine.

"Don't forget next Wednesday morning. We need to work on the water supply and the council mower will be here again," I said to Luke and Simon as they got into Simon's car and drove off after Peter and Wicket.

They were halfway out when there was a screech of brakes and their car stopped in the entrance. Someone ran in front of Simon's car, followed by several others. I recognised Jafar and the rest of the lads. They came running into the field like laughing circus acrobats, spreading out, pretending not to be aware of the need to be with us at the netting.

Fardeep was astounded. He stood there motionless, only able to mutter something in Punjabi.

"Hey, Fardeep!" Jafar shouted. "Throw us a ball."

With a great whoop of delight Fardeep took one of the balls from the ground and danced on tiptoe a few paces towards them, then bowled it with a very high loop. It landed in Jafar's easy reach who made a feint to miss the ball at first, but then spectacularly dived and rolled with it. Springing up in one movement he tossed it to Dwayne who caught it left-handed and threw it high in the air to Anas. Anas missed it and Alan chased after the ball on his bike.

As it was late spring the ground was still soft from the winter and easy to dive onto and slide along safely. First Anas showed one way, with his arms by his side, and stopping the ball with his leg; then Jafar made it more stylish with an outstretched arm. Then Alan and Dwayne flung their arms wider and squealed as they closed on the ball from different sides.

They ran and jumped and dived and slid along to execute stops and saves which could not possibly have been attempted in a hard-floored indoor area full of gym equipment. Indoors they had been restricted and bored, not free to express themselves. Here, each movement they took was full and not checked by the environment they were in.

When they settled and came to bat they had to watch the ball more because they couldn't see it so well in the gloom.

Indoors you couldn't see the result of your shot. Here you could see how far it went in all its glory. The boys loved to hit it hard and far. Jafar and Alan and Dwayne ran vast distances to throw back the balls that Anas hit. Stationed on the other side of the field, Jafar made spectacular catches running to high balls.

"You are like a gazelle, Jafar!" shouted Fardeep to one of his athletic jumping catches.

And when Alan bowled Anas with a turning ball, he cried, "Well done! You outfoxed him with a beauty!"

After half an hour they left, tired but laughing after such a frenetic session.

After they had gone, I said to Fardeep, "See Fardeep, you did teach them after all. They have learnt. You are a good coach. I never doubted you, but I know that you doubted yourself at one point when you could not see what they had learnt."

"Who would have guessed this?" said Fardeep with a slight tear in his eye. "How would you know they had learnt so much? This is just what the doctor ordered. I did not know that I had been able to teach them. I was ready to give up except for your faith in me."

"Ah yes," said Claire," but I knew it would turn out OK. They are basically only children still, like my own class. They are interested but scatter-brained. But you seem to have a need for so much respect all the time and immediate feedback of what you are doing. You must learn to trust your own instincts more. They do take it in, but it is hard to believe it at the time."

We took the netting down and locked it away and I went back to Claire's for another, all-too-brief massage.

CHAPTER TWENTY-THREE

"Can I have a word?" Luke shouted into the cabin from the door, afraid to come inside because his boots were heavily caked in mud.

Wicket, Claire, and I had been cleaning the inside of the cabin, and we met him at the doorway.

He said, "Me, Simon and Peter, we've found the old water mains in the car park and have taken a branch off it for the cabin - the tap in the loo and the toilet cistern."

"Great!" approved Claire.

"At last! I should think so too," Wicket grunted.

"Only, there's just one thing," Luke said, pressing his face closer to ours and speaking quietly. "We can't get down far enough to the main sewer. Peter's tried as hard as he can."

I recalled Peter had been using a pick to break up the ground down to the water main. Few others would have the strength to wield this pick more ferociously through the compacted gravel and old hardcore.

"We've tried digging down a few feet below the supply," said Luke. "Yet we still haven't located the main sewer. At one stage we thought we had it, but we hadn't. It was a large stone that the spades kept slipping off. So we'll have to put in a soakaway from the toilet."

"So what will happen to the waste?" I asked.

"It will just soak away into the ground. The soil pipe itself will stop just above ground to allow for air circulation. The toilet flushings will just run away. But the toilet will only be able to take liquids. No solids. If it's solid, it'll just lie on the ground."

"Well won't it be hidden by the grass and weeds round the back there?" asked Wicket.

"It would have been," Luke said. "But I've just seen the council gardener spray it with weedkiller."

"We've got to make sure that when they come they don't flush any solids down there or do any poos. I'll put up a notice," Claire said.

"But we can't have a notice on there saying "No Solids" because it will imply that the ground is not up to scratch for a grant," I said.

"So we don't tell them!" laughed Wicket.

"But what if they go to the loo and find out?" said Claire. "It will be doubly difficult for us then. They'll criticise us."

"In which case the project will fail," I moaned.

"Let's take the risk and say that the project won't fail," said Wicket. "Let's not tell them, and assume that they'll not notice or not ask the question."

"Yes, but what if one of the inspectors is a civil engineer and he's got a dicky tummy?" asked Claire.

"Squidgy poo," said Luke. "Not solid. Therefore we wash it away with disinfectant afterwards."

"Suppose he has a dicky tummy and he goes to the loo, and he inspects the back before he goes and he sees that people have lied to him?" said Claire.

"Make sure he goes round the back at the start of the day and not afterwards," Wicket said.

Unconvinced, Claire took an A4 pad out of her bag and a large black felt tip pen and wrote 'NO SOLIDS'.

Sticking the notice on the outside of the toilet door with Blu-Tack she said, "Just for now. We'll make a decision for the big day later."

"Yes, that'll do for now, but hopefully in the future, we'll get it properly plumbed in," I said.

"Yes, hopefully," said Wicket.

"That'll be a big job when it's to be done," said Luke. "There might not be much time. When is the inspection again?"

"During the tea interval," I said. "First Sunday in May. It's a special match before the Enterprise Cup Competition begins a few weeks later. We'll be playing against the County All Stars, a team organised by Sir Richard. Fardeep will be playing for us and he's formidable, as you know. To add interest to the opposition Sir Richard has obtained the services of a couple of county players and an Australian semi-pro to join the All Stars. They'll relish a game like this. If we're short then Wicket will ask some players he knows from Darbury and Lampton Ambo."

"Ah, but there are problems in transferring my players to Moxham," said Wicket. "The original club doesn't want to let them go. It thinks it owns them and that the players owe the club money, et cetera. So they might be slow to appear. Anyway, I think we'll have it solved soon. Stodgy plays for Lampton Ambo and is a slow steady player. Neil is a big hitter and is a big fish in a small pond so needs lots of persuasion to move but will play the odd game, especially against the rival Lampton Ambo for he currently plays for Darbury."

"Who will the inspectors be?" asked Claire.

"A representative from the County Council Board, a representative from Moxham Council, a representative from London," I said.

"Sounds like big poopers to me," smiled Wicket.

"What about the Friends of Moxham Cricket Club? What will they be doing?" Claire asked.

"They'll be holding it in, I hope," laughed Wicket.

Claire frowned, wanting to get a sensible answer from me.

"They'll have a stall and display," I said. Wicket was still tittering, but I carried on seriously under Claire's stern gaze. "They'll be using the gas stove and providing tea and home-made sandwiches and cakes, and running the tombola."

After more general nodding and murmuring of approval Wicket went off with Luke to see the hole they were filling in. "I'll see if they're ready to turn the water on in the lane," he said.

I turned my attention back to connecting the calor gas bottle to the camping stove. The stove was standing on an old piece of kitchen cupboard and the gas bottle was inside underneath. I had to put my head and shoulders inside to reach it.

"No!" I shouted as the spanner once again slipped off the nut.

"Left-handed thread, you know," said Claire.

"Yes, I know. It's almost there, I think. Oh, no! Not again!"

"Try it by hand first."

"It's not that so much. It's just a matter of lining up the thread and then turning. Ah, turning. Turning it a bit more till it catches. Yes. It's getting there. Yes."

I heard the council groundsman start the mower again at the top of the field, and start cutting in rows, going backwards and forwards, as regularly as measuring time as he cut across from one side to the other. On previous days he had gone round and round in a diminishing spiral towards the centre. Today however, as each sweep was completed, the mower' sound grew louder, gradually working down towards us, row by row across.

"Surely you can't light it inside here?" asked Claire, as I stood up to try the stove.

"I'm just testing it for a minute. I can see the flame better and smell any leaks in here. On the day we'll have it set up outside with windbreaks."

"Careful it doesn't explode."

"No. It's all right."

I turned it on and applied a match.

Outside, the mower turned and the engine note rose again as it came back on a closer run.

"How are you?" I turned to face her as we were now alone.

"Fine," she shouted above the mower noise, and started to fold some tea towels.

"I haven't seen you in Marmaduke's recently," I said.

"We don't go in there much these days."

I had half-expected the use of the word "We", but it was still a shock when it came.

"We? You mean you and Mark? You're not interested in me so much now?" The mower was right under our window. I was upset at having to say this so loud.

Claire stopped folding the tea towels and turned to face me.

"Oh I am, but as a friend. Mark is very kind as well. I hope we can all be friends," she shouted back. "Maybe you and he will both join GSS and we can all work together."

Suddenly the mower's engine stopped.

The ensuing silence seemed even more deafening. I felt as though we were both waiting for something.

"Please turn down that flame," she said. "It worries me."

CHAPTER TWENTY-FOUR

The first Sunday in May. A clear day, but cold and damp from short overnight rain.

On the Moxham cricket ground red, white and blue bunting ran from the cabin to three simple open-sided gazebos in a line along the edge of the playing area in front of the small car park.

It first ran to the Friends of Moxham Cricket Club tea bar. Ann was helping two well-rounded middle-aged women to cut up pieces of cake and set out blue and white ringed Albion mugs onto a tray on a trestle table. Behind the table, protected on three sides by a windbreak, was the camping stove.

The bunting ran along next to the gazebo of the Friends of Moxham Cricket Club jumble stall, its trestle tables offering jumble for sale, CDs, cassettes, books, seaside souvenir ashtrays, and disowned Charles and Di mugs.

Finally the bunting finished at the Friends of Moxham Cricket Club tombola stall, its trestle tables displaying an assortment of plastic bottles of bubble bath, packets of biscuits, boxes of chocolates and a multicoloured striped glass ornament in the shape of a fish, all with a cloakroom ticket cellotaped proudly on. By the side was the cardboard box which the packets of crisps at the tea bar had come in, now ready to receive the speculative hands of petty punters hoping to fetch out cloakroom tickets ending in a nought or a five.

On either side of the cabin door were hanging baskets of pansies, violas, tulips and ivy, giving an impressive air of spring abundance.

Then I remembered the soil pipe problem of the cabin toilet and wondered how bad and obvious it was. I went round and took a sly glance at the back of the cabin, making sure that no one was watching me. I could see Rod across the other side of the stalls talking to Mark. He might have been able to see me clearly, but I think he was looking in another direction.

There was a silver sports car up against the back wall and I had to squeeze past. It was a convertible and looked familiar. A Mazda MX-5. It certainly did not belong to our team, and was too sporty for the Friends of Moxham who were all local. I remembered I had seen it at St Margaret's School.

A wide soil pipe extended from the bottom of the cabin's back wall and turned down into the poisoned weeds. One might assume that it would go into the ground as a proper drain. It certainly looked normal enough. Yet on closer inspection it could be seen that it stopped an inch above the ground, and traces of toilet paper had collected there already.

There was a shout from behind me in the car park. Mark was now with Claire and they were in a heated debate. He grabbed her arm, but she wrestled herself free and then walked stiffly off towards the tea tent with Mark calling to her back as she went.

As I watched, Fardeep came up to me and said, "If we win the toss, what shall we do, bat or bowl first?"

"Well I think that we should bowl, because then it will be more thrilling for the spectators to see us score runs to win."

"Yes. I agree. Also, it is still a little damp this morning and consequently the ball might swing. So if we bowled first we might be able to bowl some difficult balls to them."

I walked round to the front of the cabin and Rod came sauntering up with a bombastic gloating smile.

"How is it? Huh? Are you discussing tactics? That won't help you against us. We've got a good strong team, two ex-county players, and two good ones from Appleton Water as well, and two from Darbury are amongst ours. That includes Ewart MacGough. Have you met him? He's from Australia. Plays for Darbury."

"Ewart MacGough? But I thought that he hadn't got clearance to stay here much longer," said Fardeep.

"Oh yes, he's got clearance all right. Well, actually, it's just going through now. But for a friendly promotional match like this there isn't an issue."

"But will he get clearance to play for Darbury?" asked Fardeep.

"Oh, there's ways and means," he said proudly. "He's in our team today. I think this should have been a Scoving versus

Moxham match, not Moxham versus a variety team. That would have more relevance with the heritage of the area."

"Ah, it's done now," I said, and looked to Fardeep who nodded in support. "This is the Moxham project day. You had your visit from the panel yesterday."

"What?" protested Rod. "You think that a few minutes gander from a panel that doesn't get out of their MPV in the carpark is a fair inspection for us? I don't!"

"They had other places to go to as well," I said. "I suspect that's why they couldn't stay long."

"Oh yes. You mean like going to look at Appleton Water's ground, which already has had tens of thousands spent on it? Yet they didn't inspect our facilities? We asked for some new sight screens, pavilion, and scorebox. We wanted to show them the plans we put in. Show them where we would put the extra car parking, and the plans we had to extend part of the building into a bar area. But all they did was come and turn their noses up at it from inside a car."

"Well, they probably read all they needed to in the bid you put in."

"Yes, but Appleton Water got a proper visit from what I heard, not just looking through the minibus window."

"I remember rightly it was probably raining when they came round to you, so you can't expect them to get wet. That would just put them in a bad mood and prejudice them against you for a start."

"No, it wasn't raining when they came round to us. Not much. What's a little spot of rain for an inspection party? They should be used to it. They inspect in all weathers, all over the country, proper panels do."

"Anyway. You'll get your chance to meet the panel when they come here today."

"Ha! But there'll only be the two of us here from Scoving."

"Sorry. Can't be helped, I'm afraid. They've really come to see Moxham. We're the bid preferred by the council."

"Hah! Fix! Where are they now, then? I thought they were supposed to be here to see it all?" He looked round pretending to count dozens of inspection panel members. "Don't tell me they've stood you up. Dear me, tut, tut, what will the world be coming to?"

"They're probably still having lunch at the Imperial Hotel in town. Then they've got a presentation and a couple of afternoon talks. They won't arrive until mid-afternoon. Perhaps an hour before tea. Then they go back straight after tea to their Hotel for a closed session to write their report."

"I see. So they're here for a couple of hours to watch you, and get some tea and everything, yet they didn't get out of the bus for us."

"That's how it is sometimes. Sorry."

"Yes, sometimes. Sorry," echoed Fardeep.

Just then, Wicket shouted across to Fardeep asking him where he had put the balls for the match.

"In my bag. I'll show you," Fardeep said and went over to the cabin.

Rod had looked round, and then turned back to ask, "Anyway, how's the new cabin?"

"Fine."

"It looks a bit basic to me."

"No. It's OK. Two changing rooms and running water." I waved my hand at it.

"I've heard it's not quite right in at least one respect."

"Oh? What's that?"

"The toilet."

"Oh, that's working. It's plumbed in. The cistern fills up and flushes." I nodded.

"Yes. But I've heard it doesn't go anywhere."

"What? I don't know what you mean."

"Ha! I think you do and I think you're covering it up."

"Look. It's a perfectly functioning toilet and, like any good perfectly functioning toilet, it wasn't built for stuff that would block it. So don't get any ideas about trying to see if you can wreck it."

"Oh no. I wouldn't wreck it or do anything to spoil your special day at all. I'm just asking how it's going, that's all. Good luck to you, anyway. You deserve all you get. You've obviously done a lot of hard work. Mark tells me that. Claire tells him you know. They're very friendly together. Claire tells him lots of things."

He looked at me in a sideways kind of way, wanting to see my reaction. I didn't give him one.

"Yes," he continued. "Very friendly. Very good friends they are. Claire is lovely, isn't she?"

I was silent.

"Yes siree, I'd say that she is the apple of many people's eye. Very bubbly and approachable and would make someone a good wife. In fact make me a good daughter-in-law."

"Oh," I said at last. "I didn't think that it was that serious."

"Yes. It is. They've been seeing each other for a quite a while now. Of course, I think they met in Teacher Training College, so their history goes way back. I don't suppose you've known Claire for long, have you?"

"About six months," I said.

"Yes, well. That's it you see. That's why they get on so well together. They're well-suited. Two peas in a pod, so I wouldn't think that she would change for someone else, you see. Mark knows her so well."

"Well that didn't seem the case to me a few minutes ago," I said. "They were having a right old battle in the car park."

"Oh? That? I'm sure it's nothing. Just a lovers' tiff, that kind of thing. Anyway, she's a good batter is Claire. She can handle some very difficult fast balls. Can you?"

"Yes, I've been practising."

"Mark can bowl some really fast balls at times. Really awkward. I've seen people get tangled up with his bowling. One or two have got themselves into trouble and got hurt. But Claire can handle it. So I hope you'll be all right handling it. It can be a bit difficult."

"I'll be all right."

"I see. I suppose it's your tennis skills that see you through. Nice bouncy pitch. Nice bouncy balls. You like bouncy balls do you?"

Foolishly I nodded.

"Got a helmet, have you? And some good pads. Only you can't trust the pitches early in the season."

"But it's only a friendly exhibition match."

"Oh, I'm sure it is. I'm sure you've nothing to fear at all in all this. No problem whatsoever. You'll be absolutely fine."

He walked away to join his team in the cabin, and through their open window I heard him booming jokes at his assembling team of County All Stars XI.

All of our team had changed and were assembling in front of the cabin. Fardeep the captain, me, Wicket, Peter, Claire, Luke, Simon; then the four boys Dwayne, Anas, Alan, and Jafar.

Wicket came over to me and muttered "What was all that about from Rod? What did he want?"

"He was just trying to big his son up," I said. "Trying to scare us."

"Ah yes, typical! Well, Peter will see to him, don't you worry. And as for that Rod's pride, Fardeep will cut him down a peg or two."

Fardeep waved to Alan who was standing apart from the others talking to a girl with dark hair cut shorter on one side of her head.

"Who's that girl?" I asked Claire who was passing with her head down in thought. "I think I've seen her before."

"Oh her?" She glanced up momentarily, her voice stiff and angry about something else, but she tried to soften a little. "That's Charlotte from Marmaduke's café by the railway station."

"Ah yes. I remember now. Yes. I thought I'd seen her before but I couldn't place where. So she and Alan are an item, are they?"

"Certainly looks like it."

She turned to look at me, her eyes red and moist.

"You all right?" I asked.

"Fine," she said hurriedly. "Are you ready? Fardeep is rounding up the troops. I think we've won the toss and are fielding."

"Yes. That's what Fardeep said we should do if we won the toss."

"Yes. Look sharp," she said forcing a mischievous smile. "You never know. You might have the opportunity to do something important in the field."

I touched the charm in my pocket and counted like Fardeep had taught me as I stepped onto the field.

CHAPTER TWENTY-FIVE

The County All Stars made a slow start. It seemed that their semi-professional players were uncertain against our bowling attack of Dwayne and Fardeep, Luke and Jafar. They did not wish to embarrass themselves so they spent the early overs in defensive play, trapped into the cautious mind-set that they had built for themselves.

Our fielders were quick to pounce on the ball after a shot and prevent extra runs being scored. Occasionally a strong shot would get past and reach the boundary. However, after twenty overs of the forty overs allotted per side they had lost four wickets for only sixty runs. Ewart MacGough, Rod's proud Australian player, showed impatience and made only a few before being bowled by Fardeep.

The scoreboard was a simple board painted black with a stick behind to prop it up. On the ground in front of it was an untidy pile of white numbers on black metal squares. These were sifted through and posted up as instructed by those keeping the scorebook.

I stood on the same spot on the field, always near the gateway and the bottom of the car park. Fardeep called it "behind square on the leg side" for one over, then relabelled it as "deep mid-off" for the next over.

I kept a watch on that gateway, expecting the inspection panel to arrive any minute.

I had asked the stallholders to keep a prime section of the car park clear. However, after about half an hour a car came and parked there. The driver got out and carried a couple of boxes of assorted ornaments to the jumble stall, and then stood talking to the stallholders.

I began imagining what could happen if the panel came through the gateway now. If Rod's account of the Scoving inspection was anything to go by, the panel on seeing no suitable place to park would promptly turn around and go away in disgust. I thought about signalling the driver to move and, as my attention flitted between the car and the gateway, I was late when fielding one ball at least.

I wondered why the panel was delayed. They were supposed to have made a swift visit with Sir Richard to the Moxham Sports Centre as well. I was glad I was not going round there with them. I don't think I could have kept a smiling face. My displeasure with the present building compared to Appleton Water's might have shown through too much for them.

Presently the car moved off after the driver had finished his leisurely discussion.

After another ten minutes Sir Richard's Range Rover came from the west lane into the car park. Two men and a woman got out with him.

The woman was in a suit. One of the men was tall, also in a suit. The other shorter man was more rugged and wore a blazer. All three of them were carrying folders.

The suits gave the woman and the taller man away as the local government people. In fact, I thought I recognised the woman from the local council. The man in the blazer I guessed was the sports inspector from London. He pointed to the hanging baskets and the bunting on the cabin and gazebos as they looked round the stalls and chatted.

Sir Richard ushered them to the plastic stacking chairs and Rod came out of the cabin with his batting pads on to join them. The panel members laughed occasionally as he leaned forward on his bat handle then picked his bat up and gestured with it to emphasise a point in one of his ridiculous tales, no doubt about his accomplishments with Scoving Cricket Club and why it deserved the money.

However, very soon they began to differ in their state of attention. The woman in the suit looked up at the sky. The very tall man from the county council nodded with his head down looking at the floor. The man of medium build from London was speaking, leaning across the others, but with one eye on the game.

A few seconds later, there was a shout from the other players and I looked round towards the middle of the pitch. The stumps had been broken, and the batsman was walking slowly back to the cabin. Distracted by the arrival of the panel, I had missed it.

Rod stood up. He passed a final comment to the group and, pulling on his batting gloves, he marched proudly to the middle of the pitch. He assertively held up one finger to the umpire, with the other hand held his bat vertically at the crease, and asked for 'centre' guard.

The umpire nodded firmly that he was correct, and, nevertheless Rod made the mark definitively his own by scraping his bat at that point on the crease.

Standing back, he looked round to study the field placements and then, having seen enough, he returned to his mark and took his stance.

Dwayne was bowling and had one ball left in the over. He bowled a fast one. Rod watched it onto his bat and played it down onto the ground behind him and the ball ran down towards me. I scooped it up and threw it back, but Rod had completed the run and was off the mark.

Over the next few overs, Rod steadily and safely accumulated runs and was unwilling to take any risks. Though Dwayne's bowling was tight, he was a young lad and would not be able to bowl many more overs. Rod was looking set so Fardeep decided to encourage Rod to take a risk.

He brought Alan on to bowl. Alan, uncertain at first, had a high wheeling bicycle kind of run-up and Rod was immediately tempted by these balls with a very high loop.

Raising his bat high in readiness behind him, Rod took a bound down the pitch and hit the ball straight in the air towards me at deep mid-off.

Judging that it would come down only a few yards away, I ran a few steps over and positioned myself in wait.

The small crowd hushed with expectancy.

I held my hands out ready and closed my hands on the ball in triumph, but at that moment I suddenly thought of Claire's words about doing something important today. The ball brushed straight through me to ground.

There were howls of disappointment behind as I picked the ball up and hurled it back.

Meanwhile Rod had completed two runs and was back on strike.

The next ball Rod repeated the stroke. The ball passed wide of me, beyond my reach, and bounced into the crowd.

A delighted middle-aged man with a green jacket and cap scooped it up from beside the tombola stall and tossed it back to me. Frustrated, I threw it back to Alan.

Fardeep came over from his fielding position in the slips and said something in earnest to Alan, emphasising with one hand about keeping it down, and patting him on the back in encouragement with the other.

Once again Alan bowled and once again Rod came down the pitch with the same stoke.

However, this time the ball did not go so high. It was travelling at head height and almost directly on a path with me.

I took a step towards it, but stopped, uncertain of whether I was running in too far, and by the time I had thought about this question the ball was on me.

Instinctively I put my hand up to protect myself and felt the ball thud against my breast, and I held it there for a long time. The pain only made me clench the ball longer.

I looked down at my hands and realised what must be the truth: I had caught it. Rod was out.

He was seething. He stormed past the inspection panel who were applauding from their plastic seats and disappeared into the cabin.

I felt I had to catch it because the committee was there watching, and it would have reflected badly on the Moxham revival if I had dropped another.

Yet had I known then the repercussions that I know now, I would have dropped that catch like a hot potato.

CHAPTER TWENTY-SIX

The next batters attacked the bowling. Rod's son, Mark, avenged his father with some good hits with the last few batsmen as his partners. Eventually the County All Stars finished with 160 off their forty overs, though they had three deliveries left unused because Mark was out bowled, attempting a final wild slog.

Now was the tea interval between the innings. Time to take stock and consider what had been achieved. Had we bowled them out cheaply enough, and did we feel confident about making those runs to win?

We queued for tea. A large rounded lady from the Friends of Moxham poured the tea from a large metal teapot into blue and white ringed Albion mugs with matching jugs for milk and sugar.

With the mug to my lips, I breathed out and felt the vapour from the hot tea rise up and condense on my face, like a steamy balm cleansing all previous mistakes and preparing the mind for the task ahead.

Under the gazebo Ann was serving drinks to some children.

"What do you want, lemonade or orange?" she said, holding out small pop bottles to a young boy.

He decided on the lemonade. Next to him his mother, who was rocking a baby in a pushchair, handed over the money.

Ann leaned over the counter towards the baby in the pushchair and laughed "Well, how are you?"

The mother smiled. "Well, when are you going to settle down then, Ann?"

"Oh, not yet, I don't think. The time isn't right."

"You haven't met Mr. Right then, yet?"

"No. Not just yet. Not yet." Ann glanced in my direction.

"Go on then, there must be somebody," the mother said.

"No," Ann blushed. "Not yet."

They laughed and then some movement by the side of the cabin caught my eye.

Claire was once again talking angrily to Mark, who was holding his arms out from his body, protesting innocence. Their

168

distance apart increased and decreased, Mark moving nearer to her as she pushed him away. It wasn't with a usual game or a joke that she was pushing him away, but with annoyance.

I put my tea down and walked over.

"Is he annoying you, Claire?" I asked.

"Just get lost! What's it to you, Freeman?" Mark said.

"Well seems to me like the lady here is getting unnerved by it all."

"No, Jeremy," said Claire. "It's OK. I can handle it."

"Yeh. She can handle it. Nothing to do with you. Keep your nose out of it."

"It seems to me like you've been annoying her all day so far."

"Oh yeh?"

"Yeh. I saw you earlier. That's no way to treat a lady."

"Oh no?"

"No!"

"Please, Jeremy, it's OK," Claire protested.

"But it's not OK if he's bad to you!" I said.

"Yeh, like she's just said. There's no problem. Keep your nose out of it, Freeman!"

"Now, cool it both of you!" Claire said, and waved her arms between us.

Just then Rod interrupted, calling across "Mark, come and talk to Ewart MacGough. He's got some bowling tips for you from Australia."

Mark turned to go over to join his father and, in leaving us, pointed his finger at me, "Just watch it. I'll deal with your impertinence later."

Claire and I watched his back, and then she said, "Thank you, but it wasn't anything I couldn't handle."

"It looked to me like it was a problem."

"No honestly, it was OK."

Claire suddenly noticed the woman from the panel was not speaking to anyone but was looking straight at her and clutching a copy of our Moxham bid.

"Oh, I must speak to her," Claire said hurriedly and went across.

I reclaimed my mug and plate from the table near the gazebo and moved towards the other two inspectors. Sir Richard had the attention of the athletic and relaxed expert from London. His navy-blue blazer had the England three lions symbol on it and he had a tanned complexion. However, the tall man in the suit was free and came over to me.

"Good simple facilities you have here. Quaint setting. " His head arched over disdainfully. He looked as though he could tolerate nothing and would as likely just swat me off like a fly if I jumped up too far above my station. He put his mug down and picked up his plate. He looked at his cake and grimaced, then carefully pulled the cherries out of it, and placed them separately to one side of his plate.

"Yes, yes," I said, balancing my mug of tea and a piece of homemade fruitcake on a plate in my left hand and holding a tuna mayo sandwich in my right. I brought my right forefinger up to my mouth and feared saying anything more before swallowing in case I sprayed him.

I felt as though I ought to say something, but thought that as long as I was interacting with the committee, then I was being useful, no matter how rambling my speech. Sometimes he seemed only to be half-listening, looking over the heads of the other people as I continued an automatic lecture. "And of course, it is a temporary facility which is plumbed in here with running water."

"Oh, running water," he suddenly looked intently down at my face. "Yes. It is good that you have the modern conveniences here. There are still a large proportion of cricket grounds that do not have running water or proper toilets. Having modern plumbing marks out the grounds that would be able to properly use grants if they were made available."

Just then Sir Richard's voice came loudly from the top steps of the cabin.

"Ladies and gentlemen. I'd just like to say a few words about the club and to thank everyone here for doing such a splendid job. This is a story of a community phoenix which rose from the ashes of Moxham cricket, and is steeped in a long tradition of community involvement. Today you see a celebration of cricket and a showcase for public motivation in the Moxham area. Thanks to the umpires who have given their time freely today. Thanks to the Friends of Moxham Cricket Club and all the efforts for Moxham sports service and council. In fact, they tell me that The Friends of Moxham Cricket Club raised seventy two pounds from a raffle and bric-a-brac sale in the church hall recently."

There was applause as we all turned to smile at the tombola stall.

"Today marks the rebirth of cricket in Moxham. It is a showcase for our community. It is an example of teamwork with limited resources and facilities to achieve function in an improvised and high quality scenario. So once again, thank you for this marvellous tea and for bringing cricket back to Moxham."

There was applause and Sir Richard stepped down.

The tall man drifted away and Sir Richard started to tell me about the lunch they'd just had. "It was the chef at the Imperial Hotel. Oh, he's good, but he uses a lot of oil. They might outsource it to other caterers in future. Apparently, they've got some American chef in mind, a woman, I think. "

I tell him that there is a problem with the loo.

"What? Why didn't you tell me?"

"Because it was too late to do anything about it."

"Well we could have got a chemical toilet for the public and claimed that the cabin was for players only."

"Oh, I didn't think of that."

"Just get some disinfectant round there and stop the stink. Is there good cover there?"

"There was before the groundsman decided to spray the area with weedkiller. There might just be enough cover for today. I'll try to keep people away from the back. It's a very odd thing to do to look round the back anyway." I said.

"I know, but there's one member of the panel who specialises in it. He seems pretty knowledgeable about conveniences and cricket grounds. He implied that we're likely to gain a lot of points through having a fully working system. I couldn't put it past him to go checking before he leaves. But I don't think the others would."

Just then the tall council member came rushing past us, heading for the cabin, with a pained expression on his face.

"We've got some time yet, haven't we? Before we have to go off?" he asked Sir Richard and brandished a copy of the Moxham bid.

"Oh yes – half an hour yet. Time to see Moxham starting to bat."

"Good," he said. "I'll be out in a few minutes."

He went into the cabin and closed the door, and a strange feeling of apprehension came over me.

After tea, most of our team lounged on plastic seats or on benches in the changing room, waiting to bat whilst the opposition took the field. Alan and Charlotte sat together on a couple of the stacking chairs which they had moved away from other people. They were holding hands and laughing at quiet jokes.

The woman panel member and the sportsman were now standing talking to Sir Richard, Wicket, and the stallholders.

At Fardeep and Sir Richard's recommendation, Claire opened the batting to show how diverse and enterprising Moxham was. Simon was her partner.

As Claire walked out to bat, there was a hush from the spectators.

"Is that a girl opening the batting?" someone asked another behind me. "I can't see properly because they're wearing a helmet."

The nearest outfielders of the County All Stars brought their heads up to their face to hide smirks as she passed.

Simon faced the first over from which no runs were scored, the balls bowled by the ex-county bowler rising up quite sharply from the pitch.

Then it was Claire's turn to face the other bowler and she guided the first ball down for four. Instantly there were cheers and wolf whistles from the spectators.

The ball trickled across the boundary not far from where I was sitting so I picked it up and tossed it back to a fielder. The rest of the over went by quietly, each of them scoring a single.

Play continued quietly in this vein and then Mark was brought on to bowl. Because of his pace and hostility he might get a considerable number of our team out. Indeed, from what I had seen earlier in the day, it was quite likely that Claire would be out cheaply to him and in a fairly nasty way if they were still arguing.

He measured out a long and fearsome run-up. I tensed and was ready to run onto the field to protect her or administer first aid.

However, he walked the first few paces of his run-up, then came ambling up slowly off the final steps, and bowled a very slow ball which Claire played carefully and mistrustfully back. Mark bowled another slow ball and Claire played this defensively back too. Mark kept shaking his head after every ball she played back to him.

Whenever Claire got to face the other bowler she timed a few strokes well and the crowd cheered. I looked round to judge the reaction of the panel members at Claire's strokes, but saw only the woman and the sportsman applauding. The tall council man was still in the toilet.

Though Mark went on to bowl brutishly to Simon, to Claire he was always very gentle, but close to losing his temper. Their cat and mouse session went on for some time.

Eventually at the end of an over Rod shouted something to Mark that sounded like "…not be here all day…"

In the next over Claire was again on strike to Mark. He had just bowled a brutish delivery to Simon who managed to fend it off and take a single to bring Claire on strike.

However, instead of coming off his shorter slower run again to Claire, Mark used his full-length run up and bowled a quick delivery.

It was not brutish or unpleasant, just very fast that broke Claire's wicket. She turned immediately and walked off, straight back to the cabin, red-faced and shoulders stiff. It was almost as though she had been expecting it, and had decided firmly what her reaction would be when it came.

As she walked back, Rod began to clap but Mark's head was down as he kicked the ground in frustration.

There then followed a regular procession of our batsmen in and out. Simon, Anas, Jafar, and Luke made 15-20 runs each. We reached a hundred runs for the loss of five wickets.

Peter would be next to bat, followed by me. I looked around to check where he was and I heard him speaking on his mobile phone in the changing room.

"Yes, Steve. What? I told him it was a universal one I fitted. He doesn't want to have to wait for almost a week for the dealers to get it from Germany! The one I fitted was perfectly good enough. Cheaper as well. Tell him that."

There was a shout from the field and Luke came walking slowly off as the wicket-keeper and the players were celebrating behind him.

"Got to go!" said Peter. He snapped the phone shut and put it back in his jacket. Then, after jerking his cap firmly on, he picked up his bat and gloves and strode towards the wicket to join Alan. I watched his back, his shoulders stiff and indignant from the phone call. I wondered how he could bat with his mind so obviously still agitated by work.

Alan continued to play well. After each scoring stroke he waved his bat in salute to Charlotte who cheered and waved back. Yet Peter played and missed many balls. After each successive delivery had gone by he swung his bat again through the air in exasperation at how he should have played.

As I would be next to bat I brought the charm out of my pocket, and went through the meditations that Fardeep had taught me, peering into the centre of the crystal in my hand. I closed my eyes and imagined myself inside the centre of it looking out, cocooned by an impenetrable glass shield. I was an innocent blameless spirit protected from the outside world, and also from the inner world of self-recrimination from my errors.

Luke had flopped down on one of the chairs next to Sir Richard to take his pads off.

The main man in the panel finally came out of the loo and asked them with a serious expression "Tell me, who did the plumbing?"

Luke stuttered "Me."

"Well it's good to see a cricket pavilion with a flushing toilet that's not chemical. I note the silver genuine jubilee handle and the single flush system with no slack or play in the flushing action. It must have cost you money."

"Oh, no, I managed to get a discount. Our plumbing merchant sponsored us with some stock from an old mansion house they were refitting."

"Ah yes. These well-made ones are always the best. Much better than mass-produced cheap imports. I thought it might have been a Torbeck at first because it was so quiet. However, there is one thing I did notice about the installation."

"Yes?"

"I took the opportunity to take the lid off the cistern whilst I was in the loo. I normally don't mention this kind of thing. Some people find it slightly weird as you might appreciate, but I am an expert on this and whilst in there I took the opportunity to do a closer examination of the working of it. And well, to cut a long story short, what I found was very intriguing."

"Yes?"

"The coupling mechanism for the handle. I saw inside that you have used a copper ball float and arm. Much better than those plastic ones which cannot withstand the wear of repeated flushing in a short time. Unlike domestic plumbing which can take plastic because you flush them infrequently and gently, in a sports setting you often get twenty-two flushings in a few minutes and all strongly wrenching on the handle and the siphon lever arm. Was that the original from the mansion as well?"

"Yes."

"Well done. I can see your attention to detail. You got the water supply from the existing one, no doubt."

"Yes, we took a branch off under the car park."

"Well this is most excellent. Most excellent, well done. Not many other clubs go to this level. To this fine level of detail. And the discharge, the waste?"

"Oh, it goes where all waste goes eventually," Luke laughed nervously.

The man laughed back. "And you used a hundred and ten millimetre soil pipe?"

"Ah yes, of course, with a suitable connector to the toilet pan." Luke laughed again.

"Oh excellent."

At this point Sir Richard interrupted "Well, we must go now, you must allow our players to carry on with the game, and I have some more specification to show you of the Moxham sports centre back at the hotel. You haven't seen these."

"Oh, more specifications?" the man said quickly. "Well, we'd better hurry. We haven't got much time."

He turned back to Luke. "Well. Nice to have met you. I'm sure you've got a career in outdoor plumbing facilities. If you like, we might be able to co-opt you onto some inspection panels in the future. If you'd like that, yes? Please let me have your contact details."

Luke nodded.

Just then, Peter had a massive swipe at a ball and hit an enormous six.

"Cop that!" I heard him shout even from my position beyond the boundary. It was an angry shout, a defiant outburst, like a further rebuttal to the person who had phoned him.

Excited, we all turned to watch the next ball. He took an enormous swipe again, but missed. He was out, bowled by a fast full ball from Mark that got underneath his bat down near his toes. So it came to my turn to bat.

With the end of Peter's innings the rest of the panel stirred from their seats and got into Sir Richard's Range Rover.

"Goodbye" I said to the head council man, putting on my gloves, and picking up my bat, "I hope you have had a good time. When will we hear?"

"Oh not till very late into the summer," he said, closing the door to the Range Rover. As the car reversed round to turn, I waved and walked out onto the field, touching the charm in my pocket through my trousers.

As I neared the pitch, I saw Rod and Mark talking out of earshot of the rest of the team and watching me as I walked to the wicket with just thirty more runs needed. We had eight overs to get them in and four wickets left.

CHAPTER TWENTY-SEVEN

I took my stance at the wicket. Alan gave me the thumbs up from the non-striker's end.

Rod was standing talking to Mark in the middle of the pitch and gestured to two fielders to come up closer. One squatted down in front of me to the leg side, the other low down behind. Fielders this close to the batsman are expecting the batsman to fend off a delivery and lob it up to be easily caught.

I thought that this kind of bowling was for serious cricketers and so it was unlikely that I would be in any real danger. This was an exhibition match after all and I was not wearing a helmet. I'd tried one in the nets and couldn't see very well through the grill. Furthermore, the Friends of Moxham would not like to see any unpleasantness on the pitch.

Although I never used to like a hard ball bouncing up at me, Fardeep had helped me draw on my tennis skills in dealing with such balls. "Duck it, drop it, or hit it," he'd told me. I was not worried. If I got out cheaply today then Fardeep would come in next and would be able to win the match for us, probably all by himself.

As Mark walked back to the start of his run-up, Rod was forcefully pointing out something to him and gesturing towards me and the pitch. Mark shook his head, looking at me, pointed to the two fielders, and stretched his arms wide as though he was asking why they had been placed there by his father. Rod urged him to stop complaining and bowl.

Finally Mark ran up and unleashed a fast one that bounced short and rose up straight to my head. I had half-expected this, and my tennis skills enabled me to see it early and follow it as it came up. I managed to get my bat on it to drop it down to the off side in front of me where there was no fielder. Someone raced in quickly to prevent us taking a run.

Rod immediately started to clap, shouting "Well done, Jeremy!" in a sarcastic manner, and moved another fielder into the space where I had just played the ball.

Again, he came over to Mark and argued a point with him. Again, Mark pointed to the fielders and shook his head, and once again Rod assertively motioned him to run in and bowl.

Mark was still shaking his head and muttering to himself on his way back to his starting place. He seemed unsure about how to hold the ball, checking it and re-checking it in his hand, and practising wheeling his arm over as he walked back.

Finally, he turned and started the run-up. However, at the moment when Mark released the ball Rod shouted at the top of his voice "Short!"

I looked at the pitch for the ball bouncing short as before but I didn't see it. Then, in that same split second I looked up towards the bowler and saw the ball coming towards me without bouncing. It had been bowled at head height. I tried to duck out of the way, but it thudded onto the corner of my head above my eye.

Claire was up there within seconds, I was told later.

"Jeremy?" I heard her ask. I must have been on my back because she was looking down at me.

"You all right, mate?" asked Mark, worried.

I could only grunt.

"Ah, he's all right, thank goodness," said Mark.

"What do you mean 'all right'?" Claire complained. "He's obviously been hurt. Why are you bowling like this? You know he's not a skilled player."

"It was an accident. I was distracted. I didn't mean to do it."

"What do you mean? It was a vicious delivery. You weren't bowling balls like that to me. He had no helmet either. It's an exhibition match."

"Huh!" said Rod. "Well he's made an exhibition of himself here. Fancy batting without a helmet. He's just asking for trouble if he can't bat very well."

"No. He put his trust in you. Just help me get him up," said Claire.

She put an arm round me and hauled me up with Mark's help, and then she took over and walked me off the field. I was reminded of the night I helped her out of her car. Now I was able to lean on her and feel her warmth again.

She helped me to a chair in front of the cabin.

"Should we get an ambulance?" asked Ann.

"No," said Claire. "Not at the moment. Let's just get a cold compress on his head to keep the swelling down." Claire held it in place for me as I tried to watch the game.

I rested my hand on hers as she held the cold wet cloth in place and we sat watching Fardeep bat. Neither the bowling of Mark nor the spin bowling of Ewart MacGough posed him any problem. Claire was clinically attentive, asking me if I was feeling all right and if it was hurting. Although it had settled down I did not want to leave her side and her softness and so I carried on playing the needy patient.

On the field the heated discussion between father and son was continuing and Mark's bowling was getting more wayward. Several times he came up to bowl and then stopped just before the delivery stride at the crease. On the first occasion it happened he looked down at the crease and rolled his arm over as if something was wrong with his shoulder. The next ball he bowled was a slow ball, a wide long-hop down the leg side that Fardeep despatched fluently for four.

On the next ball Mark pulled up short of the delivery stride, and dropped the ball onto the ground. He called over to Rod, motioning with his shoulder, pointing to the ball and walking away from the pitch, shaking his head.

"Looks like something's wrong," said Anas behind me.

"It's the yips. I bet he's got the yips," said Wicket.

"And no wonder," said Claire. "It's all been catching up with him for some time."

"What is it between you and Mark?" I asked Claire.

"He's done the dirty on someone at work," she said. "Instead of turning a blind eye to a nothing incident he went and told the head teacher. The other teacher was innocent but got blamed for it. I stuck up for her and got disciplined. Mark is a bully and is nasty to me but he cannot stand up against his father."

There was a shout from the pitch. Alan was out.

Wicket stood up, and pulled on his gloves and picked up his bat. "Yours was a No Ball, Jeremy, and we've got you down as

Not Out Retired Hurt. So don't go away. We might need you to go back in."

Wicket joined Fardeep and made little soft dabs to keep the strike moving. Fardeep hit the winning runs with a fluent drive through the covers for four.

They came off the field to vigorous applause and cheers from inside the gazebos. The opposition filed off behind them and all our players stood in single file to shake their hands.

Claire and I remained seated as we shook hands with them, and then Mark and Rod were the last to approach.

Neither I nor Claire offered our hands to them.

"How is he then?" asked Mark. He seemed concerned.

"He's still groggy, thanks to you," said Claire.

"Well it was an accident. I slipped. It was supposed to be a bluff. We set the field for a bouncer, but then I was trying to bowl a low full toss in at his feet as a surprise like my dad told me to."

"I didn't tell you to bowl a beamer. I told you to bowl a good length," said Rod.

"You shouted and put me off. I couldn't help it. I slipped," he said, looking up at his father then looking away at the ground.

Claire ignored him and spoke directly to Rod. "I've told you it's not fair to bowl so fast. This is merely an exhibition match."

Rod said, "Oh is it? Well, he's made a fine exhibition of his ability to play cricket and manage a cricket team if he can't even play a simple ball bowled to him."

"It wasn't a simple ball! It was vicious," I mumbled.

Rod turned to Claire: "You had some bowled to you and played them. And he should be able to. He's the manager, and a bloke."

"That doesn't make any difference," said Claire.

"Yes it does," said Rod. "He should be able to play these. He plays and coaches tennis, I believe. In which case he must be able to deal with this type of delivery. But now we see he can't. He can't return the faith and the money that is shown in him by the community. It's a good job that the panel weren't here to see it, for his sake. They would have thrown his bid out straightaway. They would have realised how bad things really are here. They missed out on seeing how terribly unsanitary the facilities are as well. I thought they'd notice that. It's only luck that they didn't see how bad the Moxham cricket is that they're being asked to put millions to."

Claire retorted "Oh I see. The panel have missed it, have they? It's lucky for you that they have because they would have seen how bad you are and how unsportsmanlike you are when you're bowling vicious deliveries when you think you are losing and the judges are not here to see. That's bringing down the spirit of cricket, that is."

"Huh! Without Fardeep you are nothing. Mark had to bowl baby balls to make you look good," retorted Rod.

Mark began to mumble again with his eyes down on the ground. "Gee, I'm sorry. Sorry."

Rod pulled on Mark's arm. "Come on now Mark, let's get changed and let's get out of here and go and watch the football on television. Let's see some real sport."

"I'm sorry about it. It was an accident. I was distracted." Mark said, as his father pulled him away.

Claire shouted after him "Huh! It wasn't an accident and you did it on purpose! You took a long run-up and let it fly at a beginner who couldn't bat very well and you intended to hit him. So as far as I'm concerned it's over between us, Mark Sterling."

She turned away from him, and towards me.

He reddened at the rejection. Then he came towards me and whispered in my ear before departing.

"Don't let it get to your head - she' still mine."

"Get away!" She screamed.

Mark skunk away.

Claire slammed the rag wetted with cold water back against my head. I winced.

"I think I'll need a lot of massage tonight," I croaked.

"Well, it's best if we don't tonight. You need to rest. And I need to speak to the Friends of Moxham with Sir Richard. I need to work out a bit more about the bid, and make sure that we can count on their support and that it succeeds."

"Ah, but, tonight is the night when I really need it."

Ann came over as I sat there, as Claire was studying the Friends working under the gazebo, looking for an opportunity when one or two had finished packing things away.

"How is he?" Ann asked.

Claire shrugged.

"I'll take over if you have to go and speak to them," Ann motioned towards the people under the gazebo, laying her hand on my cold compress. Without need for further excuse, Claire got up and went over.

"This is not cold enough," Ann said, glancing at Claire now in earnest conversation under the gazebo. "Let's get you home to put some ice on it."

She helped me back into her car, saying, "Leave your car locked up here. We'll get it tomorrow."

As Ann drove me away, I saw Claire engrossed with the others. It seemed that she had forgotten about me, once relieved of her first aid duties by Ann.

Just as we were reversing, there was a roar and the silver sports car sprung to life. I could see Mark at the wheel. He motioned that we should go out of the gate first.

Ann took me back to my flat and settled me in an armchair. She wrapped a towel round my head with ice in from the fridge. A large bruise was coming, the size of an egg.

"Here, take these co-codamols," she said as I sipped some water and then I leant back in my chair and closed my eyes.

The room started to swim and I felt drowsy. Next thing I was sunbathing with Claire, Sir Richard, and some famous tennis players on a yacht in a beautiful blue sea without a cloud in the sky.

I heard Claire's voice say, "Federer and Murray are here to see you for their lesson."

"Tell them to wait. I'll be there in a minute when I've had my nap."

"But they can't wait. We can't wait. No one can," I heard her say and the sky suddenly changed to a dark grey. A cold wind whipped up, and the boat was being ravaged by the storm. Claire and Sir Richard jumped into a life raft, but I couldn't make it.

I was suddenly in the sea drowning in the salty water, and watching them float away. I called to them, but they couldn't hear. They just looked blankly back from the raft as though they were searching for me and couldn't see me.

I took a mouthful of seawater and struggled as I felt someone was holding my arm and shouting "Hey! Hey! Calm down! You're at home!"

It was Ann's voice. I opened my eyes to see her standing over me.

"You've been dreaming!"

"What time is it?" I said dizzily.

"Half past eight. You've been out for an hour. Perhaps you'd better lie down on the bed."

With her help I staggered onto the bed in the bedroom, and she covered me with a blanket.

I dozed off again and woke up feeling a lot better. Ann was still there.

"Do you want me to stay the night?" she asked as she handed me a mug of herbal tea.

"No. I'll be all right. You have to go to work early tomorrow."

I took a sip of tea.

"Yes, and I don't think we'll see you till later in the day. I'll pop in at lunchtime. If you're feeling better we can get your car."

"Yeh, thanks. But no thanks to Rod and Mark."

I reached over to put my hot mug on the bedside table. Ann cleared some space for it by moving the digital alarm clock a little.

"That ball was an accident," she said. "You saw how upset Mark was. And Rod was upset about the Moxham bid having a better hearing than his. Apparently the panel weren't interested in his club. He said it was a fix. Somebody had nobbled the panel before they left the hotel. He has put so much into cricket over the years locally and he couldn't stand Wicket coming back from nowhere and succeeding. He didn't like it when they started using schoolchildren to boost their chances. Mark lost his temper because Claire goaded him. You saw what it was like when she was batting and all the tales she told about him at school and the arguments they had beforehand."

"No, Mark is the liar, you know."

"Who told you that? I can guess! It's Sir Richard that's the problem. I can prove it now. Rod's wife Irene works in a solicitor's in town. She has access to search records in central government and has found that Sir Richard's name came up regularly with expensive projects – high cost projects all over the country. She reckons he must make a lot of money out of it. This Moxham project, six million just to repair the sports centre roof."

"It's not that, it's the whole of the infrastructure – you wouldn't understand. Six million is cheap for the whole service."

Shaking her head, she leant over me closer.

"Irene's tracked down that GSS Company. It's been used a lot in projects in the past. Do you know what it stands for? Gregory, Spedman, and Singh. That's what. It's a front that takes the money from successful sports bids, takes a big cut for itself, and then hires out a group of little companies to do the business. It takes all the credit, disappears, then moves on elsewhere. You know what he is? A serial project expenses claimant."

"So what?" I said. "It's better than staying here. If I joined their national consultancy team I'd earn a lot more and see a lot more."

"Ah yes, and one of them would be in prison soon for embezzlement I shouldn't wonder. Don't do it."

She clutched at my lapel and looked me straight in the eye.

"Don't leave me. You can't Jeremy. <u>We're</u> the team. Not them."

CHAPTER TWENTY-EIGHT

A few weeks later, it was the first match of the Enterprise Cup against Darbury here at Moxham. Claire had opened the batting again with Simon but she was soon out. One wicket down already and only two runs scored. 2 for 1.

I was inside the cabin frantically trying to get my batting gear on.

"Hurry up, Jeremy!" Wicket shouted to me from outside the door. "You'll get timed out at this rate. You've only got two minutes left,"

"I'm coming! I'm coming!" I shouted. "Where's my box?"

"Keep looking. It'll be here," said Luke, intent on getting ready himself.

"Jeremy, why haven't you made a start on the teas?" Claire shouted from outside.

She had been away for just two balls, and in that time she had expected me to make a start on the teas when I was desperately trying to get myself ready. We had had to go in to bat early so that we would be finished in time to do the teas, but we didn't think it would be this disastrous a start. Annoyed and disheartened at being caught and bowled after a couple of balls from the Australian spin bowler Ewart MacGough, she was now putting her energies into criticising other people's efforts.

"I'm coming! Look I'm trying to find my box. Ah, here it is." I stuffed the deluxe Lillywhite protector down the front of my underpants.

"Hurry up Jeremy! You've got ninety seconds!" announced Wicket.

I strapped a pad on one leg, but the Velcro on the bottom strap came undone as I was doing up the top. I then realised I had pulled out some old pads from the team kit bag. I decided to leave that one half-done for the moment and put a pad on the other leg.

"Jeremy, is the stove lit in there?" asked Claire.

"No. You'll have to light it."

"No. Don't be silly. I can't come in there with them all changing still. You'll have to light it. Anyway, trying to light that with a lighter burns my fingers."

"I've got to bat. I can't. Luke and Anas…" I turned to them. "I say, Luke, Anas, can either of you light the stove and give Claire my car keys to get the sandwiches out?"

Luke ignored me, intent on getting his pads exactly right, but Anas muttered, "We'll see if there's time after we've got ready. Got no matches, anyway."

"Hurry up Jeremy you've got sixty seconds!" shouted Wicket.

"I'm coming!" I shouted.

I stumbled down the cabin step with my bat and gloves in hand and my pads flapping on my legs. I hadn't had time to do the meditation with my charm before running out to bat. My mind was whirling and unsettled.

"Where are the car keys for the sandwiches?" asked Claire.

"In my jacket!"

"Are you going like that? You'll have to have a helmet on."

"I can't. I haven't time."

"Thirty seconds! Run Jeremy!"

"Take mine," said Claire, forcing hers on my head, and pulling the strap tight under my chin.

I started running, but I could hardly see anything at all.

"Not that way, Jeremy," shouted Wicket. "Towards the middle! Left!"

As I reached the pitch the umpire was looking at his watch, but he said nothing. I felt my pads flapping and the buckles were rubbing against each other. This they normally do not do. Looking down through the grill, I saw the fasteners were on the inside. They were on the wrong legs. This was why it had been difficult to run in them.

Ewart MacGough who had just caught and bowled Claire the previous ball was standing at the bowler's end as I passed him. Fair-haired and tanned he was intent on his purpose and boosted by having taken an early wicket.

"Well, g'day!" he said with a smile as he was getting his arm loose in anticipation. "Glad you could join us, but you needn't have gone to so much trouble. You won't be here for long."

While I staggered to the crease and took a sort of stance I wondered if they had got the stove lit yet. I glanced over to the cabin, just to check that Claire had been given the keys. Yes, the car back door was certainly open, so they should be unloading the sandwiches. I hope they don't crush them.

Claire and I had spent all this time in the Moxham sports centre kitchen making them. Ann had complained that we were getting in her way when she was trying to make the chips for the kids' morning snack. Nevertheless, she had done a lot of work in buttering the sandwiches and making the egg and cress mixture.

I had been surprised that Claire couldn't calculate how many eggs we needed and how much cress. She had just opened the fridge and expected everything to be there.

"Can we use this ham from stock?" she had asked Ann.

"All right, I suppose so," Ann had said grudgingly. "It's just that I had ordered that especially for the children's party. It's little Jimmy Moorhouse's and his mum's just come out of hospital and it's his fifth birthday and he's been fretting a lot while she's been in. So they're having a big celebration for him. Still, I can order some more, though. It should get here in time. If not, I will have to go out and buy the extra on the day myself."

There was a noise in front of me. I suddenly realised where I was. MacGough had taken a couple of strides and released the ball. It was coming, I could see it. He must have turned and come off a shorter run whilst I was thinking about the catering.

And here was that ball! Or rather it had come and gone, for my grill had got in the way and I had lost sight of it. I felt a clunk against my bat and the ball went spooning up into the air back down the pitch.

MacGough ran to it, clutching it with both hands as it dropped in front of him and he rolled with the catch.

"How's that, then?" he asked of the umpire, who extended a finger towards me to give me out. We had scored only two runs for two wickets lost.

I turned and walked back towards the cabin, with my pads flapping around my legs, being aware of only what little ground I could see in front of me between the bars of the grill.

I felt so foolish and incompetent as though I had let the team down. I reached in my pocket for a handkerchief. There was no charm there. Of course, that was the problem! In all my haste to get ready I had forgotten about preparing my mind properly with the charm. It was still in my bag. If only I had had more time, things could have been different.

Luke passed me as he walked to the wicket, his head down in concentration preparing in his mind how he would face the balls of MacGough. At least Simon was still there, but only just, having survived several leg-before-wicket appeals from MacGough.

"Bad luck Jeremy," said Wicket from the plastic chairs as I reached the cabin.

"How did we get into this situation?" I asked.

"Simple," Wicket said. "We've been drawn against one of the strongest sides in the league to play our first match and we had Fardeep only for the Exhibition Match. He can't help us anymore. His contract is to play with Appleton Water. Furthermore, that bloody MacGough's a ringer. It's obvious. He's way too good for this standard. Two wickets in two balls. You heard Fardeep the other week. He reckons he's an illegal alien and overstayed his permit. Been months here coaching, and doing one thing and another. I'm going to have it out with the umpires during the tea interval. This is no good."

Wicket rose and started to make his way to the cabin to get changed ready to bat.

Claire was getting boxes of sandwiches out of the car and laying them on the trestle table that Jafar and Dwayne were setting up.

"Jeremy, check that they've lit that stove, will you?" asked Claire as I followed Wicket into the cabin to take my pads off.

The stove was indeed alight with a large kettle on top of it.

"I reckon that Rod's got something to do with it, had a hand in it somehow," continued Wicket, strapping on his pads. "Just think. Wasn't it him who arranged for MacGough to play in that Inspection match? Then leading people on to believe he was all right? He's been coaching round here for three months already. He's just stayed on. I don't know if he's got a permit. I mean, Fardeep's properly registered. You can tell Fardeep's been away and got more permits or whatever over Christmas. All the proper documents and more he doesn't need. That's what I think."

He pulled his cap firmly down onto his head.

"Aren't you going to have a helmet?" I asked.

"No. Can't stand them. Never have been able to."

Just then, there was another shout from the middle and Luke came walking back.

"Three now - all to MacGough!" tutted Peter in disbelief. He was sitting outside keeping the score in our book alongside a young lad who was keeping the score in Darbury's book. I went to look over Peter's shoulder. There was a zero alongside Claire's and my name and a four by Luke's.

"It's diabolical," said Luke as he came back to the cabin. "I've never known anything like it. Six for three we are now. That ball just seemed to move in two directions. It spun and dipped, then turned sharply in. He can turn it both ways. I'll tell you."

As we watched Anas stride purposefully to the wicket, we knew that we would be having tea much earlier than usual. If the exhibition match was anything to go by it should be at least another hour and a half before the tea would be needed, but in this game today it would be different. We were now ten for three, but since Simon and Anas were batting I hoped that they might put up a better display.

After a short while there was another shout and Simon was walking back towards us. Wicket muttered to himself, put on his gloves, picked up his bat and went to join Anas out in the middle.

I turned the gas right up under the kettle in the cabin and came outside to look at the scoreboard.

Simon out. It was 12 for 4.

Only ten runs had been scored in the time since I had been out, interrogated by Claire, and lectured by Wicket.

Dwayne was in charge of the scoreboard and sifted through the plates on the ground to find the right one, skilfully memorising which numbers were on the reverse of others. The tin squares clinked as their holes found the hooks on the board. The low numbers swung on those hooks like dead men.

Claire had unpacked the cake and I began to cut it on the trestle table.

"Are we going to have to do this every time we play?" she asked. "I mean, what if we have to field first? Who's going to get the teas ready then whilst we're out playing for two hours?"

"I don't know," I said.

"Or what if it gets rained off? What will we do with the teas then?"

"Obviously it'll go to waste or be sold off cheaply at the sports centre."

"Can't we see if we can get somebody else to do it?" she asked. "What about Ann?"

"Oh no, she's got too much to do otherwise. Looking after the desk and cooking the children's snacks. She would go mad if we asked her. She's not too keen on the project. She says she'll only do things as an emergency."

"Some other teams have even more than one tea lady," said Claire. "Scoving for instance have two: Charlotte and her mother, Margaret. We've got none."

"Ah yes, Charlotte," I said. "Isn't that Alan's girlfriend?"

"Yes. Perhaps that is why he's looking miserable today then. Charlotte is not here watching him. I wonder if that means anything."

"You mean, have they split up or what?" I said.

She shushed me as Alan came out of the cabin with his pads on. He looked glumly at the sandwiches and cakes on the table.

"Don't you dare start eating yet!" admonished Claire, who started to tidy the cake trays.

"You look fed up. Don't you like it here?" I asked Alan.

"Yes. It's OK."

"So, why is Charlotte not here watching you today?" Claire asked.

"Charlotte helps her mum when she can with the teas when Scoving play at home. That's all alternate Saturdays and these Sunday Enterprise Cup Days. I'm playing here today, and she has to be there. I didn't realise it would work out like this."

"Well, I'm sorry," I said.

"Things might change in the future," Alan said.

"Oh?" I prompted.

"Yes, Rod says if I wanted to be closer to Charlotte all the time that wouldn't be a problem because he could register me with Scoving."

Alarm bells rang in my mind. If Rod wanted Alan for Scoving then this might trigger a mass migration of all four boys.

I was about to say, "But please, you're not serious?", or something like that when there was another shout from the middle and Anas came walking back. It was now 20 for 5.

Alan went out to join Wicket in the middle but lasted only a couple of balls and so came back at 20 for 6.

As he saw Alan walking back, Peter gave a loud harrumph and he handed the scorebook over to Stodgy Joe. Then slowly getting up, he announced, "We're not finished yet," and joined Wicket batting.

Peter hit some entertaining aerial shots off the other bowler, and Wicket confined himself to defence against Ewart MacGough.

At 40 for 6 Peter was caught on the boundary attempting one hit too many. Thus this became 40 for 7.

Stodgy Joe handed the scorebook over to Simon and strode out to bat.

Stodgy was one of Wicket's old friends, and took Fardeep's position in the team, but he was no equivalent replacement for Fardeep really. He did not bowl and his idea of batting was just patting the ball for singles. He was not going to get out and was not going to score runs. He was an expert in marking time, no matter what he was doing.

Wicket took the bowling of MacGough, protecting Stodgy most of the time, but occasionally he would take a run and leave him with one ball from MacGough to play for the over.

Wicket and MacGough squared up to each other several times, although I couldn't hear what was being said.

The fielders were at fever pitch, and had been screaming after almost every ball from MacGough. One close fielder was wearing a helmet and sunglasses, rushing up and waving his arms at the umpire, and another close fielder frequently came right up to Wicket and shouted in his face.

Eventually Wicket was given out caught off bat and pad, but he gestured to the umpire and to MacGough that he was sure that the ball hadn't hit his bat. Wicket's protestations certainly did not please the umpire for I could see him still talking to Wicket's back and pointing to the cabin as Wicket trudged grudgingly off.

We were 44 for 8 now and Jafar went out to join Stodgy.

"It's terrible," Wicket said to me. "Eight of us out to the bowling of Ewart MacGough. I don't know where they get him from but he's absolutely awesome – deadly accurate and spinning sharply. He's not a player from round here, this Ewart MacGough character! Darbury are fielding a ringer. I've told the umpires he's much too good for this level of cricket. Does he play for an Australian state, I wonder? He's so good. It's definitely unfair; I don't know where they got him from."

"Let's just accept the fact that we're being done over here. Let's just resign ourselves to it, and be polite and not blot our reputation," I said, wanting to avoid any trouble.

"No, I won't," said Wicket. "If we lose this, and it's likely we shall, then it'll be difficult to recover from as we'd be out of the Cup. And as regards other fixtures, I know it's only mid-May but almost all the other friendly teams that are worth playing will be booked up for the season by now. As a result of that, we'll lose the impetus and the momentum. Our bid will lose credibility because we haven't been tested against other teams in the area. That'll be lovely for Rod and Appleton Water, won't it? They'll go ahead to split the money and the Moxham Area won't be regenerated. All the resources will go either out of the area to Scoving or to a private body like Appleton Water. And all because of this Aussie ringer here."

Wicket pointed directly at him.

"Well, it's true, I suppose," I said. "I was depending on this Enterprise Cup to be the showcase for the renascent cricket team. If we got knocked out we would have to invent some kind of Mickey Mouse fixtures against other people's Invitation XI's just to provide an outlet. Then that won't be the same as a prestigious tournament. The Enterprise Cup is linked with all big businesses and the charities they support. It's where the money and kudos is."

"Yes, and I'm going to have a good talk with those umpires during the tea interval. It's clear to me Darbury are up to no good. He's a ringer."

I glanced at the pitch just in time to see Jafar lash out and be bowled by MacGough.

Dwayne went to bat and hit a couple of runs before he was bowled.

We finished on 56 all out, after only 18 overs. MacGough had taken the lot.

Darbury trooped off the field and lined up for their tea, then sat around in their changing room and on the plastic stacking chairs eating sandwiches and cakes, chatting to each other with a confidence that comes from frequently winning games.

MacGough was holding forth to a group of his players in a loud enough voice for everyone to hear. He said how he knew Hayden and Ponting the Aussie Test legends. In fact, it was only necessary for a member of his team to mention a name for MacGough to say that he knew that person as well.

Wicket was still annoyed about his dismissal and sat listening, slowly eating his sandwich, and muttering sarcastically under his breath "I'm sure you do mate, I'm sure you know these people."

Claire stood apart from the group, quietly relaying events to Sir Richard on her mobile.

Returning his empty plate to the table, MacGough was courteous to us like a sports star would be, especially complimenting Claire on the quality of the sandwiches. Though we had misgivings about his role as a player there was something honest and generous in his praise and we thought that we should be courteous back in our position as organisers. It might be possible for our team to retain its equanimity and dignity if we were courteous to the opposition even though Wicket our captain was obviously disgruntled and impolite.

Wicket cornered an umpire and told him that he hadn't got a straight answer from MacGough when he asked him about his authority to be in the country and how long he had been here precisely. Neither had he got a proper reply, he said, from the captain of Darbury, a young thin character who kept looking about him and laughing, always edging away and trying to cut the conversation short on the pretext of having to see to various captain's duties.

After tea, MacGough of course opened the batting for Darbury.

From his position behind the stumps Wicket said things like, "That's well done, that's a good job. You ought to be in the

Test side," each time MacGough hit a four off our bowling. Far from being meant to compliment MacGough, it was said with a snarl and an over-polite smile.

At the end of one over when MacGough had hit three fours Wicket said loudly, "Oh thank you sir! I wouldn't have missed that for the world! Such a great shot!"

Later, as Peter was marking out his run-up to bowl, Wicket said to MacGough's back, "Now, sir, let's see how you deal with this person's bowling."

As Peter ran up to bowl Wicket muttered under his breath "Steady, now, steady."

At this point MacGough pulled away out of the shot early and looked round at Wicket whilst the ball sailed into the gloves. Wicket caught it and appealed for a catch, which the umpire disallowed, saying instead, "Right, that's enough of that. He clearly didn't hit it. No more distractions, please."

Wicket answered back "I wasn't distracting him. I was complimenting him on his skill. Surely a person of such talent deserves to be praised? Otherwise what has he come here for?"

MacGough looked at him, and then took his stance again, saying "All right. Let's get on with it."

Peter came up to bowl again and Wicket made another comment about how wonderful his backlift was just at the moment the ball was bowled. MacGough defended relatively easily, but without the interruption he might have been able to execute a powerful attacking stroke.

The umpire immediately called to the scorers and said, "Right, that's it. You've been warned. Unfair distraction of the batsman by the fielding side. Dead ball. Five penalty runs." He signalled to the scorers by patting his shoulder.

At that point Sir Richard's Range Rover came into the ground and parked facing to watch the game.

Wicket was silent for a short while afterwards, but after MacGough had hit a rather spectacularly well-timed off-drive on the back foot that sped from his bat as if from a cannon, Wicket immediately started again.

"Oh, what a wonderful shot!" he snarled in an affected voice, and when Peter came to bowl the next ball with only four runs needed by Darbury to win he said loudly, "I bet you can't do that again!"

The umpire intervened again. He called "Dead ball", and said, "Right. That's it. You've been warned about this. I'm going to make a full report to the league about it, and the Enterprise Cup Panel. As captain, you should know better. Now carry on with the game."

MacGough hit the next ball for four and Darbury had won. He had knocked off the required fifty-seven easily with the help of just one other batsman. I recognised him as the one who had been in a Manchester United shirt that football night I went out searching for players with Peter.

Wicket called over to Sir Richard who was still in his Range Rover and said loudly so all could hear, "Why should we have to put up with more of those internationals coming in? He's a fraud that bloke – he's obviously too good to be a regular player at this level."

Sir Richard got out and drew the umpires over to his car, discreetly away from everyone else. He stood there smiling with head politely bowed, as the umpires were making points and opening their arms, apologetically giving deference to a Knight of the Realm for having to take disciplinary action against the captain of his local cricket team.

After they had gone Sir Richard called Wicket and me over.

"The umpires say the opposition captain said it was a bona fide transfer from Scoving and Rod Sterling's set-up. He played in the Exhibition Inspection Match. However, Fardeep's bowling and batting kept him quiet then so we never saw how good he was. Rod didn't use him to bowl much, preferring his son Mark, and MacGough left the game early and they used a substitute so we were not exposed to him. This has come as a complete surprise today. What did the umpires say to you?"

"He told me to keep quiet and not be so complaining," said Wicket. "As far as the umpire is concerned he's a player on the team sheet and he's saying its only sour grapes from our point of view and we should accept the situation. I argued with him and he says he's going to report me to the league for perpetually distracting during the game and arguing with his decision. He said as far as he's concerned we lost to Darbury and we're out of the competition."

"Oh, that's all very unfortunate." Sir Richard shook his head. "I tried to put in a good character reference for you, saying it was provocation in what we thought was an untenable situation. But, if the umpires decide to pursue the matter we might have a great deal of difficulty getting credibility again for even friendly matches."

"If only we had Fardeep here," I said. "He would have kept him quiet again. Got him out early. Still, that's it I suppose. We're out of it."

They shrugged. We all fell silent.

"Anyway," I eventually said. "How is Fardeep getting on? He played for Appleton Water today in their match?"

"Yes," said Sir Richard. "That's where I've just come from. They were playing against a side that's out of district. Fardeep hit 60 and took 4 for 20. Fabulous performance."

"There you are, you see," Wicket said. "These internationals are such a high standard. Well done everybody else! It isn't fair. It'll kill our cricket." He walked off to his car, slinging his bag forcefully into the boot and slamming it in disgust.

Claire and I swept up the cabin after the teams had gone. We cleared away the little things in life that are left over when something big has happened. The remains of sandwiches, cakes, crisp packets, cans, plastic bottles, discarded energy drinks, and clods of mud from studded boots. I reached down with the dustpan and brush to the level of all this debris that Darbury had left us.

We dumped the waste into a black plastic bag and we put the plates into a bowl for me to take to the dishwasher at the sports centre kitchen.

"Any chance of a massage, then?" I asked Claire.

"No thanks. I'm just too tired," and she climbed slowly into her car. "But never mind, if nothing comes of this you can still join our consultancy team nationally and start off something new elsewhere."

"Thanks," I said. "Maybe I might have to do that."

As I arrived back at the sports centre, Ann was just locking up as I came in with the plastic bag and plates.

"How did it go?" she asked.

"We're out. It's all over. We're finished."

"I told you not to trust them. Their scheme was bound to come a cropper sooner or later."

"No. You've got it wrong, Ann. I can trust them. It's the other teams you can't trust. If this fails I've got so far with it now that I might have to leave here and join the national group."

"Oh, no, don't. You'll end up even worse. Look what's happened here now because of them. A club resurrected then sunk. And we'd never be able to recover the service without you if you go. No. Please stay."

She burst into tears.

I held her and felt as though I was comforting a child. It seemed such a big and painful reaction. For me it was not the end of the world, but for Ann it seemed as though the world's worst catastrophe had struck.

She clutched me tightly, tighter even as I relaxed my hands. After a while she relaxed, and as she pulled away I looked into her red eyes.

"Ann, it's not the end of the world. You said this place would survive in these times. And it will. It will. Now cheer up."

She searched my face, her doleful eyes shining at me in adoration.

"Yes. I'm sorry," she said with a sniff. "You do what you want to, of course. I'd better finish clearing here. It's OK."

I was concerned and a little puzzled at her reaction to me. To me my affinity with Moxham was not a big deal. I had hardly been here a year and could easily move on if things did not work out. Yet for Ann there seemed to be a stronger thing going on and I could not put my finger on it then. She wanted things to go smoothly at Moxham and she thought my presence was a big factor in that. I could not tell whether it was something about her being reluctant to act up in a managerial role, no matter how temporary, after I had gone, or whether it was something specific about my presence that she favoured. In a way I liked her, and strangely, it would be a big wrench to leave her if I went. I would miss the comforting, cosy homeliness of everything here. Nevertheless, I knew that I would relish the challenge of something new with Claire if only I could get closer to her than I had so far.

Frustrated, I dumped the black bag into the bin outside.

The bag split. A cake knife that we had left in by mistake poked out. An ordinary sharp knife with a black plastic handle, "Ever-sharp" it was called. I got it out and cleaned it to use again. Strange how something hidden in a bag by mistake would force itself back into this world, erupting from the rubbish of the day.

When I got home there was a phone message from Sir Richard on the answer phone. "We've been invited to discuss the events. I think they are trying to investigate and form a due process of enquiry. It's an emergency investigative disciplinary panel tomorrow evening and they want to see Wicket as well. Especially Wicket. Seven o'clock at Appleton Water."

CHAPTER TWENTY-NINE

"Come back here and tell me what happens, promise?" Ann said as I left our sports centre early the next evening to go to the disciplinary enquiry at Appleton Water.

I took the road past St Margaret's School, just to see what Claire might be doing now. To get a glimpse of her window.

I slowed down as I passed the car park. Claire's Fiesta was outside the accommodation block. The evening sun was glinting on it, making it shine like a little red treasure. However, ominously alongside it, lurking in the building's shadow, was Mark's silver sports car.

It was early evening and there were not many other cars about so it was not as though it was a school function for Mark to be working late. He had also parked it right where Claire lived, not next to the main school building.

Mark must be in her flat. Perhaps it was just harmless. He might have just popped round to check off some schoolwork. In which case, surely they would have met in the staffroom in the school block. On the other hand, perhaps he might have come round to apologise to her for his dangerous bowling during the Inspection Match. Yet it was to me he should be apologising because I was the one who got physically hurt.

The Inspection Match had happened weeks ago. It was hardly timely to come round with a quick apology now. I pressed my foot hard on the accelerator as I passed the last of the school buildings. I wanted to get away from there fast, and I was trying to dismiss from my mind the thought that I had been betrayed.

As I drove up the landscaped approach to the Sports Resource Centre, I remarked how once again Ann had sacrificed herself for the service, electing to cover the reception desk at short notice. This time she had cut short the time spent in the personal care of her mother, in order to cover for me at my meeting and be there to comfort me when I returned with what we both now guessed would be a dark day for Moxham cricket and the project.

The electric doors opened in salute as I walked into the Reception Area of Appleton Water Sports Resource Centre.

The foyer was large and open, with plush red carpeting. Brown leather armchairs were grouped around glass coffee tables. A circular reception desk was set in the middle of the room. On the other side a wide circular staircase swept up to an upper balcony which had a café area. At the far end was the glass window wall of the Appleton Splashland through which came screeching voices from pale-bodied youngsters, mums, and dads. The smell of chlorine leaked out to give an invigorating and convincingly hygienic air.

Sir Richard was there already in one of the brown leather armchairs. Wicket followed me in. He was calmer than yesterday, wearing a sports blazer and tie trying to look his best, but his mostly downward gaze showed he was obviously very tired after yesterday's exploits.

"I don't like the idea of appearing before a Board and being disciplined by Rod," Wicket said.

"What do you mean?" asked Sir Richard. "He won't be there."

"He told me he was secretary to the Board."

"Like hell he is! That's what he tells people. He hasn't been elected to it even as an ordinary committee member yet."

Presently a young man in a suit came through some swing doors.

"Ah, Sir Richard, glad to meet you," he said, holding out this hand. Then, turning to us and shaking our hands, he said, "And this must be Mr. Turner and Mr. Freeman. I am Lance Coulton, secretary to the Board. Please come this way."

We followed him back through the swing doors and along an elevated corridor that overlooked the Splashland pool. The corridor was very hot and even more pungent with chlorine along here. Several youngsters clustered around a giant toadstool at the shallow end that acted as a shower, sending down water under different coloured lights. In the deeper end, which was still only a metre or so deep, there was an inflated plastic smiling hippo monster which several of the children were climbing over and falling off, joyfully splashing into the water or diving off into their mum's and dad's arms.

We climbed some more stairs, turned into a quiet carpeted corridor beyond another door, and were led into a small office in which two men were sitting at a table.

Lance Coulton introduced the Chairman of the Moxham area cricket league, Fred Higham, who was an elderly thin man with red cheeks and half round glasses on the end of his nose. Next to him was Max Bauer, introduced as a representative from the Enterprise Cup Panel, a chunky man in his forties, also in a suit, who looked like he supervised building sites.

"Good evening gentlemen," said Fred Higham. "Please sit down. I trust you had no problems finding us?"

We shook our heads. Appleton Water Sports Resource Centre dominated the hillside for miles around. His question was a rhetorical show of power.

"First of all the matter of William Kenneth Turner of Moxham. It has been reported that you as the Moxham wicket-keeper and captain deliberately and repeatedly distracted the batsman by continually making comments about his professional standing and registration.

"I understand that during the match five batting points were awarded. The captain of the batting side, the captain of the fielding side (yourself), your deputy, and the other umpire were all informed.

"Since the batsman was not seriously impeded, and in fact many of the deliveries were hit for four, and Darbury won the match, they have asked for the matter not to be taken further. We are therefore to record that you have been cautioned, but that circumstances might not be so lenient should there be a next time. However, we shall not take the matter any further this time. Although, what you did was against the Spirit of the Game."

He moved a sheet of paper away from him on the table, and picked up another.

"Which brings us to another matter before the Board. One that is more serious. Mr. Bauer?"

Bauer, the Enterprise Cup man took over.

"Yes, Can you tell us please what you know of Ewart MacGough?"

Sir Richard outlined to them how he had been given the player by Rod in good faith as an available player legally in this country and had arranged for him to play in the Exhibition Inspection Match, which was a unique non-league friendly match.

"So Rod had then vouchsafed his transfer to Darbury," Bauer said. "In effect he introduced this illegal player into the Enterprise Cup competition."

"Well," said Sir Richard. "We cannot vouch for how other teams play. We just expect them to play like us. I am sure whatever the Board decides will be an appropriate strategy to move things forward."

Bauer nodded gravely.

"We cannot ask this player for his account because he has disappeared. Darbury have not attended this hearing. They have merely sent word that they do not know where this player has gone and they claim that they cannot be held responsible. However, rest assured that we will be speaking to the Darbury committee over this very serious matter, and also in view of their flagrant non-attendance today. We have a witness sheet signed by Rod Sterling for his statement, but that will not excuse their non-attendance.

"It seems now that the transfer to Darbury was invalid because he had not been registered. Though he did not need to be for the friendly Exhibition Inspection Match, it was crucial he was registered somewhere along the line as the player claimed he was when transferring to Darbury. The Darbury captain should have checked his status."

He looked down and rustled his papers for a moment in order to prepare himself for his verdict.

"Thus he is an illegal player and for this infringement Darbury will forfeit the match. Let the records show that Moxham is awarded the fixture and will progress into the next round to meet Lampton Ambo."

He held the pose for a moment. A smile flickered over Sir Richard's face, which was returned by Bauer's as he concluded "Thank you gentlemen for coming. Let us hope there will not be a repeat of this. Thank you."

We all shook hands. Coulton was going to show us out, but we said we knew the way.

As we stood in the foyer afterwards Sir Richard said, "What Rod has effectively done was to send in a booby trap in the shape of this player so that any club who tried to play him would be removed from the competition when the truth got out."

"Hah!" said Wicket. "I see. Rod can claim he didn't know about the status, whereas he probably did. It's his way of sabotaging the strong Darbury club if MacGough is detected, or of making sure that other clubs (for example, us) are knocked out by that club if he is not detected. Scoving and Darbury were in different parts of the draw and might not meet. Either way it would have been one less club for him to worry about and one step nearer his being the only side left in the bidding."

"Yes," I said. "But he won't get very far with it because although he might not have to play Darbury now with this Ewart MacGough being exposed, it is likely he will still have to play Appleton Water in mid-August which has got Fardeep and he's bound to lose to them."

"Unless of course Fardeep has gone back to India by mid-August," said Sir Richard. "That's when his contract with Appleton Water ends and he's hoping that he will be selected for an Indian touring side then."

"Huh!" said Wicket. "It seems to me that with Scoving being in different parts of the draw from strong teams like Darbury and Appleton Water that he must have planned that it would happen like this."

"Yes, but let's concentrate on us," said Sir Richard. "We've got a weaker side next – Lampton Ambo."

"Oh," I said." They're from the East of Moxham. I've seen how they can't play football - so they'll be no good at cricket."

"Yes, but watch it. You never know what might happen next. They might have a ringer as well," said Wicket.

"I can't see it somehow!" I said.

We laughed.

Then Sir Richard said, suddenly pointing to a poster on the noticeboard, "Well, what do you know? Claire told me you are looking for a tea lady. What about this for a culinary solution?"

Printed plainly and amateurishly, but on expensive paper, it read "MEET ESMERALDA FIORA, TV PERSONALITY CHEF. DEMONSTRATION OF THE NEW REVOLUTIONARY FIORA SPORTS DIET. All sports people welcome. Sports clubs are invited to tender for a chance to participate in a high profile multicentre trial of this fantastic dietary programme. 7.30 pm Tuesday 22nd May in the Empress Suite, Appleton Water Sports Resource Centre."

"Ah yes, this is the woman who's been e-mailing all the clubs," said Sir Richard. "That's tomorrow night if you can get to it. Well, we can pay for her from subs, but it will only be a basic tea lady fee. I don't know if she's after anything more in the short term. I think she's trying to get people to support her in a bid for funding. She'll be trying to get the Health Education Council on board. Look at this internet quote here: '....a portfolio of salubrious side-dishes in a prospectus of diverse healthy delicious delights.'"

"Great!" I said. "A celebrity who might be externally funded. All we have to do is supply the ingredients which we would do any way from club funds. A high profile professional chef. Great for the team if we can get her. That'll be all our problems solved. What can possibly go wrong with that?"

CHAPTER THIRTY

"Welcome everyone to another in our Appleton Water Sporting Life Evenings. Well, we've had previous ones on important matters such as golf clothing and equipment from the John Brown Sportsmaster Chain. Tonight we have a real treat for you." Matthew Goyt the presenter was an impish man in his early forties in a grey suit with open neck pink shirt, and   short, greying hair. He stood at the front of the fully-carpeted Empress Suite with its heavy red curtains and soft upholstered dining chairs arranged in rows.

Claire, Sir Richard, and I sat in the middle of the audience of approximately thirty or forty people. I guessed many were from other clubs but I recognised a lot from Appleton Water. There were several older women with their husbands and presumably connected in some way with the catering or committee side of cricket clubs. I saw the back of Rod Sterling's head across the room in front of us.

"Our attention tonight is on something very important - looking after the inner cricketer. We are pleased to welcome the distinguished cook Esmeralda Fiora. Many of you will know of Esmeralda from her appearances in magazines and television, and for her Fiora Diet which has been a great success both in America and here. Tonight she is going to cook for us a dish which can be eaten in place of a normal cricket tea. Afterwards she will be signing copies of her new book 'Cooking from US' over on the side table there."

He pointed to the book display on a table by the large side window with its view over the cricket field in fading light.

"But now, here's Esmeralda."

There was applause as a woman came from the side to stand behind the long table at the front of the room. She was in her forties with bouffant platinum hairstyle and a stars and stripes apron over a bright red dress. She was of medium build, neither anorexic nor obese. Her face was hard, heavily made-up, but smiling in a self-assured way behind thick wide black-rimmed square spectacles.

On the table was a collection of bottles, dishes, bowls, and a stand with lit gas ring and griddle. A white tablecloth hung most of the way over the front, but one could still see her red high-heeled shoes and the large calor gas bottle underneath.

"Thank you, Matthew. Hi. I must say it's wonderful to be back in England again and at your beautiful Appleton Water." Her transatlantic voice rang out confidently and clear. "Tonight I'm going to share with you a superb experience. I will show you how to make something delicious, simple, healthy, *and* sustaining. And of course, it is just right for your cricket game. It's grilled chicken in a lime and ginger marinade served in a sushi nori wrap, and there's a bountiful fruit salad for your dessert."

"So it's like being wrapped on the cricket pads, only it's wrapped on the chicken pads, and with a fruity appeal." Matthew chuckled, and the audience tittered.

"Yes, that's right." Though Esmeralda's face had a mystified expression, she joined in with the joke and smiled anyway. "Now I have the ingredients here and the recipe is in my book."

She pointed to the bottles and jars on the table.

"Why are you using chicken?" interrupted Matthew.

"It's healthy and cheap and manageable in a wrap and many people like it and can eat it. It's not red meat."

"I see. Tell us what you're going to use here." He pointed, his hands poised up high near his shoulders, his arms partly folded up like bird's wings. Frequently he would bend forward at the waist and dip his head down near a dish to smell it as Esmeralda named the ingredients on the table.

"Well, I have some garlic salt, and some peeled and grated ginger. Some limes, plum sauce, red onions and extra virgin olive oil. And of course, chicken breasts. You want them boneless and skinned."

"Now, the plum sauce – why is that?"

"Well that's because it's a sweetener for the marinade without using unhealthy white sugar. And plums have a long history of going with birds."

"Yes. A partridge in a plum tree, Ha!"

"No, Matthew. It was a pear tree."

"Oh yes, quite." The audience laughed as Matthew pulled a face at being corrected.

"And I also have a packet of nori wrap, normally used for making sushi, but in this case we will wrap the chicken in it. It is much healthier than bakery rolls. And of course we don't want all that unhealthy carbohydrate to weigh us down after the break."

"No. Of course not. But isn't carbohydrate supposed to give you energy?"

"It is and it does, but from what I've heard there is too much of it in the ordinary cricket snack. But there will be plenty of energy in this. You'll love it." She formed a ring between her first finger and thumb and moved it smartly away from her mouth in salute. "It gives you protein to restore what's broken down and used up in the muscles whilst you've been playing. Now I will make the marinade. You need two red onions which I shall chop up like this."

"Ah yes. You can smell the onions." Matthew said, leaning towards her as she worked. "Do they ever make you cry?"

"No. These don't unless they're very strong Spanish cooking onions."

"No. It's usually the cricket scores that make me cry!" He said turning to the audience for another laugh.

Esmeralda smiled slightly but was already picking up a teaspoon and reaching amongst the dishes and jars.

"Now I am going to add garlic salt - one teaspoon. Then two tablespoons of ginger. Six tablespoons of plum sauce. One tablespoon of extra virgin olive oil."

"Yes."

"Then I will cut three limes in half and squeeze them into the mixture."

"Hah! So much lime. I wonder what Fardeep would say about that if he were here. It would meet with his approval. He would want to make a curry with it."

"Yes, but you know Matthew for all you curry-loving guys I really do have a variation in my book which has black pepper and curry powder in it."

"Hah! I was right! See!" He shouted to the audience.

"Now you watch that marinade doesn't boil whilst I take the chicken fillets. I slice the chicken fillets into wafers, as thin as I can. See? I turn the fillets into thin pads. Now with these you want to make a shallow cut lengthwise down the middle end to end, like this, and then make short cross cuts all along."

"Oh, this is warming up and you can smell it. Hm! It's lovely. All that ginger and onion," he said, stirring the saucepan.

"Yes. Now I take a large plastic box with a lid and I place the chicken fillets in here and I pour the marinade on, like so, and work it into the fillets with the spoon. Just like that. See? Now we seal the lid and put it in a cool place overnight. Just turn it every few hours. Or if you've got a box with a tight lid like this you can shake it up without taking the lid off."

She shook the box vigorously and Matthew stepped back. He looked to the audience in mock amazement.

"Oh, you do that every few hours through the night as well, do you?"

"No. I do not. Silly! Just a turn before bedtime and another as soon as I get up on match day."

Matthew looked at the audience and pretended disappointment.

She put the box under the table and brought out another.

"Now this is what it's like after about twelve hours." She opened it. The chicken pieces were no longer white but a mixture of various shades of light green and red.

"Wow, yes. Just smell that!" Matthew sniffed the box after she had opened it. "All those flavours in the marinade."

"Now we shall grill them. We have a hot griddle here and I shall lay them out. Cricket teams could barbecue them. Just you keep an eye on these whilst we make the fruity appeal."

"Ah. Yes. How's that?"

Matthew raised a finger and got a laugh from the audience, but Esmeralda was impervious to the joke and carried on with her lecture.

"We have some bananas, some pears, pineapple, shredded coconut, lemon halves, and strawberries. I chopped the pears up after peeling them. You want to use Rocha pears since they will be softer to eat with the other ingredients. What you do not want is a hard pear. Then peel and slice the bananas. I like to use ripe bananas, just before they go brown."

"This looks good. I can smell the different fruits now they're cut up. Mmm lovely."

"Then cut up the strawberries, and add the shredded coconut and the lemons. Just the juice of them. This stops the fruit from going brown and gives everything a really healthy tang. Just what you want in the tea interval to revive you. "

"I see and you've got a healthy main course and a healthy dessert."

"Yes. You know Matthew I have done some research. And in fact, the teams that are fielding second are at a distinct disadvantage sometimes if they have had a big snack. In fact, I have found that some teams elect to field first before the snack so that the opposition team has to do the running around after eating. So why not have a situation that is much fairer where the snack is very healthy, light, *and* self-sustaining? Now some cinnamon and vanilla and the fruit is ready. So let's get the chicken fillets off the grill."

"Hmm! They smell delicious. All that ginger heating up. I don't know if those at the back can smell this like those of you at the front, but you will soon."

There was a murmur from the audience.

"So what you do now is to take a chicken pad and place it in the sheet and wrap it up carefully like this."

She placed it on the little square bamboo mat and carefully rolled the matting with the wrap and thin chicken fillet inside and some lettuce leaves, keeping it tight all the time.

"Sushi nori is basically seaweed," she said. "It is high in iodine, calcium and zinc. So you get lots of good metals there. Also it is high in lignans which help reduce the risk of cancer. The sushi matting stops it all breaking up as you roll and helps keep the shape. Then when you have it all rolled up, you take the mat off, and you cut it across the middle into two shorter pieces so you can better handle them."

She took the fruit compote and spooned a little into a plastic dish.

"There you are." She stood up tall, faced the audience, and pointed, "The alternative healthy English cricket tea."

Matthew cut off a thin slice from the end of one of the two pieces and made a great display of putting it in his mouth. Esmeralda smiled and watched him chew it.

"Hmm. This is absolutely delicious," he said patting the side of his mouth with a paper napkin. "All those wonderful flavours. You have the zinginess of lime, combining with the ginger, and the sweetness of those plums really settles and soothes it and balances it – and then the garlic intensifies the balance. You have all the flavours from the cricket-playing nations of the world in this. You really have the spirit of cricket in this snack. A wrap around the pads and a fruity appeal! How's that?"

They both stepped back from the table to applause.

"Ladies and gentlemen you can now come up and try this," said Matthew. "We have prepared a few earlier that we are bringing up out of the back kitchen here and will be with us in a few moments. Alternatively, some of you might like to start by trying to make your own wraps."

The audience queued up to the table, some of them getting the idea of rolling the chicken up better than others. Claire and I did quite reasonably, but Sir Richard's was more like a loose bundle and was splitting apart at the sides.

"Make it tighter, Sir Richard," yelled Rod from across the room, who was now obviously on his second wrap and was taking more than his share.

"It's easy for us – she can use the Moxham Sports Centre Kitchen and then bring it to the ground," I said to Claire and Sir Richard. "There will be no problem. It will all be done. The club will only have to endorse the Fiora Diet in its adverts. Maybe also put up a sign at the matches."

Rod came across to us, his mouth full of the chicken and said, "Just the kind of thing to revitalise our club. I want to get our team a lot fitter and if we can get on this low carb diet so much the better. With Esmeralda at our helm catering-wise we'll wipe the floor with anybody else. I'll get her to lead my hospitality team of Margaret and Charlotte and we'll put on functions and attract crowds and bring in lots of revenue. She won't be able to resist our facilities. Then we'll have a proper cricket centre over to the west of the county. Coach these youngsters. We'll be able to do a lot of coaching of youngsters. Yes. By the way, how is your coaching coming on?"

"We had Fardeep and it went well."

"Ah yes I see. Went well whilst he was with you, you mean. But now he's gone to Appleton Water. Well I suppose you miss him."

"Anyone would miss Fardeep," chirped in Claire. "I expected him to be here tonight."

"Yes. These youngsters need coaching in my opinion to develop them. And they need a lot of coaching. TLC. Tender Loving Coaching to bring them on. They also need transport to grounds – that's another form of coaching," he laughed.

"Most of our matches are at home," Claire said.

"I see. So that's why you need a tea lady. You've got to look after these lads. If you don't, they'll go elsewhere. Mark my words."

He was interrupted by Esmeralda approaching with a smile.

"Hi, how's it going, guys?"

"Fantastic," I said, quickly swallowing to talk. Claire, Sir Richard, and Rod nodded.

"We launched it at the Mets and at the Bulls," Esmeralda said. "They needed something to chow down onto quickly and it went down a sensation. Then naturally, I thought about you English and your cricket game and came over here to launch it. To bowl it to you, as you say."

Rod spoke up. "I'll take it. I can give you the lot. All the publicity you want as an existing club. Also I've got a team of tea ladies already who, although they're not here tonight, I'm sure they would love to learn from you what to do and all your recipes. I'll see to that. Definitely. You can be our head cook, the team leader. It'll be famous. Just think of it. The Scoving Diet."

Rod raised his hand as if to point out the phrase up in lights across some advertising somewhere.

Esmeralda loudly sucked through pouted lips.

"But this is the <u>Fiora</u> Diet," she said firmly.

"Well, yes. Then - the Scoving Fiora Diet."

"Perhaps. But my problem is that I have some promotional work still to do and therefore I can't commit too much. I just want to see how it will go locally. I am expecting to hear from a major player soon."

"But in Moxham we have no tea ladies at all," I said. "There is no one to do it and the position is wide open. Please come and cook for us. This season we are only in the Enterprise Cup and so therefore we will only have a couple of matches at home, so there will be no great demand on you. Also we will have a lot of publicity because of our bid and you will be associated with it. It is a rebirthing, a relaunching of an established club and there will be a lot of publicity surrounding the bid, as I've said."

"Ah, but that's true of Scoving as well," said Rod. "A lot of publicity here and a worthwhile cause, an established club."

"Ah yes, but it's not like as though it was a new club or a reborn one like Moxham," interrupted Sir Richard.

"It sounds as if this Moxham will have a high profile because it is a new one in a way, or at least, a new endeavour," Esmeralda said thoughtfully.

"Yes," said Sir Richard. "That's right. You can launch your own set-up first and then start teaching other clubs. You can use the fully-fitted kitchen at the Moxham Sports Centre and would not have to cook stuff in outdoor prairie conditions as you would have to with other clubs."

Rod frowned at that remark.

"One other thing – this is forty pounds for a team tea, not twenty pounds," said Esmeralda.

"What! We don't spend that much! We only spend twenty five at most, fifteen if we can." Rod was aghast.

"Hah! As you can see for just a tiny bit more you can make some really good food. And remember I'm giving my services free: I should be charging you a hundred pounds an hour for this as a celebrity chef."

Sir Richard nodded.

"Yes of course," Sir Richard said. "In fact, we have the resources for you because we are only having a few games– I think our budget will go that far. I think we can give you a platform to launch yourself."

Esmeralda's eyes grew huge behind her heavy black-rimmed square spectacles.

"Ah, thank you, Sir Richard. I was hoping to find an appreciative audience, but I never expected to be engaged by a team of such cricketing gourmets."

CHAPTER THIRTY-ONE

"OK," said Claire, pensively swallowing a mouthful of lunchtime lasagne in Marmaduke's. Her shopping bags fell against my ankles under our table. "We'll check with Sir Richard that his budget will run to sixty pounds to Esmeralda for the tea, even though she said forty on the presentation night and Rod reckons he does his for fifteen."

We had arranged to meet here urgently on the Saturday afternoon after I had received a phone call from Esmeralda asking for more money for the tea for the match against Lampton Ambo at Moxham in two weeks. I was taking my lunch break late and was frazzled. I had needed to get out of the Sports Centre after a long tiring morning with groups of kids running wild. Claire was also worn out after searching the whole of Moxham for shoes and having to go back to get them from the first shop.

Marmaduke's seemed also in a tired phase. Although there were few people at the tables, the remains of a busy lunch hour were still there. On the little blackboard behind the counter one of the chef's specials had been rubbed untidily off by hand, and only the smell of the braised pork remained. We had to settle for the lasagne. The staff had tried to compensate for the sadness of its being second-choice by making it mouth-burningly hot from the microwave.

"She can use the Moxham Sports Centre kitchen and then transport it to the ground," I said. "We'd have to work out what facilities she might need and at what time, because Ann would be in and out of the kitchen making chips all day on the Sunday and they might get in each other's way."

Just then, one of the catering staff came out of the kitchen with an empty tray. I recognised the dumpy build, heavy mascara, dark hair combed on one side, short on the other exposing a pierced ear and dangling earring. Charlotte. She hovered by the tables and took a long time clearing and wiping the table next to ours as though she was ready to say something.

It was Claire who spoke first.

"We saw you at the Inspection Match with Alan."

"Yes." She flicked her hair.

"But you weren't at the next match when we played Darbury."

"No. I help my mum out at Scoving when I've got the Saturdays off here. That other time Scoving were also playing so I couldn't come to Moxham."

"And do you get to see much of Alan?"

It was a direct question, a harmless one I thought, but Charlotte blushed and frowned.

"Not much. As far as Saturdays are concerned, I'm either working here or helping my mum out with the teas at Scoving for the league games. The only way he can see me is for him to come to Scoving."

She collected some dirty cups and stacked them on her tray on a neighbouring table.

"Some Sundays we can get together when we're not working. But now a lot of those are Enterprise Cup matches where both teams are playing in different places. Soon they'll play each other at the same ground."

"No, since they are both in different parts of the draw that won't happen," I said.

She wiped a spot on the neighbouring table very hard until the moisture from the cloth was making the table messier.

"Rod asked him if he wanted to play at Scoving because then he would see me more, but he said he'd got his mates at Moxham and it would mean him giving up there. But if his mates wanted to go, he might go."

"He's a good player. I wouldn't want to lose him, or any of them," I said.

"Well, Alan could go to Scoving," said Charlotte. "He hasn't got too much to lose by not going to the garage on Saturdays, because all he does is hang about all day and helps Peter for next to nothing. It's a kind of semi-job you could say. Something to show future employers if he went for a proper job after he's finished college."

"If he does, he'll miss some good food. Moxham will soon have a better cuisine then Rod's fifteen-pound budget. We're in negotiations to have a TV chef come." Claire said proudly.

"Who?" Charlotte started. "Not Esmeralda?"

"Yes," I said. "Do you know her? We went to her promotion night. It was really good. It was a grilled chicken marinated in ginger and lime. Absolutely delicious."

"Huh. We had her at college. She was a visiting cook. A special treat it was supposed to be for us in Domestic Science." She screwed up her face in disgust. "She got us making something Hungarian in the first week which tasted dodgy but some people thought it was all right. But the next week she had that seaweed stuff with some chicken, but it was in a different marinade - a kind of cheese which smelt really like somebody had been sick in it. And then she gave us some fish heads, and we had to wrap them up into it. It was raw fish and they still had the eyes in the fish heads and people had to eat it like that. It was disgusting, absolutely disgusting. And if your fish had lost an eye you had to put a frozen pea in the socket instead. And it was horrible. You could see this horrible green eye from miles away across the other side of the kitchen. And people were expected to eat it. Half the class ran out to be sick while making it and nobody could eat it. That's these famous TV cooks for you. Sounds like she's done a nice one for you as a demo but when she gets going you'd better watch out."

"Well I don't know about that. This was good, especially the fruit compote," Claire said.

"Alan won't like her stuff. He only likes my cooking – proper English country food that my mum makes. She bakes her own bread for the sandwiches, and her own cakes. She's won awards, she has. Rod says there's too much butter in it and it isn't healthy. But the rest of the team love it. But Rod, he's trying to get them on a health drive to improve their fielding and stuff, and trying not to give them so much tea that they can hardly move. Some of his team are really gi-normous."

"Ha! I know," Claire murmured. "Yet that night she made some really good stuff. Some fruit compotes. They were good!"

"Yes, she can do that, and that's what she's famous for. But then very soon, you mark my words, she'll go really wild. You'll see it when she starts putting a bit of extra something fishy by the side of your plate. You might like it at first because it'll just be a little garnish but in time it'll get more and there'll be a bigger dollop. But still nothing you can't move to one side if you don't want it. Then one day without warning it'll be diabolical, absolutely diabolical. She'll think that's good and everybody will have to eat it and be sick and you'll lose the match and that'll be the end of it. Anyway if Esmeralda comes to Moxham and she really starts up and then starts on her stuff, there's no way that Alan will be able to stick that and he and his mates will walk out and come to Scoving."

Just then, a man in a suit came out of the kitchen behind and looked in our direction. Charlotte smartly turned, picked up the loaded tray, and went off back to the kitchen.

CHAPTER THIRTY-TWO

I went into the Sports Centre late morning on the day of our next match, against Lampton Ambo, just to check up on things. I don't know why. Just a feeling. I hoped I was being over-cautious.

When I arrived Ann was standing annoyed with arms folded across her chest in front of the kitchen door. Normally jolly and even-tempered, today her body was stiff with indignation.

"How much longer is she going to be in there? She's locked me out! The serving hatch is bolted as well! I've got all these chips to fry and the kids are going to be coming soon from their morning activity. I should have the oil hot and ready by now."

There was a crash of pans from beyond the door and swearing in an American accent.

"Hey, now," I said to Ann. "Let me go and see."

I knocked politely on the door. Yes, I actually knocked very politely on the door of my own kitchen in my own sports centre of which I am the manager.

"Hello, Esmeralda?"

A muffled stressed voice came from behind the door. "Don't come in here! Don't look. It's not ready yet. You folks told me four 'o'clock for your tea. Not noon. "

"Esmeralda, can I just speak to you for a second?"

"No. Goodbye. I need privacy for my creation."

"No, but…"

"I'm not just someone turning up and making you a ham sandwich you know. I am trying to give you a masterpiece. Leave me alone to work."

"Yes, but it's just that I didn't realise you would be in here all day as well!" Ann decided to inject her annoyance into the interaction through the door.

"What! You didn't realise it would take so long to make? What do you think I am - a burger maid? Of course it will take some time – it will take a long time to do all this. If you want the highest standard, you must accept that it takes the highest level of skill and effort. Now please, I need to concentrate."

"We need to just sort out the chips for the children," said Ann.

"What? Chips? You put such things above my efforts? I don't believe this."

"She didn't mean it like that," I said. "Is there some way we could get the little electric mini-fryer out and set it up in the storeroom out here so that Ann will still be able to cook her chips for the children?"

"Yes, yes. I see what you're saying. Take it if you must."

"But it'll be contrary to health and safety not to cook food in the kitchen, but somewhere else," grumbled Ann.

"But it's only the chips." I whispered to Ann, sensing the conversation getting complicated. "You've got the microwave already out here at the back of the serving counter if anybody wants pies. All you do is warm them up."

There was the sound of scuffling and the door opened a little way.

Ann was behind me but she was being barred from entry by Esmeralda who guarded the door, opening it only by a slight amount and closing it as soon as I had squeezed through.

On the table in the middle of the room a tablecloth had been spread over to conceal an array of dishes. She seemed to have used all the pots and pans in the town, for there were many dirty in the sink. I thought there was a slight fishy smell, but I might have been wrong. If Charlotte hadn't prompted it the other day then I wouldn't have thought anything about it.

"There's the fryer," Esmeralda pointed, carefully making sure I focused on nothing else in the room. "That's it now. I'll be along with your tea at the ground at four 'o'clock. I know where to come. You told me where the ground is."

I took the fryer to the storeroom where Ann had hastily wiped down an area and had opened the little window to let out the smoke that would be generated.

She looked at me and raised an eyebrow. I raised mine back.

"Well," I said. "Let's hope this works."

"Yes," Ann said. "Otherwise I think there'll be more at stake than a cricket tea and some children's chips."

I plugged it in, switched it on, and left.

CHAPTER THIRTY-THREE

"This is some of the Lampton Ambo team." I told Sir Richard as we watched two full cars arrive at our ground. "They can't play cricket much. I expect we'll beat them. Most of them are from lads playing football in the trailer park. They kept on losing. I recognise some of them. Their dads make up the rest of the team."

Sir Richard said, "If we get through this we have to go up into high farmland to play quarter-finals against either Ploughton or Laxendale. If we beat them then the semi-final draw will be tough. We will have to play one of the three most powerful sides: Dry Langford, Appleton Water, or Scoving. The remaining two play each other. That is, assuming they all run to form and they all get through."

"Yes. I've heard about this current Appleton Water team. There's this particular player. He's a high flier banker and he is the main one in Appleton Water. He flies back from Zurich every Friday night just to play cricket on the Saturday for the team and then goes back again on the Sunday evening."

"I know," Sir Richard said. "They've got Fardeep as well. They've won this Enterprise Cup for the past two years and are keen to make it a hat-trick. However, I think that Fardeep will have to go back to India after the quarter-finals because his contract and money will have run out. So that will weaken Appleton Water slightly, but they're still a good team. They could easily beat Scoving for instance, especially now."

"Why especially now?"

"I've heard that Mark is still registered with Scoving, but has made himself unavailable for them because of 'work commitments'. He still feels bad about upsetting Claire."

"Tough!" I said in disgust.

"Yes," Sir Richard smirked. "Looks like Rod and Mark are shooting each other in the foot. They won't have much chance of winning matches and rivalling the credibility of our bid if they carry on like this. Ah well, I'd better nip over to see how Fardeep is getting on at Appleton Water. I'll be back to see you later."

He got into his Range Rover and drove off.

I turned to watch Wicket greet the Lampton Ambo captain and go off to the middle of the pitch with him to toss up for choice of innings.

I looked at the opposing team. I recognised the person who had said his father wouldn't like it if he tried something different from that first night when I had gone out with Peter. Once they were all back in their changing room they kept the door shut.

Though generally a meek team, one of them was exceptional in that he was annoyed rather than lacking confidence. He was their fast bowler, a big bloke they called Bill. He was very bombastic and had parked his car in an imposing position near the boundary.

As a host I felt I should warn him about safety in a friendly way, so I half-joked to him, "Don't park it there, it's dangerous. I hope you've got good insurance because it might get hit."

He looked round at me as if he was in charge of the ground. "No. If anybody hits that, there'll be trouble." He turned smartly and walked authoritatively to the changing room.

Wicket returned from the middle of the pitch after the toss. "We lost and have been put in to bat," he said. "It has been raining a bit overnight and they think that it will be lively to begin with. They don't want to bat on it, so they have put us in out of fear."

As the opposition captain returned to his team changing room, I could overhear Bill's loud voice.

"What do you mean by leaving my brother Ted out of the team?"

"Well, Bill, it's a big decision and I had to make it," said the captain. "We needed an extra bowler and we also need to give everybody a chance. I've got people who haven't had a game for weeks and I need to keep them fit. If they don't get any practice then they can't see the ball so well. So I thought I'd better give one of the young ones a chance and let him have a bowl first. We can bring you on to bowl later."

"Well I don't think much of it. Ted's an in-form batsman — you can't go chopping and changing," he continued, as he followed the captain out onto the field.

I took up a chair a short distance behind everyone as Luke and Simon walked out to open the batting. I was due in next and wanted to have time to use the charm and have a good innings today, not like our last match.

Seeing no one else was looking at me, I surreptitiously took the charm out of my pocket and held it in my hand.

I stared into the centre of its amber heart. I felt that I could see something deep in there, like a glint of a little ghost of something. As I moved the jewel in the light, the centre of it seemed to glisten and I imagined that I was following the light around inside a cave as though it was a will-o'-the-wisp.

I imagined myself catching the will-o'-the-wisp and blending with it to become an entity, then looking out at the world from the centre of the charm. The charm around me was a crystal armour protecting me from harm, distancing me even from any of my own negative thoughts.

I closed my eyes and counted as Fardeep had taught me, then opened and closed them again. When I finally opened my eyes after I had finished the world seemed to have slowed down and become dream-like.

The knocks from the bats out in the middle now seemed to be both frantic and slow. Frantic because they were hurried, ill-thought-out, last-second dabs at the ball, and slow because my mind saw them in so much detail that they appeared so imprecise and late, that a more retarded way of making those strokes could not be imagined. Normally I do not see any minor flaw in Simon's and Luke's batting in such detail. Today was different. And once I saw where their imperfection lay I saw what I needed to do. I understood how much more smoothly I might apply the bat to the ball if I watched it all the way and made only a clean contact with the ball at the essence of the moment.

I put the charm back in my pocket and relaxed.

When the score had reached 32 Luke dabbed at yet another in an untidy way, not quite over the ball, late and angled, and the wicket-keeper caught it. He was out after making 17.

I shadowed a few shots and swung my arms as I walked to the crease. I passed Luke coming back with his eyes down, who said nothing.

I went up to Simon, the other batsman, to ask for advice.

"Just watch this one at your end, he's swinging it away a bit," he said. "The other one is swinging it in. But it's not moving much for either of them."

The fact that it wasn't moving much rang alarm bells for me. If it was straight and then would suddenly swing a little – just enough to find the outside edge of the bat – it made me feel even more uncertain than if it had been swinging a lot. In the latter case you might be able to judge the swing and follow it and play with it, or safely miss it. But a small amount of swing occurring late was difficult to counter.

"Another thing," Simon whispered to me. "They've had some kind of argument with each other and haven't opened the bowling with that bloke Bill. I don't know, maybe out of spite. Yet that's good for us, because this young lad's poor."

He meant Fred, a spindly youngster who was bowling many wayward balls which Simon had struck well.

I took my guard. "Middle please," I said to the umpire, and he directed me exactly to the same mark that Luke and Simon had been using.

"Four balls left in this over," he said.

I looked round at the field. There were fielders in a ring around me, all at a distance of a pitch length away, except for two: one back on the boundary behind the wicket across from me at third man and one behind me at fine leg.

The wicketkeeper was standing about ten yards back from the stumps. There were two people to his right, occupying first and second slip.

The young bowler walked back about a dozen strides and then I took my guard with my weight on my toes and tried to make sure that my head was level and watched the ball in his hand as he ran in.

Around me, the fielders who had been chatting as I was getting into position became still. They disappeared from my mind as I focused on the bowler. Slightly shorter than me and with short dark hair, he ran up and swung his arm.

I said to myself "Easy. Watch."

I did not see the ball leave his hand, but saw it after it had gone a few feet. I leaned towards its path, to meet it with the bat. I tried to lead myself to its line with my head, as Fardeep had taught me. It bounced in front of me and I watched it strike my bat with a heavy clunk as I leant forward defensively with bent front knee, almost kneeling onto the ball. I was taking no chances. I felt the clunk vibrate all the way up the bat handle.

Yet there it was now, stationary at my feet. My bat had taken the full force of that bombard as though it had been a castle wall of fortified thickness. I relaxed and stood back.

The fielders around me shouted "Good ball!" and one of them in front of me retrieved it.

The bowler had started walking back to his mark. I relaxed and looked around. Everything went hush. The fielders were in the same position, and a wood pigeon cooed over in the western bushes.

I took my stance, focusing once again as the bowler ran in to bowl.

The bowler passed the umpire as before but this time his boot seemed to have a firmer footing on the last stride and his head and arm came over with a prolonged swing. I had followed his arm and saw it go the whole way down almost to the ground.

I turned round square to the bowler to try to follow the ball. It hit the ground with a phut just in front of him and was rising quickly towards my right shoulder.

I was uncertain what to do. My weight wanted to come forward but this unexpected shorter ball made me flinch back.

Instinctively I moved the bat at it, in an effort to defend myself or to try to flick it away.

There was a faint nick sound as the ball, rising steeply, caught the edge of the bat.

The fielders cried, "Catch!"

Simon shouted, "Run!" and I started off, unaware of where the ball was and just kept on running.

At the other end I turned round and saw Bill throw the ball heavily and angrily to the wicketkeeper at the end that I had just left. Though I had not designed it, I was off the mark and had scored my first run in the innings.

Simon played the other two balls in the over, cutting each for four runs.

After each ball I played I took a step back from the crease and touched my hand against the charm through the outside of my trouser pocket. It was merely a small touch that no one would notice, as part of a negligible mannerism. Just like swinging my arm as I walked away to breathe out and prepare for the next ball. But to me it was like a recharge of energy. A flash of power surged through me each time.

That was how I mastered my mind to make twenty runs that day. Compared to other players it was not a lot, but I knew that it was good for my development.

After half an hour the captain shouted to Bill and pointed, "This end Bill, after this over?", inferring that he would like him to take over the bowling from the young lad.

But Bill turned to the captain and said angrily, "No, you've bowled 'em in, now you bowl 'em out!"

He stood stock still and neither spoke for several seconds, each looking at the other.

Then the captain broke the pause with "Please, Bill."

Bill grudgingly took the ball, saying, "The great Sydney Barnes wouldn't have done this. I think he would have stuck to his guns when he said he wasn't going to bowl."

The first and only ball he bowled to me was a fast yorker. It landed perfectly at the base of my middle stump and spread my stumps aside.

CHAPTER THIRTY-FOUR

After my innings I sat down next to Claire who was looking out for Esmeralda to arrive.

"What could have happened? Do you think she is all right?" I asked.

"Give her time yet. She'll be here. It's only quarter to three and she would have phoned if there was a problem like not being able to start her car," Claire said.

"Do you think she could have done something silly in the canteen and fallen out further with Ann?"

"I don't know. I wouldn't put it past her."

During the next hour my attention was divided between watching our innings build in the hands of more capable batsmen than myself, and watching out for Esmeralda. At five to four, we were close to the end of our innings. Just five overs were left, and only five wickets had fallen.

Just then, a little white van appeared through the gateway with the words "Fiora Catering" on its side. It screeched to halt, sending up a shower of gravel on the car park. As she jumped out her red dress seemed so intense in the bright sunshine, it almost hurt my eyes.

"I left it close to time because the food has to be served warm," Esmeralda shouted. "I know you have no facilities here for heating it. I have foil-wrapped it as much as I can and kept it in an insulating bag. Call them over and tell them it's ready."

"Well, there's just a couple of overs to go yet."

"What do you mean? It's here, now. Tell them to wash their hands and get ready. Call them over."

Esmeralda looked at me, then at the players on the field still engrossed in the game. She thought of saying something more, but instead started to prepare something at the back of her van.

"Can I do anything?" asked Claire with one glance at the game in case she was called to bat, and the rest of the time trying to look in the van. But Esmeralda carefully blocked the view of her culinary secrets.

We finished on quite an accomplished total of 180 for 5, with Neil and Wicket being the not out batsmen. Claire would have been next to bat but was not needed in this innings.

Esmeralda opened several large insulated pizza satchels to reveal the nori and the chicken that we had had on the presentation night.

In addition, there was a dip that tasted like a raw fish mixture. It didn't go with the chicken and so after half a mouthful I scraped it off my chicken wrap.

The reception from the team was a very mixed one. They stood around eating carefully, seeming to be afraid of making eye contact with Claire and Esmeralda, occasionally confiding a whisper to each other or me.

Alan eyed it mistrustfully, saying. "It's foreign. I don't like seaweed. Why should I eat this when I could be eating Charlotte's cooking if I were at Scoving?"

Peter loved it, especially the really hot lime in it. "It's like a curry. Great!" Then he turned away from Esmeralda to say to me, pulling a face. "But the garnish needs work. That's not quite a fish curry."

Wicket said he hated it. "Why can't we have a proper tea with sandwiches like we used to? We've had it in the other matches. So why not in this one?"

Claire's reactions were like mine. We were uncertain about the fish, but could eat a little. However, we loved the fruit and the chicken.

"Fish is a psychological thing," Claire said. "If you are at all afraid of it or have too much of it all at once then you will develop a complex about it. But this is OK. Pretty good taste. Nice seasoning. A fish paste."

"Yes," I said. "But a fish paste of what? A fish paste of fish brain, fish eyes, fish gills, for all we know."

Lampton Ambo's captain was a meek man who liked chicken, hated fish, and took little mouthfuls, chewing thoroughly. When I saw him again a few moments later, he no longer had it in his hands. I wasn't quite sure what had happened. He couldn't have eaten it that quickly. He talked a lot about the fruit, not about anything else, saying that he wasn't "a fish person".

Bill, the fast bowler, it was clear, didn't like any of it. He ate nothing. On his nerves all the time and angry he spat out what little he tried immediately in front of his teammates. His captain reddened at being powerless to prevent Esmeralda from seeing Bill's behaviour.

She said nothing, and turned her back.

One of the older opposing players, a large fat man with a grey beard, ate all of his portion and part of another. He came up to Esmeralda, with bits of fruit salad still in his beard, holding a pocket diary open to a fresh page early in the year.

"I've seen you on the telly. I think you're good. Can I have your autograph? Anywhere on this page."

Another even fatter player, but clean-shaven, was another slow eater. He only ate half of it before saying politely "Very full. I had a meal before I got here." A few minutes later I saw him eating a sandwich of his own with a banana and cake in his car.

Soon a queue of people formed for the loo, either holding their stomachs or standing with crossed legs.

"'No Solids'," said Wicket. "I don't think it will be very solid."

Esmeralda came up and asked us if we liked it.

"Yes. It's different." I said, a little uncertainly.

I was worried that as everyone was so quiet and negative it would put Esmeralda off. At least we had a tea lady at the moment. If we upset her, we wouldn't have one and there were games still to play that needed teas.

I said to Claire, "I sense a big team fall-out coming. Perhaps you can have a quiet word with Esmeralda. Get her to do a different type of tea. Esmeralda will surely realise that if she wants to promote her cuisine these future remaining teas will be important. So she will want to make sure that these teas count."

After I had repainted the worn creases during the interval with a straight edge and some whitewash, we took the field to bowl as Lampton Ambo began their batting reply. They needed 181 to win and had 40 overs to get them. They had to score at an average of 4.5 runs per over.

The captain opened the innings with Smith whom I recognised as the clean-shaven slow eater with his own secret food. After a mix-up the captain was run out cheaply for 5. The score was 10 for 1 in the third over.

The large man with the beard came into bat next. His name was Hamp and his scoring was restrained by our bowlers. Lampton Ambo began to get behind with the run rate, crawling to thirty off twelve overs.

Smith was slow and lacking in confidence and refused many runs. The run out incident with his captain seemed to have made him even more dithering and unconvinced that more runs should be risked.

The captain shouted "Get on with it!" from the cabin, but the batsmen seemed unable or unwilling to speed up. At the end of one over he went out to them, with a water bottle and glove on the pretext that they were asking for refreshment, and further exhorted them to speed up from close range.

Soon afterwards, Hamp set off for a single. Smith refused and sent him back. Hamp slipped, spreading his legs wide and collapsed on the ground, tweaking a hamstring. He managed to stand up and took a couple of feeble steps towards the cabin, hobbling in pain.

"Stay there! I'll come as your runner!" the captain shouted.

A minute or so later he came out of the cabin with his batting gear on, and jogged to his position alongside the square leg umpire to be a runner for Hamp.

After several dithering calls over the next over from Smith, the captain must have decided to force the situation and run Smith out to get someone else more athletic and positive in his place. He called for increasingly tighter runs, and eventually he went for a run stranding Smith midpitch.

It would be an easy run out.

I threw the ball to Wicket, who smoothly caught it near the stumps. Unbelievably he did not remove the bails to run him out.

He stood there and allowed Smith to just amble back out of breath into the crease.

"No," he said to Smith. "You can stay in. It's not you we want out."

On hearing this the captain realised that we might never run Smith out and shouted in dismay to him about the slow scoring rate. "Only forty runs off twenty of the forty overs! Smith, what are you doing?"

Smith, however, on hearing that Wicket would refuse to run him out, was transformed. His behaviour flipped to the opposite extreme and became more animated, now attempting runs that put his captain in danger.

He hit a subsequent ball in the next over smartly and set off. After a couple of steps, he saw Dwayne reach the ball. Suddenly realising his mistake, he shouted and sent his captain back in panic.

However, Dwayne overran the ball, so Smith changed his mind, calling the captain to set off again after all. Though Smith was powering down to make his ground, the captain was slow to re-start.

Dwayne recovered quickly and threw the ball at the stumps. It was an accurate left-handed direct hit and the captain was run out. Hamp, for whom the captain had been his runner, was thus out.

Hamp and the captain plodded together dejectedly back to the cabin, the captain turning twice to glare and shout back at Smith, who was shaking his head bemused and invincible at the crease. Now they needed 140 off 18 overs. The rest of the middle order came in succession with the captain barking orders at them from the boundary to run or to get out. Many of them were forced into hopeless panic by the situation and others cheaply run out by Smith. For Smith, still feeling invincible despite his annihilation of Hamp and the captain, was running more frantically and taking more risks when he did decide to run.

At 91 for 8 Bill the bowler came out to bat in the thirtieth over and needed to get ninety off the last ten overs with just two partners left: the historic Smith, and Fred the new young bowler to come. Bill began trying to hit sixes. Many went near his car but none of them landed on its windscreen. However one bounced on its roof. After clearing the boundary 4 times, he finally perished to a catch by Peter.

Fred the young bowler was out cheaply trying for a second run with Smith when eight off each over was needed. They finished on 135 all out off 35 overs, having lost by forty-five runs.

They packed their bags and drove away in silence, leaving Smith to follow them at his slower pace.

We watched him go. A match winner for us? He was a match loser for them.

We were through to the next round and would be away to Ploughton at Ploughton field. Therefore, our next home game for which we would have to provide the tea would be the one after that, assuming we got through.

As we were packing up after the game, I asked Claire if she would give me a massage again.

"It's a bit difficult tonight," she said. "It's Sunday and I've got an awful lot of schoolwork to prepare for tomorrow. Sorry."

At that moment of rejection my back which had been behaving very well for the past few weeks suddenly gave a sharp twinge. I grimaced, but tried to focus back on our conversation. I wondered if she was getting cold feet about other aspects of the project, or whether she was just too tired and busy to care about me today, so I changed the subject.

"Did you find out from Esmeralda what she was doing in the Moxham Sports Centre kitchen so early in the day?" I asked.

"No. She wouldn't tell me."

"Hmm. Did you manage to speak to her about changing her menu a bit?"

"Yes. Even better. I suggested that she might like to go and cook for Scoving."

"What? Why?" I was stunned. "We'll have no catering for any home games now. Surely, this gives Rod all the cards? He will have the best cooks in the league. Three of them. One of them a high profile chef. He's bound to sweet-talk her into staying, and cooking normal food at matches. And what of us? Are you thinking that we won't get any further than our next game? Or do you know something I don't?"

"Yes, I do know something, but... trust me," she said, holding my gaze as she got into her car and drove off.

CHAPTER THIRTY-FIVE

It was mid- July and we were in the quarter-finals.

Journeys to new grounds for important matches are fraught with problems. You never know what might happen until it does.

Therefore everything was planned in the finest detail and nothing was left to chance for our away match to Ploughton. Claire, not trusting her car, had had it serviced for the occasion. The local garage I had recommended had scrupulously replaced all the tyres except the front nearside one, assuring her that this had no apparent defect even by their high quality standards.

From the Moxham ground three cars drove off filled with people and their kit. I followed them in the little Jimny with the usual combination of team bag and scoring books. Claire would bring Alan and the large kettle for the tea. Our opponents' kettle was leaking, and they had asked us to bring ours.

I had just got as far as the next village when the phone went. It was Claire. Had I driven off with her car keys from when I had opened her car to help her load up? Yes, I'm afraid so. I turned round and dropped them off to Alan who was waiting at the bottom of the lane.

I texted Wicket to say that we had been slightly delayed, but never mind – just to carry on and we could catch up with him. It was a two o'clock start, and everyone should be there at twenty to two. Wicket should make that, but now I wouldn't be there till ten to two. Wicket would toss up since he was captain. The lads could have a practice knock-up before the match because some would have a ball and their own bat.

I started off again. I had now reached the end of the town and the Rose and Crown. So far, there had been no further problem. I put the radio on to catch the cricket commentary on Test Match Special. England was doing well at 210 for 3 against the Australian leg-spin attack.

Feeling inspired, I thought that I might bowl my leg-spin today, and I started to think about how the opposing batsmen might be outwitted.

Yes, I think I might turn it from the leg side if I can only get it through their defences. If it bounces sharply early on then it might ride up the face of the bat. The only way a batsman might be able to stop himself from going through with the shot early and knocking it up in the air will be by stroking the ball with a slowing velocity, bringing the bat down on top of the ball and smothering it. But with sharp turn and dip then the ball might go straight through his defence and bowl him.

At that moment, "Eine Kleine Nachtmusik" started in my pocket. I pulled over.

It was Claire, but the reception was very poor because of the high ground I had reached and I could only make out the words "Have you got it...got it?" She evidently wanted something she thought I had.

I threw my hands up in horror.

Everything we were taking was either in the team cars, which had just departed, or in her car. I had only the team bag and scorebooks. The clubhouse must now be empty of everything else. I had bolted all doors and windows, and locked them with the clubhouse keys. That was many miles back behind me.

I told her that now she had the car keys she should stop worrying about anything else, start the engine, close the gate after her, and go. Never mind about doing anything else, not even touching the horseshoe on the cabin door or whatever for luck.

Her line was crackly and alternated with the sound coming and going like someone holding the phone close to them and then moving it away. There were noises in the background like Alan grunting and heaving baggage about in a small space, with the occasional clank of metal.

But yes, I thought I heard her say, she had touched the horseshoe for luck, started the engine and driven it out of the field, closed the gate, and then suddenly realised that she wanted something else which I couldn't make out, and did I have it? She had been looking for ten minutes.

No, just leave it, I told her. You must have everything. Wicket would be arriving at the ground soon and they would be getting ready to start. She still had a member of our team and herself to bring as well as the kettle. If Wicket lost the toss and we were told to field first by the opposition, then our team would be in danger of not having enough people there in time to control the flow of runs. Indeed, if she was any later she and Alan might even be forced to forgo the right to play because they would be too late. She should get out of there fast.

Get out of there fast? Get out of there fast? Didn't I realise that that was what she was trying to do? Hadn't I heard a single word she'd said? How dare I tell her how important it was to get out of there fast! It's all right for me to sit up near the motorway smug in a nice little Jimny. How could I have the faintest clue about what was really happening from up there?

I told her this was no time for anything other than a goal-directed deployment of concentration, putting aside distraction, staying on target, and focusing on the practical matter in hand.

Staying on target? Staying on target? Where did I get this from? It's not a shooting range, she said. Staying focused? What did I mean staying focused? Did I think she was training for the Olympics?

Look, I know what's wrong, I told her. I could understand it. Look, she was just having a normal reaction to it, I told her. People do. It's only natural. When you've got your first away match and it's an important one as well you're bound to feel on edge and all keyed-up. Maybe over-keyed. And you're bound to feel upset when you realise it's time to go. It's quite human. Some people get it out of their system early and others it takes them by surprise on the day. It's nothing to worry about. You just have to pull yourself together and focus. Just count slowly from 1 to 10.

Count? Count slowly? From 1 to 10? I was telling her to count slowly from 1 to 10 in a situation like this? I was telling her to keep calm and yet that was what she was doing. I would realise that if only I myself would stay calm and listen for one moment. Hadn't I heard that despite the interference on the phone line? Didn't I know what she was on about? If I would only listen a moment she would say it again slowly so that I could take it in and not blame the reception.

Yes. I am sorry, I said. I will listen if you say it slowly.

Yes, right, then here's how it was to be. I would just listen. She would ask me one simple question and I'd better keep calm and listen and think carefully then give a simple answer. And it had better be right. She doesn't want any put-off delayed kind of answer like she's been given up to now. She just wants a straightforward answer. No ifs, buts, or maybes. I either know the answer or I don't.

Yes, I told her. OK I will listen, if that will do any good. But I had been trying to listen to her all along. So in turn I told her that this question she was going to ask, it had better be necessary. Time was precious. We were falling behind schedule and I couldn't stress again how important it was to get out of there fast. So, just ask the question I told her, and let's get on with it.

All right, now I will ask you, and don't you start pretending you haven't heard, she said. Never mind about my question being good. It will be. It's your answer that's got to be better.

I closed my eyes and took a deep breath like the Maharishi Yogi Bajan, and asked her what was this simple question which she so desperately needed answering for which the universe must stop its irresistible revolutions.

Her voice started clearly "Did I know ….." and then the interference rose to a peak louder than before like breasting from a trough in a high sea. It dropped suddenly and then I heard the question again "Did I know where the …was." And the word sounded like "tyre jack".

I started the Jimny back to the ground again, this time at an even faster speed. I reached the end of the lane and stopped.

I don't know if you remember those John Wayne films when he becomes diverted from tracking Indians who have disappeared over the far mountains. Typically he comes upon the remains of a wagon train with a wagon tilting over its front nearside wheel, the entire contents of cooking utensils on the ground, and an angry woman with a blackened face and young lad aiming scowls as menacing as a shotgun at a would-be rescuer they have strong doubts about.

Quickly sizing up the situation he says something like "You take my horse and leave this to me, ma'm".

She took me at my word and climbed into the Jimny with Alan, anxious to catch up with our advance party leaving me to find the jack and change the wheel on her car.

I managed to do it and then started on what for me was my third attempt to get to the match in the space of half an hour.

In fact it turned out that in spite of this delay I did in fact catch her up because she had stopped down a country lane to check the map.

As I came alongside she said haughtily out of the window "Huh! Jeremy Freeman! A real man would have organised this much better and not sent me to an incompetent garage in the first place. Look at how late we are now. If we're out of this Enterprise Cup and if the project fails it'll be your fault. I'm getting fed up with you. Fed up to the back teeth!"

She revved the engine, let the clutch out fiercely, and sped ahead.

CHAPTER THIRTY-SIX

I expected the match to have started, but incredibly, half an hour after the match was supposed to have done, I arrived with the large kettle in Claire's Fiesta to find them still rolling the wicket.

Ploughton field, although it is high ground, is a field more in the shape of a bowl. The pitch is in the middle of this basin-shaped field and the pavilion and car parking is over to the right from where you come in.

There is no gravel in the car park. It is all a rambling field, uneven with dips and hollows, so it is difficult to drive a car over at speed without the chassis bottoming against the suspension. If I had had my little Jimny then there would not be a problem, but driving Claire's Fiesta meant I had to take it steady even though my insurance allowed me to drive any car. Any car yes, but across any field?

I parked up next to my Jimny at the end of the line stretching round from the pavilion.

The pavilion was a small wooden hut with a veranda and three rooms: a changing room on either side of a central room which had a gas ring on a worktop near the window and a calor gas bottle beneath. There was a pissoir round the back.

I went over to the pitch where the host team were pulling a heavy roller backwards and forwards watched by Wicket and the two umpires.

As they reversed the roller at the end of each run their feet came dangerously close to being squashed underneath it.

One of the men was not in cricket whites, but in a boiler suit and had a farmer's floppy hat on. He looked like a country yokel, so I presumed he was the groundsman.

He suddenly shouted "Stop! Stop! No! No! Whoa!"

Fearing the worst had happened, all quickly applied their forces in the counter direction.

"What? What?" another shouted.

"Push back! Push back!" shouted the groundsman.

"What is it?"

"My keys! My keys!" he said.

"What? Where?" one said, looking round and expecting to be asked to fetch them from the pavilion.

"No, no, here," said the groundsman and bending down behind the roller put his finger into the pitch. He laughed in triumph as he pulled out a set of dirty keys covered in soil leaving a large divot. "I wondered where they were all this time."

The younger umpire grinned, but his older colleague did not see the joke. He coughed loudly, and his voice boomed out, "Now surely you are not going to leave that divot there?"

"Oh no," said the groundsman. "I'll fill it in."

The groundsman went off to his shed and came back with a bucket of soil and a shovel.

He scooped a shovelful of the soil into the divot and directed the rest of his men on the roller to haul it forwards and backwards a few times over the piece of ground before hauling it away.

The umpires and Wicket inspected the pitch. It was terribly pot-holed with similar divots, where it might have been repaired after previous treasure trove.

"Look here," the senior umpire said. "And here. And all over here."

He pointed with his foot to patches, and his colleague tut-tutted and shook his head as the gravity of the situation began to dawn on him.

"It's not dangerous," said the groundsman.

"It's not totally safe either," said Wicket.

"Yes, but it won't harm you - at our speed and with helmets on. We played a league match on here yesterday without any problem."

"You played a league match here yesterday?" asked the senior umpire. "I can hardly believe that. How come the umpire let you do that? I don't know about this. I think it's very borderline."

The groundsman shook his head. "There weren't any umpires yesterday. They couldn't be spared down for this division. We rarely get them to the league matches. Just the Cup."

"If I was the umpire you wouldn't have played on it. I must offer it to the captains to see if they agree to play on it. Otherwise we won't play today and it'll have to be re-scheduled. We're running late as it is. You're lucky that there's no system for deducting points for ground fitness in this competition. But it may lose you general points in the end of season rating for your programme as a whole."

"Perhaps," said the groundsman. "Anyway, let's see how it plays, shall we? And then see if it makes any difference later on."

"Oh," said the umpire. "I think it will. We've the two captains here and I suggest we ask them whether they want to play on this. Or perhaps you have some other pitches that might be better?"

The groundsman shook his head.

"Very well then, let's ask the captains," the umpire turned to Wicket and to the Ploughton captain, a short rotund man in his forties with a cap pushed back over his head which revealed the full ruddiness of his farming face.

"Oh, it'll be all right," the Ploughton captain's voice had a rough rural twang.

Wicket paused and studied the ground. "I think if it plays up then we might consider moving it, even though it will eat into the playing time and shorten the time available and thus the match."

"Agreed" said the Ploughton captain, pleased that a compromise had been reached. "So let's toss then."

Wicket called "Heads".

We gathered to see. It was tails.

"You bat first. We'll field," said the Ploughton captain.

Claire had not come over to see what was happening but remained in her car, out of contact with the team, ostensibly getting ready.

As the rest of the team were in the changing room Wicket told us in a low voice that we should be cautious. We had been put in to bat by them and he felt sure that this was because, unlike our opponents from Lampton Ambo last month, these were confident, knew the pitch conditions, and had the team to beat us.

He said to Luke and Simon, our opening batsmen, "Be careful out there. It looks like it's very unpredictable and dangerous. Full of potholes. If it's no good, we'll have to see if we can move to another strip."

We watched from the pavilion area as Simon took guard for the first ball. Their fast bowler came pounding in off a few paces and used all the force in his shoulders to hurl the ball down onto the pitch in front of Simon.

It bounced hard and fast, rising vertically just past Simon's ear and over his head.

The opposing team applauded and Simon shook his head in disbelief. He went and prodded a divot from where the ball had taken off.

Wicket said to me "There you are. That's an example of what's to come. First ball."

Another ball was hurled down by the bowler. This time it shot along the ground after pitching and Simon just managed to get his bat down in time to block it.

The opposing team's fielders shouted in approval at the speed and difficulty of the deliveries.

Balls continued like this, fast, shooting up or down unpredictably, until the over had been bowled.

Simon went over to talk to Luke mid-pitch, and then Luke took his guard at his end.

However, when the next bowler tried a gentle run-through before bowling a ball for real, his feet slipped in the final delivery action. He pointed to this spot and said something to the umpire.

The first bowler shouted from his position on the boundary at fine leg "Are you sure you've got the right boots on?"

The bowler nodded, then marched back and started on his proper run. He managed to stutter through the spot where he had had difficulty before but then fell down on one knee and rolled, ending up in the middle of the pitch. He sat up dazed.

The captain and several fielders gathered by the crease where the senior umpire was very carefully testing the area with the toe of his foot. They were joined by the younger umpire from square leg, shaking his head.

Sensing that this was becoming a crucial discussion point in the game, Wicket walked out to them, and I followed in some kind of official backing up capacity.

"I can't bowl here," the bowler was saying from his sitting position.

"Of course you can, just try it again. And this time, put your right boots on," the first fast bowler had come up from the boundary and was urging him back to the pavilion.

"But I've got my boots on," he said, shaking his head.

"I think this pitch is very poor, and dangerous," said Simon. "Several balls rose nastily to me."

"That wasn't the pitch," explained the first fast bowler. "That was my bowling."

"Yes, that's right," agreed their captain. "It was his skill."

"Well I don't like the look of it," said Wicket. "As I said at the beginning, this pitch is very poor and pot-holed. That groundsman's dug up part of it to get his keys."

The senior umpire turned to his colleague and shook his head. "Well, Len, I think that we need to have a re-start on a different pitch if this is much too dangerous to use."

"What? This is perfectly all right, ha!" The first fast bowler interrupted the umpire. "As I said this isn't the pitch, this is my bowling. Let's get on with it. Let someone else finish your over if you can't manage and then I'll get some wickets my end."

"No," said Wicket. "We'll get another pitch, thanks. A proper one."

The umpires looked at each other and then the senior umpire turned to the Ploughton captain. "What else have you got?"

The captain motioned to the strip next to where they had been playing. "Well, there's that."

The umpires examined the bowling foothold area, and then searched the middle of the pitch for divots.

"There's still some problems with that, but not as many, Dick," the younger umpire said to his colleague.

"No, don't let them change this," said the first fast bowler to his captain. "It's not all that bad and I was getting some zip from it. You saw those first few balls I bowled in my over. That was a good over. I could have got half the team out by now."

Simon began to rub his arms to remind the umpires how the ball had grazed him, muttering, "Pretty nasty this is. I don't think it's a good idea."

"No," said Wicket. "It's too dangerous here. You'll get somebody hurt and you've a duty of care."

At the phrase 'duty of care', the umpires stopped, looked at each other, and then the senior umpire said to the captain, "How long will it take you to get the new one prepared?"

"About half an hour at the most. Just cutting it and a quick roll, you mean," said the Ploughton Captain.

"Then I think we'll abandon the first match even though it only lasted six balls and have a re-play here. If the captains are willing." The senior umpire looked at Wicket and at the Ploughton captain.

Wicket said, "Aye, we'll try it, but it's not much better as you can see."

The Ploughton Captain nodded to the groundsman, "Get it ready then."

"No, don't do this!" shouted the first bowler. "It's all right, believe me, it's my skill!" He turned to the captain. "Look, tell them. If they go through with it, it'll make a nonsense of things. Tell them. They won't believe it's my skill, not the pitch. I've never been in a situation like this. I've never been so insulted."

"Now look here, Pete." The Ploughton captain took him aside. "You are a good bowler. And I know you're skilful, but this pitch isn't for everyone. You are doing well, but what about Sam here? He's having trouble keeping his grip even with his proper boots on."

"He says he's got his proper boots on – but what he's wearing are not proper boots, not like mine." He raised his foot and pointed to the studs on the underside of his sole.

"Look, Pete, I know. But what about when it's our turn to bat on this? It'll be much worse for us because it'll be worn out by then as well as pot-holed."

"No. We can sort out our batting later. That doesn't matter. Let's get them out cheaply. I've almost got him out four times in my first over. Just another over like that one and they'll collapse in no time. I can do it. No. No. I tell you. This is my final match before I leave for London. This has always been my favourite strip. I've done wonders on here in the past. Please, please I can get you through to the semi-final. It will be my leaving present to the club."

"Pete, Look. When you've gone to London they'll remember you up here and see your name in the record books. It's in the record books already for all those great performances. For all what you've achieved with the club, everybody will look back on your name in years to come and say what a great bowler you were. All those wickets!"

Pete's face shone.

"And then someone will say," continued the captain. "Someone will say that last cup match against Moxham – he took those wickets but it was on a bad pitch, and that's why he got them. And that's how they might remember you and your final performance. The day the club cheated."

Pete said hotly, "Don't you call me a cheat! Just you keep them on this pitch here and I'll see that they're all out! Just you trust me on this. You're throwing the game away."

But the captain's reply was interrupted by the rest of the team coming between them hauling the roller.

"Well if that's your attitude, if you're not listening, I might as well go to London tonight, and never come back," said Pete, starting to walk away.

"And I'm never coming back!" he shouted at them as he reached the pavilion.

A few seconds later he had reappeared, still in his cricket whites and carrying his bag which he slung angrily into the boot of his car. Then with one final pause to glare quickly at the captain, as though giving him only the very briefest opportunity for reconsideration, he climbed stiffly into his car, reversed violently away from the line and sped out of the field.

CHAPTER THIRTY-SEVEN

Half an hour was spent by the groundsman mowing and the Ploughton team rolling, whilst the Ploughton captain made calls on his mobile to track down a player to replace Pete.

"I don't know if this is going to work much in our favour," said Luke. "This could be an even more dangerous bowler they're trying to get."

"No, I don't think so," said Wicket. "If they had wanted someone like that then they would have made sure he was in the original eleven. No. I don't think so. I think that they'll be trying to get a junior."

The captain snapped his phone shut and looked in Wicket's direction. "We've got someone," he said. "Let's toss again for this new game."

This time we won the toss and Wicket decided to bat first. He said that although it might have some gremlins in it like the other one, at least we will have first go and it would surely be worn a lot more for a team batting second. It certainly wouldn't improve. Luke and Simon opened the batting again.

Unfortunately we lost wickets early and were five down for only forty.

I would be batting soon so I took the amber charm out of the side pocket of my kitbag. This time I desperately needed to make sure that I would stay there and hold the batting together, even if I didn't score many. I looked deep into the charm, and stared to find the glint at its heart again.

I imagined my mind fused with that glint and once again I visualised myself inside the charm, looking out and surrounded by its crystal armour. I closed my eyes to count and re-opened them the mystical six times. Then I put the charm in my pocket and tried to maintain that focused state of mind I had created.

Claire had been watching me studying the charm.

"Huh! We'll need more than magic to win this!" she said.

When I walked onto the field to bat at the fall of the next wicket my mind was settled, and although I did not score many, I resisted resolutely in partnership with Stodgy and later with Alan.

It was as though my mind was playing from deep inside the crystal, for I felt invincible. My mind was completely attuned to the ball, and to that ball only. It was irrelevant who bowled it, it was my ball and I could control it completely.

Fortunately, I was insightful enough to realise that I was not a great batsman. I did not attempt brilliant shots, but was doggedly determined to block defensively and stay there. The charm gave me the power to control my mind. In these circumstances I knew that there was only one person who could get me out, and that was myself, through attempting something beyond my skill level. So long as my mind stayed inside its crystal armour then I could stay there for a long period.

The tension with which I gripped my bat was wearing the rubber on the handle. It would need replacing soon, perhaps after this innings.

Finally, my end came when I defended a faster ball down onto the ground, but it still had freakish life in it. It rolled onto the stumps. I was out, bowled.

Though having contributed only ten, I had held on and blocked difficult balls.

During this time, the score had gradually climbed to eighty for seven wickets down.

I had the feeling that Ploughton would know how to bat on this wicket in order to get something like eighty or ninety. We had not yet put the game beyond their reach.

Claire went out to bat walking past me without acknowledging my presence. The fielder's cries of "Catch!" that had occurred regularly throughout my innings quietened down when Claire was at the crease. She played carefully and straight down onto the ground, delicately tapping the ball for singles. Slowly she built up over a dozen runs in a partnership with Alan who was eventually out, bowled. Then Wicket came to bat.

Wicket was basically a slogger who was experienced enough to often succeed. He had two shots: anything in line with the stumps he would block, but anything off target he would thrash at. His strategy paid off and he made several high shots over the covers that bounced for four.

Eventually he decided to take risks with a straight one and was bowled for 15.

Dwayne was our final player and was soon caught out by their junior replacement player, who at last made a fielding contribution on the last ball of our innings.

Claire thus finished on 15 not out and our team had made a total of 118. This, we felt, would be a challenge for Ploughton on this pitch.

CHAPTER THIRTY-EIGHT

The tea interval at Ploughton was a basic affair. The pavilion had a central room that served as the kitchen, and people queued up outside the doorway to be given a little plate of sandwiches and cake with a mug of tea. If you wanted crisps you could buy these additionally.

Being a farming community, the sandwiches were of thickly-sliced ham which had been boiled by the captain's wife, and made up into sandwiches at home. It was natural and organic.

I went over to Claire who was still angry and she stiffened as I approached. I had been taken aback by her outburst on the journey here and wondered what the future would be like if I joined the consultancy team nationally. Then we would be travelling about the country to different venues that might be further away and the logistics of getting there would certainly be more problematic than needing to fix a flat tyre on a simple trip over the hills to Ploughton.

I wondered whether it was me in particular she was annoyed with or whether she was suffering the general stress of the situation. We still had not heard about the project bid and I suppose someone in her school position would need to know about future job prospects well in advance.

I also wanted to know why I wasn't getting the massage like I used to and where our relationship was now going.

I thought I'd open with something neutral. So I asked her about how her scheme with our catering was going.

She said that Esmeralda was now at Scoving. She had been there a week and Rod was very keen to have her work for him.

"So, you don't mean to tell me that it's perfectly good food she's cooking?" I asked. "If so, she's certainly changed her ways."

"Let's put it like this," she said. "From what Alan said, Rod has made some kind of business deal with her. He's put some extra money of his own to finance her to do some fancy stuff for some banquet functions he's got. In return she's moderated what she does for the cricket team."

"Oh yes? Then to reduce the options, I shouldn't wonder? So where does that leave Charlotte and Alan?"

"Charlotte is still catering there, being told what to do by her mum who is being told what to do by Esmeralda. Alan says they have more time together, but he is continually being approached by Rod to transfer across."

"Huh!" I retorted. "So that gives them a terrific army of cooks! Meanwhile we have none! If we get through this, we'll have to play the next match at home and we'll have to provide a tea for that without any tea ladies. I think I'll find that stressful."

"Oh well, trust me."

"Huh! That's what I have been doing and look where it got us. You've lost us a tea lady and have probably lost us a player and maybe all his mates. The whole team could be cut by a third in one go."

She reddened. I was angry at her prevarication and put all my concerns out in the open. I asked, "Tell me straight, what's your real connection to GSS? I've heard it's a company that doesn't exist, and acts as a front to launder project money. Isn't it?"

"Oh, that. That's Sir Richard's company. It does exist. It puts up money for the national project team. It would employ you. There's already finance for your new job there."

"Huh. I'm not sure I trust it."

"If you don't believe me you can ask him yourself," she said as there was the noise of a car engine and Sir Richard's Range Rover came into the field.

We waited in silence for him to park and walk over. Then I asked him directly with some anger still left over from my interaction with Claire, "What really is GSS? Tell me straight."

Sir Richard stopped short of us, and then glanced at Claire and then at me.

He smiled and said, "I see. Been having a deeper think about joining us, eh? Well, GSS is a consultancy built on the specialised knowledge and skills of highly brilliant people who work to pool their abilities. We've got elite experience. We develop solutions for projects and then co-ordinate with other contractors who deliver the services. If you joined us, that is what you would be doing on the sports coaching side. Your sports centre management experience would be helpful. I suppose that's what you want to know. I admit that it might sound uncertain to you, but that is how projects are conceptualised and delivered on a national perspective. We don't always win projects but when we do it's usually very lucrative. You would take your money from the project fees as a whole, as well as from the twenty percent contingency factor. If the project is successful then everybody wins. If you join us, you could go national next year instead of being stuck here in Moxham for the rest of your life. Just think about it."

I wasn't sure what to say in reply, so this allowed him to ask, "Anyway, what has been happening here? Why are you so late with the tea interval?"

I recounted the problems of having to restart the match.

He listened, occasionally raising his eyebrows, then tutted.

"Pete Bairstow again. He's a good bowler. Or he was."

I nodded. "How are the other teams getting on? I thought you would stay at Appleton Water's match until the finish?"

"It has finished. Fardeep finished it for them. He took six wickets for next to nothing with his doosra ball. Then hit fifty in record time. He's getting stronger all the time. Their opponents Parlside, an unknown club from out of the district, barely made sixty. Fardeep opened the batting and hit them everywhere in record time. It was a one-man class act. Incredible."

"Incredible," I echoed. "And just to think that Appleton Water who are now through to the semis will be losing him for their next match because he has to go back to India. At least he might come back next year to give us some more coaching."

So many imponderables. Although we were making progress, I had a funny feeling that it was going to get really difficult soon with the matches going to be against stiffer opposition, and with the unsolved catering question.

"Ah, but, listen, I've been speaking to Fardeep after the match and it seems he's been given some news," said Sir Richard.

"Oh?"

"Yes. We thought all along that Fardeep would be leaving the country to go back to India at the end of July. However, he has some extra weeks' leeway before going. His club in India had signed somebody else who had become instantly available. So he's got a few spare weeks. He could theoretically stay on here for a month if people could fund him. But Appleton Water can't get the money to keep him here for the rest of the season, so whoever has got the money to pay Fardeep can have him for these final four or five weeks of the season coming up."

"Oh, that's wonderful!" I say. "Let's get some money to pay him and then we can have him in our team."

Sir Richard shook his head. "I'm afraid that's impossible. The County Fund has completely gone now. You know yourself how things have deteriorated Sports Centre wise. The swimming pool is closed for refurbishment and might not re-open on schedule because there's no budget left. As for paying Fardeep's wages? No way. He'd need thousands. He's on the threshold of the Indian National side. A player like that. There's no way we could afford it. Particularly at the present time. Fardeep's got money problems with his business at home in Northern India. So he's looking for extra cash and he won't be able to stay on here just for peanuts."

"Can't some clubs form a consortium for coaching with Appleton Water?"

"No way. They've got no money either. Some clubs including industrial clubs like Darbury maybe, but the conditions are so poor there that he might not be tempted."

"Oh God. That's a shame."

"Yes. From our point of view it gets worse."

"Oh?"

"Yes. There's one club that is close to finding the several thousand apparently."

"Oh, which?"

"I don't think you want to know that."

"Go on. Tell me."

"Scoving. Rod is trying to borrow money and put some of his business up as surety. If he can win the Cup it will promote his business and he'll get back his investment money. Teamwork in the building trade. Add to it his lifestyle consultancy and he'll have a fitness empire stretching across the county, and in competition with the council's."

I was dumbstruck.

CHAPTER THIRTY-NINE

Frozen by the news, I could only stare at Sir Richard.

At that point Wicket called, "Come on. Chop. Chop. Let's go. We're fielding. Ploughton's batters are there already."

Most of our team were now on the field, and the Ploughton opening batsmen walked out to start their innings. Wicket was throwing the ball in catching practice to Claire and then threw it to me. I had no time left to talk more to Sir Richard as I threw the ball back and stepped over the boundary onto the field of play.

Ploughton had to get 119 off 40 overs.

I overheard the Ploughton captain say loudly to his team from the pavilion doorway so we might hear. "A gentle pace of three runs an over, lads. We don't need to take any risks. Just take it easy."

However, no sooner had he spoken than Dwayne bowled the first opening batsman. The ball pitched on the line of leg stump and I expected it to be struck away by the batsman for a boundary, but in fact he missed it. It should have been an easy shot to a full-pitched ball.

That occurrence seemed to install some fear into the minds of the opposing team as they came out to bat. It was the captain who appeared next and he played all round a ball from Dwayne, which he almost nicked to the slips.

Alan bowled the next over and although two of his balls were accurate and were met with a stiff defensive reply from the batsman, four of his balls were quite wayward and two of them were struck to the boundary.

The score moved to 20 for 1 and I could sense Ploughton were beginning to gain control. We would have to bowl Ploughton out rather than trying to stop the flow of runs as their target rate had now come down to less than three runs an over.

Wicket changed the bowler to Claire for the first time in the competition. We had seen her bowl accurately in the nets. Claire measured out her run, much to the amusement of the Ploughton players in the pavilion.

"How the hell did they get this far in the competition? They're so bad that they have to send in girls to do their bowling." I heard one of them say from my fielding position near the boundary.

The Ploughton batsman due to receive held up play for a little while.

He stopped her in the middle of her run-up claiming he wasn't ready and he went down the pitch to tap it and check for divots. He wanted to tease her and make her wait.

Eventually the umpire said, "OK, batsman, you've had your time, get ready now."

Claire ran up and bowled a ball which pitched on one of those divots, and swung in to hit him on the pads in front of the wicket.

We all shouted an appeal, but the batsman was looking down at the pitch, tapping down the divots, ignoring us as if nothing had happened. When he did finally look up, he saw that Claire was still standing there with hands on hips alongside the umpire who was holding up his index finger.

"You looked too busy gardening, so I waited till you'd finished and looked up again before I gave you my opinion," said the umpire. "Out – LBW."

The batsman opened his mouth to speak, but seeing both Claire and the umpire glaring at him, he walked slowly back to the pavilion, head down, tapping and gardening the divots along the way as he went. He looked as though gardening was his job, and it had been briefly interrupted by some batting he'd rather forget.

The opposition were now 20 for 2 and this put a slightly different light in their minds, especially as Claire next bowled the captain who had decided to have a swipe at the ball. Evidently their policy on a troublesome pitch was to hit out as much as possible and hope that somebody would succeed. The next few batsmen attempted to do that and perished cheaply, the ball chipping up in the air off a divot into an awkward angle on the bat and being caught in turn by Peter and by Stodgy who were close in on either side of the wicket.

At 60 for 8 they realised that they were not going to do very well. Their last man was the new junior bowler who had replaced Pete Bairstow and he was bowled by the third ball he received from Dwayne.

We came off the field victorious. In the changing room Sir Richard summarised his news for the team, saying in these quarter-finals we had beaten Ploughton, and Dry Langford had beaten Erping Cross, Scoving had beaten Oxburgh, and Appleton Water had annihilated Parlside.

"Fardeep completely destroyed them. None of their top batsmen could pick his doosra, six of them stumped going out of their crease trying to chase it. It spun viciously without warning. They say you can't see any difference in delivery action from his others. I doubt if anyone in the world could play those deliveries of his at the moment. There's just no way you could tell. I've just been on the phone to the Board for the results of the draw. I can tell you now we shall be home to Dry Langford. Moreover, Appleton Water without Fardeep will play Scoving, who are putting in a bid to buy six week's worth of him. If they get him, it'll be a titanic clash between Fardeep and that Zurich bloke."

I came out of the pavilion and Claire was just about to drive off in her car.

"We're at home to Dry Langford next," I said. "Have you sorted the teas out, yet?"

"Not yet. I'm working on it." She didn't unwind the window much.

"I don't suppose there's any chance of another of your massages tonight?"

She turned round and pulled that screwed-up kind of face with an apology down only one side.

"Honestly, Jeremy, I'm sorry I've got so much on for school tomorrow, otherwise I would."

"Oh, yeh, yeh," I pretended to understand. "A lot of work to do at school, in line with another colleague."

She blushed. "None of your business, Jeremy Freeman."

Nevertheless, it was, and she knew it as soon as she had said it. She knew she had to keep me sweet for the sake of the present project and for trying to get me to join GSS later. I knew they needed someone with my sports centre experience.

"I'm sorry, Jeremy, I'm sorry. I shouldn't have said what I did today."

I wanted to say something smart that would hurt her, but I thought better of it. After all, you have to live in peace with people and work with them in future, so I just left it.

On the way home, I called at an off-licence in Moxham to get a few cans of lager and then drove up past St Margaret's School and Appleton Water to my flat a few miles beyond. I felt compelled to slow down as I passed the accommodation block. Claire's car was there and next to it was Mark's silver sports car.

Maybe she might change her mind about things later, but for now things were not going to work out between us.

CHAPTER FORTY

Claire and I were at lunch in Marmaduke's. Our relationship was awkward these days and we did not meet as much as we used to. We had come here today to discuss how we were going to provide the teas for our home semi-final against Dry Langford. Her saying "Trust me" all the time had finally got to me. I had decided to call her bluff.

"What are you going to do?" I asked.

"I'm working on it," she said, taking a bite of her sandwich.

She wasn't as hungry as me. I had ordered lasagne and chips. Charlotte had put it in the microwave and then said from behind the counter "Oh, I've got something else for you," and disappeared into the back.

Claire and I looked at each other across the lunch table. I mime "What?" to Claire as she takes a sip from her large coffee, elbows on the table, both hands either side of the large cup. Staring back at me, she gives a slight shake of her head.

Charlotte reappears with a crockery bowl, glazed with the label "Moxham Council" on the outside. I recognise it from the Sports Centre Kitchen.

"How did you get it?" I asked.

"Esmeralda left it here a few Sundays ago from one of her 'Creations'."

"It figures. Freelancing."

There was a ding from the microwave, and Charlotte came back with my lasagne and chips, plonking it down in front of me with a knife and fork wrapped in a purple serviette.

"How is the cooking at Scoving? We've heard a lot from Alan about how successful Esmeralda is," Claire said to Charlotte.

"Is she? You could have fooled me." Charlotte wiped down the table next to us, moving the salt and pepper pots and the little flower vase and menu around.

"Isn't she?" asked Claire.

"No. No way. Flaming rows all the time between her and Rod. I can't stand it. Best thing for her is to go back to Moxham. Honestly, Jeremy, I don't know how to tell you this as well. Believe me I had nothing to do with it. But Alan is thinking of coming to Scoving and bringing the lads with him. He's thinking of handing in his notice to you. Rod has signed a form for him ready and Alan only has to get you to countersign it. Rod has promised them all specialised coaching from Fardeep."

"No," I said, unwrapping the serviette. "There's no way that's true. Rod's got Fardeep now so he hardly needs anyone else in the team. Alan might get some coaching from Fardeep. Yet it won't be anything more than he's got already – going to one of Fardeep's occasional open coaching days at Appleton Water. And those'll stop soon. However, if Alan wants to go to Scoving and wants me to sign the form then I won't stand in his way. And if Alan wants to ruin his sporting life chasing opportunities that don't exist, he can."

"And as for you, Charlotte," said Claire. "You'll be stuck in the middle. You won't be able to leave Scoving because Alan will be there waiting for an opportunity that he might never get."

"But Alan says he can't stand Esmeralda's food and she should go back to Moxham where she came from in the first place," complained Charlotte. "And then he'll come over to Scoving with me like it should be."

"No, Rod needs Esmeralda for business purposes so I don't think he'll let her go," Claire said.

Charlotte was stunned. "You mean, you mean, Rod won't sack Esmeralda?"

"No. He needs her and we don't want her back," said Claire.

"So Alan and you'll have to eat Esmeralda's teas forever," I said, picking up a salt-cellar and pausing with it.

"You might get put off a career in hospitality permanently," said Claire. "That's not the real thing up there at Scoving. Only one woman's fantasy, a delusion."

"So that's it, then. Isn't it? We're in a right mess. I don't know what to do." Charlotte was reddening.

I shook the salt-cellar over my chips but no salt came out.

"Well, it's obvious what to do," Claire said. "It's obvious."

"What? What?" Charlotte asked.

I looked at the next table. I put the salt-cellar down over there and picked up the fresh one.

"There," Claire pointed to the salt-cellar. "That's what to do. Swap. Come to cook at Moxham."

I shook the fresh salt-cellar from the other table over my chips. It sprinkled out in satisfying plenitude.

CHAPTER FORTY-ONE

We were at home to Dry Langford. They won the toss and batted first, reasoning that they would have first batting use of the new pitch and that their spinners would get more purchase when the pitch became worn later on.

Our pace bowlers Dwayne and Alan got the opening batsmen out, and then we turned to our other bowlers who were medium pace or spinners. A seventeen-year old came to bat when their second wicket fell. Classically coached, he had had private lessons with Fardeep. He played beautifully against all the spin bowling variations of Peter and Anas.

His name was Alexander. No part of the field was left unconquered by his speeding boundaries. Sometimes he would impishly dab the ball. Other times he was so quick-sighted that he would step broadly forward and let his bat flow through.

To be hit for a four by him was not like the brutal beating that other people might give your bowling. Peter and Anas told me afterwards that to be struck for four by him was like being a partner in a beautiful event. That afternoon we felt privileged to watch the skills of a young master at the crease.

Yet though we felt hypnotised by his presence, we knew that this could not be allowed to last. We were the opposition and the more we worshipped him the more set he would become. Therefore, we had to think of a way of getting him out.

Peter and Anas were our spinners, but Dry Langford was a land of spinners. Dusty and arid, the sandy ground the opposing spinners had come from was set on the southern side of a hill so it always dried quickly.

Playing at their home ground, they spent half their time with spinning deliveries. Yet, they were not so skilled at playing fast deliveries, especially left armers like Dwayne. Only their openers had been good at that. They knew their role was to flourish for a few overs in order to see the shine off the new ball. The ones who came after them would be greater players against spin, yet possibly less experienced against fast left-arm bowling.

As Alexander had been brought up on spin and had been coached by Fardeep, a master of spin, then it seemed logical to us that he would be a great spin player who might not be able to play fast bowling so well.

Realising this Wicket brought back Dwayne and instructed him to flick the ball like an off-cutter at first and for us all to say that there was a lot of swing about today with this ball.

"It's definitely moving, Jeremy. You get to second slip," said Wicket aloud so all could hear.

"Now then Dwayne," he shouted down the pitch so Alexander would hear. "Remember what I told you - let's get this really swinging now. See if you can make it swing more."

Dwayne gave a little grunt each time he flicked the ball, in an effort to build up an association in the batsman's mind of his doing a particular action and the swing it would produce.

Dwayne flicked the next one and it moved in towards the batsman off the pitch as before. Alexander executed a glorious on-drive for two runs.

This was ominous for both teams for different reasons. Firstly, it was ominous for us because Alexander was getting better at hitting it. Secondly, it was ominous for Alexander because it showed to us that we were training him to hit the ball how we wanted him to hit it. I might add that, of course, no one in their right mind would want to be punished by a great batsman like this – but it showed us that if we put the ball in certain places then he would willingly oblige by preparing for the ball's turn and hitting with it. Between the grunt and the swing was growing the idea.

The next ball Dwayne, as Wicket had secretly pre-arranged, did not flick it but bowled it straight. Yet he still made a loud grunt.

Alexander had got so primed by the grunt that his bat had begun to search out for the movement already. He didn't seem to realise the swing wasn't there this time until it was too late. Only the outside edge of the bat hit the ball and it deflected straight into my hands at slip. I clutched it to me as an egg, as though I had been entrusted with the young master's life-force. I was privileged, but sad.

After that display I cannot remember the rest other than to say that they managed to get themselves to quite a reasonable total of 130.

Then it was time for tea, a splendid moment.

Charlotte, our new tea lady, made good old-fashioned English ham sandwiches, egg and cress or cheese for vegetarians, tuna mayonnaise cobs, pork pies and sausage rolls. And slices of fruit cake. It was faultless English food.

During the tea interval I overheard Peter on his mobile. "Well, I don't know what you're talking about Steve. I put that exhaust on properly and you're telling me now that he's saying it's fallen off and he wants his money back? No way. No way. I welded that completely top to bottom. You look on the computer and tell me how much oxy I used on that job. I remember I had to change the bottle that day. Two cars he brought in and I did them both. You say he's bringing it back in ten minutes? But I can't be there, can I? I'm playing cricket! You tell him to put it on a ramp if he will and you look at it underneath and tell me if it's not been properly welded and it's all a con on his part. Yeh. Cheers. Cheers. Yeh."

He flipped the mobile case closed and breathed a deep sigh of indignation. "I don't know," he said to himself. "I don't."

Dry Langford opened with a spin attack, as they had no skilled and reliable pace men.

Luke and Simon were used to pace and were not expecting this. They gave catches, and very soon we had lost two wickets for twelve runs. We were chasing 131 to win against one of the top three sides in the league. It did not bode well. Needless to say, with my more defensive batting ability I was demoted to last man.

Anas went in next to bat and often mishit it tantalisingly in the air just beyond the reach of the fielders, whereas Stodgy played a much more controlled and slower game, coaxing the ball around. It was not a great asking rate of just over three per over, but it was the tightness of the bowling and the fact that the ball spun uncontrollably up into the air after hitting the bat that made it so difficult.

After a while Dry Langford changed the bowlers and we hoped they might bring pace on but they did not. They brought on another couple of spinners.

Peter would be in next and was padded up and it was clear his mood had been darkened by his phone call from work. I thought that this would be another of those days when he would be out cheaply. During the inspection match he had been out for just six, his only scoring shot, swinging wildly at fast bowling. Then the bowler had speared in a yorker and he had just swung over it.

He sat watching the match, brooding, when his mobile went again. He checked the number and there was a wary hesitation in his voice as he answered it.

"Yes, hello? Steve? Yeh?" he listened intently, but then he brightened.

"No mate. Fine. Say no more. See. I told you. He was trying to con us, that bloke. Trying to pull a fast one, I knew something had to be wrong. I don't just weld it all up like that and then they fall apart of their own accord. Yes. He's gone over some rocks. Must have done. You're telling me for it to be smashed like that. He was trying to tell us that the welding just fell apart as he was driving along the road in a built up area? No way. See, for that kind of impact, that what you've described, he must have been doing a ton – easy. Well at least fifty and probably straight across those cobblestones at the junctions with the bypass. He did it himself at those junctions and he's trying to cover up and blame us. I expect the cops'll be after him next. He'll be on CCTV. Yeh.yeh. I hope you've sent him packing? Yes, yeh!"

Then a pause. Then "Cheers mate. Ace."

He snapped the mobile shut triumphantly. "Huh!" he shouted, putting the mobile back in his jacket on the hook.

At that moment there was shouting from the middle of the pitch. Stodgy was out trying to deflect one down to third man but only succeeded in giving a catch to a slip fielder.

Peter picked up his battered and dirty bat, jerked his cap on tighter, and strode out confidently to the wicket. I had not seen Peter draw himself up to so full a height since the first day I met him in Mechkwik. Moreover, we needed a hero now at 25 for 3, with over a hundred left to get.

As he took his stance at the crease he looked like he had the power to demolish anything with his bare hands. And he did. In his hands it seemed not a bat, but an exhaust tailpipe with a baffle box he smashed the ball with. We had not seen such hitting since the outdoor nets. The sixes sped from him as though they were from a powerful precision engine. He blasted the car park so much that some of us moved our cars further back out of range.

Peter shouted, "Cop that!" after each six.

By the time he had finished he had blasted fifty-seven and our score was now almost ninety.

However, we still had forty to get. I was last man and I was hoping that I wouldn't be called upon to do something ridiculous like having to strike a handful of runs off the last over with only my wicket to fall and the whole of our campaign and project dependent on my final efforts. How fitting it should be for me to play the innings of my life and yet how risky a burden this would be.

Though the game was still a long way from its climax, I was convinced it would be me who would be there at the end. And I knew the opposition would bring back their best bowlers for this showdown.

I got the charm out of my side kitbag pocket and sat apart from everybody else to concentrate on fusing my mind with its deep sparkle. I did my routine of counting and opening and closing my eyes and slowly built up an impenetrable wall of concentration.

Next I took out my bat to play a few preliminary shadow strokes in preparation and looked at the rubber grip on the handle. It was worn from the tension this season. I would definitely need another grip fitted after today.

With the charm now in my pocket I settled down in my invincible focus to wait for the eventual showdown.

Neil and Wicket carried on the batting attack and they gave many chances to the slips and wicketkeeper, but the ball was spinning too viciously for them to catch it. Eventually it was Claire who, with Alan as her batting partner, scored the winning hit – one of her gentle dabs down between point and the slips for a single.

My batting had not been needed after all, just the power of my wishing. I felt a strange mixture of disappointment and relief. Disappointed that I had not batted and had thus been denied a rightful part in the glory of success. Relief that I had been saved from the ignominy of being exposed as a culprit in the disaster should I have failed.

Dry Langford's wicket-keeper was not as adept as Wicket, and had missed the ball quite a few times, possibly because their bowlers had put so much spin on it. They had given away about twenty-five byes in that total.

Therefore, the kings of spin had been spun out themselves, spinning too hard for their wicketkeeper to reliably catch the ball. We had a motivating phone call from a garage manager to thank for our victory, as well as the peace of mind that one gets when provided with proper cricket food. We were thus into the final.

Sir Richard, standing by his Range Rover, here again to see our last few overs, had just arrived from the other semi-final at Appleton Water.

Claire, Wicket, and I went over to him. He was smiling.

"Congratulations!" he said. "Meanwhile at Appleton Water, that Zurich bloke – Fardeep got him out cheaply. He didn't let him settle. Rod brought Fardeep on as soon as he came to the crease. That's how Scoving won. Fardeep got another five wickets and hit fifty."

"If you see Fardeep, can you tell him to pop by into the sports centre and put a new rubber on my bat handle ready for the match?" I asked. "I presume that although he'll now be the opposition for next month's final he'll still be friendly enough in the meantime to sort out my bat handle. He's got the tool there with him."

"Yes. I'll see him this week," he replied, then with a triumphant glint in his eye he added, "But, in fact, I've got something to tell you. The outcome of the final doesn't really matter."

With a gleam of satisfaction, he brandished a letter from inside his jacket.

"This is from the government's project selection panel, with a covering letter from the County. GSS has won part of the money for the project and will get a first instalment of the six million soon. This is based on our plans, the bid, and our progress. Though it would be nice to win the final and the prize money, we don't need to in order to finalise the project money."

"Hey! That's fantastic! We've got it! Hooray!" rejoiced Claire, jumping and clapping her hands. She snatched the papers from Sir Richard's hands to read.

Wicket said, "Yes, perhaps we don't need to beat them, but I'd like to. We've come all this way now and we need to. I reckon we should fix the beggars after what they've said about me and Moxham in the past. They've claimed to have fresh evidence now about that trophy years ago, but they haven't come forward with it. It's all lies. It's a slur. I say we set out to beat the beggars."

"Well no, we don't have to," said Sir Richard. "Let them have their bit of glory. We've got the project bid money and that's enough. Fardeep needs to be in a winning team for his references for when he gets back to India. It won't look good for him if he failed to win the Enterprise Cup for his club. He is a very proud man and it might break him."

"Are you suggesting," said Wicket, "That we therefore let them win? That we don't try? That's tantamount to match-fixing. We can't have that. No."

"I think what he means," said Claire, "is that there's obviously a lot riding on this for Fardeep. So why don't we accept the fact that he's such a brilliant player and that he's going to win anyway, and not beat ourselves up too much about it?"

"I'm not going to accept nothing!" said Wicket angrily. "Never mind about Fardeep. If he beats us fair and square because he's a good player, which he probably could do, then that's fine. But I'm not going to give in before we start and hand everything to the likes of Rod and Mark. No. I'm going to put everything I've got into this match. We've got the bid money. Now let's get the bloody Cup as well."

"Anyway, did Rod's bid succeed?" Claire asked eagerly, handing the papers back to Sir Richard. "It doesn't say anything about him there. Did he get any money?"

"He got a provisional acceptance of a very small amount. Hardly anything," said Sir Richard.

"Oh," Claire's face fell. "He's put so much in. So much. Rod and Mark have put so much in and they didn't get it."

She shook her head in disbelief, walking away from us, dazed by the news.

CHAPTER FORTY-TWO

On the evening of the Grand Final, I was in my flat looking at Sir Richard's new website and thinking about the future.

It would be a hard wrench to leave Moxham now that I had grown friendly with the people. In particular, I felt as though I had known Ann for years even though I had only been there twelve months.

However, I could sense opportunities out there with Sir Richard's consultancy. Perhaps the reason why Claire was cold to me was that she found this Enterprise Cup stressful. Perhaps she might turn back towards me once it was over and we had won. Mark was only a friendly teaching colleague, I was sure.

A tinny Eine Kleine Nachtmusik started from my mobile on the desk. It was Wicket.

"Hi," he said. "We've our best team ready for the Final tomorrow. Everybody is fit. Fardeep rang me to check how things were going and tell me Rod was ready. It should have been Rod ringing but he won't speak to me directly still. He's delegated Fardeep to. Also seems they've got Mark back in the side."

I stiffened at the mention of Rod's son.

"Yes," he said. "And also Fardeep tells me you're thinking of joining up with their consultancy and leaving us after this."

"Ah, but, I have to think about my future career," I said, scrolling through the list of Sir Richard's projects. "There are some opportunities with them."

"Hah, but you won't get far with that Claire. I know that you're sweet on her, but she's still got Mark no matter what you say."

"Well, I think there's still hope," I said. "She'll come round again."

"No. She'll two-time you behind your back. Take my word for it. You stay here and let her go. We can build the service all up together again. We've got a start now. We need you, you're part of us now."

"Well I'm touched, Wicket, I'm touched. But I haven't helped you much at all. You've done it all yourselves."

"No. We did it all with you and we're not going to lose now. Fardeep will be trying his hardest to beat us, but I'm going to go down fighting against that Rod. And I think I can say that for everyone in the team. Peter will certainly want to settle his score against Mark. If we win, the world will be our oyster and you will be a big part of it. Now that Charlotte's the tea lady, we've got a stable young group. We'll be revived and important. We can't give in."

"I'm glad to hear it, but I still don't think you'll need me next year."

"We will if we lose. We'll still have a share of the bid money, but only that. That's not fully come all the way through yet. And if you're gone then the council won't want to spend the money on a bunch of losers like Moxham again. They could divert it from source at County Level to another part of the service like Scoving or Appleton Water. That would be bad. After the match Sir Richard, Fardeep, and Claire will be off – they'll have done their job. So I say you should stay because you're the only person who can rescue us next year if we fail tomorrow."

"Look, don't start to think about what would happen if we lose. Keep focused, for goodness' sake. I'll see you tomorrow. Good night."

We had to win. It was not just a Moxham thing, it was my future escape route.

CHAPTER FORTY-THREE

The morning of the Grand Final. I went to the Moxham Sports Centre to pick up my kitbag. I unsheathed the bat out of the compartment on top of the bag. Fardeep had done an excellent job of putting a new grip on the handle. It was a nice green colour, as green as an English summer cricket field. The whole bat seemed refreshed. It balanced well in my hands and felt as though there would be plenty of runs in it.

"Fardeep came and did it yesterday," said Ann. "You missed him. He did it here in the staff locker room. He didn't have to take it to a workshop or anything. He rolled it onto a wooden stick and then rolled it off onto the handle. But I didn't trust him. I was with him all the time except when the phone went."

"Well, you don't have to worry about Fardeep," I said. "He's done a really good job with this and I'd trust him with my life."

"Huh! I wouldn't. I'll be along to watch the final today, though. Charles will cover for me. I'm looking forward to seeing us win."

"Well, a win's not so important now that we've got some of the project money. In fact, as regards the future, now Moxham's got the project money I can choose what to do either way. If we win then I'm sure Moxham could carry on without me and I might go and join the consultancy."

"Oh no, don't go," Ann reddened and took a step towards me. "Why would you want to do that? No, stay here. I don't want to stand in your way, but don't go."

"I've been thinking," I said. "Maybe Sir Richard and Claire are right. Sir Richard said there's a lot of work to be done nationally. There are lots of places round the country that didn't succeed with their bids. Lots of places that will need the money and would have got it if they had had a determined firm of consultants like GSS behind them. After all, Sir Richard's done a lot here to liven up this area. It's all benefited from his input, as well as from Fardeep's and Claire's."

"Huh, oh no. They've not done much. There's been more from the Friends of Moxham I should think. And, as for Rod and Mark, they've contributed a lot behind the scenes, and hardly got any money back from the bid for their efforts. That's what irks me."

"Oh how, exactly? What have they done?"

"Well, for instance, Rod has single-handedly put in his bid without help from others and against a lot of opposition. He's also put a lot of his own money into Scoving, and he's paid Fardeep's wages out of his own money. Also paid for coaching and hire of Appleton Water for some of his team. In all, several thousand pounds. So you'd think that if anyone deserved to win the Cup it would be him."

"No. I can't stand him. His son tried to kill me."

"No. It was a slip-up. He apologised. You saw how shocked he was."

"I couldn't see. I was only half-conscious."

"Well I know. I've known the family for some time. You've only been here for a year, like Sir Richard, Claire, and Fardeep. Me and Rod's wife Irene go back years. I know they wouldn't do anything like that - it just slipped. It looked bad, but it just slipped."

"Claire thought it was on purpose."

"She made it worse. She got upset about it and stirred it all up."

"No. She didn't. She was right."

"What? She's a bitch! She'll lead you up the garden path, she will. Stay here with me. If we lose, we'll need you even more then."

CHAPTER FORTY-FOUR

Appleton Water Sports Resource Centre. Little did I think that I would be coming up the drive here to play in a cricket cup final instead of giving one of my private tennis lessons.

I drove past a sign saying "PLAYERS AND OFFICIALS ONLY" along a narrow driveway that ran off round the back of the main building. It finished in a smaller car park by the cricket pavilion. Some of the grass there had been laid over with grid-panelling to form a honeycombed hard-standing that would accommodate an extra dozen cars.

I parked and went to look inside the pavilion whose security-shuttered windows were just being raised.

There was a large middle central hall with a servery and small kitchen on the back wall with a ladies' toilet, and on either side wall the entrances to the changing rooms, each equipped with their own toilets and showers. They were grades above the rustic cabins without proper toilets that we had been used to.

Around the walls were photographs of Appleton Water cricket teams through the ages and a glass case in one corner with a bat, a ball, and a framed newspaper cutting about the outstanding performance of one of their past heroes.

Inside our changing room the white walls were unblemished, the floor swept clean and the varnished wooden benches had ample storage space underneath for our bags.

I looked out of the window at the bright early September day. We were due to start at twelve o'clock and it was now eleven-thirty. A small crowd was gathering, many of whom had brought their own chairs, and were opening their lunch boxes. There were at least two dozen people whom I had not seen before and there was still half an hour to go.

What had this crowd come to see? They had certainly never come to see Moxham play. Although we had seen extra faces at the

Inspection Match, I had attributed that to the publicity and the Friends of Moxham.

I stepped back outside. As I passed a pair of old men in short-sleeved shirts with floppy hats and sunglasses in adjacent deckchairs, I overheard one say, "Yes, well, he hit fifty – did you see that? And he did some fantastic bowling as well to knock us out. Of course, if only we had the money! I think we should have kept him on our side."

I realised that they were talking about Fardeep.

Just then Fardeep's little brown saloon pulled up. As he got out he looked tired and worried, not his normal self.

"Hi, what is the matter?" I asked.

"Jeremy, I have worries," he frowned. "I have to sort out some business interests at home. This game can't last very long. I have to catch a plane down at Heathrow. In order to do that I must be on the evening train from York. So I must get the 7.10 from Moxham. I have luggage in the hotel lobby and will be off as soon as I can. I am under great pressure from my family."

I thought he usually polishes the opposition off in half an afternoon - but if he's in a hurry, how long will it last?

"My family, they expect me to win all the time because I am so good. You have got the bid money through so it is not so important to you to win, but Rod did not get as much as he wanted and he has sunk his business into this now. There is so much upon my shoulders that I cannot afford to lose. You know, he has spent two thousand pounds of his own money to develop the club when the council has given him nothing. Also, he has paid me one thousand for match fees this month and he has put another three thousand at the bookmakers on this match. All his family business money. So I cannot fail him."

I had never seen Fardeep like this. He barely looked at me, interspersing looking into the far distance with shuffling his feet, and looking at the ground, and shaking his head sorrowfully.

"Also I think that Mark, his son, is depressed. This I am certain. He is fed up with his own performance with the ball, being bossed around by his father so much. He has not been his own man. He has listened to people against his better judgment, and upset Claire."

I was sad for Fardeep, but there again I wanted to win to justify our efforts with the project. To show everyone that the club they had seen born on that Inspection Day was not just an idle idea that would come to nothing and squander folk's efforts and money.

We were interrupted by a little white van that pulled up with the words "Fiora Catering" on the side, and Esmeralda sprang out in her dazzling bright red dress.

"Hi guys!"

"So you are catering here today?" I asked.

"Yes, But I prefer the main building, not here. There is a good kitchen over there."

She looked round the field.

"Ah I see a small crowd is gathering already," she said. "Well I didn't realise I would be expected to provide an exhibition fare. They didn't tell me that. I've been given no extra help other than my usual Scoving staff."

"Ah yes," she stretched to her full height and breathed in deeply. "I feel a speciality coming on today. We really need the press here." Then, noticing a man wearing a sunhat in a deckchair holding a camera, she called out. "Yoo-hoo! Are you press? Do you want to interview me?"

The man looked round behind him to see whom Esmeralda was waving to.

"I think they're here for the cricket," I said, seeing some of them were already eating some sandwiches and crisps they had brought with them.

"Yoo-hoo! Go and get your reporter friends. Tell them. This is the great Fiora Catering. I am Esmeralda, as you know. With two a's and two e's. Not three e's. It is Spanish for emerald. You see. Emerald, not Emereld. It is a very precious stone, as you know. Get your camera ready now."

"But I'm only taking some holiday snaps," shouted the man. "Just me and the wife."

"What? Oh! I see. Very well. You can interview me later then." She turned stiffly away towards the back of her van.

"Need a hand unloading?" I asked. Maybe this was a rare occasion for me to see inside it. She always guarded the inside well and would only let people see a few of the things in there. She half-opened one of the back doors to her van and pointed to a stack of cardboard boxes near the back door.

"OK. Do you guys mind taking those into the kitchen for me? That'd be swell."

I got one box, Fardeep got the other, and she swiftly closed the van again.

"OK. You guys, into the kitchen. Lead the way."

As we entered the kitchen, she uttered a cry of disgust.

"Huh!" she said. "There's no gas. Now guys, before anything else, would you know how to turn on this electric? Is there a main switch somewhere? I don't like too much electric, and I am used to using the direct flame of gas. How am I supposed to know where the sockets are? Where is the switch? Oh! Don't I know it? You English, you're so antiquated."

She put a hand to her forehead.

I threw some switches that appeared to have no effect. Fardeep also went around looking in the cupboards for a master switch and fuse box.

"Guys, I am so late and so stressed! Myself, I just cannot possibly imagine you working for me. How can I create my fabulous creations here if you guys cannot even turn on any electric? Huh!"

"Look we don't work in kitchens – it's not our job to do this kind of thing," I said stiffly.

Finally, we found the master switch. It was there in front of us, disguised as a cooker switch.

"Hah. Definitely not the Ritz, but it will have to do. Now there's just two other boxes, guys."

We went across with her and she once again opened only one door and rummaged around inside the van without letting us see what else was there. Finally, she stepped back and motioned us to two cardboard boxes she had wrestled near the rear door. Mine was cold with a smell of fish.

"Put them on the table. I'll follow you in a minute when I've locked up and parked it away from the action."

We put our boxes down on the table in the centre of the room and Fardeep asked me "How are you getting on with the charm?"

"Very well. It's been most helpful at our matches. It helped me concentrate."

"And the new grip? You like it?"

"Fine."

"Remember to hold it properly. I could see by the way it was worn that your bottom hand was very tense. You should relax it more. It is not tennis."

"How do you mean?"

"Well you need to hold it much lighter on the handle with the bottom hand. Like this."

Seeing a cucumber sticking up out of one of the cardboard boxes, he seized it firmly with his left hand and held it lightly with his right.

"You see like this." He motioned a forward drive. "If you hold it so then all the work is done by the top hand, and it can't get out of control with the shot. Here, see that tomato?"

He pointed to a group of vegetables in one of the boxes.

"Toss that onto my bat and I'll show you what I mean," he waved the cucumber ready from across the other side of the table.

I tossed the tomato and he hit it back to me. I caught it.

"Howzat!" I shouted.

"Ah yes," said Fardeep. "Notice how I had hit it in the air because I had a tight bottom hand, swooping it into an arc. Toss it again and I will now grip it lighter with my bottom hand and so my top hand will do all the work and angle the bat forward so the ball stays down. Bowl it now."

Once again, I tossed the tomato to him and this time he hit it down hard onto the table. It splattered.

"See" he said. "The ball is kept down."

Just at that moment, Esmeralda came back in after locking her van.

"Hey! What are you doing, guys? That's food!"

"Yes," I said. "We are just helping you unpack."

"Yes, well guys, I don't need you to damage the salad. Thanks, but I'll take over. Huh."

She took the cucumber out of Fardeep's hands.

"Er, if that's it, we've got to get changed and ready to play." I said, exiting rapidly.

CHAPTER FORTY-FIVE

I went back to get my bag out of the car and saw the silver Mazda MX-5 parked under a tree round the back of the pavilion. It was well away from all the others, like it was on a special mission there.

There was some movement in the car. I put my bag down behind my car and pretended to rummage in it. I only had to look up a small way from behind my car to see Mark was kissing someone in the front seat. I recognised the blond hair. It was Claire.

I felt a pang of anger attack my heart. I knew all along but had blanked it out of my mind. I had been uneasy but had believed her when Claire had said that Mark was a liar and meant nothing to her. Now she was the liar. They both were. They disgusted me.

I wanted to go and bang on their car roof and shout at them, "You bastards!" However, I held back. Surely, that would be going down to their level.

It had been her behaviour at bottom all along. To have lured me into the project and then to have dropped me when it was announced the project had succeeded. Or was it her plan even to have dropped me? Indeed, had she dropped me a long time ago and kept up the pretence? Like Rod had said, was that not just a lover's tiff I had seen at the Inspection Match? They had obviously got back together again and once I was on board with the project and my back was better, there was no need from her point of view to be giving me any special attention.

I slunk away back into the pavilion with my bag, and pondered the truth. How could I possibly join her now in the consultancy, touring the country? I had been well and truly stitched up here. She had lied to me all along. She had been in love with Mark all this time and her friendliness towards me was just to get me on board with the project and for her and the rest of them to get their cut of the project money.

If I joined the consultancy there was still no guarantee that I would get closer to Claire. It could be a battle all the time.

Well, she can go off with him. I don't feel that I have the stomach now to react much with her. I might join the consultancy, but if so, I will be very wary of being with her. Whether she will change her mind later, I don't know. If I hung around with the consultancy team then she might come back to me eventually when she gets fed up with Mark.

It was not for me to judge her. I would leave her to the company of Mark. Two liars together.

As no one else from our team had arrived yet, I put my bag down in the changing room and came out to see Ann who had just arrived and was talking to Rod at the bottom of the steps.

"Looking forward to a good day, Jeremy?" asked Rod, arms akimbo. His smooth tanned skin and assertive manner exuded the confidence of certain victory.

"Oh yes, definitely," I said. "And you've got a lot dependent on this, or so I've heard?"

"Ah, yes. Private money and proud of it. Not public money like you. Living off the taxpayer and being paid to play tennis all day long."

"Huh, no, we are providing a service," I said. "It's a valid job. Just like building contracting."

"No. It's not. Consultancy isn't contracting. Contracting is a fair day's work for a fair day's pay. Consultancy is thinking of a number, and multiplying it by ten to get your cut out of it. Then hoodwinking the government into giving it to you, and then making an enormous profit by selling it on down the line to other firms who have to do their bit on a shoestring to make ends meet. No way."

Ann interrupted. "Please Rod, don't get too worked up."

Then to me she said, "You just think about what you're going to be doing if you do leave. You'll be going into the lions' den. You need to stay here and manage our share of the project money. There's no one else who could do it as well as you."

Mark and Claire came round the corner. Mark stopped and put his bag down whilst Claire carried on into the pavilion to get changed in the ladies.

Mark turned to me. Instinctively I shied away from him. He had hurt me and offended Claire and I didn't feel like speaking to him.

"Jeremy. I'm sorry about that day. I didn't mean it to get out of hand like that."

I was silent.

Rod brushed off the matter. "Yes, well, we all made mistakes that day. No harm done."

I let them carry on. I was damned sure that I hadn't made any mistakes myself, and I didn't have to say that aloud to believe it. I didn't need to hear them say sorry to prove it was me who was innocent and wronged against. However, I did need to hear them say they were sorry in order to forgive them.

"I'm sorry to Claire as well," Mark said. "It's difficult when you upset people and then you realise that you have to work with them. I've found it difficult. For a while we were walking past each other at work, not speaking. I'll never do it again. OK?"

Mark offered a hand.

Like a bullied victim, I grudgingly took it. We shook and smiled, and there was a silence as everybody had said what they had to say and then stood there expecting something else. It never came. I wasn't about to say any more. I just shrugged and went back into our changing room.

The rest of our team came in the next few minutes in vans and cars. Peter brought two of the lads, Anas and Jafar; Wicket brought Alan and Dwayne. The rest of the team arrived soon after. Charlotte came with her mother Margaret to help Esmeralda.

We lost the toss and Scoving batted first. Rod batted well but did not make 50. He was out for 49, caught at extra cover by Luke off the bowling of Jafar.

Fardeep scored very slowly. It was clear his mind was somewhere else. He gave several chances to fielders. On one occasion, he tried to free himself from the shackles of his thoughts by attempting a desperate shot that was almost caught near the boundary. Occasionally he would hesitate over a run, at other times he would speed up and shout in panic when he thought his partner slow. I was sorry for him, how the preoccupation with his worries and business and other people's affairs had affected the performance of this great man. Finally, he was put out of his torment by being bowled by Claire for thirty.

During the play, Wicket attempted a diving catch to try to dismiss Fardeep, but he fell awkwardly. I noticed that after that he was sometimes hesitant when walking between overs to keep wicket at the other end, gingerly testing his calf muscle, stretching to keep it supple, trying to extend its working life that afternoon.

As we walked off the field together after the forty overs, I noticed he was hobbling even more.

"What is it? Are you all right?" I asked.

"It's going to be a problem, I think, Jeremy. But let's see later."

As we reached the pavilion, the scoreboard updated the score. Scoving had made 140 for 8. Thus, we were set a high target, and up against Fardeep's bowling as well.

The tea was a grand affair. For the first time ever we had a proper plated tea, where we sat on either side of two long tables, one team to each in the large middle room.

On the plate in front of each person's place was already set a slice of chicken breast, a slice of dried fish and a dollop of pink sauce.

On the middle of each table were piles of open sandwiches on plates, and bowls of fruit salad.

Not surprisingly, people rarely touched the fish portion. We all agreed that the chicken breast was delicious. It was Esmeralda's famous marinaded chicken. In fact, that and the fruit salad was the only dish that I had seen Esmeralda make and I wondered if, despite all her self-promotion, that was the only dish she could do. Perhaps it had been different people's reactions to variations of the same dish that had given her the reputation of providing a variety.

Though half of each team had their backs to the other team, this did not stop Claire and Mark turning round and feeding each other with titbits from their plates.

After tea, Luke and Simon set about trying to make the 141 required to win.

Faced with such a large total we had to attack fast so I knew that I would be batting last as there were more capable batsmen than me. Nevertheless, I reasoned that because it was a tough task I should get the charm out and start to meditate on it early so that my mind would be fully prepared when the time came.

I reached into the side pocket of my kitbag but it did not come into my hand.

I drew out the packets of mints, the spare boot studs, the little spanner, the scissors, mini-bottle of Savlon, the first aid plasters, and put my hand in once again. Nothing else.

I touched my cricket trouser pockets in case I had already absent-mindedly put the charm in there. It wasn't there.

I checked the other pockets in my kitbag. Just an abdominal protector in one, just a bottle of water in the other. Nothing. Nothing visible in the main compartment under my pullover and plastic bag that I brought my boots in.

I checked my jacket hanging on its hook and my jeans. Nothing.

I had a dread feeling that some awful event was about to happen and that we might lose the match all because of this.

I came back outside and slowly sat down next to Ann on the bench. The rest of the team, including Wicket nursing his outstretched leg, was scattered about on the grass out of hearing of us, intent on watching our batters in action.

"What is it?" she asked.

"The charm. It's gone."

"Gone?"

I nodded.

Her eyes narrowed. "It's that Fardeep, I'll bet. He doesn't want you to win. He's a scheming devil."

"No, surely not."

"Yes. He's got money problems. It's well known. I said never trust him."

She sat up straight as a thought occurred to her. "I know when it was. It was when he was doing your bat the other day. The phone went and I only left him alone for a minute. He got into your bag, the devil. It must be him!"

Wicket stretched his leg out and rubbed his hamstring, grunting, but didn't turn round.

I whispered back to Ann. "It can't be him – he wouldn't do that."

"You don't know. I bet he would. No money. Business collapsing in India. Not in Test Side again. He needs to win. He's got the motives."

"It doesn't make sense. He's my coach."

"He taught you to use it. He knows your weakness. He that giveth can also taketh away."

She glanced through the pavilion doorway. "That's their changing room. It's open. They're all out fielding. There's no one in there. I can see there's a bag open on the floor with an Indian sticker on it. It's open."

I glanced round at our team idling on the grass. Still all were intent on watching Luke and Simon who were finding the opposition's opening bowlers a struggle.

"Watch out for me," she whispered, getting up. She paused to make sure that everyone's attention was on the game, and then slunk into the opposition's changing room.

Luke pulled a ball for a single and we all applauded.

Peter switched his legs over and asked Wicket, "How many balls left in this over?"

Wicket said, "Three."

Peter said, "I think I'll get up and go to the loo at the end of this over."

Alarmed that Ann might be discovered by Peter walking past I waved to her but she didn't see me. She was too intent on looking through the bag.

Luke hit the next ball for a single, and then Simon played the next defensively.

I coughed loudly and Ann turned. I waved for her to get out of there fast. She crept back out to sit next to me. A second later, the final ball in the over was played defensively and Peter got up and walked swiftly past us.

"It's not there," she whispered to me. "I've looked in the whole lot. Bag and coat. Nothing."

The anguish on my face must have been obvious to her. She put a hand on my shoulder.

"Don't worry Jeremy, love. You can do this. You can win without it."

"No. I can't. I've got into a routine now. I can't concentrate on the ball without it. I'm so used to the routine. It's not magic, but it seems like it to me now. That's how I learnt to play. If it all comes down to the final last man and me then I'm afraid I'll fail."

"No Jeremy. Have faith in yourself. You can do it."

She thought a moment, and then another idea hit her.

"Look," she said. "Fardeep says he's going to Heathrow late tonight straight from here without going back to his flat. That means that his luggage must be in Moxham in the Imperial Hotel near the railway station rather than up in the outskirts of Scoving somewhere."

"Yes. So?"

"Charlotte is here watching Alan. She is not on duty."

"Yes. So?"

"So the hotel is down on staff and they'll take people off the reception desk and general duties and put them in the café. They'll only have one person on reception now in the afternoon. Now, before the evening rush."

"So?"

She took a plastic discount card out of her wallet.

"I used to work there years ago. I know where the baggage store is, and it's still the same simple Yale lock that can be slipped back with a sheet of plastic. All you have to do is to phone the desk up at the precise moment when I tell you and distract them. Keep them busy and I'll get in there. In and out quick. His bags'll have Air India stickers on them."

"No, no. You can't. It's illegal. It's dishonest," I said.

"What? Dishonest? He's been dishonest to you! Can't you see that? I'm not stealing anything. It's yours all along. Just getting back what is rightfully yours."

I could not believe that Fardeep would do something like that: to break his own cricket coaching code and sabotage a pupil's performance for his own financial ends.

"Look, now, there isn't much time," she said. "Come on. If you want Moxham to win then you have to have that charm to concentrate your mind when you are called upon. Unless you can do it with something else? A rabbit's foot or horseshoe or something?"

"Well, no. It's not magical or supernatural or anything like that. It's just what I'm used to. Just how I've trained myself to concentrate. There's no time to start to do it with anything else now. It would take days to build it up."

"Precisely. Look." She brought a tattered glossy leaflet out of her bag and thrust it into my hands.

"Imperial Hotel. There is the telephone number. Just ring them, say you're thinking of booking, and ask them a load of questions. Like, what is the menu for today? What will it be tomorrow? What time do they stop serving it? How many rooms overlook the moors and how many overlook the town, and stuff like that. That should keep whoever's on duty busy for ages so that I can get in and out."

"Ah, but..."

"Look. I'll ring you on the mobile when I'm there and ready to go in."

"But it's a crime. Breaking and entering."

"Never mind. It's a crime what he did. I can see you need it back. It's yours. They don't deserve to have a good man like you with them if this is how they behave. But I shan't stand in your way if you want to go off with them. I just want to see you right. I don't want you taken advantage of like they have done. Roping you into this, then ditching you because it suits them."

And then, she did a surprising thing. A thing I didn't expect. She took hold of me and kissed me. I was stunned.

It wasn't a kiss of manipulation or of fleeting playfulness like Claire.

It was a kiss of genuine affection.

It was a last kiss by someone setting out to make a sacrifice for another and to risk being caught committing a crime.

I was overwhelmed by how much my success and peace of mind must mean to her and could only watch her go to her car and nod at me as she started the engine.

It now all began to make sense. Her sacrificing that day with her friend back in February to put up all the notices when she didn't have to. Staying behind for extra shifts for the evening nets to help me when she didn't have to. Her misgivings over the project team, and how she felt that they had all suddenly come into the area together indicated their conspiracy. How I had been used by Sir Richard, enchanted by Claire, with a fake car crash no doubt, and drawn in by Fardeep. Ann had been right all along and had not wanted me to leave. I knew I wasn't infatuated with her like I had been with Claire, but I did feel a sense of smoothness when she was about. With Claire, the world was often a struggle, alternating ecstasy with depression. Ann was making a sacrifice for me, a sacrifice that Claire would never do.

As I watched her drive away I wondered whether I would next see her in police handcuffs and why I hadn't tried to stop her. Damn it! I was her manager. I couldn't let this go on. Yet I couldn't leave the game. I must take my chances here, and master my concentration if called on at a crucial stage.

I turned back to the game. They had changed the bowler and brought on Mark. He slowly loped up to the crease to bowl his first ball well within himself. It was off target, and Simon cut it for a boundary square of the wicket. Mark's head went down, and he kicked at the ground.

"Come on, come on, get focused, Mark!" shouted Rod.

Mark tried again. It was another bad ball, this time down the leg side, and Simon flicked it away for four.

"Come on! Come on! What's the matter? Get back on it!"

"OK. OK, Dad. I'm on it!" Mark shouted back.

Mark's next ball was another off-target, but this time Simon only managed to play it into the covers for just one run. Mark bowled his fourth ball and Luke played this away confidently for a single.

The next two balls Mark bowled were just patted away by each batsman for a single. Twelve off the first over, and Rod came over to say something to Mark who then took his cap roughly from the umpire, and strode off to his fielding position on the boundary.

The next over was bowled by one of their less regular bowlers and only three runs were scored from it.

Mark came up to bowl his second over and there was a lot of discussion between himself and Rod whilst Mark was handing his cap to the umpire.

From my position at the pavilion, I couldn't hear it, but Rod was pointing and setting his field with great precision.

Eventually he decided on two fielders on the boundary either side of the playing area: covers and midwicket. Rod, at first slip next to the wicket keeper, was at one of the few close-catching positions.

After all this discussion, Mark shook his head, walked back to his start, and ran up to bowl. He hesitated in his delivery stride and lost control. The ball flew over the batsmen's head.

"No ball!" the umpire shouted with one arm outstretched.

He started his run-up for the next ball, but stopped after a couple of steps, and turned back. He shook his head and repeatedly swung his arm, trying to smooth out his action.

He turned and ran up to bowl yet again. Again the tic in his action, and the ball whistled over the batsman's head again.

The umpire signalled no ball again, and said loudly, "Come on now, you'll have to be taken off if you continue like this."

"Come on now, concentrate!" shouted Rod.

He tried again, but this time as he delivered the ball he collapsed his front leg too soon, making him drop the ball short on the off side. It was easily hit away for four through the covers.

We cheered.

I was glad at this, to see our score improved, and glad that Mark was doing so badly with this nervous tic he had developed. His arms flew sideways in exasperation as his next ball was well struck again by Luke and Simon. Another six runs off the rest of that over making another twelve in all. Yet only one run from the next over by the bowler at the other end. Obviously Luke and Simon were saving themselves up to attack Mark's overs.

The pressure was mounting on Mark to perform like his father wanted. Yet a third over by Mark produced more runs and the score had risen to 30 off 10 overs, and we now required 111 to win off 30 overs.

Cricketers talk about the score of 111 being significant and being associated with the fall of wickets. But at this point 111 were not the runs achieved so far, but the further runs that needed to be scored. It proved to be equally significant, however. For when Rod called Mark up to bowl the next over in the sequence Mark shook his head and pointed to Fardeep.

Rod had persisted with his son and delayed the introduction of the match-winning Fardeep, content in his belief that Fardeep would rescue any situation he was presented with as soon as he came on to bowl.

Fardeep immediately set about directing his field. Several men in close catching positions, and three people only on the boundary: one at square leg, one behind the bowler at long on, and one across from the batsman in the covers on the off side.

As I watched my hero bowl I couldn't believe that he knew where the charm was and was responsible for it.

I wanted to go out and confront him, let him reassure me it wasn't true, but I couldn't interrupt a match. Yet what if Ann was wrong and I had just lost the charm after all? Simply genuinely misplaced it, or indeed, if it was another person who had taken it?

No. I couldn't be sure. I could only sit there and brood on the possibility of it being Fardeep.

I tried to concentrate on thinking back to what it was like to meditate with it, but my anger and uncertainty about the whole affair was interfering with any vestiges of an image I could create.

The action on the field served only to increase my tension. As in the match against Dry Langford, Luke and Simon were not used to spin bowling and were quickly out caught by the close fielders off Fardeep's bowling.

However, Anas and Jafar came in to bat and played Fardeep's deliveries quietly enough so the score trickled along, 40 for 2 off 15 overs, still needing 101 off 25 overs.

At 50 for 3 Fardeep bowled Jafar and this brought Stodgy Joe to the crease who played steadily until he was also out bowled at 60 for 4.

Eighty-one were needed off 20 overs when Peter came to bat.

At that moment, I heard the sound of Eine Kleine Nachtmusik from our changing room.

I went inside to answer it.

"Right. I'm in the lobby now," said Ann. "Remember what you have to do. Just keep the receptionist talking."

"Ann, listen, you don't have to."

"I do. I want to. You'll see now I was right all along. Then you'll stay. You'll stay here with me. Remember me."

Her voice was calm. I knew at that moment that she must think deeply of me to be doing this. Risking her job and her livelihood and freedom to restore to me just a little whim of a thing that I had been trained in all ignorance to rely on.

"But Ann."

"What?"

I paused then said, "Thanks."

"OK. Phone up now."

She was so sure she was right that Fardeep had trained me all along for this moment as a defensive batsman who could not be got out, and then as his masterstroke, he would remove the charm to pull the plug on my performance. What better than that as a failsafe trick to win? I still couldn't believe it, but I certainly couldn't doubt that something had gone seriously wrong with the project team for it all to turn out like this. I had been outsmarted in my position of manager, and it was clear that I had been manipulated. All along Ann had been right.

Behind me, through the open changing room doorway, there was a shout of "Good shot!" and applause. Peter was beginning to let fly, and I was missing the spectacle.

I pulled out the hotel pamphlet and dialled the number, then turned round to face the wall to concentrate.

"Moxham Imperial Hotel," came the woman's plum voice.

"Ah yes, I was thinking of maybe booking and I wanted to be sure of what your menu was like."

I could hear the music of the hotel lobby and various people talking in the background.

"Well, we have a fully resourced menu that is available a la carte and haute cuisine with twenty-four hour room service. We specialise in the highest quality game when in season and we have a full vegetarian menu."

"Ah yes, what form of vegetarian menu? Do you do vegan, for instance?"

"Yes sir, we cater for all tastes and diets. Our chef can prepare food to all medical diets and we have a TV Celebrity chef on call for that special occasion. What particular diet were you requiring?"

"Er, it's very specialised. It's the …" And I looked round the room for inspiration.

There was another shout from outside of "Good shot!" and "Run them up!", "Two there!"

"Yes. It's the Slazenger Diet. Very specialised."

"Oh, yes, can you tell me what it is?"

"It's very specialised, as I've said. You have to have everything pure."

"I'm sure we can accommodate that sir. Purity is one of our quality concerns."

"Yes. Quite so. And what time are your evening restaurant hours?"

"Seven till eleven for a fully waitressed service, but there are snacks in the bar and a room service which specialises in individual gourmet food available twenty four hours a day every day."

"I see. Yes. Now. Can you tell me about the views there? I know it is very good walking country."

"Yes, sir. The hotel is situated on the lower edge of the moors and you can see the Old Man Tor from our windows."

"Is that all of the windows you can see the hills from?"

"All of the bedrooms to the rear of the hotel have a view over the mountains."

"Yes, but precisely how many of the rooms have that rear view?"

"I believe that all the rear windows have views, sir."

"Ah yes. Just how many is that. I might be coming in a group."

There was a pause as if she was consulting a document. "Well, sir, there are … twenty seven …with rear views I believe."

"Yes, and how many without the view?"

"Well, that would be the remainder. Let me see…Hey! Stop! Guests aren't allowed in there! What have you got there? Stop! Stop! Sorry sir, I'll ring you back. "

The line went dead.

I wondered if they had chased Ann, or called the police. She might have been able to elude them because she knew all the backstreets around there. On the other hand, they could have caught her. She might have miscalculated the number of staff on duty.

Stunned. I put the phone back in my pocket and eased my way back outside, careful not to attract the attention of others for I didn't want them be able to be place me on the phone at the time of the Robbery. They might have my mobile number come up on their screen and might suspect me as part of a distraction. My phone call and the strange questions might be too much of a coincidence. They would be able to trace me and prosecute me as part of the Imperial Hotel Robbery Gang. As an alibi I would say, how could it have been me when I was with the rest of the team watching the cricket match all the time? Someone could have taken my phone.

I slipped quietly back onto the bench behind everyone to see Peter begin to hit Fardeep's bowling for six as he had done to the other bowler, shouting "Hee haw, cop that!"

Anas tried to copy him but he was out, bowled in attempting a big hit.

This brought Alan to the crease.

At this point Fardeep had still two overs of his allocation to bowl and 60 runs were needed off 15 overs with 5 wickets left.

I was beginning to feel that this was an achievable target for our team. Rod was desperately trying to motivate his players, clapping his hands between overs shouting, "Keep it up lads! Keep going!"

Then I saw Fardeep go across and speak to Rod and the next over Mark was brought back to bowl in his place.

I did not expect this. I thought that Mark had decided he had finished for the day because he had lost control. Fardeep could sense a piece of strategy that had escaped Rod.

Peter by now was very confident and hitting out cleanly and hugely. However, Mark, as in the Inspection Match, bowled a yorker to him that splayed his stumps. He was out for 25. Forty were still needed off ten overs with four wickets left.

I expected to be last in the batting order, but Wicket said to me from his lying position on the grass. "This muscle is still playing up, Jeremy, so I won't be any good at running. You must go in ahead of me at Number Ten."

"But you're so much better than me," I said. "And that might make all the difference if it comes down to it. Surely you can have a runner?"

"It won't be the same. Runners get in the way and make things complicated. Best avoid them if we can. No, you go in at Number Ten."

I had expected to have at least a quarter of an hour more before I had to go in, or before Ann came back, but now time had been shortened. I sat down and desperately tried to concentrate on my memory of the charm, but without its physical presence I still could not summon up the same mood state. I certainly would not last very long if I had to bat with a mind as unsettled as this.

Claire joined Alan out in the middle. She played beautifully with a flowing, graceful cover drive. It seemed like part of a dance with a lovely crisp follow-through of the bat. There was a sumptuous smooth action as she just leaned on the ball and it sped away.

Alan was next out, bowled for five attempting a big shot. Then Dwayne went to join Claire.

My mind had been paralysed by the awful task that lay ahead of me. I alternated between trying unsuccessfully to visualise the charm and pacing about fearing the worst had happened in the hotel lobby.

Dwayne suddenly swiped at the ball and was bowled.

I knew then that it was my turn. I got up and started walking onto the field to join Claire.

Suddenly Ann's car came into the car park. Relief filled my mind, but I held my breath to see if she was being pursued by a police car.

She wasn't.

As I was halfway to the wicket Ann came rushing out of her car to me, leaving the driver's door open in her haste, gave me a hug, and slipped something into my pocket. She patted the outside of my trouser pocket and said, "Hit them. Big boy. Hit them."

My gloves were on and their thick padding prevented me from doing anything more than patting my pocket from the outside.

"The charm? Thank you," I said, gratified. Just to have it in my pocket instantly cleared my mind.

Now twenty were needed off six overs with two wickets left. That left me with Claire who was on five. Wicket the last man was still to come.

As we batted there together, I felt that we were true partners again. She had bewitched me with her eyes, her mouth, her laugh. Now all would be forgiven and forgotten. Touching the knuckles of our gloves together after a ball had gone for four, making jokes about cream cakes and Marmaduke's. It all seemed to be back in the old days. I forgave her a thousand times over for all the heartache she had caused me. I felt that old dreamy conviction once again that we might become natural lovebirds, and that the gods had manifested that we should score the winning runs and then go away together.

I even joked, "Can I have a massage tonight?" as we ran past each other to make our ground at the other end.

She forced a little enigmatic smile just to keep my spirits up, an inscrutable look, and I knew that it was probably not on. Nevertheless, I might be able to work on it, given time.

Yet, the closer we came to the target score, the stranger and more careless Claire's behaviour became. She began taking enormous risks, more than was necessary to keep the score moving. She was so careless that on several occasions she would have got either herself or me run out.

I did not know what had gotten into her. Then on the last ball of the penultimate over with only five runs needed she took an almighty swipe at the ball as though she was trying to hit it for six. She missed and was bowled.

Why, I wondered, why could she not have just held it together just a little longer and not been so risky so near the end?

It was almost as if she wanted us to lose. I dismissed that thought as ridiculous, instead putting it down to something I had not realised before about Claire – how she gave in under extreme pressure. On the other hand, perhaps she had done this on purpose to say sorry and make amends for all her wrongs by allowing me the privilege of this moment of victory. Somehow it was a sign from fate she loved me so much that she would give me the honour of starting the batting of the final over to score the winning runs.

That must be it. She had thrown down a gauntlet that said, "If you want me, you must score these winning runs for me." She was like a damsel to be rescued, and it was up to me to do it. I felt honoured, but it was a trifle naughty of her to test me out like this. Nevertheless, I might win her heart if I could pass this stiff test. High stakes for a high lady.

There was honour in this moment, and yet also horror, when I saw Wicket come hobbling out of the pavilion to stand off-pitch at the non-striker's end with Claire on the pitch as his runner.

Fardeep was practising his action in readiness, viciously spinning the ball, directing his fielders to new attacking positions. The wicket-keeper was standing up to the stumps hoping for a stumping or a close catch and there were two close fielders in front of the bat.

Any mistake by me would mean that we would lose. Yet armed now with this charm I could once again focus my mind on getting five runs from those last six balls.

If Fardeep was the thief, then his bowling should be punished and he should lose for that.

But when I saw him face me, I felt a pang of remorse and sorrow. This was the original Fardeep, the Fardeep who had taught me all I know about cricket, who had given me the cricket skills to help me get to this final. It was unbelievable that he should be a mastermind behind all this, and be able to turn my progress on or off at will.

There was a solid determination in his eyes, yet focused no doubt by his obligations to Rod's money and his own reputation. I saw my Fardeep, but also a ruthless adversary. This was not a friendly coaching session now.

I decided to be confident and to use the methods he had taught me.

I remembered what he had said about trying to watch the ball and to believe. I said to myself that I believed in flying saucers and I wanted to see one now and as I watched the ball come spinning from his hand towards me I got down to the pitch of the ball and saw it hit the bat. It sped away for four. The fielder at mid-off dived yet it was through to the boundary.

Now I was feeling confident and faced up to the second ball. With this, I attempted the same shot and I missed. Fardeep had put so much spin on it that it had thudded onto my legs and he appealed for leg before wicket.

The umpire brought his hand from his pocket, but he was merely changing a counting stone over to another pocket.

"Not out," he said. "Going down past leg."

Having had one appeal so far, and this indeed off the second ball of the over, I was shaken and began to doubt whether I would survive these last four balls, let alone score the necessary one run. Fardeep bowled and, once again, the ball thudded into my pads.

"Howzat?" Fardeep appealed again.

"Not out, going down leg again."

Claire had taken several steps down the wicket towards me preparing to run on those balls, but now gritted her teeth and got quickly back to her crease.

I settled again for the fourth ball of the over. Fardeep came in to bowl it, and it started to drift down the leg side. Instantly I saw that here was a failure-or-glory shot and I swiped at it. The ball hit the bat, onto my pad and then went behind me.

Claire called for a run and I started for what could be the greatest sporting achievement in our summer: the winning run in the Enterprise Cup Final. Yet if I were run out here, then though the scores were tied, Scoving would win because they would have lost fewer wickets. Tied scores was not an option for us: we had to get that extra run to win.

"No! Get back!" shouted Wicket, from his position of the injured non-striker at the side of the pitch.

I turned and hurled myself back into my crease as the ball came thudding into the wicket keeper's gloves from a smart fielder behind. I was sprawled on the ground, but I had got back in. It should have been Claire's call, and strangely, she wanted a suicidal run, but Wicket had intervened. Even though it was not his place to call, I was glad that he had.

There were thus two balls left in order to hit this one run for victory.

I thought of the meaning of this for Fardeep if I could pull off a victory. Fardeep would have lost his all-important final match, and for him this might bring disgrace. I wondered whether I could do that to him, but the urgency and excitement of the situation and the extra prestige that the bid might get from a win swayed my mind.

No, there must be no weakness now. There would be none on his part and there must be none on mine.

I settled myself and recalled how I could use my strategies for ball-watching derived from tennis. Never mind what Fardeep had taught me. That was all out of the window now. Though successful with the first ball, that kind of thinking and knowledge had failed for the following three balls in the over. I must play a tennis shot to this. It was my only hope. I was never any good at cricket and it was clear that I never would be and I certainly wouldn't be suddenly good now at this moment. But tennis – tennis had never deserted me and I knew I had two shots at this, to make this count.

I mused how it was like tennis when you could serve a fault and have a second go. I had a feeling which started in the back of my mind and which grew stronger and now took over with total certainty that I would have two attempts and I would do it.

I would try to score it off the first of these last two balls. Yet surely, if I failed I would take my time and score it off the second.

So I decided to be careful with this next ball and then let fly on the second one – the last one of this final, the last ball of summer.

I touched the charm through my trouser pocket, and took my stance as Fardeep was walking back. Then I thought, well what if I go easy on this ball, too easy, and then I can't score on the last one? What if something happened on the last ball and Fardeep bowled me one of his beauties that no batsman alive would be able to play?

I suddenly changed my mind and decided that I could not leave it until that last ball. I must act now. I must attempt to strike it now. Hard and firm. Even though I might be taking an enormous risk, I must strike it hard, for if I did not intercept it right then at least it had the chance of flying away a safe distance.

As Fardeep turned and was coming up to bowl, I thought what is he thinking? What has he really been thinking and surely, he must be under pressure himself? Or, on the other hand, was he just a well-practiced player who has been in lots of these situations before?

Then I realised that I had been concentrating on what I thought Fardeep might be thinking and had not been preparing my mind for the ball that had just been released and was now coming towards me, fizzing with spin.

Instinctively I stuck to my plan of trying to hit it hard and thrashed out.

There was a shout from Fardeep, and he jumped up in the air.

I had missed it, but probably not by much. It thudded harmlessly into the wicket-keeper's gloves.

Wasted.

One ball left.

The thought crossed my mind that subconsciously we would lose the match because they all wanted me to stay. I dismissed this as an extraneous negative thought. I knew from my tennis games that the strangest thoughts cross your mind in tense conflict situations.

I watched Fardeep walk back with a confident swagger. I concentrated on the back of his turban, on the labyrinthine twists.

He turned and came up to bowl.

Some say that it is vital that you should be looking only at the ball. However, in that moment I must admit I failed on that criterion. I looked at the ball in his hand first and then something made me flick to Fardeep's face before I looked back to the ball again. In that moment if you don't concentrate hard enough, all will be lost, for you will never find the ball again through the air to play a proper shot. Something made me want to see his face, as a victim and executioner must look at each other before that final moment. I was floundering when I brought my attention back to look for the ball, but I knew what I had seen in that face. I had seen the same grimace I had seen in the outdoor nets, the same grimace when he had been trying to bluff at poker. The facial expression when he would bowl the leg-spinning doosra.

I prepared myself to be able to pounce on it, to flick it square for a quick single, but still keeping the option that it could be straight if I had read him wrong, and half of my mind was still wanting not to believe my hunch but to come down and play it straighter onto the leg side.

He bowled it and I saw it pitch a little way from my bat and I flashed at it, expecting to make contact with the doosra or at least if I didn't make contact then I would go for the run whatever.

But I did not feel it on the bat and instantly I started to run, Claire was running too towards me and behind me I heard the thwack of the ball hitting the wicket-keeper's gloves and then the oomph as the keeper hit the ground in his dive, and the sound of the wicket behind me being broken for a stumping, and an appeal from the keeper.

"Out- stumped!" The keeper shouted. "They're all out! Scoving wins!"

I swung round and saw the square leg umpire's finger up.

Claire's face relaxed from concentration to joy as she ran towards me. I thought why was that, why was she happy? Didn't she know we had lost?

CHAPTER FORTY-SIX

As Claire ran towards me I saw behind her, out of her sight, the umpire at the bowler's end. His hands came out from behind him and moved to his side to prepare to signal. But it was not one hand and its damning finger to give me out that he raised. It was both as he spread his arms to signal.

"Wide ball!" he shouted.

Claire immediately stopped in her tracks and her face fell.

Whilst my face was now lifted in triumph, hers for some reason had registered despair, and she slammed her bat angrily into the pitch.

Fardeep had bowled a wide! In his desire to succeed, he had tried to spin the ball so much that it had spun away and out of my reach.

Fardeep turned to the umpire. "But surely sir," he said. "Surely ..."

The umpire would have none of it. He said firmly in a loud voice. "The one run penalty for the wide is always registered first before whatever other outcome. He might be stumped, but that is after Moxham have won by one penalty run."

"You stupid idiots!" Claire shouted and stormed angrily off to the pavilion.

CHAPTER FORTY-SEVEN

We gathered in front of the pavilion for the presentations, facing the fifty or so crowd, with Sir Richard on top of the steps behind us.

Fardeep was muttering into his mobile phone and Sir Richard was waiting for him to finish before starting.

I heard him say, "Yes, hello. Yes, I am Fardeep Singh. Who? The Imperial Hotel? Yes. What has happened?" before he turned away to face the pavilion wall to speak privately.

I stood next to Claire, proud to have won. Proud that I could now go off with her and the project team. Yet strangely, she looked annoyed as though she was a damsel who resented having been rescued by a knight. The excitement of batting over, she had now gone back to her cold self and was more interested in standing nearer to Mark and a downcast Rod then me. I wondered how I could have upset her by winning. I couldn't understand her reaction.

Switching off his phone, Fardeep turned round to speak to us.

"The hotel texted me to ring them. They said that there had been a break-in and they were going to report it to the police. But I have my valuables here with me. There was only equipment. They are not sure if anything was taken even."

"Yes it was," said Ann, pointing a finger. "I got back what you stole."

"What I stole? How can this be?" asked Fardeep, looking from Ann to me. "Jeremy, tell me. What is this all about?"

"Ann says you stole the charm when you repaired my bat handle the other day," I explained.

I looked round the group. They had all fallen silent.

Ann pointed at Fardeep. "And Jeremy still won even though you stole the charm!"

"What?" he said. "What do you mean? I never."

"Yes" she said. "Look at this. Show him, Jeremy."

In that moment of condemnation, I knew I had lost the greatest sporting coach I had ever known. The man who was destined to be the greatest. On the verge of the Indian Test Squad, he would now, because of the contents of my pocket, fall from grace. Moreover, I would have had a part in his downfall. How could I work with some deceitful man who groomed his pupils only to be able to switch their abilities on and off as it suited his betting tactics? Indeed, by Ann exposing Fardeep not only had I lost my will to work for GSS, but with it my opportunity with Claire.

The truth sometimes appals and, ashamed by what I was to do, but knowing it was the right thing, I slowly got the charm out of my pocket for all to see. I did not want to have to finger Fardeep, glum with the problems of defeat and now this latest news, to accuse him in front of everyone. Yet Ann was making me do it, making me do the right thing. Tense with the moment, I closed my eyes as I got the charm out and then opened my hand for all to see.

There was a gasp from the group. Then I opened my eyes and looked. As soon as I did so I realised there was something different about the faceting of this charm.

"But Ann," I said. "This is not my charm."

CHAPTER FORTY-EIGHT

"But it is," Ann said. "It was in his kitbag. Along with a load of other ones. They were all like this."

"No," I said. "Mine is different."

"What?" said Fardeep. "So it was you in the hotel?" He looked at Ann and laughed. "Those charms are for the juniors at Appleton Water. They are nothing to do with Jeremy. I would never hurt a pupil of mine as you say. You all know that."

"Then where is the charm?" asked Ann.

Fardeep was instantly absolved in my eyes and I breathed a sigh of relief. However, Ann was in shock. Once pleased at having exposed what she thought was a master criminal, she now looked round the group for the real thief in our midst. A truth much darker.

Wicket seized the moment. "Now Rod, you've got the motive for this. You've always been needling us over that silverware years ago. Are you sure you don't know anything about it?"

"No, surely, not. Oh no please," Ann said.

Rod was indignant. "What? Are you accusing me of this? That's typical of you, Wicket. I didn't even know that Jeremy was using a charm to help him focus. I always play fair. I have sunk all my own money in this and bet on the outcome but I would never interfere with the due process. Never interfere with another team's abilities. If I lose I go down fair and square."

"Then who has it then?" Wicket scoffed as he turned to Mark.

If it was true that Mark and Rod had stolen it, then I could not see why I should stay. It would just show that the whole district was corrupt and it was still stuck in the same old Scoving–Moxham feud.

"I don't know why you are looking at me," Mark said. "I didn't do it."

"You had motive as well," said Peter. "You would lose money."

"I never did. How could you accuse me?" he glared and took a pace forward.

"Is this what you mean?" said Claire suddenly, opening her hand.

It was my charm.

I gulped.

My knees weakened.

"I took it because I couldn't stand to see Mark's father lose the rest of his money today after all the effort he had put into the bid. I knew it could come close so I did it to make sure Rod and Mark did not go down the tube. I was wrong. I thought I was doing it for the best. Part of me was spiteful. I'm sorry if I wronged you Jeremy, but I had to get the project to succeed and then I had to make sure we got money back from the bets. I see now I was wrong. I tried to make everyone succeed."

She put her arm around Mark. "Mark and I have just become engaged." She turned to me. "The Sterlings need the money. They have lost so much. Moxham are rolling in it. Will you forgive me, Jeremy?"

Then I knew that she would never be mine. There would always be some new way in which she would deceive me. Now I saw what a depth I would be taken down to if I teamed up with her, and I was afraid. My face began to get hot.

"Come and join us at the consultancy and forgive me," she said coolly. "I only tried to do it for the best."

After all the times she had betrayed me, now she had betrayed me a final time. I had no more strength left to carry on liking her. I gulped and felt myself welling up.

I turned away from her, unable to look. I felt so foolish. I went red. I felt so foolish and so angry that I began to cry.

A friendly arm touched my neck. It was Ann and I turned away from them and sobbed onto her shoulders.

Sir Richard interrupted us all as he said, "Well, I can see what a mess this has got everybody into. I'm sure there's some way we can help Fardeep and keep Scoving going for a little while until the money comes properly into the district."

Then seeing the crowd was getting restless at not understanding what was going on, he drew himself up and spoke in a loud voice to all.

"Ladies and gentlemen, how very honoured we are today to witness the revival of cricket here and have seen such a glorious match. This is the fertilisation of the epitome of modern sports endeavour. We pay tribute to the many who have made this possible and to the brilliant end that we have seen here today.

"The energy and the body and the growth for Moxham Cricket and indeed the whole sports infrastructure is notably well-served by this great expression of energy and motivation. I feel confident that Moxham cricket is alive and well as is the whole of cricket in this county as a result. The bid that the government has promised will soon be authorised to allow us to rebuild the sports and leisure service.

"Now to the prizes. For the excellence of the teas we award the catering prize to Esmeralda Fiora".

Esmeralda came up the steps and took the placard with the enlarged mock-up of a certificate from Sir Richard to warm applause. A photographer sprung forward from the crowd, motioned for a pose and took a photo. As she came down the steps she nodded thanks at Charlotte who was standing arm in arm with Alan.

"Now for the sports prizes. The Player of the Match award for his batting goes to Rod Stirling."

Rod held up his placard and, though he fleetingly smiled, he stepped back in line sullen and depressed.

"Now to the captain of Moxham, Mr. William Kenneth Turner. To receive on behalf of Moxham Cricket Club, the Enterprise Cup."

As Wicket posed there on the steps with the cup for the photographer, my mind went back to the old photos in his front room cabinet. Ten years had passed but it seemed the same shy pose, as though Wicket had once again been caught in a private reflective moment. He only smiled after the photograph had been taken.

"Now to the manager of Moxham, Mr Jeremy Freeman to receive on behalf of the club the Enterprise Award, a cheque for three thousand pounds."

I saw Rod's bowed head close to tears. I took the cheque and the photographer sealed the moment.

"I'm ruined, I'm ruined," Rod muttered.

Mark came forward and extended a hand to him "What is it Dad, you're OK. It's OK. We're back together now. You couldn't help it. "

"No," said Rod. "I'm ruined. I've lost six thousand pounds. I've sunk all that money into the club to buy Fardeep to keep him here for the final. So that we would win. I was sure that we would win. How could anyone forgive me?"

I was touched by how, out of all of us, Rod the surliest and least sporting, was the one most dedicated to the future of cricket in the area. Always criticised by others, he had risked all his own money in this venture; he had alienated and welcomed back his own son; and he had maintained single-handedly his purpose of developing his players and club to their benefit. Yet it was he who was now ruined.

I went down the steps and, putting my hand on his shoulder, I said. "It's OK Rod. Even though you lost the government bid, you showed it wasn't necessary. You paid out of your own money to keep Fardeep on to draw the crowds so we could have this day. Without you, there wouldn't have been a competition. Here, you have this three thousand because you have put up such a good contest."

There was a ripple of applause that got louder as people realised what I had done.

"Thank you ladies and gentlemen. That concludes the ceremony," said a smiling Sir Richard, stepping down to mingle with the crowd.

I felt an arm around my neck from the side. It was Ann. I wondered if she would criticise me for giving the prize money away but her touch was soft. She kissed me on the cheek.

"Well done Jeremy, that's fantastic. Never doubt yourself. You don't need any charms."

Rod said, "I don't know what to say, Jeremy. Thanks." Then he turned to his son and said, "I'm sorry I made you almost lose your girlfriend as well by making you be so bad to Jeremy."

"It's OK Dad," said Mark, squeezing Claire's hand. "I've found a new job as a sports teacher and coach with Sir Richard's project team, GSS".

Claire laughed "Sure thing. You'd better watch it. I'll be your boss."

As we broke up Rod came across to Wicket and offered his hand. "I'm sorry I kept criticising you. You don't deserve it. You're not so bad. I can believe now it wasn't your fault about that silverware years ago."

"That's all right," said Wicket. "Let's work together now. There'll be plenty of money in the bid for us all when it comes through."

I looked across with Ann on my arm and saw Fardeep loading his bags into his car. He started the engine, then reversed towards us and wound the window down to say goodbye.

Shouting over the noise of everyone laughing and congratulating each other, Ann said to him. "I'm sorry, Fardeep. I wasn't thinking. I shouldn't have jumped to that conclusion."

Fardeep laughed "Ha! So it was only you? Well. Good job there's no harm done. My charms are so popular. Anyway, Jeremy, you'll stay here at Moxham to manage the bid money?"

"Yes," I said, "Now that I know everything."

"Hah! Are you sure?" he laughed and drove away.

At the beginning I thought that it seems to fall to the one who knows nothing to play the most important part. And for a lot of the time I thought that would be me. But now I have learnt that it is each and every one of us.

ABOUT THE AUTHOR

Stuart Larner is a chartered psychologist, has worked in the National Health Service for 34 years, and was mental health expert for XL for Men magazine. He also writes plays, poems, and stories. He is a cricket enthusiast in North Yorkshire, UK. His previous book is "Jack Daw and the Cat." http://stuartlarner.blogspot.com/.

Lightning Source UK Ltd.
Milton Keynes UK
UKOW03f1502260114

225275UK00001B/92/P